S. M. Gaither is the author of multiple bestselling romantic epic fantasy books. And while she's happiest writing stories filled with magic and spice, she's also done everything from working on a chicken farm to running a small business, with a lot of really odd jobs in between. She currently makes her home in the beautiful foothills of North Carolina with her husband, their daughter and one very spoiled dog. You can visit her online at www.smgaitherbooks.com

ALSO BY S. M. GAITHER

The Shadows & Crowns Series:
The Song of the Marked
A Twist of the Blade
The Call of the Void
A Crown of the Gods
The Queen of the Dawn

The Flame & Sparrow Duology

The Serpents & Kings Series

The Shift Chronicles

The Drowning Empire Series

S. M. GAITHER

PENGUIN BOOKS

PENGUIN BOOKS

UK | USA | Canada | Ireland | Australia
India | New Zealand | South Africa

Penguin Books is part of the Penguin Random House group of companies
whose addresses can be found at global.penguinrandomhouse.com

Penguin Random House UK,
One Embassy Gardens, 8 Viaduct Gardens, London SW11 7BW

penguin.co.uk

First published by S. M. Gaither/Yellow Door Publishing, INC 2025
Published in Penguin Books 2025
001

Copyright © S. M. Gaither, 2025

The moral right of the author has been asserted

Penguin Random House values and supports copyright. Copyright fuels creativity, encourages diverse voices, promotes freedom of expression and supports a vibrant culture. Thank you for purchasing an authorised edition of this book and for respecting intellectual property laws by not reproducing, scanning or distributing any part of it by any means without permission. You are supporting authors and enabling Penguin Random House to continue to publish books for everyone. No part of this book may be used or reproduced in any manner for the purpose of training artificial intelligence technologies or systems. In accordance with Article 4(3) of the DSM Directive 2019/790, Penguin Random House expressly reserves this work from the text and data mining exception.

Cover Art by Lila Raymond (@lettersbylila_)
Nova art by Chrissa Barton (@chrissabug)

Printed and bound in Great Britain by Clays Ltd, Elcograf S.p.A.

The authorised representative in the EEA is Penguin Random House Ireland,
Morrison Chambers, 32 Nassau Street, Dublin D02 YH68

A CIP catalogue record for this book is available from the British Library

ISBN: 978-1-804-95866-7

Penguin Random House is committed to a sustainable future
for our business, our readers and our planet. This book is made
from Forest Stewardship Council® certified paper.

For Grant:
The reason all my books are love stories in the end.

Author's Note

Please be aware that this is an adult/new adult fantasy book that contains explicit sexual content, violence, and adult language. It also contains depictions of death, emotional abuse/manipulation, and trauma that may be upsetting for some readers.

This is also the first book of a planned trilogy, and it does end on a cliffhanger.

Read and enjoy at your own risk!

Prologue

I HAD NOT DISTURBED THE GRAVES ON PURPOSE.

Truthfully, I'd forgotten they were even there. I rarely visited this corner of the palace grounds, after all. No one did. The shadows cast by the walls around me were long, the pebbled paths beneath my sandaled feet overtaken with weeds and the rotting corpses of long-dead foliage. Most of the headstones were lost to the ravages of time, whatever secrets they held unreadable and unremarkable to the average eye.

At any rate, the graves marked by those headstones had certainly not been my *targets*.

My aim had been higher. Focused on the withered flowers clinging to the twisting tree branches that formed a canopy over this tucked-away corner of my home. I felt a sickness in those shriveled blooms whenever I stared at them; their fading life force moved as a tingling sensation along my arms, raising little bumps across my skin.

Death took many different forms to me. I was still

learning what forms I could detect, what I could decipher, what I could control...

And what I was better off leaving alone.

But the dying flowers, I'd decided, would be excellent practice targets. A good chance to exercise my powers, which had been growing increasingly restless with all the extra attention being paid to me over the past week.

It should have been an easy task, extracting the decaying energy from them and temporarily bringing them back to something that mimicked the brightness of life. It was a trick I'd managed with relative ease in the past.

Yet, for all my familiarity with this trick, I'd failed.

So there I stood, still surrounded by withered blooms—and now by cracked gravesites, too. Little bits of white danced in the air above the broken ground, drifting and sparkling like snowflakes—the faint auras of the long-deceased. When those cold flakes brushed my skin, the tingling in my arms became more like the sharp prodding of needles...

More like a warning.

The air smelled of freshly turned soil, with a rotten, musty undercurrent. The night seemed eerily quiet, save for the occasional groan of the slow, cold wind.

But at least there were no accidental *bodies* rising up, this time.

My mother—the queen—still would not be pleased at the messy disturbance I'd caused.

My father, meanwhile, would find it all wonderfully amusing; I could already imagine his laughter, his eyes dancing as he gently teased me about my wayward magic. Thinking of his laugh gave me courage enough to shake off the needling sensation in my skin and keep going in spite of my mistakes.

Everything is fixable, My Star. You just have to keep trying.

The sound of plodding footfalls made me jump.

I rolled the tension from my shoulders as Phantom—the silky-haired puppy my father had given me a year prior—clambered into view. He took one look at the ghostly specks of energy flitting through the air and clumsily settled onto his haunches with his head cocked in curiosity.

A trio of blackbirds alighted on the nearby wall as well, their feathers glistening like oil in the pale blue moonlight.

I ignored my audience and focused on soothing the bits of lingering energy in the air, guiding each one back into the broken ground with precise movements of my fingers. It helped to imagine the bits attached to my fingertips, I'd learned over the years—to tether myself to such energy by way of invisible chains.

Once the air was clear again, I took a fallen branch covered in blooms, closed my eyes, and tried to refocus on the precise feel of the flowers' decay.

Nothing had changed in those flowers when I opened my eyes—but the cracks in the dirt had widened in several places. The space again grew hazy, thick with my misguided magic and the uneasy, partially-roused energies of the dead.

I cursed under my breath.

Why couldn't I do this?

Phantom yipped his disapproval. His keen blue eyes had a human-like awareness to them, I'd always thought, putting his judgmental looks on par with my mother's.

"No one asked your opinion, now did they?" I muttered, hiking up my skirts and trudging toward the disturbed ground. I dropped down before the first grave and started to smooth it with my bare hands, raking my fingers through the cold soil to break up the uneven clumps, paying little mind to the grime collecting beneath my freshly painted nails.

Phantom panted and whined loudly behind me. I shot him a disagreeable look, but he didn't seem bothered by it; I would have sworn the damned dog only smiled in response.

Secretly, however, I was glad he was here, judgment and all. He was fast becoming my constant companion. The only being in the court—aside from my father—who didn't flinch when they saw me coming.

I crawled from one grave to the next, putting the dirt back in order and pulling a few weeds along the way. The shimmering hem of my silver dress was soon streaked with grass stains and growing heavy from the clinging, damp earth, but I persevered nonetheless.

Soon enough, the job was finished, the dirt smooth, the air crisp and clear.

I gathered up another handful of fallen blossoms. Most would have admitted defeat by this point, I guess, but I was stubborn—determined to follow through with my original goal, however silly it seemed after so many failures.

I glanced over my shoulder, making certain I was alone save for my dog. I took a deep breath.

And, this time, I allowed the shadowy markings along my neck and arms to lift from my skin as I focused on the flowers' decayed energy.

My shadows were very adept at grabbing hold of dead things. But they also made me feel like I was unraveling whenever they lifted away from my body—which was why I hadn't called on them at the start.

Thankfully, it was a quick spell. The auras of the flowers were small, weak, easy enough to manipulate and pull out with my shadows. My hands were soon filled with blooms that glowed at the edges—the subtle shine of organisms drained of their morbid energy.

Faint as it was, the glow seemed bright against the deepening night. It cast a thin light over the cracked gravestones, drawing my eyes to their weathered, unreadable names once more.

I tossed the now luminescent blooms over the freshly-smoothed dirt, one after the other. "Whoever you are," I said softly, "I'm sorry you've been forgotten here."

This was far from the only dilapidated and disregarded area of my family's estate. We had not lived among the sweeping grounds and ornate buildings of Rose Point for very long, and prior to my parents' arrival, the place had sat empty for more than half a century. The king and queen had done a great deal to restore the central palace itself, along with the main grounds, but there were still plenty of overgrown corners and dust-coated corridors to explore. Plenty of buried secrets to dig up; a wealth of treasure and trouble to find…which was one of the things I loved most about my home.

One of the many things I would miss after tonight.

Because after tonight, everything would change.

I tossed the remaining flowers down with a slow, reverent sort of precision—save for a single, stubborn blossom that stuck to my palm.

I moved to show off its illuminated loveliness to Phantom—who had, by this point, fallen asleep in a pile of damp and rotting leaves—but before I could rouse him, the dog suddenly lifted his head of his own accord. His pointed ears twitched as he sniffed the air.

A smooth voice parted the quiet a moment later: "Lady Bellanova?"

Just Nova, I corrected—or at least, I did so in my head.

I couldn't get my mouth to form words, however. I'd frozen in place, newly aware of the dirt staining my dress and hands, and of the shadows still circling lazily around my body. I clamped my hands over those shadows. Pressed them back to my skin, bit by bit, where they settled like swirls of ink tattooed upon it.

Slowly, with as much dignity and poise as I could muster, I turned to meet the man approaching me.

Like the magicked flowers, he stood out with a subtle yet certain brightness against the darkening twilight. His hair fell in short, thick waves around his face, framing his sharp jawline. The strands were a peculiar shade of silvery white, a color that seemed to have been absorbed from the cloud-covered moon itself. The sight would have been ethereal enough on its own, but combined with the shade of his eyes…

Let's just say, he was difficult to look away from.

The first time I'd met his gaze, many years ago, I'd been sure the light was playing tricks on me. I'd never come across anyone with eyes of such deep, arresting gold—eyes the color of a sun-kissed wheat field. I'd soon learned the hue was common among his regal family, but at the time, he'd just been a young boy lost in the same courtyard where I'd been attempting to hide from my lessons; I hadn't recognized him as royalty.

I recognized him well enough, now, though: Aleksander

Caldor, Crown Prince of Elarith. The soon-to-be-ruler of that neighboring kingdom.

And it was a wonder the light in his eyes had not gone out; in the year since we'd last seen one another, his mother had passed away, the result of a gruesome riding accident. Her husband had followed after months of self-imposed solitude and suffering—taken by his own hand, if rumors were to be believed. Aleksander was an only child—and now the sole remaining ruler of Elarith.

The Elarithian throne had been stewarded over the past months by the Keepers of Light, a council largely made up of the descendants of powerful magic-users who had first settled Aleksander's kingdom. That council was eager to place their young prince on the throne and return their mourning lands to order and stability. Which was partly why he was here tonight—to shore up their relationship with Eldris before he began his rule.

We should be honored they looked to us first, my mother had reminded me, countless times, over the past days. *We need this alliance. Our* kingdom *needs this alliance.*

Phantom got to his feet and trotted over to my side, nuzzling his sharp nose against my leg and letting out a whine. I gave him a reassuring scratch between his ears, just above the burst of white on his forehead—the only splotch of color in his otherwise jet-black fur.

My eyes never left the soon-to-be-crowned-king.

"A little dark for gardening, isn't it?" Aleksander did a poor job of hiding his amusement as he looked my dirty self over from head-to-toe. His suppressed smile accented his dimples, the only hints of softness in his otherwise sharp features.

I did my best to appear completely unaffected by those

dimples. "Some things bloom brighter in the dark," I countered, holding up the blossom still clinging so stubbornly to my palm, "so that's when I tend to them."

He considered the words, studying the flower with an intensity that made my heart beat faster.

The flower was already fading. Withering at the edges. Not surprising—the glow rarely lasted long. Even though I could sense and occasionally manipulate death's hold over things, I couldn't truly, permanently remove its grip.

"That makes sense, I suppose." As he spoke, Aleksander carefully took the flower from me. His fingertips brushed mine, sending a shiver up my arm and making the shadows on my skin shift slightly. My heart pounded even more furiously.

I kept my eyes on his hand as a soft white glow rose up from the lines of his palm, engulfing the shriveling bloom. As I watched, the edges of that bloom smoothed out and began to shine once more.

The *King of Light*. That's what he would be called once he ascended the throne—just like his father and grandfather before him. He was a descendant of the most powerful line of those magical beings who had settled his kingdom. And unlike my own shadowy powers, his had been celebrated and nurtured since birth.

In all five kingdoms of the Valorian Empire, his magic was revered and welcomed.

I couldn't help but marvel at it myself, if only briefly, as he placed the flower back in my palm and gently closed my hand over it. I could see a gleam through the cracks between my fingers, one much warmer than the glow I'd caused. Where I had drawn out the decaying energy, he had simply forced light—life

—back into the bloom. The end result was similar, and yet...

"Will I see you at the party soon?" he asked. "I believe the queen was looking for you. She seemed a bit frantic."

Mother always *seems a bit frantic*, I thought, biting my lip to keep the comment to myself.

I looked to the main house. Even from here, I could feel the buzz of activity within it. Could hear the music and laughter getting louder, could smell the delicious aromas of roasting meat and vegetables, along with the sugary desserts waiting in the wings.

I forced my eyes back to Aleksander's. "Sorry," I said, "I must have lost track of time."

I hadn't lost track of time at all.

And something told me the future Light King knew this. He said nothing, however, merely waving my tardiness away—as polite as he'd always been.

"I'll be in shortly," I assured him. There was no avoiding it. Because it was *my* party, after all—a celebration of my eighteenth birthday.

And the gossip spreading throughout the Kingdom of Eldris like wildfire all claimed the King of Light was here to bring what they considered a most *incredible* gift: He was going to ask for my hand in marriage.

I fought the urge to pick at the grime under my nails, trying to maintain my composure.

What did one say to a mere acquaintance who they might have to call *husband* soon?

How did I say it, when I must have looked positively feral in the moonlight, with my clothing covered in grave dirt and my hair hanging in disheveled waves around my sweat-streaked face?

I really owed my maids an apology for how thoroughly I'd sullied my appearance after all the work they'd put into it.

Luckily, Aleksander seemed to sense my discomfort and diffused the awkward air between us by way of a gentlemanly bow.

"I'll be waiting for you inside, then," he told me, sweeping a kiss across my knuckles before turning and heading back towards the palace.

My heart behaved strangely as I watched him go—simultaneously trying to soar and clench into a tight, protective ball.

It was kind of him to come all this way and make a show of officially proposing. Romantic, even. But any marriage between us would be purely political; I was not foolish enough to believe otherwise. Our kingdoms had once shared a powerful alliance, and it was simply the wise thing to do—focusing on rebuilding the connection.

Aside from this, it was the wisest move for *me*. My magic would be far less restless in the Elarithian Kingdom. My mother had assured me of this—that being around Aleksander and his light-magic-wielding court would help balance and temper my powers. Father seemed less convinced, but he was not one to argue when the Queen of Eldris truly put her foot down about a matter.

I rarely agreed with my mother about anything, but in this case...

Well, there were worse birthday presents, surely. Far fouler things than being married off to a wealthy, handsome king who, by most accounts, was well-liked by his subjects.

The Kingdom of Elarith was said to be breathtakingly beautiful, too. I wouldn't know; I'd only been there once when I was younger, and my memories of it remained a blur, no matter how hard I tried to focus on them. The way others spoke of it, though, made it seem as if I was soon to be whisked away into a fairytale.

Of course, most fairytales had a darker story lurking underneath—a fact I'd started to mention several times after overhearing whispers about my supposedly enviable future…

But I held my tongue every time.

I would not complain. For my kingdom's sake, I could bear any burden. For my *family's* sake, I could carry the weight of a foreign crown, endure the pain of being a stranger in a strange land, leaving behind all I knew. It was just another form of death, I'd convinced myself.

And I had never feared death.

I drew myself up to my full height, settled my nerves, and marched inside with Phantom trotting at my heels.

I avoided the party for a little longer, sneaking my way toward my room first. Once there, I changed quickly out of my soiled clothing, opting for a sleeveless, simple gown in my favorite color—a rusted shade of orange—mostly because it was easy to slip on and secure without the help of any servants.

I picked stray flower petals and bits of mud from my long, dark tresses, redid the braids keeping the unruly locks away from my face, and assessed myself in the mirror.

Good enough.

Yet I lingered, noticing how dark the markings on my arms still were. They had not fully settled since Aleksander's hand had brushed my skin; occasionally they twitched, the darkness rippling like strands of silk ribbons caught in a breeze.

The markings—and my magic—were an ill-kept secret within this palace. Most knew about them at this point, because although I could make them disappear completely if I concentrated hard enough, burying them beneath my skin never lasted long before the restless itch to let them out again overcame me. Death was everywhere in this world, after all, in all its different forms, and my magic called to the different morbid energies.

Oftentimes, it was safer to let the darkness breathe. That's why I'd been hiding in that corner with the gravestones—because I'd desperately needed to *breathe*.

I needed to be under control for this party.

"I *am* under control," I told my reflection.

Phantom gave a concerned yip, drawing my attention. I knelt before him, straightening his jeweled collar.

"Are we ready for this, you think?" I asked, running my fingers through his silky fur.

He let out a happier bark before twirling in a circle.

I smiled, wondering if the King of Light was a dog lover—and then promptly decided that I didn't care; Phantom was coming with me to Elarith, either way.

"Come on, then," I said, standing and turning for the door. "Let's get it over with."

I went to the door and, with stiffened resolve, pulled it open—

And found my mother standing on the other side, hand outstretched toward the handle. She'd clearly had no intention of knocking.

We stared at one another.

The queen spoke first, per usual. "Nova, that isn't the dress we agreed—"

"The other one is dirty."

My mother pursed her lips.

"Ah, but *this* one looks splendid on her, doesn't it?" my father offered, appearing behind his wife. He quickly stepped between me and her critical gaze—just as he'd been doing for the past eighteen years. "The color brings out her eyes."

The queen breathed in deeply through her nose several times before managing a smile. "I suppose it does," she agreed with a soft sigh, her gaze flicking up to mine.

Our bright turquoise eyes were one of the few things we had in common—one of the few things I had in common with either of my parents' appearances. As she stared into them, maybe she was reminded of this—that I was, in fact, her daughter. Maybe that was why she gave me a quick embrace before hurrying me on down the hall.

Phantom raced ahead, nose lifted into the air, eagerly following the smell of the feast awaiting us.

"We've been ready to announce you for the past half hour," my mother said as we practically jogged down the portrait-lined corridor. "Everyone is eager to see you."

I doubted this last part, but didn't say so; I merely nodded along as she launched into yet another recap of the events she had planned for the evening, and how they would now have to shift due to my lateness.

My father rescued me again as we came to the massive double-doors of the banquet hall, insisting he wanted to escort me inside himself. My mother let me go without a fuss, her attention catching on a servant who was sorting silverware in a way that was apparently *all wrong*!

"She means well," my father said, wincing a bit as we watched her hurry off and fix her frantic energy on the poor servant.

"I know."

He veered away from the banquet hall and beckoned me to follow, pulling a small, wrapped box from the inside pocket of his waistcoat once we were out of Mother's sight.

Inside the gift box, I found a bracelet with beads painted in almost the exact shade of my eyes. A few had symbols painted on them as well, drawn with precise, painstakingly neat brushstrokes.

"I commissioned it from Orin," he said.

Orin Greenbark was one of my many teachers. Mother was not particularly fond of him and his unorthodox views on magic—among other things.

And there was magic in this piece he'd created, no doubt; I could already feel it coming to life as I slipped the bracelet on.

"You like it, I hope?"

I couldn't take my eyes off it. "It's beautiful," I breathed.

"Good. Happy birthday, My Star." He planted a kiss on top of my head. "Now, let's get to this party before your mother disowns us both."

Though he did escort me through the doors as planned, after my appearance was officially announced, the king was swallowed up by his own admirers, everyone clamoring for a chance to speak face-to-face with him.

The King of Light was having a similar effect on the partygoers on the other side of the room.

Because of this, I found it easy to disappear into the shadows, even though I was the guest of honor.

The hall was even more impressive than usual. Dozens of tables spanned the space, draped in layers of silk and lace, glittering with silver and gold cutlery, overflowing with platters of exotic fruits and delicacies. The scent of spices mingled with perfumes worn by guests, wrapping me in a rich, heady embrace. The music of string ensembles and flutes filled the hall—a soothing backdrop to the conversations growing more raucous by the minute, thanks to the countless wines flowing freely from stations in every corner.

I found Phantom hiding under a table, devouring scraps of some slab of meat he'd managed to pilfer. At the sight of me, he gulped down the remaining bits and scurried to my side.

Heads turned my way as I continued my walk through the dazzling room. Most offered a polite bow or a generic well-wish for my birthday. Few made prolonged eye contact or conversation.

I was not revered the way my parents, or my alleged husband-to-be, were—but I was not hated, either. I was... *tolerated*. The odd daughter of a well-liked king and queen. Despite my strange magic, I'd never caused any *real* trouble for the royal city I called home, and so I was mostly left to my own devices. Overlooked, save for the rare occasions when my mother insisted on celebrating me.

I doubted any of the people here would care if I left this kingdom.

Most probably wouldn't even realize I'd gone.

Some days, I wondered if it would have been easier if they all hated me. If that would have been better than being overlooked—better than being able to blend perfectly into a party but rarely asked to dance.

It was unsettling to feel so alone in a room full of hundreds of people who knew my name.

"Maybe a change won't be so bad," I mumbled to Phantom as I slipped him a slice of roasted beef.

Maybe things would be different in Elarith.

For the next several hours, I drifted through the glittering spaces, sipping my favorite red wine and slipping in and out of daydreams about what awaited me in the weeks to come.

The night pressed on. The crowd grew more inebriated. The full moon rose higher, the skylights allowing its beams to press in and strike chandeliers, sequined dresses, and dangling jewelry, turning the room into a shimmering kaleidoscope of color and movement.

It was easy to get swept up in the magic of the event, however detached I might have felt from the people around me. Easy to enjoy the moment. To appreciate all the work that had gone into it—and it soon occurred to me that I should find my mother and thank her for that work.

After a bit of searching, I found her standing by my father on the largest of several verandas attached to the banquet hall. Speaking with the future Elarithian King.

Of course.

Aleksander was accompanied by an impeccably-dressed servant who held a beautiful weapon—a blade secured in a sheath of white and gold—which the future king was busy presenting and describing to my parents. A gift for them, I assumed.

He was the first to notice my approach. He tilted his head toward me, pausing his speech long enough to offer a small smile. My heart reacted just as it had in the garden—with an odd combination of desire and uncertainty.

The music around me slowed.

The world seemed to slow with it.

I could sense my parents' eyes shifting my direction, the weight of their expectations growing heavier with each passing second. My chest tightened. It felt as if I was approaching the crux of this night—the moment that would divide my life and legacy into *before* and *after*.

Aleksander went back to addressing my parents. My pulse skipped several beats, wondering what other gifts he planned to lavish on my family and kingdom before the night was through. I wanted to hurry closer, to hear the ideas he had for his rule, for our alliance…

And yet, something slowed my steps—a feeling I couldn't name.

So I didn't reach the veranda before…*something* struck the ground between Aleksander and my parents with a vicious *crack!*

Smoke exploded from where it hit, throwing up a thick curtain that billowed into the banquet hall.

The riotous laughter and chatter of the hall faded into confused silence. The music screeched to a halt. The clattering and clanging of dishes echoed in the stillness for a moment before ceasing along with everything else.

The sound of boots hitting stone came next—dozens of bodies dropping onto the veranda from somewhere above. The smoke made it difficult to see, but I could tell my parents were being surrounded.

Shouts rang out.

Palace guards surged through the panicking crowd, shoving partygoers aside and barreling toward the king and queen.

I hiked up my dress and sprinted after them.

Phantom darted after them as well, his large body further clearing a path for me to follow. I kept my eyes narrowed on my dog, trusting him to find the quickest route

—I was so focused on him, I didn't see a man crossing into my path until it was too late.

We collided. *Hard*. As I fell, a strong hand caught my arm, jerking me back upright, and I found myself staring into a pair of warm brown eyes.

I didn't know his name, but I'd seen this man at Aleksander's side throughout much of the night. He looked like a muted version of the Elarithian king—more earthy than ethereal, but with glints of gold in his eyes and hair. His rolled-up sleeves allowed a glimpse of tattoos that appeared to cover most of his right arm.

After a few seconds, his eyes widened in recognition, and his hold on me tightened. "Princess, it isn't safe—"

I ripped free and sprinted onward. The bracelet my father had given me was trembling, clenching painfully around my wrist. Like someone taking a merciless hold on me, jerking me onward through the panicked crowd, continuing to pull even when my steps grew clumsy.

By the time I hurtled onto the terrace, the smoke had cleared enough for me to see Aleksander standing tall and clear in the moonlight. His hand was wrapped around the hilt of the blade he'd been presenting to my parents.

The blade that was now buried in my father's chest.

He yanked it out and turned to my mother next.

I moved faster. Without pausing to think, I threw myself in front of my mother, knocking her to the ground. Palace guards swarmed over her, gathering her up and carrying her to safety.

I spun to face Aleksander. The tip of his sword came within an inch of my throat, where it collided with an explosion of shadows that lifted from my skin without any effort or control from me.

Little fissures appeared in the sword as it was struck by the shadows. Light leaked from the cracks, radiance rising up to meet my darkness.

Our competing energies swirled faster and faster, engulfing us. The tangled power raked like claws over my skin, whipping my clothing and hair wildly about, leaving me breathless and shaking.

Our eyes met through a hazy cloud of light and dark, his golden irises burning like twin suns ready to implode and devour the world.

I heard the *thump* of knees hitting the ground, followed by the rest of a body. *My father's body.* I glimpsed it crumpling down into a motionless heap behind Aleksander.

Rage blinded me. My shadows swelled, and I would have sworn they turned solid for a moment, shifting into monstrous limbs that knocked everything and everyone—ally and foe, alike—to the ground.

When they faded to mere haze once more, Aleksander was gone.

The sword he'd used to stab my father was now embedded in the stone floor of the veranda. It had cleaved straight through the marble tiles as if cutting through dirt.

My father's blood dripped down the blade.

Another rush of rage overtook me. My shadows became solid extensions of my body once more, talons that dug into the world around me, grappling for control.

The veranda cracked apart, a chasm opening in the middle and swallowing up the sword.

The cracks swept outward, forcing me to jump back to avoid being swallowed up myself. A renewed chorus of screams filled the air, followed by the thunder of footsteps as people scrambled to put more space between them and the breaking terrace.

Phantom grabbed a mouthful of my dress and tried to pull me toward safety. I stumbled a few steps backward until my gaze fell upon my father again, on his body that was rolling precariously close to the opening chasm.

A dozen feet separated us, yet I reached out my hands as though to catch him. My shadows swept forward with the movement, spiraling, wrapping around his lifeless figure. But, try as I might, I couldn't get my magic to turn solid enough to secure him—to stop him from meeting the same fate as the sword.

The ground shook, rolling him forward, swallowing him up.

Gone.

Just like that, he was *gone*, leaving only a trail of blood and bits of broken shadows in his wake.

The few people who hadn't fled were staring at me, horrified. Everything was spinning. Unraveling. I felt out of control, out of options, out of ideas. I turned away from the widening chasm...

And I ran.

Shadows followed. *Destruction* followed. Wherever I went, darkness flailed alongside me, occasionally catching on living things and draining them, felling bodies, cutting swaths of grey through what had once been lush courtyards.

I ran faster. Faster, faster, *faster*, until, finally, I stood alone atop the highest hill overlooking Rose Point. Gasping for breath, I gazed back at my home, trying to make sense of what had happened.

I willed myself not to be afraid.

Death, after all, took many forms to me.

But the day I watched the future King of Light murder my father was the first day Death's shadows took *my* form, wrapping me in a merciless embrace, turning me into a vessel of lethal darkness.

And it would not be the last time my shadows raged out of control, seeking both solace and vengeance, but finding neither.

Chapter One

Seven Years Later

AFTER MONTHS OF SEARCHING, I'D FINALLY FOUND IT: A *crimsonlith* tree. One in full bloom, heavy with the fruits that contained the last ingredient our spell needed. Now, all I had to do was steal one of these fruits, carry it back, and let Orin work his magic with the seeds inside.

And then I would finally be ready to die.

I'd been told, over and over, that these trees no longer existed in the southern region of the Valorian Empire. Yet, here one was, standing tall right in the middle of Lord Roderic's home, kept in a glass-covered atrium flooded with light and all manner of other rare plants, just mere feet away from my spirit-self.

If only my spirit-self could have collected them right then and there...this mission could have been over in minutes.

Still, this was a start.

Having successfully located my target, I released the

tethering spell I'd been using to guide my ghostly shade, sending it snapping back toward my physical self. It was a useful trick for spying and seeking—though not so much for *stealing*; one needed a corporeal body capable of holding objects for that.

Minor details, you know.

Absently, my fingers closed around one of the four bracelets I constantly wore. As my thumb traced black, rose-shaped beads, I bowed my head and closed my eyes, waiting for my dizziness to subside. I'd grown quite skilled at projecting shades of myself around, but putting my pieces back together would likely always be a jarring experience.

A chill brushed over my hand—Phantom, rubbing his nose against my fingers and letting me know he still stood by my dazed body, watching over me.

Spirit-walking could be dangerous magic to wield—leaving the wielder in varying states of inebriation or outright oblivion—but I always took care to hide my body, and I never feared as long as Phantom stayed close to that body.

He kept most stray passersby away by his frightening appearance, alone, and he'd done this enough times to become something of a legend around here; the haunting, spectral beast of the once-royal city of Luscerna. When appearances alone didn't work, he could also exert a terrifying energy that left his targets feeling ghastly ill—a rather useful power he'd gained after dying.

Or mostly dying.

I say *mostly* because, thanks to my magic, he wasn't as dead as he should have been.

Three years ago, Phantom had fallen ill and passed

away. But I hadn't been ready to let him go. He was the only family I had left, and so, without thinking, I'd unleashed my shadows and given them free rein in a way I never had before, hoping they might pull him back to me… a desperate attempt that had actually *worked*.

Sort of.

To this day, I still didn't fully know how I'd kept him with me—or how long the spell would last.

Limboed was the term my mentor, Orin, used. The constraints of Phantom's physical body had been broken, his spirit had risen to dominance and headed for the Underworld…but that spirit had been stopped in its tracks by my frantic spell. Stopped, and imbued with enough of my strange magic that he was now anchored to me and, in turn, to the world I inhabited.

The same magic had also tied us together in other ways, allowing us to communicate with perfect clarity. For better or worse.

(*You weren't gone very long,*) came his voice, echoing softly through my mind. (*Are you sure you have a clear vision of your next step?*)

"Clear enough."

He sneezed. (*Hasty. Impetuous. As per usual.*)

Occasionally, I missed the silence between us.

I flashed him a crooked grin. "If you think I've been impetuous thus far, you *really* aren't going to like the next part of my plan," I warned, patting him on the head. My hand went through him, coming away covered in a viscous, shadowy substance. It was a matter of habit, petting him; even after three years, I still missed running my fingers through his solid fur.

He bared his teeth—his displeasure obvious—but

settled back on his haunches, expectantly. (*Well? What is your plan?*)

"I'm going to walk straight through the front door."

(*Brilliant,*) came the reply, dripping with obvious sarcasm despite the way his thought-speech tended to soften and blur his tone.

I was used to such sarcasm from him, so I continued without commenting on it: "Luckily for us, Lord Roderic lives alone, save for his servants. We only need to get them to open the door. Then, you'll make yourself as horrifying as possible to create a diversion and chase them away, and once they've fled, I'll slip in and take care of the rest. I have the route to the atrium memorized. It's an easy path. I can be quick."

(*Your optimism is exhausting.*)

"Some might argue that optimism is a virtuous trait in a person."

(*Some might argue that pessimists live longer.*)

"Why are you so worried? You're already practically dead."

(*Yes, but* you're *not.*)

"This is going to work," I insisted.

Phantom snorted, unconvinced.

"Also? Lord Roderic is a monster, if it helps you focus on becoming a distracting monster yourself. He's King Aleksander's puppet, responsible for plenty of unjust arrests and disappearances."

I bristled as Aleksander's name left my lips, fighting off a wave of nausea along with a rush of white-hot fury. Even with no audience save for my dog, I refused to let my hatred for the Light King show. He wouldn't control my emotions; to allow such a thing felt too much like bowing to him.

Something I would never fucking do, regardless of how many admirers and supporters he collected.

When I was finished carrying out my full plans, *he* would be the one bowing to *me*. Or groveling, more like, while begging for mercy I wouldn't give.

I leaned against the wall of the run-down, unused shed we'd taken refuge in, forcing myself to inhale several calming breaths. To hang on to my *exhausting optimism* like I always did, even when I felt like I was cracking apart from the inside out.

(*You should rest for now,*) Phantom urged, rising to his feet with an uncertain wag of his feathered tail. (*You still look dizzy.*)

I didn't argue. But there were too many people passing too close to the shed for comfort, so first, we moved to a less conspicuous location, tucking ourselves away in the small forest behind Lord Roderic's estate.

I dozed against a thick oak tree while Phantom kept watch. We waited until well after sundown—until most of the lights in the manor had flickered out—before we put our plan into motion.

I donned my hood and pulled my scarf up to cover most of my face; I didn't plan on being seen, but one could never be too careful. The bounty on my head was impressive at this point—between the lies the Light King had told about me and my family, and the occasional…ah, *questionable* missions I'd taken on to obtain the things Orin and I needed to get by. I didn't have time to deal with an arrest, or to pull off yet *another* elaborate escape from the city prison.

Not when I was this close to achieving the goal I'd been working toward for *years*.

I quietly scaled the front gates—while Phantom simply shifted into shadows and passed through the narrow bars—and then I tiptoed to the massive double-doors and gave several swift knocks, lingering there until I caught the sound of what might have been footsteps.

(*They're coming,*) Phantom confirmed, ears twitching.

I darted out of sight, hiding in the nearby hedge to watch my companion work.

After his death and near-resurrection, he'd gained the ability to shift his not-quite-solid body into different shapes. At first, they were mostly his same lanky, canine form—only larger or smaller, depending on his mood. He'd grown more talented at it as the years passed, though, and now he was constantly surprising me with the different forms he managed to twist himself into.

He was brilliant tonight, as usual. First, he shifted into a vaguely-human shape—that of a hunched-over old man, convincingly pitiful enough that Lord Roderic's servants heaved one of the doors open after only a brief glance through the curtains.

Then, as soon as the door opened fully, shadows engulfed the porch and everything around it.

When the darkness fell away, Phantom was transformed again, his shape now that of a hulking wolf with its fur bristling, its mouth open and breathing out cold, sparkling fog.

While the servants scrambled away from him in panic, I slipped inside and crept quickly in the opposite direction.

More servants soon arrived to aid the others; the sounds of their clashing with Phantom echoed loudly through the house, and I had to fight through the sudden surge of fear that tried to grip me and slow me down.

I wasn't sure what I would do if anything happened to him. Over and over, the grim, sobering fact played through my mind: *He's the only family I have left.*

I couldn't stop thinking of it, even once I shook off the fear and pressed deeper into the manor.

I'd never recovered my father's body, no matter how many times I'd risked sending my spirit-self back into Rose Point to search for it. My mother still lived, but in the same way that most who had been at our home on that horrible night seven years ago 'lived'—that is, she stood like a cursed statue. Still breathing, but otherwise unmoving, her pulse a barely-there fluttering beneath her pallid skin. Her eyes remained wide-open, too, as if the darkest depths of hell were the last thing she'd glimpsed before the curse settled… and even after all these years, she still couldn't pry her gaze away from those depths.

The halls and grounds of my old home were full of bodies in similar poses—bodies of both my family and our court, as well as most of the guests who'd come to celebrate my birthday.

Phantom and I were the only two members of our kingdom who I knew had escaped this fate; I'd spent years searching for others with no success. They existed, I believed, but nobody wanted to admit they'd been at Rose Point that night. To admit they'd been exposed to the cursed shadows that still twisted throughout the grounds to this very day.

I gave my head a shake and carried on. Tonight, I just had to steal this last ingredient. Then I would be able to go where I needed to go. To fix what I needed to fix.

I continued toward the center courtyard as quickly as I dared, pausing only to occasionally run my fingers over the rose-shaped beads of the bracelet that helped channel my projection spell, sending the spectral version of myself ahead to check my route.

As long as that projection of my essence stayed within a few dozen yards of my body, the side-effects of separation were minimal; I could move while simultaneously seeing the path ahead through my specter self's eyes—eliminating any chance of being ambushed by stray servants or, worse, by Lord Roderic himself.

Within minutes, I was pushing open the glass door to the atrium, bracing myself as a *whoosh* of hot air rushed over me.

The stifling air reeked of ripe and borderline-rotten fruit. The tree I sought was said to be especially pungent, its smell similar to that of burned flesh. This proved accurate; once inside the glass-walled room, I could have found the way to my target with my eyes closed.

The ground turned uneven and spongy beneath my boots as I approached the tree. With a slightly trembling hand, I reached up and plucked one of the lowest-hanging fruits. They were bright red with appendages that seemed to be alive, moving like scrambling spider legs.

The seeds in the center of these legs were the edible parts, but only when properly prepared. Without proper preparation, they were poisonous—which was likely the main reason behind this tree's near-extinction. Well, that and their known association with the world of the dead; they supposedly bloomed only in soil where bodies were buried and carried the essence of the underworld in their crimson blooms.

Which was, of course, why I needed them.

Lord Roderic loved to boast about his chef being able

to prepare edible dishes from the potentially fatal seeds; the fool's careless bragging was what had led to the rumors that ultimately brought me to his doorstep.

I plucked a few more of the spidery, waxy-skinned fruits for good measure. Carefully, I placed them in the special container Orin had provided, then secured that container in the canvas bag slung across my body.

The vastness of the central courtyard was more apparent now that I truly, *physically* stood within it. I couldn't help pausing for a moment to take it all in. My gaze swept over the abundance of colorful, rare plants—most of which I couldn't identify. Insects, equally colorful and unusual, buzzed loudly around my ears. The air no longer smelled purely ripe and sickeningly sweet; now, there was an undercurrent of salt and a tinge of smoke. A scent that felt familiar, though I couldn't say what it was.

My eyes kept returning to the crimsonlith tree. To its pale roots that rose above the ground, crisscrossing the dark soil, intertwining like skeletal fingers. To its silver leaves and the blooms I'd plucked…

Blooms that had already been replaced by new ones, several of which were starting to unfold, their flashes of crimson burning in the moonlight that filtered in through the glass roof.

My pulse skipped at the incredible, impossible sight. The air above the tree's roots flickered. The soil between the pale fingers seemed to shift, veins of sparkling, bluish black popping up through it.

I blinked, and the sparkling colors disappeared.

My skin crawled as I thought again of the legends surrounding this tree—the claims that its supernatural flourishing came from soil filled with decomposing dead.

Even knowing the legend, something about witnessing that flourishing in real time was unnerving.

I breathed in deep and exhaled slowly. Calmed my racing pulse. Settled the magic that had begun stirring in my blood and smoothed the chill bumps from my skin.

I would not allow myself to be unnerved by anything concerned with death.

In a matter of days, I planned to greet the world of the dead with a confident smile, knives in hand, steps unflinching. All my life was now centered on this one goal.

And I would not be turned away from it now.

Chapter Two

THE SUN WAS RISING, PAINTING THE SKY WITH STREAKS OF gold and red, as I scurried my way across the bridge that led to the home I shared with Orin.

For decades, he'd lived alone in this small cottage near the banks of Echoing Creek. My father and I had visited it occasionally when I was a child. Its cozy, chaotic interior was a place of wonder and laughter, alongside lectures and lessons in magic and a myriad of other topics. After I lost my parents, it had become a place of refuge, too—though it had taken months before I agreed to stay and consider it *home*.

I scaled the ladder propped against the right side of the house, making my way to the flat stretch of roof and the trio of skylights spaced across it. The middle window opened like the hatch on a ship, and we'd hooked another ladder to the rim of it, allowing for an easy descent into the cottage.

We had a door, of course. But the bits and pieces of Orin's latest experiments had stretched their way all around the perimeter of the living room, as they so often did, and a table had been dragged in front of the door to accommodate them. When I'd left that morning—by crawling through the kitchen window—said table had been covered in books, scraps of parchment, and countless gadgets in various stages of completion...all of it so precariously balanced that I didn't want to risk flinging open a door and creating an even *bigger* mess.

It was simply easier to drop in through the roof.

Phantom followed my lead, falling soundlessly to the dinged and scratched-up plank floor. His shadowy body sent chills rippling through me as he passed.

He threw a disapproving glance at the mess in front of the door before plodding to his typical spot underneath the stairs. He didn't really need sleep, considering he wasn't truly alive, but he tended to become grumpy when he didn't get his time alone—so I made a point of keeping a comfortable bed for him.

My mentor stood by the kitchen sink, humming a jovial tune as he washed a teetering stack of ceramic mugs. Smudges of ink stained his brown skin despite the soapy water sloshing all the way up to his elbows. His long waves of grey hair were tied back by a strip of leather at the nape of his neck, and he wore his favorite coat, even though a healthy fire blazed in the hearth. I'd mended that coat countless times over the years—a different scrap of fabric for every ill-fated experiment that ended in flames, or sharp edges, or some seepage of cloth-eating liquid.

At this point, I wasn't even sure what it had originally been made of.

"Morning, Orin," I said, cheerful in spite of my exhaustion.

"Nova, my beauty!" He spun around, throwing soapy water in all directions. "What a relief to see you in one piece."

I arched a brow. "You doubted I'd return this way?"

"Never," he proclaimed, waving a dismissive hand, flinging even more suds onto the crooked cabinets. "And even if I had, I'm a senile old man. You can't take my doubts seriously." With a properly stern look, he added, "Or my certainties, for that matter."

I grinned.

Old was an understatement, really. He'd never revealed his true age to me, but he'd served my grandfather, and his grandfather before that. Orin was one of the *Aetherkin*—beings with a connection to the old magic in our world that, among other things, tended to grant a longevity not seen in most humans.

He couldn't wield any magic directly—there were few who could, even among the Aethers—but he could sense it and, with the tools he expertly crafted, he could channel some of it. It's why my father had introduced me to him in the first place; Orin was the main reason I had *any* sort of control over my powers.

I still wore the bracelet my father had given me on my eighteenth birthday, and I'd been gifted several more like it in the seven years since. Each one was crafted by Orin. Each one helped me channel a different strand of my power, allowing me to access specific spells—such as the projecting spell the rose-bead bracelet helped me call upon. They'd helped calm the restless shadows inside of me, too; those dark ribbons hadn't emerged upon my skin in years.

I was up to four main bracelets now, and I was somewhat proficient at—or at least knowledgeable about—each of the spells they channeled. Spells that all centered around matters of death and souls, exits and endings—*necromancy* was the overarching term Orin, and other magic scholars, used to describe my innate powers. Powers that needed to be tamed, by way of enchanted jewelry or otherwise. For everyone's sake.

It was a crude system, but these bracelets were the best we could do; there simply weren't any true necromancers left to teach me how to properly wield my powers.

Once, it was said that the five kingdoms of Valor had been home to hundreds more like me. But not anymore. I was the only one Orin had encountered in a century, despite his extensive searching for others. Which I'd always thought was part of the reason he'd agreed to take me in: He *did* love collecting his oddities.

Even my parents had shown no signs of possessing the Shadow magic I did…though, I did have a twin brother—Bastian—who had carried markers of emerging magic. He'd died when we were just shy of a year old.

I had no real memories of him. But apparently, they'd found him dead in his crib, a dark scar running the length of his abdomen, with more scars splitting through the centers of his arms. As if something had tried to peel apart his skin and escape…

Ripped apart by his own magic, it was decided.

My parents almost never spoke of him, except to remind me of why I needed to keep my magic under control. Shortly after our first conversation about the matter, I'd found myself under Orin's tutelage. Given the alternative of losing another child, my mother had begrudgingly allowed me to continue honing my powers with him, even as I grew, despite her misgivings about his methods...and despite the fact that the old codger refused to swear loyalty to anyone but himself.

"Have some tea to warm yourself," Orin said, motioning to a steaming cup by the stove as he returned to washing dishes. "I'm sure it's been a long night."

I picked up the drink but didn't sip from it right away; every concoction in this house warranted caution. And a quick sniff told me I was right to be suspicious—whatever was in this cup smelled like poison and the wrong end of a horse.

"This is...I'm fairly certain this isn't tea, Orin."

He shot me an indignant look before stalking over and taking the mug from my grasp, inhaling the steam for himself.

"...*Ah*. So, that's where I put the foxglove elixir." His disgruntled expression turned sheepish. "Yes, right, no—don't drink that. It might lead to a mild case of...erm... *death*, I'm afraid. And not at all the kind we've been planning for."

I gave him a wry smile as I searched through the cabinets and grabbed a clean mug. "I'll just make something for myself, thank you," I said, moving to the sink to wash the mug a few more times...just to be safe.

"Very good, very good," Orin mumbled, offhandedly, having already carelessly placed the foxglove elixir down and moved on to the next object that grabbed his attention. A book, in this case—one with multiple, colorful slips of paper marking almost all of its pages.

"Judging by your mood, your mission was a success, I take it?" he asked without looking up from the book.

"Of course it was," I replied, retrieving the container of

crimsonlith fruits from my bag and plopping it onto the kitchen table.

He glanced up. His flicker of interest became a fixed stare, his eyes widening, mouth falling open. Clearly astonished—and now it was my turn to fix *him* with an indignant look.

"You *really* didn't think I was going to manage this heist, did you?" I pouted. "You should know better than to doubt my skills by now."

"I plead senility, once again." He chuckled, tossing the book aside and moving to the table. "But Nova...this is well done. Well done, indeed!"

I gave a little bow before returning to my cup.

While he inspected the fruits of my labor, I mixed up my usual comfort drink of piping hot black tea with sprinklings of cinnamon, sugar, nutmeg, and a dash of vanilla. The same drink my mother used to make me most mornings—though I rarely managed the perfect balance of bitter and sweet she always had.

This morning, in my exhausted state, I accidentally dumped enough sugar in it to render the damn thing nearly undrinkable.

I swallowed it down, all the same. The warmth felt good sinking into my bones, even if the sugar made my stomach twinge.

Orin had placed the crimsonlith blooms carefully in a row on the kitchen counter—after shoving away the mess that had already occupied said counter—and now he was sweeping around the room, plucking different containers from the shelves along the walls; mumbling to himself as he measured this and that; nodding as he lined up more ingredients.

I watched him, silently sipping my tea. After a few minutes, his collecting ceased. His soft lavender eyes fixed again on the blooms I'd gathered. He let out a low sigh, like a man who had traveled around the world and finally laid eyes on his destination. "The last piece. *Finally*."

A weight settled over the room, but neither of us acknowledged it with more than a meaningful look at the other; that was all we needed. We'd both already made peace with what came next.

Or as much peace as we were going to make with it, anyway.

"I'll prepare it all from here," he said, quieter, his eyes still on the blooms. "Then it will need a few hours to properly settle into a usable spell, and a few more after that to infuse it into a new piece of jewelry for you. What say you get some sleep in the meantime?"

I agreed, draining the rest of my drink before climbing to the loft where my bed awaited me in the same cozy, hastily half-made state I'd left it in.

I kicked off my boots and flopped onto the lumpy mattress without bothering to change, or to fully disarm myself, or to even pull the privacy curtains closed.

I'd planned to at least *attempt* rest, but I ended up sitting cross-legged on the mattress, instead, staring at the shelf directly in front of me. It held the few objects I'd dared to collect from Rose Point over the years: a violin that had belonged to my mother; a journal of my father's; an assortment of Phantom's toys, which had gone untouched since his death and the loss of his solid body.

From the shelf, my gaze lifted to the spiraling swaths of gold-flecked paint across the low ceiling. The paint had been added to cover the deep grooves crisscrossing that ceiling; gashes left behind by my magic after a particularly bad nightmare summoned it and sent it lashing violently out of control.

Six years had passed since that incident—the last time my shadows had clearly appeared on my skin.

Orin hadn't flinched when I'd woken him in the middle of the night, sobbing over the destruction those shadows had caused. And he hadn't immediately kicked me out, or threatened to lock me away in some 'safer' prison, or done any of the other awful things I'd feared he would.

He'd simply made a new bed for me on the couch, left me there with a cup of chamomile tea, and set to work purifying the magic-wrecked space with various herbs and enchantments. The following morning, I'd woken up to the sound of him humming as he covered the deepest grooves with paint.

The shimmering spirals had faded only slightly after all these years. They still reminded me of the *Zephyra*—the lights sometimes seen dancing in the southern parts of the Valorian sky on cold winter nights.

I crawled to the edge of my bed, peering sleepily down through the loft's floorboards. There was a decent-sized notch in the board just to the right of the bed, which I sometimes used to spy on Orin and the occasional interesting company he invited into our chaos.

He remained alone today, however. The door stayed barricaded, and he'd even closed the blinds, something that he—a lover of natural light—rarely did.

He was moving recklessly fast, now, fully caught up in the fervor of spell-making. I winced as he upended a bowl of what appeared to be beef stew; likely his dinner from last night, entirely forgotten about. He simply let it be, oblivious to the thick broth oozing across the table as all his focus zeroed in on some sort of smoking powder he was leveling off in a teaspoon.

I blinked, trying to clear the sleep from my eyes as I swept my gaze around the rest of the space, studying it.

I'd been gone much of the past week while working on planning my theft from Lord Roderic's manor, and the house had grown even messier than usual in my absence. If I disappeared for good, there was a very real chance Orin might lose himself entirely within the waves of clutter surrounding him.

How was he going to manage without me?

There were security concerns, as well; this house had no shortage of priceless artifacts, ancient tomes, and other specimens that would likely fetch a good price—assuming someone could pick their prize from among the mess.

Various wards surrounded the property, but it was typically *me* who chased away any threats.

I'd maimed an impressive number of would-be thieves, by this point.

And that was merely my work with a knife—to say nothing of the shapeshifting, spectral dog often seen hunting at my side; or my strange magic; or the outlaw reputation I'd carried since the night I fled from my old home.

Then again, Orin had managed to survive without me for years before taking me in. He'd be fine.

Wouldn't he?

He was back to singing his tune from earlier, much louder than before, and likely so caught up in taking notes about his spell-making that he would never hear me leaving.

Even if he did, I doubted he would interfere; for better or worse, he'd always let me come and go as I pleased.

I just needed to breathe some fresh air. To clear my head. To return to the place where this all started so I could remind myself of where I was going next.

Where I *had* to go next.

Without making a sound, I pulled my boots back on, double-checked the knives still secured to my belt, and then crept to the other side of the loft. There, a narrow staircase led down into a nook that I often cozied up in to read. A window took up most of the back wall—one I could pass silently through, as it was already unlatched and partially open to allow the soothing sounds of the babbling creek to filter in.

Once outside, I followed the familiar path along Echoing Creek, jogging through the early-morning mists with only birdsong and the occasional bounding deer for company.

It was only twenty minutes or so to the edge of my family's fallen estate, and a few minutes more before the shadows came into view.

For seven years, these shadows—the same kind that had chased me from my home on the night of my eighteenth birthday—had been colliding with a barrier of protective Light magic wrapped around the grounds of Rose Point. As a result, the air here had a beaten and battered, ragged and thin quality to it. Like it would never truly fill up my lungs, no matter how many deep breaths I took.

There were signs posted all around at the points of the colliding powers, all declaring essentially the same thing:

Off-limits, by order of His Majesty, Aleksander Caldor, King of Light and Fair Elarith; Elected Steward of the Eldrisan Throne.

That King of Light had erected the barrier of his magic to keep the curses in, and to prevent anyone from crossing over to get a better look at what lay on the other side. Protecting Eldris's people, he claimed, from the rot their own royal family had unleashed upon them—which was how he'd ended up with the title of *steward* to the Eldrisan throne.

It was all a lie.

A giant, fucking lie.

He was the one who had unleashed the very rot he claimed to be saving my kingdom from.

The night of my birthday celebration had been pure chaos, but in the seven years since, I'd untangled some events. Uncovered some truths. I'd ventured into the rotting lands multiple times, too, typically using my spirit-walking abilities to return to Rose Point.

So I'd seen for myself where the darkness flowed from: From the spot where Aleksander's sword had stuck into the stone—a deep, supernatural wound cleaved open by his blade after he stained it with my father's blood. A wound that still had not healed.

Luminor was the blade's name, I'd learned—the infamous, magical Sword of Light that had been passed down through the Elarithian royal family for generations. He'd never planned on gifting it to my parents, as I'd mistakenly believed; he'd always planned to wield it against them.

That sword had been swallowed up by the ground, along with my father, but dark energy still wept from the wound it created. Energy from the dead world below, Orin theorized. A world reserved for the deceased, but one that, centuries ago, was much more intimately connected—and accessible—to our living realm.

We'd studied the power enough to conclude it was separate from the magic that came from my own body. But for years, I hadn't been able to tell—or believe in—the difference. I'd assumed *I* caused the destruction and draining power. Because the shadows had chased me that night, driving me from my home and everything I'd ever known.

But now I understood they hadn't truly been *summoned* by me; the blade and the breaking world had let them in, and I had only channeled the darkness from underneath, briefly and inadvertently giving the dead energy a foothold. Orin had tried to convince me that I'd likely *saved* lives that night, by drawing the shadows toward me and running away from the manor.

Even so, I wasn't sure I could consider myself a savior of any kind. Not yet, anyway.

And the rumors perpetuated by the King of Light and his followers, of course, called me the exact opposite. They reminded my former subjects at every chance they could that I was the odd princess they had never fully trusted or embraced—the Shadow-marked woman who had allegedly cursed her entire home and everyone she loved.

Now, it was only a matter of time before Aleksander moved to *officially* annex my small but prosperous kingdom—a move that would likely be met with little resistance, unless I could stop the cursed shadows bleeding out from Rose Point and find a way to reveal the truth about the Light King's treacherous actions.

To do that, I needed to close the wound and recover the

sword that had caused it—a plot Orin and I had been working on for years.

And now, the most pivotal part of this plot was finally upon us.

My eyes fell on the main gates in the distance. After seven years, they should have been overgrown with weeds, overtaken by the elm trees flanking either side of them.

Instead, they were perfectly intact.

Nothing had grown around them, though the color of it all had faded in an unnatural way; it was like looking at a painting in need of restoration.

I'd physically pushed through the Light King's barrier a few times in the past, but it was always a draining, difficult experience—which was why I typically opted to send only my spirit, instead.

I traced my thumb along the rose-shaped beads around my wrist, thinking of projecting now. It was risky to do while I was alone. But the chance of anyone stumbling upon my incapacitated body so close to this cursed place was slim; too many strange things had happened here over the years—enough that even the bravest of thieves and trespassers had long ago abandoned Rose Point in favor of easier targets.

And I couldn't help the longing in my chest.

I *needed* to go inside.

Chapter Three

I whispered the word Orin had taught me—*SOMNIS*—and I tapped on the largest bead of the rose bracelet.

My soul separated from my body with a feeling akin to sinking into a snowbank—brutal cold, sudden darkness, and a muffling of all the noise around me.

But then I was emerging, digging myself back into brightness and sound and striding up to the manor, which looked as unnaturally faded as its gates.

I went immediately to the final destination I'd envisioned; another advantage of this projection spell—or *disadvantage*, in some instances—was the way time and distance could so easily blur while I moved as a ghost, allowing me to reach my target without too many thoughts or doubts getting in my way.

In the span of what felt like heartbeats, I was summiting the steps outside the banquet hall as if carried up by a favorable wind.

I walked the short, empty corridor to the massive

double doors that remained open, as though the guests on the other side were still waiting for me.

If I'd been in my physical body, sweat would have been beading my skin, just as it had on that last, fateful night.

I could still hear the sounds. I could still smell the food. As I passed through the doors, the memories swirled around me like elegant dancers, bright and mesmerizing—yet always fleeting in the end, skipping off the stage before I could look too closely at any of them.

They always got away, because there was no *true* life in this place. There hadn't been for seven years. I was the only conscious being here, as far as I knew.

There were the bodies, though.

In a small room off the main hall, dozens of those cursed, frozen bodies waited for me—breathing faintly, but otherwise unmoving.

This was the room I always ended up in, despite the ache it caused in my chest.

The queen stood closest to the door, a sword in her hand. She'd been guarding the ones behind her, I'd surmised.

Or trying to, at least.

But though her eyes remained wide open—eerily aware, even now—her head was bowed, as if she'd ultimately accepted whatever curse had come to take her. And, if the terrified expressions of those at her back were any indication, that curse had arrived baring teeth and horrors beyond anything this kingdom had ever known.

I could only guess at what had really happened. At what might have gone differently, if *I* was different. If I didn't have my own horrifying powers that frightened so many in my kingdom—including me.

If I'd stayed to fight instead of fleeing.

I reached to cup my mother's face, as if I could lift her eyes to meet mine.

But, of course, my hand went through her. Because I didn't belong here. I'd scarcely belonged here when it was a living, breathing place. I'd felt like a ghost in the crowd then, and now…

The far too-familiar feeling of being an outsider in my own life gripped me, making me lose focus on my spell.

I tucked my head toward my chest and willed myself back into my physical body, slamming into it with far less than my usual amount of control. It took my breath away, leaving me feeling like a specter for several more seconds, even as I became more aware of the world around me.

Finally, the floating sensations subsided. I rubbed the last of the memories from my eyes and gazed around at my current reality. My stomach clenched, again, at the sight of the shadows lashing against the Light King's barrier.

Not my darkness, I reminded myself. *I did not summon this curse.*

And yet.

And yet.

Darkness was darkness, according to so many in this kingdom.

I carried more darkness than most. I'd never wanted my death-related powers. I'd embraced them out of necessity, trying to negate the damage they could do. But here in the quiet morning—alone, and still haunted by the memories of all I'd lost—I openly loathed them. I wanted to reach inside of myself and rip them out, or just twist them into new shapes…

I just wanted to be *different.*

A sudden gust of cold energy lifted the waves of my hair, making me jump. Once my heart stopped racing, I searched the bushes behind me and quickly found exactly who I expected to.

"Phantom." I sighed. "Announce yourself next time, would you? You frightened me."

He might have been mistaken for a wayward scrap of shadow, if not for the way his bright blue eyes caught the sunlight when he blinked.

(*Paranoid, are we?*)

"Yes—likely from no sleep, and from staring down my own impending death."

(*Death is a bit of an exaggeration. You won't truly be dying, not if Orin does things properly.*)

I laughed to hide my nervousness. "You would know about not truly dying, wouldn't you?"

He bared his teeth at the reminder of his condition.

But, as usual, he was right.

I—much like my spectral companion—was not descending into our world's afterlife with permanence in mind. I was merely going to locate the magical sword that had passed into it, and then take care of the wound it had caused, whether by destroying that weapon or otherwise.

And then, with any luck, I would return to the living realm.

It wasn't as implausible as it might have seemed.

There was once a time when living beings could visit their loved ones who had passed on, if only for a short period of time. The Kingdom of Eldris was well-known for this, in fact; legend stated that the most-traveled route between the living and the dead—the infamous Nocturnus Road—came about because an ancient ruler of Eldris,

King Argoth, couldn't bear to be entirely separated from his wife when she died.

It was a story I'd heard often while growing up, given how thoroughly it permeated our society. Parts of the elegy he'd written for his queen were often recited in wedding vows and toasts to long-lasting loves across the empire.

> *...And if death should take you*
> *I will meet you there;*
> *look for me where the light*
> *gives way to shadow*
>
> *Seek me where pain and sorrow yield*
> *where time no longer flows;*
> *I'll find you in the stillness*
> *before any heartache grows...*

It used to be much more than a romantic story; people had traveled to Eldris from all reaches of the empire to pay homage to its first queen in hopes that her spirit would grant them passage to visit their lost loved ones.

It had been well over a century since the last known visit. Such travel was now forbidden—even talking of it was considered taboo, and a punishable offense in some places.

But that didn't mean it was impossible.

The barrier between the worlds was not impenetrable. There were plenty of hauntings and odd phenomenon serving as proof of this—not to mention the fact that the Sword of Light had been swallowed by the ground, and the energy radiating from the wound was clearly from the Underworld.

And, most importantly, there were spells that could still

open Nocturnus, that long-abandoned road between the living and dead worlds. It had taken Orin a lot of time and research to find one with true potential to work, but he'd managed it.

Of course, no one ever returned from such descents these days. Even with the proper preparation, to walk this road was the equivalent of signing off on your own death. But I was prepared to die if that was what it took to make things right—so long as I took care of the sword and its distorting power, first.

If I couldn't make it back, my only regret would be that I wouldn't *personally* be able to deliver justice to Aleksander. But Orin and I had an agreement, in the event that I didn't return. I'd written a series of letters for him to deliver to the queen. So when the wound was healed—and the curse over her and the others ended—she would know what to do next.

I pictured her frozen body. The sword in her hand. The fearless, stoic pose she'd held for seven years.

When she woke, my mother would see vengeance carried out, I was certain.

And the King of Light would pay for all he had done, one way or another.

Chapter Four

After leaving Rose Point, I ended up wandering through the surrounding wilderness for several hours, still unable to stomach the idea of trying to sleep.

Orin was waiting on the front porch when I finally returned. His eyes darted between the trees as I approached, narrowing at every odd sound as if expecting to see some dangerous fiend following me.

He didn't ask where I'd been.

I suspected he already knew, given how sensitive he was to the various magical energies of the world; I likely reeked of the magic bleeding from that wound the Light King's sword had left behind.

It was an energy specific to Rose Point—although, in recent months, weaker shades of this rottenness had started to spread beyond the borders of my old home, despite Aleksander's magical barrier. Truthfully, it felt like the rot was stretching farther outward with each visit…which was partly why my step was more hurried than ever, my tiredness forgotten as I met Orin's gaze, hoping for good news.

He offered that news immediately, holding up a small drawstring bag. "Your ticket to death, my lady."

I mirrored the grim smile he gave me as I took the bag and carefully pulled it open, dumping its contents into my palm.

A bracelet fell out. One far, far heavier than any of my others, yet still delicate in its appearance, with leather segments braided like twisting vines and holding pale amethysts between them. The two largest jewels were evenly spaced, so that when I slipped the piece on, one sat on top of my wrist while the other pressed underneath. One radiated warmth. The other pulsed with occasional bursts of cold. It made me think of the world above and below, with my racing pulse caught in between.

I stepped off the porch and into the daylight, holding the bracelet up to better inspect it. The sun's rays pierced through the pale purple jewels, revealing a swirling cortex of different energies within them. In one of the larger crystals, I thought I caught a glimpse of blooming red—the essence of the crimsonlith flowers, maybe? There one instant, gone the next.

The same unnerving sensation that had overtaken me in Lord Roderic's manor tried to sink its claws into me again, but I quickly shook it off.

"Stunning, as always," I told Orin.

He waved the words away, the way he always did when he was pleased with himself but didn't want to admit it. "More importantly," he said, "it's infused with all the substances necessary to guide its wearer into the Underworld. Though I caution: It will work differently than anything I've made for you before."

"How so?"

"Well, all your other accessories channel your own innate power. The crystals on this bracelet, however, were forged and spelled so they would draw in magic from *outside* of you—but only a specific type of magic, of course."

"The type flooding the road that once connected the living and dead worlds, I presume."

"Exactly." He beamed, as though this was just another routine lesson—one I was actually paying attention to, for once. "Now, according to all the research I've done, there is a lot more chaos on that route than there used to be. But this bracelet should help you navigate through it, drawing you to the right energies that will lead you fully to the other side."

"…How much chaos should I be expecting on this road, just out of curiosity?"

He propped a hand under his chin, considering for a moment. "You may have to dissolve some of it with your own power—absorb the excess to help you see things more clearly. Your siphoning bracelet should serve you well, regarding that."

I reached for that bracelet, absently squeezing the red beads making up the bulk of it. Soundlessly, I counted them, feeling my way toward the triangular golden charm hanging from the center.

It was one of the four bracelets I always wore. I had other accessories spelled with minor powers that I sometimes experimented with, but these four—well, *five*, now—were made of something stronger, both physically and magically speaking.

The original four were all intimately tied to my innate magic. The power the red bracelet helped me channel more effectively had been one of the earliest kinds to naturally manifest: The ability to drain energy from things.

It was the same ability I'd been practicing in the garden the night of my last conversation with Aleksander, before everything had gone to shit. I couldn't forget any of the details of that night, no matter how hard I tried—and maybe because I associated this power with that moment in time, I'd struggled to practice it every day since.

So *of course* it would be the one I needed to use.

I spoke none of my concerns out loud, but Orin picked up on them anyway.

"You are more capable with siphoning magic than you give yourself credit for," he insisted.

I ignored the praise and promptly changed the subject. I could handle my fears better when I didn't dwell on them —which was why I'd made myself a master at burying them so I could remain, as Phantom put it, *exhaustingly optimistic*.

"And what about Phantom?" I asked Orin. "Will he be able to follow me through this chaos?"

He looked to the trees again, to where the creature in question was a blur of darkness weaving in between the trunks, likely chasing a squirrel. Some doglike habits persisted, however much he'd changed after his near-death experience.

"I'm afraid I can't say. It will be an interesting experiment," said Orin. "He exists just fine within this world that he doesn't fully belong to, though, so hopefully, he'll manage in the netherworld, too."

I watched Phantom for another moment, fighting off a frown. Part of me didn't want to risk bringing him. But I knew he would never let me go without him; he hadn't even let me go as far as Rose Point on my own.

"Tomorrow, more will become clear," Orin said, giving my shoulder a comforting squeeze before nodding toward the house. "Now, this time I'm ordering you: Get some rest. I'll finish packing your things. We leave for the Nocturnus Door at first light."

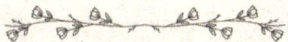

How does one pack their things for a trip to the afterlife?

It was the question I'd fallen asleep pondering, and the first one that came to mind as I blinked my eyes open to dreary sunlight.

The scent of spiced tea wafted up from below. The *tip tap* of rain on the thatched roof fell from above. Most of the windows were open in spite of that rain, allowing the sound of the creek to rush in—not with its typical babbling, comforting trickle, but with a roar of swelled-up and swiftly-moving water; I'd slept through what must have been a heavy storm.

I imagined myself caught in that creek's rushing current, letting it pull me toward my destination. It yanked me around, tumbled me out from under the covers and through the motions of dressing, before it tossed me—off-balance, but doggedly onwards—toward the stairs.

I descended with as much steadiness as I could muster, greeting Orin the same cheerful way I did most mornings.

Breakfast was a quiet, resolved affair. I tried not to think about how this might be the last time I sat at our table, with all the scratches and dents and burn marks I'd come to know and love over the years.

After breakfast, I went through my bag one last time, took a few quiet moments to mentally bury the fears trying to wrap their fingers around me…

And then it was time to leave.

We took a carriage out of Luscerna, driven by one of the few acquaintances Orin trusted in this city—Alistair Finch.

Finch had always seemed a bit…*off* to me, with his heavily-scarred skin and a penchant for bursting into strange songs without warning. But he also never questioned Orin whenever we needed a favor from him. And we needed his indifference this morning; anybody else would have surely wanted to know what the hell we were doing— why we were asking him to take us to such an odd location.

While Orin made small-talk with Finch—and occasionally hummed along with his songs—I stayed curled up in the back corner, watching the countryside blur by.

I'd left my newest bracelet on my left wrist, separate from the others. Keeping it alone on one arm helped me feel more balanced, given how heavy it was.

I absently plucked and pinched at the beads and bands of my original four as we bumped along. The black-rose bracelet—probably my most-used and trusted piece. The red-beaded bracelet I'd apparently have to rely on once I was on the Nocturnus Road. A wide bracelet made of colorful string, woven tightly into a pattern featuring multiple diamonds, which helped bolster my innate ability to speak with the dead; I suspected it was also a force that kept the communication between Phantom and I consistently smooth.

And finally, there was the bracelet my father had given me on my eighteenth birthday—one that still occasionally vibrated with the same, unmistakable power I'd felt when I first slipped it on…though it was a power I remained clueless about.

Orin proved evasive every time I tried to press him for details about it. He was the one who had made it, but it seemed my father had pressured him into the task; without my father mandating the lessons, Orin seemed content to let me figure out this particular power on my own.

The most I'd ever pried from him was a cryptic reply that the magic it channeled would reveal itself on its own… *if* it was meant to be.

As our ride stretched on, I found I couldn't take my eyes off the turquoise beads of my father's gift. Couldn't bring myself to stop studying the strange symbols carved and painted on some of the larger orbs—letters, I'd decided, but ones I'd failed to decipher, despite many hours spent flipping through Orin's books full of ancient languages and long-forgotten history.

Thunder rumbled in the distance.

Phantom—who had shifted himself into a small, shadowy, mouse-like creature and curled up in the pocket of my cloak—poked his head out and swiveled it around. He sneezed. He was not a fan of storms. His spectral body trembled, and my chest tickled with the nervous energy rolling off him.

I curled a finger under his mousy chin, giving it a reassuring rub even though my touch went right through him. "It's fine, Phantom. We're heading away from it, I think."

(*And likely into something much worse.*)

"Must you always be so pessimistic?" I said under my breath.

(*I like to think I balance out your ridiculous optimism.*)

"You can always stay here in the land of the living, you know."

(*You'd be lost without me.*)

"True enough," I muttered, grinning slightly as I sank deeper into my seat.

Finch dropped us off, as requested, at the head of an overgrown trail, right at the edge of a forest known as Ashenveil. He helped me down from the carriage, his eyes and his touch both lingering a little too long. A frown twitched at the edges of his thin lips as I pulled away from him.

His expression unsettled me. It felt like the lingering look of a person watching a knight heading off to war, knowing their return was unlikely—but how would he know? And why would he care? Finch and I had rarely spared each other more than a glance. He knew little about me. He certainly knew nothing of the war I had ahead; no one did, except Orin and me. We'd made certain of that.

Convinced I was imagining his concern, I offered a brisk *thank you* and then quickly turned to the path we still had left to travel on foot.

Once well-used, the trail before me now appeared ominous at best. Weeds and fallen tree limbs claimed much of the walking space. Bits of broken, rusted lanterns gleamed in the sunlight—the remnants of ornate, bright sentinels that had once stood along the entire route.

Our real destination was a few miles south along this ruined path.

We started down it without a word. The silence—an

unusual occurrence between us—settled deeper during our walk, lasting until the top of a steeply-pitched roof came into view. This was our true target: an abandoned shrine to Calista, Argoth's beloved queen. It was one of several scattered throughout Eldris.

Once upon a time, through the doorways within these shrines, one could supposedly access various points along the Nocturnus Road with relative ease.

Now that I was truly approaching it, doubt threatened; I still wasn't entirely sure portals like this could truly be real, even through the use of the correct blessings and spells or whatever else. But Orin was convinced. And his spells were successful more often than not—however messy that *success* ended up being—so I didn't hesitate to jog after him when he called on me to hurry up.

We made our way down paths that meandered through dried up fountains, through bits of crumbling statues, and then up the leaf-littered steps to the doorless shrine.

Inside, it smelled of dust and dead flowers. There was a hint of something waxy, too, as if melted candles had been stashed somewhere, though I never managed to spot them. The windows were missing most of their glass, but judging by the colorful, jagged teeth still around the edges, they had been beautiful during their better days.

Those teeth glinted in the early morning light, throwing radiant patterns across the entirety of the large space—save for one corner.

There, a spot for a door was set into the stone wall…but there was no actual door in place. There was only a frame with strange symbols etched deeply into its dusty wood.

The bricks within this frame were different from the walls around it. Newer—as if there was a room on the other side that had been closed off well after the shrine was completed. The whole area was cast in darkness. It seemed to absorb all the bright colors from the broken windows, no matter how the sun shifted and threw its beams through the glass.

Unnatural.

There was definitely something about it that was—

Orin cleared his throat. "Come look at this, Nova."

I hesitated, my gaze still on the odd doorframe.

Phantom leapt from my pocket, his mouse body twisting, turning into shadows that reshaped themselves into his usual canine form. He hit the floor silently and, ever the curious one, he padded over to the long, narrow table that Orin stood before. Lifting onto his back paws, he appeared to brace against the edge of this table—though in reality, his near-weightless body was merely hovering over it, studying the art it contained.

I followed slowly, taking the space beside him.

It was a story that stretched before us—one told through scenes carved into thirteen separate slabs of marble affixed to the table's top.

In the very center was a particularly eye-catching panel. On it, a man stood before a coffin covered in flowers and flanked on either side by two crimsonlith trees. Countless soldiers surrounded him, their heads bowed while the man's face was lifted, staring upward. Looking at the scene, I was gripped with a feeling I couldn't easily describe—a strange kind of...*grief*. A hollowing cold that was survivable, yet miserable. That look in his upturned gaze...

Alone.

Despite the dozens of people set in stone beside him, he appeared utterly lost and alone.

I shuddered. I knew the feeling. I'd spent most of my life trying to *bury* that feeling. And something about looking at this man brought it rushing to the forefront of my mind with a quickness that took my breath away.

I forced my gaze to Orin. "King Argoth?"

"Indeed."

"He built all of these shrines, didn't he?"

"So it's said," Orin replied. "All intended to bring him closer to his beloved, dead queen. It took him several tries to create the first one that properly opened into the Underworld, however. After he managed to open that first path, he went back to the shrines he'd previously attempted to build, making them functional as well, and continued to build upon the road on the other side—a road they all lead to."

"Nocturnus."

"Yes. The temple we stand in now is the last one he built, but the first one to succeed at his ultimate goal." His voice was somber, his expression more serious than I'd ever seen it. His eyes misted over as he swept them around the dilapidated space. "Quite a miserable state it's fallen into, isn't it?"

He didn't seem to be expecting an answer; he looked lost in his own thoughts. I wondered at the breadth of those thoughts and the memories he had—how many times had he visited this shrine, and others like it, when it was still a functioning throughway?

So much had changed in Eldris over the past century, alone. And I shuddered to think about the changes to come, should the King of Light go unchallenged in my kingdom.

I searched for something to say to soften the mood, but I came up with nothing.

Orin inhaled a deep, rattling breath—one that reminded me, again, of how old he truly was. "It's time, I suppose," he said, his gaze lingering on my new bracelet for a moment before jumping up to my face. "Trust yourself. And don't be afraid of your darkness. Your magic will protect you, if only you let it."

I nodded, even as I fought the urge to recoil. I didn't want to be reminded of that darkness within me; I merely wanted to use it to get through what I needed to, and then go back to my usual survival method of pushing it all down deep enough to ignore it.

"Nova, seven years ago, when I first offered to take you in…" He trailed off, fidgeting with one of several rings on his gnarled fingers, swiping at what looked like spell-ingredient residue underneath the gold band.

I let out a nervous laugh. "We don't need speeches, Orin. This isn't goodbye forever."

"I just wanted to say…"

"I know. I'll be fine."

"Yes. Of course you will." He molded his mouth into a forced smile and rolled up the sleeves of his patchwork coat. With a quick wink, he said, "Now, stand back and watch me work."

I stepped aside as he moved toward the corner where the strange doorframe stood. Once he was facing it, he reached into the bag slung against his hip. He pulled out a small jar sealed with cork and twine and started to carefully open it.

Humming a tune under his breath, he swiped a finger through the violet-colored contents of the jar, and then he proceeded to mark the bricks within the frame.

For several moments, nothing happened.

Orin closed his eyes and whispered something under his breath.

A deep rumble vibrated through the room; I couldn't tell if it was coming from inside or outside of the shrine, but it made both Phantom and me jump. I braced a hand against the table while Phantom curled behind me, pressing into my legs, his ears flat against his skull.

We watched as a spinning vortex of black and grey appeared in the center of the bricks, swallowing up the marks Orin had painted.

Another rumble. This time, a cold breeze swept through the room along with it, leaving the taste of ash and decay on my tongue when I breathed it in. The colors on the bricks continued to spin for a few beats before stretching into a more defined image, one that flickered and seemed to be a glimpse of a realm beyond—a shadowed landscape filled with jagged mountains and swirling mist.

I blinked, and the scene was gone.

In its place was a door.

It looked perfectly average and unassuming, as though it had always been there. The longer I stared at it, the more I found myself questioning how I'd missed it before.

A sudden, unseen force grabbed at my body, pulling me forward.

Before I could lose my nerve, I reached for the silver handle in the door's center and pulled it open.

And with Phantom at my heels, I stepped over the threshold, immediately falling into darkness on the other side.

Chapter Five

Falling into death was a lot like falling asleep.

Waves of black rose up on either side of me, tunneling my vision, making my balance sway. I hit the ground and a heaviness immediately followed—one that made my eyelids droop and my limbs feel sluggish and clumsy. If I could have just rested a moment, then maybe…

(*You can't rest here.*)

The voice in my head was familiar, yet far away, like something from a memory. I tried to pinpoint its origin, anyway, stumbling along with my too-heavy body, reaching out with tingling hands.

The very air seemed to be fighting against me. *Collecting* against me, too, the particles of it settling on my chest and making it harder and harder to breathe.

Panic started to sink in, until, somehow, Orin's instructions parted through the drowsy fog in my brain. My fingers fumbled along my wrist until they closed over the bracelet I needed—my red-beaded bracelet with its golden charm.

Just touching that charm was enough to send a jolt of confidence shooting through me.

"*Siphonus*," I whispered.

The air sparkled with a myriad of colors, suddenly—all the different shades of life and magic surrounding me. With some effort, I could partially make out the shape of the Nocturnus Road itself—a relatively clear outline beneath everything else.

The second most prevalent energy swirling around me held no definite shape. It was the color of a sky at twilight, rippling like a protective shroud over the road, masking large swaths of it.

This was the *chaos* Orin had warned me about; likely made up of the residual memories of all the ones who had walked this road an age ago. An energy contained within the stones of the road itself, at one point, but now it had grown restless after being left to fester and swell on the abandoned path for so long. I'd seen similar colors swirling around abandoned graveyards.

Life left a lasting imprint, even in the most desolate, forgotten places.

With a flourish of my hand, I pulled bits of the chaotic energy away from the road, trying to drain them and clear my path forward. They resisted. I dug in my heels, clenched my bracelet more tightly, and tried again. And again.

Finally, I felt a line of it shifting—like a stubborn vine breaking free from the grip of thorns, nearly throwing me off balance as it snapped toward me.

Like it always did, the spell left me feeling like I might topple over with the slightest breeze. *Draining* did not mean dissipating; energy did not simply disappear. It had to go somewhere—into me, in this case—and I'd yet to learn how to stay balanced while the bits and pieces of other things redistributed themselves into my body.

When it all finally settled, I looked up and tried to orient myself.

I'd cleared my path, but it was one that seemed to stretch endlessly in both directions.

Remembering my newest bracelet, I lifted it in front of me and grasped both of the large amethyst stones—the hot one above and the cold one below. I thought of where I wanted to go, as Orin had told me to do, and I squeezed tightly. The hot and cold of the gems seemed to meld inside of me, bringing a comforting, warm certainty into my limbs.

As I relaxed into the feeling, I felt a pulling sensation taking hold of me—the same kind that had urged me to step through the doorway in the shrine.

Once again, I followed it.

Dizziness still threatened, but I broke into a jog, determined to reach the end of the road before the twilight energies I'd absorbed had time to be replenished, to converge and block my path once more.

After what felt like a mile of pushing my way through thickening darkness, the same heaviness from earlier began chasing me. The farther I went, the more tempting the heaviness became. It nearly made my knees buckle more than once. If I could have simply knelt for a moment, maybe rested my head…

(*You can't rest here.*)

There it was again—closer this time. I clambered toward the voice as if caught in the crashing, pulling surf of a restless ocean, trying to make my way back to the shoreline.

My foot caught on something. I tripped, only just catching myself against the road I could barely see. I twisted back around, searching, reaching for the knife near my boot.

Phantom's eyes blinked back at me.

If not for those familiar blue eyes, I likely wouldn't have recognized him. He was in a strange shape as he slinked closer; something serpentine, but with powerful legs, clicking talons, and a sharply-tipped tail.

And he was...*solid*.

Solid enough that I'd actually *tripped* over him.

"Are you...?"

He lifted his tapered snout and huffed out a breath that sent a puff of shimmering, warm dust into the air. Though his shape was more dragon-like than dog-like at the moment, he was still covered in waves of sleek black fur. *Solid* black fur. It glistened in the breath of energy he'd exhaled.

(*Let's just hurry and get away from this road. It feels chaotic. Unstable.*)

Despite all my burning questions, I followed his lead as he broke into a sprint. His footfalls were quiet—yet not the silent steps I was used to hearing from his more ghostly form. We ran together down a gradually steeper slope until, soon enough, my feet fell upon soft, spongy ground.

I slowed, taking in my surroundings. The scent of damp, rotting earth overtook me at first, but a sweeter aroma—like freshly-picked berries—eventually fought its way toward me as well. Ethereal wisps of fog snaked through the air. Beyond its swirling, I could see the outlines of distant trees draped in shadow and edged in what seemed to be starlight—though there were no stars above that I could see.

It was desolate. Foreboding. Frightening. And yet…

It was one of the most beautiful places I'd ever seen.

Walking through it made me feel as if I were floating. As if all of the questions and fears weighing me down were suddenly gone. Not simply dead and buried…but *gone*.

The feeling of liberation, unfortunately, didn't last.

As we reached the starlight-edged trees, the temperature dropped alarmingly quickly. An odd wind whispered around us, making it feel even colder. My skin tingled with warning, as though lightning was building somewhere nearby, preparing to strike.

I jerked my head up in search of an oncoming storm.

The entire 'sky' might have passed for a tempestuous cloud; one continuous, lightning-filled cloud, shifting between shades of black, red, and grey. The way it simmered and seethed reminded me of the volcanic fields I'd once visited as a child, in the Ember Islands off Valoria's eastern coast—only the colors were more muted, and somehow more ominous because of it.

My stomach flipped.

How had I already let my guard down?

Beautiful though it might have been, this was a dark place. A dangerous place. I didn't truly belong here, and I needed to stay focused so that I could accomplish my task and then leave it all behind as soon as possible.

I abruptly realized Phantom was not behind me, and the anxious fluttering in my stomach became painful.

I found him just before panic truly set in; he stood beside a narrow stream of silvery water, gazing at his reflection. He was back to something that resembled his original canine form.

"You're almost solid," I commented, still unable to fully believe it.

(*More suited to the dead world than the living, it would seem.*) He wagged his tail, and was promptly distracted by the sound of it actually *thumping* against the ground. He chased it for a few seconds—clearly enamored with the fact that he might actually be able to grasp it in his jaws for the first time in years—before collecting himself and settling back into a more dignified sitting position. (*I feel light here, even though I'm more solid.*)

I frowned; I still felt that way, too—as if I could float away and forget about the world above, if I really wanted to.

It was unsettling, how dangerously alluring death could be.

"Let's not get used to it," I told him. "We have a job to do here. Nothing else."

Phantom stood, giving his body a hard shake. He lifted his gaze to mine, expectant.

I adjusted the weight of the bag on my shoulders and set off, and he didn't hesitate to follow.

"From a topographical standpoint, the dead world mirrors the living, in many ways," I said to Phantom as we walked, reciting the lessons Orin had given me on the matter. "So we'll follow the route east, just as if we were returning to Rose Point in the world above. That will hopefully lead us to the place where the Light King's sword carved out a path for the rot of this realm to bleed through…"

Phantom trotted along beside me, mostly listening, though his ears occasionally perked and his hackles lifted at what I assumed were distant sounds too quiet for my own senses to pick up on.

My eyes darted all around us, scanning for landmarks I might be able to orient myself by. I was trying to maintain my optimism, to keep myself grounded in the knowledge that this place was only a reflection of where I came from; I wasn't that far from home, really.

But the longer I studied it all, the more this particular swath of the Underworld seemed entirely removed from the living realm I'd left behind.

To my left, a great chasm split through the ground, wild and twisting, a murky ocean of dark fog and scattered wisps of white energy filling it. I veered farther and farther to the right as I walked, trying to put more space between myself and the chasm's precarious edge, but that only led me to looming mountains with cracked and crumbling faces. There were piles of rubble at the base of these mountains, and stripped, gutted grooves that suggested prior landslides, making me hesitant to wander too close.

Despite the ominous surroundings, however, our journey proved uneventful for several miles—until I saw something moving out of the corner of my eye: Dark, shadowy bodies with strands of gossamer white energy tangled like spiderwebs around them.

The restless, wandering souls of the dead.

They were a jarring sight, even though I'd expected to see them here.

Orin had warned that, given my innate magic, there was little chance of me being able to walk through this morbid landscape without causing some sort of disturbance. It was only a question of *how much* and *how many* I would disturb—and how dangerous that disruption might prove.

I kept my eyes straight ahead, determined not to get distracted. The amount of chaos my power and I could potentially wreak in this dead world was immeasurable. It was imperative that I chose one path to follow and followed it to the end.

But the souls continued to follow me down my chosen path, too.

Perhaps it was my magic inadvertently fueling them somehow, but they seemed more sentient than I would have expected. They slowed when I slowed. Turned when I turned. A few made movements on their own, too, sweeping wider and out of my line of sight—almost as if they were dividing and preparing to attack from all sides.

Phantom voiced my fears a moment later: (*They're trying to surround us, I think.*)

I broke into a run.

Ahead, the terrain became messier, the mountains I'd been traveling alongside easing into my path, into foothills full of uneven ruts, path-blocking boulders, and jutting rock formations of all shapes and sizes. I set my eyes on two particularly large slabs of stone rising up in the distance, a narrow passage cutting between them. If we could get through that narrow gap, hopefully...

I didn't think beyond this. I only ran faster. Just as I reached the opening to the gap, I caught a flash of swirling white energy diving toward me.

A terrible coldness wrapped around my ankles. Fingers slipped beneath my pant leg and clenched into my skin—not quite a solid touch, but enough to knock me off balance. I stumbled. Stayed on my feet. Kicked at the reaching fingers, gasping as my boot went through them. As an even deeper cold sank into my bones—

And then *something* struck the fiend that was attacking me, drawing a sound like howling wind from it as its hold on me slipped.

I was free.

I didn't stop to try and make sense of *how*, or of *what* had just happened—not until I was on the other end of the gap.

Phantom raced ahead of me, bolting out onto a sweeping expanse of dark, uneven, but mostly clear ground.

Breathing hard, I straightened and glanced over my shoulder. The sound of howling wind persisted. An odd energy funneled through the gap behind me. I risked a few steps back into that gap, just until I could see the opposite side again.

Nothing else was there—dead or otherwise—aside from the creature that had tried to attack me. It was shriveling up, turning to nothing more than wisps of smoke that occasionally curled into the vague shape of a human.

Disturbing—but harmless now, I thought.

An arrow lay on the ground beside it. One that seemed to have sucked the sentience out of the wandering soul and put it to rest, somehow. Whoever—or *whatever*—had fired that magical arrow…had they been trying to help me escape?

"Thank you?" I called out, unsure of what else to say, and hoping good manners might coax my protector out of hiding.

I received no reply.

Curiosity getting the better of me, I climbed the rocks to my right until I came to a large, flat ledge that afforded a better view. I searched for several minutes, but...no sign of anything, spectral or otherwise.

Oh well.

I jumped down and continued on my way. And as I emerged on the other side, I quickly forgot about what I'd left behind, my attention grabbed instead by a grove of flowering white trees that had suddenly appeared in the distance.

"That grove wasn't glowing so brightly before," I whispered to Phantom as he raced back to my side. "Was it?"

He growled in response, the air around him darkening as he stalked forward. His body shifted as easily as it had in the world above, but arguably more impressively, now; rather than shadows tumbling chaotically about as they had in the past, watching him change here was like watching ink spill upon a page, only to arrange itself into the shape of a perfectly accurate drawing.

This time, the ink became the dragon shape he'd taken on the bridge—with the addition of wings. He flexed those leathery appendages but didn't take flight; only pressed them back against his lean shape, streamlining his body, making it even faster.

I lost track of the blur he became as he hurtled into the trees.

Those trees reacted strangely as I stepped into their embrace, their white flowers blooming with sudden ferocity and expanding to their full diameter in the span of seconds—only to shrivel up in the next breath. Several of them burst as they withered and compressed to their most compact point, showering me with fragrant petals as they did.

Incredibly *bright*, fragrant petals.

After so much time in the darkness outside of this grove, the effect was blinding.

Squinting against the light, I carefully picked my way down a narrow path. Even as my eyes adjusted, the brightness made my head ache. Deeper inside the grove, the trees grew more scattered, which meant less petals to blind me—but countless other things seemed to be glowing at this point, too; the veins of leaves; clusters of berries; little mushrooms lining the trails. And the warm, close air, while pleasant at first, soon became sweltering. Paths crisscrossed in a labyrinth-like fashion—well-manicured, yet leading nowhere clear.

I finally caught up with Phantom at the center of four of these paths.

(*I think we should leave this place. It was a mistake to enter it.*)

I was nodding along with him before he finished the thought, but I couldn't bring myself to follow him as he turned and slinked away in search of an exit.

Something in the distance had caught my eye.

I stumbled a few steps closer, until I was certain of what I saw, and I froze.

Less than a hundred feet away, reclining against a massive silver tree with his eyes closed, was a man who looked *exactly* like the King of Elarith.

Chapter Six

"Impossible," I breathed.

Phantom let out a low snarl. (*If the King of Light is here, then who is that on the throne in Elarith?*)

"Good question."

I crept closer.

How could I not?

For seven years, this face had haunted my nightmares. For seven years, I had been working to heal the damage he'd done. *Seven years* of planning my revenge against him and all the curses he'd brought upon the world above. Upon my kingdom. Upon *me*. I'd hoped to face him myself, to someday personally introduce my dagger to his neck, but this man sitting before me now...

It couldn't have been the King of Elarith.

He wasn't moving, aside from an occasional slow, deep breath. A stunning statue of taut muscles and tense, frozen limbs, seemingly alive underneath its stone casing. He looked eerily similar to my mother and all the partygoers caught in their frozen poses back at Rose Point.

(*Be careful,*) Phantom warned, as I came within a few feet of the reclining man.

I gripped my bracelets. Not necessarily for the sake of spells, but for comfort. Everything felt as if it was tilting around me, but squeezing my familiar charms—reminding myself of the power they could channel—kept me balanced.

I was balanced. I was solid. Not a ghost, the way I usually was whenever I visited my mother in the living tomb that was my old home—and I couldn't help but crouch down and reach my solid hand forward, eager to touch and see what one of these statuesque beings might truly be made of.

Aleksander's face was not comprised of stone after all, though it felt similar. His cheek was incredibly firm and shockingly cold beneath my fingertips...but it gave slightly beneath my touch, and after a few seconds of pressing against him, the pulse of life underneath became apparent.

A pulse that clearly grew stronger for every moment I kept my fingers against him.

It felt like the opposite of the sort of energy my magic usually created. And I hadn't even called upon any of that magic—yet his body was clearly reacting to my touch. I couldn't pull myself away from the strange sensation of his stirring, even as my own pulse started to pound and my skin flushed uncomfortably hot.

Phantom slithered closer, his lithe body arching up as he reached me, his bright eyes searching the trees with purpose.

A single word hissed into my thoughts: (*Company.*)

I jerked my hand away from the frozen king. There was movement all around us an instant later—the brush shivering, the ground trembling, the light flickering. I could sense gazes settling in our direction, too. We were being surrounded. But by what, I couldn't say; I couldn't take my eyes off Aleksander.

Because he had just started *glowing*.

Like the flora strewn throughout this grove, only brighter, and with warmer tones woven through the strands of light—the fiery oranges and golds of a faint, dreary sunrise.

I reached a tentative hand back toward him, wondering if the light felt as warm as it looked.

It was hot enough to burn.

And this time, his skin seemed to crack at my touch, jagged fissures appearing and crisscrossing over his face, down his neck, disappearing beneath the loose linen shirt he wore.

He gasped.

I tumbled back, nearly losing my balance. Catching myself, I rose back into a more formidable crouch, lifted my gaze to his face—

He was *awake*.

Awake, and staring at me with a hatred so intense it felt like my skin might melt from the sheer heat of it. The moment stretched on for several horrific seconds before he finally blinked, and his expression changed; his first instinct had been fury, but his second seemed to be confusion. Disbelief.

Finally, his eyes narrowed once more in rage—and recognition.

"*You.*"

I withdrew the knife at my boot before quickly rising and taking several steps back.

He was on his feet just as quickly. He swayed for several seconds, as if he'd been holding his pose for long enough that the muscles in his legs had atrophied. But just as I started to lower my guard, thinking he might be too weak to actually fight, he rushed forward.

Crackling light surrounded his fist.

He swung.

I managed to avoid the fist itself, but not the bolts of energy that flung from it. They fell like a hail storm across my body, the larger beads of energy stinging straight through my clothing and leaving painful welts on my skin.

In the corner of my vision, I still saw covert movement. People were still darting around, just out of sight, surrounding us. Phantom stalked along the edges of the trees, hissing and snarling, trying to flush them out.

I kept my attention on Aleksander—was forced to, as he was already preparing another attack. This time, the crackling energy around his clenched hand tapered to a point, like a makeshift sword.

Before he could finish forming the weapon, I rushed forward, swiping my knife toward his neck.

When he moved to parry my blade with his half-formed sword of energy, I slammed my other fist into his stomach. He doubled over. I considered plunging my knife into the exposed back of his neck. I could picture it so disturbingly clearly: a river of red staining the silvery locks of his hair; his body crumpling, returning to the statue-like stillness of before...

Two things stayed my hand.

First was the need I felt to keep him alive long enough to question him, to make sense of how he could be *here* when he was also in the living realm.

And then, there was the way more cracks had appeared in his skin when my fist connected with his body; there were dangerous flashes of magic sparking out from the fissures, reaching toward me like bolts of living lightning.

I squeezed the handle of my knife more tightly and backed away, attempting to put distance between myself and those currents of bright magic so I could think more clearly.

He remained bent over for several seconds longer, clenching his stomach, cursing.

I shook out my wrist, letting the clinking and clanging of my bracelets ground me once more. The red-beaded bracelet slipped down over my palm, falling over the others as if urging me to use it first. I traced my thumb over its triangular golden charm. I whispered the word Orin had taught me.

The distinct energies of my surroundings swirled into view, but they seemed…*wrong*.

All the colors were skewed, and strange halos appeared around it all, blurring everything together and making it impossible to focus my magic on anything specific.

Was I still too weak, too disoriented from the amount of power I'd used on the Nocturnus Road?

Or was something about Aleksander's magic throwing mine off?

I tried to level a glare in his direction.

The amount of energy surrounding him was blinding.

Blinking, I spun away, abandoning my attempt at a draining spell, and considered escape routes. Aleksander still seemed off-balance from his time spent in repose. I could have gotten away. He might have followed, but someone had saved me from the restless dead chasing me earlier; maybe I would get lucky again.

I made up my mind to run—

Until I looked down and, suddenly, I was too stunned to take another step.

Because for the first time in *years*, bold, shadowy markings were rising upon my skin.

What the hell was going on?

I was so distracted by the ribbons of black lifting from my body that I almost didn't see the arrow, made of pure Light magic, flying straight toward me.

I twisted aside. It only grazed my thigh, but even the shallow wound sent buzzing energy skipping through my veins. Between it and my emerging markings, I was too dazed to make myself move fast enough.

The Light King, on the other hand, was blazingly fast and focused all of a sudden—a blur of power that slammed into me, knocking me further off balance. His arms wrapped around my waist. He threw me against the nearest tree. My knife slipped from my grasp and my breath left me with a violent gasp.

He pinned my arms at my sides, pressing them into the rough bark.

"Seven years," he said, his face tilting uncomfortably close to mine. "I've suffered *seven years* in this hell after what you did."

"After what *I* did? You—"

His hand caught my throat, choking off my reply.

I stopped trying to talk and instead tried to free myself, thrusting my knee upward. He narrowly avoided the strike. The movement shifted his hold, and I nearly slipped free;

he caught me by the arm and twisted it painfully, forcing me to go still.

"*Seven years*," he repeated in a low, growling voice. "And you aren't escaping me now."

"You'll find I'm very good at escaping," I snarled back.

He pushed harder against my arm.

The biting pain woke something desperate inside of me. The swirls of darkness on my arm grew bolder. They started to lift and twist and spin around us, and I panicked a bit at the sight, remembering how calling upon these shadows in the past had always left me feeling lightheaded, removed from my own body—not a feeling I wanted to experience while trapped in the king's deadly embrace.

I didn't know how I would fare, allowing them to rise after all these years.

And I never found out—because Phantom was upon us in the next instant, bringing a cold wind and a storm of his own shadows with him.

He shifted briefly into an inky, amorphous essence, making himself small enough to slip between Aleksander and me. Then he exploded back into his solid dragon form, talons thrusting outward toward the king's chest, forcing Aleksander to stagger backwards to avoid impalement.

The force of Phantom's re-solidifying body threw me back against the tree, taking my breath once more. But when I caught it and the dizziness subsided, I realized I was free. I stumbled my way from the tree, snatching up my fallen knife as I went.

Aleksander darted furiously around Phantom's coiling form and dove after me.

I ducked his reach and then swiped upward, catching

his wrist with my blade. I danced several feet away before turning back to face him.

Blood poured from his wrist; he didn't spare it a glance.

"I'm *very* good at escaping," I reiterated with a nasty grin. "Because I've had *seven years* to practice, after your kingdom's sabotage and lies made a criminal out of me."

Whatever response he gave, it was swallowed up by Phantom's hiss as he shot forward.

I watched, applying pressure to the wound on my thigh, as Phantom wrapped his long, powerful body around the king and bent him toward the ground. His bottom jaw unhinged, allowing him to open wider, putting his full, terrifying set of fangs on display.

I wouldn't be able to question that bastard if his face was ripped off.

I realized this.

But the stinging pain in my thigh and the ache in the arm he'd nearly snapped in half made me less inclined to care.

Before Phantom's fangs could crush him from existence, however, the ones surrounding us finally rushed out from their hiding places.

Ten soldiers, that I managed to quickly count. All carrying bows. They didn't try to interfere with my shapeshifting companion. Instead, they all nocked and drew arrows with practiced, synchronized precision, pointing them at me. With the same disturbingly coordinated sort of movements, they hurried several steps closer, tightening the circle around me and leaving no gaps for escape.

Phantom and I both froze. I tried not to wince, or to show any kind of weakness, despite the burning pain blazing through my leg. Phantom remained tightly wrapped around the king…or the king's body double, or whoever the fuck he was.

A man walked into the clearing a moment later, his own weapon—a broad sword—sheathed in an ornately-decorated case at his side.

He surveyed the lawless scene without speaking, drawing respectful gazes and bowed heads as he moved into the circle surrounding me. His right arm was wrapped in a complex tapestry of inked designs. Light brown hair; a tall, wiry frame; honey-colored eyes that seemed determined to take in everything without truly focusing on any of it.

He looked familiar, though I couldn't think of where I'd seen him before.

His expression was the complete opposite of Aleksander's as it met mine; there wasn't a hint of rage to be seen. Pure curiosity brightened his gaze, tempered further by an easy smile that spread across his face as our eyes met.

"Call your beast off," he said, nodding toward Phantom, "and I'll call off mine."

My gaze darted around the clearing, calculating. I didn't trust him to *call off* anything. But I also didn't trust my ability to survive all of the arrows currently pointed at me.

Seeing no other option, I gave a single, curt nod. "Release him, Phantom."

He let out a reluctant hiss.

"Now."

Slowly, my beast uncoiled himself and allowed Aleksander enough space to drop to the ground. The king—or his lookalike—braced a hand against that dark, muddy ground, bowing his head as he fought to catch his breath. Once he'd managed to do so, he calmly straightened to his full, impressive height and strode over to a group of the bow-wielding soldiers. Whereas the tattooed man had clearly commanded their respect, the king himself drew complete, deep bows, with a few of the circle dropping fully to their knees before him.

Even with their heads lowered, they kept stealing glances at him; they all seemed astonished to see him walking upright.

How long had he been sleeping against that tree?

Despite how fluidly he'd moved during our battle, he moved somewhat stiffly, now, as if slowing down had reminded his body of how it had been a statue only moments ago.

He didn't so much as look in my direction anymore.

Instead, it was the tattooed man who spoke, stepping in front of me, blocking my view of Aleksander as he asked, "How did you do it?"

"…How did I do what?"

The man cocked his head. "The king has been asleep in this cursed forest for a very long time, despite all of our best efforts to save him. How did you wake him up?"

"I…all I did was touch him."

Though his smile never truly disappeared, it was obvious he didn't fully believe me. His gaze hardened. I braced myself for an onslaught of difficult questioning, and perhaps some form of torture to force the answers out.

Instead, he only asked, "What is your name?"

There was a faint glimmer of recognition in his tone. I averted my eyes, unwilling to indulge it, but it didn't matter; he guessed correctly after only another moment of looking at me.

"You're the Princess of Eldris, aren't you?" I glanced up

at his face and found him studying the shadows on my arms. "Bellanova Halestorn."

"*Exiled* princess," I corrected. With a furious glare in Aleksander's direction, I added, "The monarchy is no longer intact after what that bastard did on the night of my birthday."

His brow furrowed. "I see."

And then all at once, I realized—I knew who this man was. "You were there that night, too, weren't you?" He was the one I'd slammed into while rushing toward the balcony.

His smile wilted a bit. "Yes. I was there, unfortunately." He seemed to disappear into his memories for a long moment before reemerging and offering me a polite bow. "Zayn Caldor, Lord of the North Reaches." Just as quickly as it had disappeared, the easy smile slid back onto his face as he jerked his head toward Aleksander. "And cousin of that bastard, I'm afraid."

My gaze darted toward the king, but I didn't let it linger. Instead, I searched all the faces around us, a seemingly outlandish possibility occurring to me…

Had they *all* been at Rose Point on the night of its demise?

None of the other faces seemed familiar—but then again, I hadn't exactly been committing any faces to memory, aside from Aleksander's. I'd kept to myself, just trying to get through the party without disappointing my family or my kingdom too badly.

"What really happened that night?" I wondered aloud.

Zayn fixed me with another long, searching look. "We've yet to figure it out," he said. "All I know is, we've been trapped here ever since."

Chapter Seven

Aleksander

"So, *this* is an interesting development, isn't it?"

I finished wiping a streak of blood from my arm before darting a look toward my cousin. "Which part?"

"All of it, really." Zayn was practically bouncing as he spoke. In all the time we'd spent trapped in this hellish underworld, some things still hadn't changed; he was still entirely too fucking excitable.

"We're all *awake*, to begin with," he said. "Which hasn't happened in a long time, for some of us."

I didn't want to think about all I had lost during this most recent sleep, but I couldn't help asking, "How long was I out for, this time?"

He hesitated.

"The truth, Zayn. Out with it."

"…This last stretch was the longest one yet. Nearly a year, as best we could track it. We didn't think you were going to wake again."

My breath hitched.

A year?

How was that possible?

It felt as if I'd only been sleeping for a day or two, at most.

My tongue felt oddly heavy. My lips, numb. I couldn't speak, so I busied myself with lifting the cloth I had pressed to my wrist, checking the stab wound underneath.

Still bleeding.

That chaotic beast had been impressively accurate with her knife.

"And all the princess did was touch you, she claims—and just like that, you woke up." Zayn glanced at the woman in question, frowning.

We still had her—and the strange, shapeshifting beast accompanying her—surrounded by our soldiers. She would not escape. But she was keeping her distance from me, at the moment. Which was for the better, as far as I was concerned; the farther away she was, the easier it was to think.

"Interesting, as I said," Zayn concluded, dragging his gaze back to me. "And she could prove even more useful to us, maybe. Given her magical affinity…" His tone shifted, a cautious hopefulness weaving into it as he quietly added, "She could be the very thing we've been waiting for, Aleks. Our way out of this hellscape."

I bristled. "I wouldn't count on that. She's the reason we're here to begin with, if you'll recall—her and that damned, out-of-control magic of hers."

His gaze danced between the princess and me, questions clouding his eyes, but he didn't argue.

"It doesn't feel like years ago that it happened," I told

him, shaking my head. "It feels as if I just woke up after that last night at Rose Point. I still remember everything perfectly clearly. And I'm assuming you do, too."

I'd tried to save her father that night.

In return, she'd attacked me. Her magic had ripped my sword from my hands, cutting open the world itself in the process—and then her shadows had overtaken me and my guards and courtiers, pressing us down into the realm of the dead, trapping us here.

We'd come to in this strange hell, assuming she'd killed us. Yet, after a time, we realized something even more disturbing: We were different from the ghastly souls who haunted this place—at least, at first.

Buried alive, in a manner of speaking.

Some of our companions had eventually succumbed to the deathly air and energy here. They'd joined the pale, dead figures who pressed against the edges of a safe area we'd created—an area protected through what magic Zayn and I could manage to summon within this suffocating place.

But my magic had grown increasingly erratic as the weeks went on, and soon, my consciousness had started flickering in and out along with it. I'd assumed death would take me and everyone else, eventually.

I'd *hoped* for that ending, more than once.

True death had eluded me, though—me and eleven others, including my cousin.

We'd all slipped in and out of consciousness a few times over the years, and I had vague memories of waking and existing in a half-life of sorts; of fighting against falling back into the clutches of a death-like slumber.

But no matter how hard I fought, the darkness always took me back.

And the last thing I saw before I slipped back into the cursed darkness was always the same thing: The face of the Princess of Eldris, glaring at me through a haze of smoke and shadows while the ground buckled and broke around us—a memory of the night we'd confronted one another in Rose Point.

I'd relived it a dozen times over.

At least.

Waking up to her face had been different than falling asleep to it, yet no less enraging. And I didn't know how she and her magic had woken me up—if she truly *was* the reason behind that—but I did not intend to go back to sleep, whatever the cost.

Zayn drummed his fingers against the symbol of his house that was branded upon his bicep, the way he always did when he was deep in thought.

I studied the emblem—an upward-pointing sword encircled in a radiant sun—as his fingers fell upon it, thinking of the world above. Of the life we'd once lived, and of what we'd lost and left behind.

The rage in my gut twisted tighter.

"That out-of-control magic of hers seems to be continuing to have an effect, even as we speak." Zayn's brows knitted together in concern as he picked up a black, fallen leaf—one of the countless number now littering the ground. They cascaded down in a steady stream, like dark water puddling at our feet.

"The entire time you were in repose, this forest around us continued to flourish," he said. "It's kept us alive, the food within it growing at an impossible pace, the stream through it remaining perfectly clear...and all of it glowing, we assumed, because it was being fed by your magic, despite your unconscious state. But now...well, what do we make of this?"

I took the withered leaf from him. Despite my gentle grip, it still crumbled in my hand.

"Whether we find a way to use her and her power to our advantage or not, we obviously can't continue as though she didn't crash-land into our little corner of Hell," said Zayn. "Things are shifting because of her presence."

I clenched my fist, crushing what remained of the leaf into dust, as I glanced her way again.

She sat in a circle of soldiers who all kept their hands firmly on their weapons. She seemed to be talking to the creature who had very nearly sank its fangs into my face—a creature that had reminded me of a small dragon earlier. Now, it looked like a mere dog with a long, narrow snout. I watched as it pressed its forehead to hers, its feathered tail sweeping back and forth through the dead leaves that had fallen over them.

A shapeshifting beast was not the strangest thing I'd seen in this realm, but it was still difficult to take my eyes off the two of them.

The princess must have felt my staring, because she tilted her head toward me and glared back, her hateful expression remarkably similar to the one that had chased me into the dark so many times over these past years.

Things are shifting because of her presence.

I wished I could disagree.

But then, why was I still aching in the places where she had touched me?

My magic had flowed to those points, as if desperate to collide with her.

Although, now that the initial rush of my awakened power had eased a bit, that magic seemed to be…*scattering.* It bounced restlessly about inside of me, fluttering with a frustrating lack of direction, like a moth trapped and beating against a closed window, able to see a light inside, but unable to reach it.

I felt unsteady, but also more alive—more aware of my magic—than I had in as long as I could remember.

But *why*?

And at what cost?

As she stood and marched her way over to us, escorted by several wary-looking soldiers, I felt compelled to stay put and watch her approach. She was walking with a slight limp; from the arrow of magic I'd managed to slice through her leg, I suspected.

She made a point of avoiding my gaze, speaking directly to Zayn as she snapped, "I want answers."

That makes two of us, I thought.

I said nothing, however; my magic tumbled and spun faster at her sudden nearness, and my head throbbed so painfully I couldn't think straight.

Zayn, always the more cordial one between us, said, "By all means. Where shall we start?"

His friendly tone seemed to briefly confuse her, as if she'd expected to have to work harder to pry information out of us. Composing herself, she said, "You told me you all have been trapped here since the events at my birthday celebration…but what about the weapon that also fell from the living world that night?"

My gaze lifted automatically at the question, the pain in

my head parting long enough to allow me to grind out a response. "Luminor, you mean."

"Yes. The Sword of Light."

"What of it?"

She reached a hand toward her shadowy beast, who had slipped free of the soldiers and now moved to sit at her side, fixing its unsettling blue eyes on me as it did. "We came to the underworld in search of that blade," she said. "Among other things."

I snorted at the audacity in her tone; she spoke as though strolling into Hell was akin to taking a short trip to the seaside.

Zayn spoke before I could comment. "It isn't here," he informed her. "We would have known, if it was; Aleksander's connection to it is a kind of magic itself. It's tied to his blood, in a manner of speaking."

If only I *did* have that blade…then perhaps I never would have lost my grip on my magic. Or my consciousness. Luminor channeled my abilities into something far more powerful than what I could manage on my own; there was a chance I could have used those powers to cut a path back to the world of the living.

If only.

"How can you be sure?" she demanded. "How much of this realm have you explored? Have you truly *looked* for the sword?"

"As much as we could," Zayn replied, evenly. "Things aren't that simple here, I'm afraid."

Her power seemed to flare in indignation, and mine only grew more restless in response. I closed my eyes, tucking my chin toward my chest to try and steady myself through the waves of unsettling energy.

"I've researched this blade and its powers," she said, matter-of-factly. "It caused a tear in the world above that's still there, still bleeding after all these years, cursing my home and the kingdom around it. It must have caused an inverse wound in this dead land. And the sword is likely near this wound, preventing things from healing."

"...We've seen nothing of the sort," said Zayn.

"There must be *something* that—"

"Your little adventure was in vain," I said, my eyes still clenched tight, pain making my voice even harsher than intended. "And now you're trapped here in this hell along with us. Sorry to be the bearer of bad news."

"You don't *sound* particularly sorry."

"No? Well, I suppose seven years of slow, miserable death have dulled my empathy."

I opened my eyes to find her watching me with a venomous gaze, her stillness unsettling—like a snake waiting for the opportune moment to strike.

Zayn stepped closer to her, blocking any potential attack she might make. His gaze fell on the pile of blackened leaves behind her. He studied them for a moment before he said, "Let's get out of this mess before we discuss things any further. There's something I want to show you, too, Princess."

"Nova," she corrected.

"Nova, then. Come with me." He offered another of his disarming smiles. He'd rendered more people defenseless with that smile than I could count—it was part of why I'd always kept him close, and why I'd intended for him to play a large role in my court when the time came. I could fake charm and niceties well enough for short periods of time, but not with as much conviction as Zayn.

His charm seemed to be working on her, as well; she followed him with only a slight hesitation, silencing the beast at her side when it let out a low growl.

I trailed the trio at a distance, more interested in reorienting myself with the land we were imprisoned in, searching for things that had changed during my latest bout of cursed sleep.

A year.

It still seemed impossible I'd been gone for so long.

We came quickly to a small structure rising up from a stretch of otherwise flat, bleak landscape—the dwelling we'd staked our claim on shortly after our fall into this world.

We had reinforced it over time, but we were not the ones who had originally built its walls of dark, weathered stone, or laid the interwoven pattern of bone-colored logs that made up its roof. The vines of black ivy crisscrossing its face had started to grow soon after our arrival, however, and they shimmered and crawled as I approached them now, newly stirred by my presence—or my magic's presence, rather.

Like so much of this realm, this house seemed to be an echo of a structure in the world above. Our theory was that the more sentient souls who arrived here—the ones unable to fully pass on into deeper parts of these afterlands, for whatever reason—were responsible for building these kinds of things; we'd even glimpsed them working on other projects, sometimes, drifting through the motions, surrounded by billowing curtains of ghostly white energy.

It was perhaps the most haunting thing about this place —the way some of the dead carried on as though they were still alive. It had caused me to question my own existence, more than once; with the line between the living and the dead so blurred, could I really be certain that *I* had survived the descent into this hell?

Maybe it was an eternal punishment of the damned, to believe you were still alive and somehow able to claw your way back to life.

The wooden door creaked as we pushed our way into the house. Little had changed inside; it still smelled of damp soil and woodsmoke. The walls were still cold and close, making it feel more like a cave than a home.

Zayn knelt before the large fireplace in the central room. His magic was not as powerful as my own, but he channeled it with a smooth, confident precision, and in no time at all, he'd used a stream of concentrated light to ignite a pile of leaves and twigs in the center of the hearth.

Others of our company continued the job as they came inside, some building up the fire through non-magical means, while others took the torches from the wall, lit them, and proceeded to ignite the lanterns spaced along the rooms and hallways.

As light and warmth spread throughout the abode, Zayn led Nova on a tour of it, explaining more about how we'd taken shelter here and survived over the years; how my magic allowed for some things to grow, even in this climate, and how this was our main source of sustenance—that, and a once-clouded and rot-filled stream I'd managed to purify with more magic.

While they talked, I walked onward into the backyard, to where a garden of withered blooms awaited. Like the ivy we'd seen on our way into the house, this garden reacted to my approach, the flowers in it shivering with awareness, some of them blooming and brightening to deep, lush shades of purple and blue. The trees along the edges of the stacked-stone fence we'd built were withered nearly beyond recognition, their fruits nothing more than shriveled husks; they didn't show any signs of life, even when I purposely tried to magic some essence of it back into them.

Three of my guards followed me outside: Elias, Rowen, and Farren. They had changed more than the house had in the last year; their features were terribly gaunt, their bodies skeletal—more like the dead beings outside our safe haven than the proud men and women who had followed me into the disaster at Rose Point.

How much longer could we withstand this realm and its noxious airs?

We sat for a while, catching up on the things I'd missed and the memories I was attempting to sort through; it was getting difficult to keep timelines clear, as much as I'd slipped in and out of my cursed, slumbering state.

As we talked, I tried to subtly infuse the air with warm magic, even though I was still feeling weak and off-balance myself. My power brightened their skin and their eyes, making them at least *appear* slightly more alive.

Alive.

I had to keep reminding myself that we were alive. We did not belong in this darkness. And one way or another, I was going to find a way to claw us back to the light.

Zayn rejoined me perhaps twenty minutes later, dismissing the guards and assessing me as he approached. "You're still conscious."

"Wide awake," I assured him.

"A good sign." He glanced back toward the house. "She still claims all she did was touch you. She certainly didn't intend to wake you up." A corner of his mouth quirked.

"And I'm pretty sure she'd prefer it if you went back to sleep."

I ignored the jab. "Did you get anything more useful out of her?"

"She's not eager to run away from us, at least. We've intrigued her. And, from what I gathered, she's already encountered some of the nasty spirits of this world…she doesn't want to face any more of those alone, even if she won't outright admit it. Fear is a powerful motivator, and it's reason enough for her to want to stay close to other living beings." He crossed his arms, his head tilting back in thought. "There's more she's not telling us, though. About her magic and her mission, and about the living world."

"Of course there's more. Did you expect her to immediately, willingly share her entire life story and all her hopes and dreams with you?"

"It wouldn't have been the first time I had a woman spilling all her secrets within an hour of meeting me."

"Maybe not—but copious amounts of wine were usually involved in your persuasions back home, as I recall. Something this realm is sorely lacking."

He arched a brow. "It wasn't the wine that loosened up their inhibitions, Cousin."

I fought the urge to roll my eyes.

"Though, I wouldn't say no to copious amounts of wine," he added with a grin, "if you think we could procure some, somehow."

I massaged my throbbing temples, sighing. "I could use something much stronger than wine."

He chuckled, nodding in agreement.

After a minute, he said, "At the very least, don't drive her away. Not yet. She was able to enter this world and navigate her way to us by using her magic—a useful talent. So think of the larger picture, please." He finally dropped his usual cheerful act, fixing me with a hard look. "Some of us have been awake in this infernal region for longer than you have, and we're getting tired of it."

With that, he disappeared back into the house without a backward glance.

After studying the dead trees around the fence for a few more moments, I decided to go and have a chat with the princess myself.

I found her near the fireplace, tending to the gash I'd left in her leg. My magic had seared straight through her pant leg, leaving an ugly slash of burned and bleeding skin in its wake.

I leaned against the wall, watching her work for a moment, trying to recall the few memories I had of our meetings in the world above. Her appearance was more striking than I remembered. Waves of dark hair fell to the middle of her back, hints of deep violet shimmering in the strands that caught the firelight just so. Her complexion was porcelain pale, an alluring contrast both to those dark waves and to the piercing turquoise shade of her eyes. The shadows upon her arms still had not receded completely, though they were faded, now, to a pale grey that made it look as if she'd painted them on with ash from the hearth. Several bracelets decorated her wrists, and I could sense magic swirling around them whenever they shifted and clanked against one another.

She ignored me, as did her shapeshifting beast who dozed by the fire, still in the form of a large dog.

As I pushed away from the wall and sauntered closer, my head didn't throb as badly as it had earlier, but the effect she continued to have on my power was undeniable.

It felt…*chaotic*.

Everything about her arrival did.

She continued to ignore me, even as I drew close enough that we could have reached out and touched one another.

"Hey. You."

She didn't look up from tending her wound. "My name is not *You*."

"Annoying, Abhorrent, Abysmal Creature of Death and Chaos, then."

"Still wrong."

"What if I shorten it to just *Chaos*?"

With a vicious flick of her wrist, she ripped her knife through the roll of bandaging cloth she'd just taken from her bag. I could only assume she was fantasizing about doing that to me, instead—perhaps wishing she'd cut my wrist a little more deeply earlier.

"What do you want?" she demanded.

"I have a proposition for you."

"Does it involve you going and fucking yourself?"

"Such foul language for a princess."

"*Princess?*" She bared her teeth at me. "The Kingdom of Eldris has no princess. Not since the night you murdered her father."

I forced myself not to react, steeling my features into an unreadable wall.

So the poor old bastard had ended up dying.

Interesting.

What else had transpired in the world above since that moment?

A thousand questions exploded in my mind all at once. All the more reason for me to try and strike up a partnership with her, at least for a little while—long enough to get answers, and to see how her magic might help us search the endless parts of this realm that we'd yet to explore, hopefully finding our way home in some part of it.

"I didn't kill your father, Chaos."

"Spare me your lies," she snarled. "I *saw* you stab him."

"What happened that night was…regrettable. And complicated. But it's not important right now."

"*Not important*? For seven years, I have—"

"Do you wish to listen to my proposition, or do you wish to continue arguing until the deadly curses and demonic things in this realm overtake and claim us both?"

She looked as though she was actually considering both options with equal measure.

Chaos was a more fitting name than I'd anticipated, apparently.

Several times, she opened her mouth only to snap it shut. Finally, she asked, "What do you propose, then?"

"That we find Luminor together."

"I would rather die a thousand excruciating deaths than willingly travel anywhere with you."

"Well, that's good to know. Because you very likely *will* die without the help of me and my soldiers."

She finished cutting her bandages and stabbed her knife into the dirt floor with excessive force, but she held her tongue.

"There were nearly three dozen of those soldiers when we landed here, you know."

She continued bandaging her leg while regarding me from underneath her lashes, her curiosity clearly piqued.

"The ones who remain are the ones who have learned how to survive in this desolate place. The rest…" I let the comment hang heavily between us.

She stared at her impaled knife, a tormented look in her bright eyes.

Without looking at me, she said, "Go on."

"They've had more practice than you at keeping the ghosts and demons of this world at bay," I said with a shrug. "And trust me: You want escorts well-practiced at this. Because living things don't truly belong in this realm—even those with magic such as yours."

"So you're offering to escort me to the sword, even knowing I don't intend to let you have it back? I'm going to find a way to repair the damage it's done and continues to do. And then I'm going to use my magic to neutralize the blade. I'm going to *destroy* it, if I have to."

"Ah, so you actually *do* have an ultimate plan? That's reassuring."

"I always have a plan," she muttered.

"We have that much in common, at least. Which brings us to the other part of this proposal," I said, calmly, "and what's in it for *me*."

She wrapped her hand around the jeweled hilt of her knife, but left it in the dirt, and she didn't interrupt as I continued.

"Something about you and your magic seems to have stirred my own magic, waking me up in the process," I said. "And it seems to be *keeping* me awake—more awake than I've been in some time—even if it's giving me a headache to go along with it."

She considered my words for a long moment, her fingers tapping against her weapon.

And then that wicked, chaotic beast *smiled*.

"Have I said something amusing?" A snarl slipped into my words.

"You need me in order to stay conscious. I give you, the King of Light himself, life. I just find it ironic how desperately you need me, even though you called me—what was it? An *Abysmal Creature of Death and Chaos*."

"And you need *me* to keep you from meeting a gruesome end in this realm."

"Debatable."

"If you think so, then feel free to leave. Best of luck on your journey. *May the road show you mercy, favor, and light*, as they say in my kingdom."

She shot me a nasty look before getting to her feet, testing her weight on her injured leg before making a few adjustments to the bandage she'd tied around it. She looked as though she was considering walking away from me, but she couldn't bring herself to move.

I took a step closer to her. Then another. The closer I drew, the more the restless magic inside of me settled. The clearer my mind became. It was such an odd, unexpected reaction that I couldn't help but draw even nearer, chasing the sudden clarity without regard to much else.

Her knife was at my throat in the next instant.

I almost smiled at the feel of the cold steel pressing against my skin; at least she was entertaining. How many years had it been since I'd felt this alive?

"You're impressively quick with your blade."

"And you're embarrassingly slow at realizing I want you nowhere near me." She punctuated the sentence with a twitch of her wrist, making the tip of the knife bite painfully into my skin.

A few pounding heartbeats later, the sound of approaching footsteps reached us.

Neither of us flinched.

"Oh, good," Zayn said, smiling brightly as he appeared in my peripheral vision. "I see you two are still getting along wonderfully."

I didn't acknowledge him, keeping my gaze leveled on the princess's. "Either join forces with us, or leave," I said, my voice low. "Our resources are too scarce to waste them on outsiders."

"Fine," she snapped, after a weighted pause. "I agree. But I'm warning you: One more questionable move, and I am going to stab you in the neck."

I met her threat with a smile. "Part of me still thinks letting you kill me would be preferable to subjecting myself to more of your company. So, by all means: If you are going to stab, aim for an artery." I pulled the collar of my shirt aside, exposing myself further to her blade.

She glared, drawing back and spinning the knife around in her hand with impressive control.

Zayn cleared his throat—loudly—finally pulling both our gazes toward him. He held up a bright red fruit, one of several from a basket balanced in his other hand. "Anybody hungry?"

The princess flashed Zayn a perfectly cheerful smile—as though she hadn't just been threatening to kill his cousin.

"I *am* hungry, actually," she said, sheathing the knife before swiping the fruit from him and holding it out to me. "You first, though."

"Paranoid, hm?"

"Plenty of others have tried their best to poison me in the past."

"What a shame they failed."

She spun the fruit between her fingers, inspecting it closer. It was one of the bright red specimens from the withered trees in the backyard. *Hellthorn apples*, we'd nicknamed them, because of how difficult it was to pluck one without bloodying your arm against the briar covered branches. Their taste reminded me of strawberries at first bite, but with an odd hint of spice and honey in the aftertaste.

"What was it you were saying earlier?" I asked. "About how I needed you more than you needed me?"

"Don't test it for me, then. I'm perfectly fine going without food." She looked as if she was considering throwing it in my face instead.

"No need for that." I caught her wrist, holding it steady. "It's safe. Don't worry." I leaned in, my eyes never leaving hers, and took a bite of the succulent fruit. Crimson juice trickled like blood from the apple's broken flesh, winding a path down the side, dripping onto her skin.

Her hand shook slightly as I drew back.

"No one here is out to poison you, Chaos," I told her, turning away. "But you might wish we had, after you see what the rest of this realm is truly like."

Chapter Eight

Nova

(*Trusting them feels like a grave mistake.*)

I finished reorganizing my bag of jostled supplies and buckled it shut before looking toward Phantom. "I *don't* trust them," I admitted. "But it feels like a better option than traveling the Underworld on our own." Setting my packed bag on one of the stone benches in the garden, I wandered through the vibrant rows of flowers, studying their hues in an effort to distract myself from the haunting memories I'd already made of our journey—the restless energies of the Nocturnus Road, the wandering spirits that had nearly ensnared us, the cold grip that had wrapped around my ankle...

We were still at the 'outpost', as Zayn had dubbed it. He and Aleksander were inside, busily making preparations to leave. I'd stepped outside to escape the king's imposing presence, and Phantom had been trying to convince me to make a run for it ever since.

We were still here because I wasn't confident of my original plans any longer; stumbling upon Aleksander and the others had rattled me. I still didn't know what to make of them—how could the king exist both here and in the living world?

Which one was the *true* Aleksander?

I hadn't mentioned the other Light King to Zayn or anyone else, yet; I wanted to observe them and gather more information for myself before I decided my next move—even if that meant staying uncomfortably close to them, against my better judgment.

Kneeling, I picked a flower with deep, luscious blue-black petals that shimmered like the sea at night. If this Aleksander was the fraud, his magic was certainly convincing; how did he make such beautiful things bloom within the deadly air all around us? And brightly enough, strongly enough, that they had *continued* to bloom even while he was unconscious?

I could feel Phantom watching me closely as I plucked the flower's petals off, one by one.

"It isn't as if we can't escape them if things go wrong," I assured him. "Have I ever *not* managed to escape when things went wrong?"

(*Your luck will eventually run out.*)

I scoffed. "It's not luck. It's skill."

Before he could reply, we were interrupted by the arrival of Zayn. The Lord of the North Reaches stepped into the backyard, his expression brightening as his eyes landed on me.

The more I saw him, the more vividly I recalled our encounter that night at Rose Point. After seven years, my assessment of him remained largely unchanged; it was clear he was related to Aleksander—albeit distantly. Their basic features appeared to have been shaped by similar hands, crafted by artists with a penchant for strong jawlines, high cheekbones, and perfectly refined noses. Yet, they bore the finishing touches of two different masters, each with their own distinct visions of beauty.

Aleksander embodied rugged elegance, quiet strength and perfect poise.

Zayn had a much more approachable look—a youthful charm, almost, even though he was the older between the two, if I recalled my mother's boring lessons about the Elarithian royal family tree correctly. As he scanned me with his warm gaze, the flecks of gold in his brown eyes seemed to shimmer. "I didn't mean to eavesdrop, but it sounded as if you were having a conversation…with your dog?"

I carefully considered my reply, searching for the answer that would make me sound the least insane.

In this case, I decided, it was the truth.

"It's a facet of my magic," I told him. "I can understand his thoughts, and he can understand my speech." With a slight, rueful grin, I added, "Although, sometimes he likes to pretend he can't, so that he can ignore me and my commands."

Zayn's eyes widened slightly.

"His name is Phantom."

Zayn crouched down, tentatively reaching to scratch him beneath the chin.

Phantom's fur bristled. (*Please tell this fool I am not a common house pet for him to coddle and caress.*)

I arched a brow. "He likes being scratched between the ears," I said. "Just above that white spot on his forehead."

Phantom started to growl in protest, but Zayn was

already reaching for the spot I'd mentioned. Phantom's tail thumped happily in response—though hesitantly, and perhaps against his will.

I gave him a wink, which earned me a flash of teeth.

(*You betray me,*) he protested, even as his tail wagged more furiously.

So dramatic, this one.

"It's been some time since he could enjoy a nice petting like this," I told Zayn. "He wasn't this solid in the world above."

The Elarithian lord stood up straight once more, giving me a curious look. "What do you mean?"

"He died three years ago. I kept him alive with magic, but I didn't quite manage to give him his solid body back; when we arrived here, though, something in the air seems to have reinforced my attempt. It's made him more corporeal, somehow."

"And he can shapeshift, as well?"

I nodded. "Another skill he picked up after losing his permanent body. I'm still not entirely sure how my magic helped with that, but…" I trailed off with a shrug.

He was quiet for a moment, his gaze dancing between mine and Phantom's, before finally settling on my face. He gave me a crooked grin. "You get stranger and stranger, Nova Halestorn."

"I've been called far worse things than *strange*."

As if to remind me of my inherent strangeness, the turquoise bracelet suddenly tightened on my wrist. I gasped at the burst of pressure, earning me another curious look from Zayn.

He studied all of my bracelets for a moment before he said, "Another bit of strangeness?"

I didn't reply, too busy searching our surroundings for whatever had triggered the beads' movement. Was it something about the Light magic protecting this outpost?

And if so, why had it already settled?

Was I *ever* going to find out what this strange, stupid, beautiful bracelet did?

"...Don't worry," Zayn said. "You don't have to answer me. I'm not usually the prying type, anyway." The grin slid back onto his face as he added, "I prefer to keep my brain as empty as possible."

I snorted. "I know what you mean; I often find myself wishing my own was far emptier."

His smile started to droop in the corners, but he quickly changed the subject, his attention shifting to the bag on the bench beside me. "All packed, then?"

"As much as I can be. Though I'm beginning to think this journey might take longer than I'd hoped, and that I didn't bring nearly enough supplies."

"We have extra provisions to share. No need to worry about that."

I frowned. "That actually leads us to a question I had."

"Oh?"

"The food and water that sustain you have been cultivated and purified through magic, I understand. But if you've been here for so long, how have you managed to find clothing and other things like that?"

"An excellent question," he replied, "and the answer is simple: Just to the south of here is an area we call 'Mourner's Rest'. A place full of impressive statues, stone platforms, and basins meant to hold offerings. We stumbled upon it during one of our earliest attempts to navigate these lands. It's one of the locations, we believe, where living visitors used to leave gifts, back when the roads between the living and the dead world were more easily and frequently traversed."

"...Gifts those people brought for their deceased loved ones, you mean."

"Yes. All manner of things those loved ones must have favored in life—fine clothing, weapons, various trinkets... you name it."

"You stole these things, I'm guessing?"

He gave me an unapologetic smile. "To be fair, the dead weren't really using them. Their spirits don't even enter the area. The whole place is a desolate expanse, devoid of any kind of energy—living or otherwise. It's an unsettling wasteland, to be sure, but nothing besides our own fears prevented us from taking and repurposing what's there. We eventually overcame those fears out of necessity."

The whole practice still struck me as deeply wrong. I found I couldn't convincingly argue against it, however. I was also in no position to choose morals over materials, so when Zayn suggested I search through one of their trunks full of stolen gifts and take what I needed from it, I begrudgingly agreed.

The trunks were stacked in one of the innermost rooms of the outpost. I located them quickly and began sifting through one before I could second-guess myself. I had stolen plenty to survive in the living world; I tried to convince myself this was no different.

Still, as I caught sight of a particularly fine-looking cloak, I found myself hesitating, wondering about the deceased person who had once worn it.

When my fingers finally brushed against the luxurious fabric, an image flooded my mind.

I saw a young woman enveloped in the cloak, her delicate fingers resting on a brooch that fastened it. The brooch was crafted from lustrous silver, featuring a meticulously shaped tree at its center, its branches adorned with red gemstones that glinted like ripe fruit. The filigree border surrounding the piece resembled intricate lacework, a testament to masterful artistry. But as the vision focused more closely on that tree, I realized that not all of the crimson dots were gemstones.

Some were glistening specks of blood.

A gasp escaped my lips—whether it was my own or that of the cloak's former wearer, I couldn't tell. In my vision, her pale hand tightened around the brooch, pressing it deeper into the velvety folds of the cloak. In my reality, an unexpected ache blossomed in my chest, as if that same hand had struck me.

I blinked, and the vivid images faded, but the pain in my chest lingered.

Phantom gently took my hand between his teeth and gave a little tug. (*What's wrong?*)

"Nothing," I whispered. "Just…just an odd feeling. It's passed."

And it had.

Yet, my woven bracelet with its diamond patterns tingled against my wrist, as if it wanted to be used.

My experience with my innate ability to speak with the dead was limited, mostly confined to my conversations with Phantom. I had never attempted to divine knowledge from objects before, even though I knew this was one possible manifestation of my power.

They said a skilled necromancer could uncover long-buried truths from the past…

Had I just uncovered something?

I heard footsteps. Hastily, I shook out the cloak, searching for the silver brooch. But there was no such ornament within its folds, bloodied or otherwise.

I shoved the garment back into the bottom of the trunk. After grabbing a few simpler articles of clothing—which mercifully caused no visions—I crammed them into my bag, slung it over my shoulder, and hurried from the room.

On my way out, I nearly collided with Aleksander.

He started to reach out as if to catch me…only to realize who I was at the last instant. He quickly pulled his hand back, though not before his fingertips brushed mine.

The touch sent an itch crawling through me. Shadows briefly arched up from my arms like the fur of a startled black cat. In the same instant, his skin cracked slightly and light bled through, shimmering faintly between us.

Chapter Nine

Nova

We stared at one another, our disdain thickening the air along with our magic.

He settled his magic quickly. In the darkness that followed, his golden eyes seemed to glow. He needed no words to explain the turmoil and fire in his gaze; he hated the effect I had on him and his power. It was a hatred I felt in return—an increasingly tangled web of animosity that made my heart pound.

Phantom growled low in his throat. When Aleksander's attention shifted to him, I seized the opportunity to break free from our locked gaze, pushing my way past him and hurrying to meet Zayn in the front yard.

The king followed a few minutes later, along with his three most capable soldiers. The others would stay behind, it was decided, both to continue to tend to the outpost, and because traveling in a large group was more likely to attract unwanted attention from whatever spirits and beasts haunted these depths. My magic alone would undoubtedly draw some of those fiends; we didn't need anything else increasing our chances of trouble.

Of course, I had my own reasons for insisting on a smaller party: It meant fewer people to outrun should my new companions prove as untrustworthy as I feared.

For now, though, I put on a façade of compliance, blending into the team. Zayn had a clear destination in mind, and the confident manner in which he struck out onto the road was contagious, urging me and everyone else onward.

I felt a flicker of relief as I realized his chosen path aligned closely with that of my own original plans; if the theory about the mirroring between the living world and the dead one held true, we were heading toward the parallel of Rose Point that lay somewhere in the darkness ahead.

As the six of us—seven, counting Phantom—walked, time stretched into what felt like hours.

Above, the sky unfurled in a tumultuous canvas of swirling colors, dominated by deep violets and somber greys, occasionally illuminated by flashes of crimson and cobalt. The ground rolled endlessly beneath us, a mixture of dark stone and ashen soil that swallowed the sound of our footsteps. The air was heavy, pervaded by a sense of melancholy, as if it bore the weight of all the former lives of the lost souls around us. We passed only a few of those wandering souls, and they all kept their distance.

But it felt as if countless more were watching us, lingering just out of sight.

I looked frequently to the sky. Violent as it was, it was

still less unsettling than the ghosts drifting around us. When the flashes of blue overtook it, it occasionally reminded me of the sky in the living world—albeit one still streaked with foreboding colors and clouds, hinting at storms to come.

Several times, I thought I caught a glimpse of what looked like a sphere of fire peeking out of the tumbling waves of chaotic energy.

"Is there a sun in this sky?" I wondered aloud.

"If it can be called such a thing," said Elias, one of the soldiers accompanying us. "It hasn't moved since we've been here, though. Least, not that I've seen. Only the clouds around it shift and change the amount of light it gives off—but that shifting does seem to stick to a pattern that mimics the day and night of the living world."

I kept watching, hoping for a clearer glimpse of this 'sun' that never came.

Finally, we slowed to a stop. Ahead of us, a strange structure stretched as far as I could see in both directions. It looked like it might have been a grand, protective wall at some point, but now it was nothing more than unevenly spaced piles of cracked and broken stone.

The physical damage it had sustained didn't seem like the kind that could be caused by mere weathering, nor inflicted by wandering ghosts and incorporeal beings…

So what had destroyed it?

Zayn took a piece of parchment from his bag, consulting the notes and diagrams on it for a long moment before seemingly making up his mind about where to go next. He led us to one of the largest openings between the rubble piles, but he stopped short of trying to pass through it.

No one else dared to step forward, either; even Aleksander had exchanged his usual arrogant demeanor for a look that could almost be mistaken for concern.

I chanced a few cautious steps closer, studying the twisted scraps of iron scattered among the broken stone. It looked like the remnants of a gate. As I stared at it, a foreboding feeling took root in my gut and began to grow.

"This is as far as most of our expeditions have ventured over the years," Zayn said. "A few went beyond this wall in the earlier days, but…"

"They didn't make it back?" I guessed, glancing over my shoulder at him.

He shook his head slowly. "No…they did come back." The words slipped from his lips with reluctance, like heavy stones forced uphill, fighting against the gravity of what he truly meant to say.

I held my breath, waiting for him to continue, but Zayn remained silent.

"They made it back, but they were never the same," Aleksander interjected, his voice cold. "All three took their own lives within weeks of returning."

Zayn cleared his throat. "Yes. But before they did, they spoke of strange things they'd seen on the other side. Most notably? A walled city rising far in the distance, much of it hidden by a hazy cloud that suggested it might have been surrounded by powerful, protective magic. And there was at least one towering structure rising impressively high in the center of that place."

"An impressive structure…" I repeated. "Like a palace? A mirror of Rose Point and the city that once flourished around it?"

"One of my theories," said Zayn. "I'm curious to explore it further, either way—which is why I thought we'd start our search in this direction. But now that we're here…"

Now that we were here, the way forward loomed impossibly dark and dangerously uncertain.

Everything safe and familiar was already far behind me, though, and turning back didn't seem like a viable option, either. So I took a few more steps forward. The red-beaded bracelet around my wrist shivered, so I gave in to the magic it channeled, just a little—just enough to let a more perceptive filter overtake my vision—allowing me to better spot and decipher the energies and potential spells surrounding the piles of stone and metal.

Most of the wall might have been gone, but someone, or some*thing*, had rebuilt the gaps, placing reinforcement spells that had been invisible to my naked eye, but which danced with brilliant color before me now—a tumbling current of black and silver magic.

"The energy shifts in a strange way within the empty spaces," I explained to the others. "It's building and stretching out like a new wall." I blinked several times, clearing away the remnants of my enhanced Sight. "The path isn't as open as it seems."

"…You can see such things?" Aleksander questioned, skepticism lacing his voice.

The doubt in his tone irritated me. "I can do more than just see it," I replied, meeting his gaze defiantly. "If I wished, I could drain the energy and create a passage for us to slip through unscathed—while hopefully avoiding the cursed magic that drove your soldiers to madness. I used a similar trick on the Nocturnus Road when I first arrived in this hell."

He still looked skeptical, but he gestured me toward the largest opening, as if to say *prove it, then*.

And I rarely missed an opportunity to prove myself.

Without hesitation, I strode forward until I was right in front of the missing gate, my fingers reaching out, preparing to explore the shimmering magic woven into the air.

"*Siphonus*," I uttered, my voice steady yet quiet, reverberating with intent. I squeezed my eyes shut, feeling the energy swirl around me, then opened them to the vivid display of black and silver forces I'd glimpsed moments before. They danced with renewed intensity, swirling most fervently around the remnants of the crumbling wall, while the stones themselves glimmered with a rich, sparkling green hue.

Orin had taught me that everything carried life. Even crumbled walls like these held the imprints of things left behind—the hopes and dreams of the hands that had crafted it, the sorrows and aspirations of those who once walked along it. To carve a path through the barrier, I would need to drain the energy that clung to the stones first, separating it from the spell barring our passage. Then I could focus more easily on the spell.

As I began the process, it felt as if I was absorbing not just the energy, but the lingering echoes of the wall's existence too—its triumphs and its tragedies intertwining with my own essence. I could almost sense it collapsing, the weight of its history pulling at my body and threatening to bring me down as well.

My arms dropped to my sides, overcome with the weight of it all.

Phantom nudged his nose into my palm, snorting warm breath into it.

"Are you okay?" Zayn asked.

I waved off his concern, shook the feeling back into my limbs, and immediately moved on to trying to take hold of the barrier spell.

Siphoning the silvery-black waves of energy proved challenging—but I had anticipated far worse. They struggled precariously against my hold, like a sail caught in a stormy wind, trying to rip free. I steadied my breath, though, allowing the beat of my heart to sync with the erratic rhythm of the magic, and soon I felt the energy flowing into me, weaving its way through my veins.

With one final surge of focus, I pulled the remaining bits of the spell into myself. It unraveled from the wall with a sharp snap that nearly knocked me off my feet.

"...Nova?"

"I'm fine," I reassured Zayn. "It's clear. Let's just cross over while we can."

I led the way, Phantom at my side, the others following closely behind.

As we passed through the opening, a visible shudder rippled throughout our entire group. Aleksander came last, little cracks lighting on his skin as he stopped to encourage the last of his soldiers—Elias—to keep moving.

Elias seemed to have forgotten where he was for a moment. The dazed look in his eyes sent a shiver skipping down my spine.

Once we were all through, we huddled together against

the biting cold that felt more penetrating on this side of the barrier.

"The energy around this wall is still dangerous," Aleksander commented, his brow furrowing. "I can't see it, but I can feel it intensifying, suddenly. It's restless."

As much as I disliked agreeing with him, I instinctively turned my magical sight back toward the gateway and nodded. "It's like we've triggered an alarm. Something really didn't want us to cross. I can't explain it, but…"

My words trailed off and my body tensed at the sound of a low hiss echoing through the air, growing louder as the seconds passed. I held tight to my red-beaded bracelet while my companions exchanged worried looks. No one spoke right away. We scarcely dared to breathe.

"…That spell was powerful." I ran my fingers through Phantom's cold fur, trying to hide the way my hand shook. "There's a very good chance that whatever created it has been staying nearby, working to maintain it."

"Should we go back?" Elias asked.

The other soldiers—Rowen and Farren—whispered between themselves, wondering the same thing. One by one, the three of them looked to their king.

"We aren't going back." Alexander's tone was grimly stoic. "But we should get away from this wall and find cover somewhere. Lay low for a moment while we feel the area out and decide our next steps."

No one argued. We followed a small trickle of a stream with cloudy water until it led us into a clutch of spindly, leafless trees that provided some measure of cover. Here, we laid our packs down along a flat, sandy stretch of ground and quietly discussed our options.

After a few minutes, Aleksander knelt by the stream, fingertips skimming the water.

I watched—mesmerized against my will—as that water swirled and brightened beneath his touch. When it settled, a perfectly clear, purified section of stream flowed before him.

He didn't look up at me as he refilled his canteen and several others, but I could see his arrogant smile reflected in the stream as he said, "It's okay to be impressed."

I briefly considered darkening the cleared water with my shadows just because I could. Petty? Yes. A waste of magic? Also yes.

But gods, I *hated* that smirk.

I bit my lip hard enough to taste blood, and then walked away without replying, announcing that I would keep watch so the others could rest.

I brought Elias along with me; he still seemed in danger of slipping back into a daze if left unattended. I tried to make small talk with him to keep him awake—something I'd never been particularly good at, which proved even more difficult than usual with my all of my nerves on edge.

I eventually gave up on trying to talk, instead stationing him at the top of the hill sloping into our resting spot while I patrolled a wider perimeter. Phantom accompanied me on this patrol, at first, but after an hour or so he grew bored and took to entertaining himself by digging holes and burying various objects in them. When I inquired as to what he could possibly be storing in the dirt here, I received only a haughty reply that it was his business, not mine.

Very serious dog business, apparently.

I continued minding my own, and I occasionally heard the same low hiss in the wind that we'd heard near the wall.

Eventually, I gathered my courage and walked back toward that wall, scanning the area for any sign of where the ominous noise might have been originating from.

I never found anything—yet I remained convinced something was there. A feeling in my gut, tightening with every strange sound or flicker in the lighting. It was more unsettling than facing a monster outright, to be able to *sense* it but not *see* it.

Our break was over, I decided; it was time to pick a direction and keep moving.

I made my way back to the others, preparing to rally them for an onward march. Elias had his back to me as I approached—staring at our temporary camp rather than watching for threats approaching it.

"Some lookout he is," I muttered, picking up my pace.

As I reached him, though, I slowed to a stop. His eyes were glazed over. He was mumbling words that didn't sound like any tongue I recognized from the living world. And no matter how I shook him, or how loudly I called his name, he didn't reply.

A troubling thought—a possible explanation—struck me. Though I was afraid to test my theory, I reached a trembling hand toward him, giving my red-beaded bracelet a shake, bracing myself to channel magic through it once more.

The enhanced Sight fell over my eyes, revealing threads of silvery-black entwining Elias—threads the same color as the spell that had tried to prevent our crossing the wall. They clung so tightly to him in places that it was hard to see where they ended and he began; and they seemed to be sinking more deeply into his energy, changing its color as I watched.

They made it back, but they were never the same.

Was this the same spell that had infected the last ones who'd crossed the wall, leading them to madness and eventual suicide?

"Elias," I said, as calmly as I could, "let's go back to the others."

"The shadows know we're here. They know where we've gone. Where we're going. We should return to them—no one escapes them, in the end."

"...What the hell are you talking about?"

Instead of replying, he broke into a run.

I was too shocked to move at first—until I realized he was sprinting straight for the wall.

"Come back," I called, taking a few numb, confused steps after him. "*Come back!*"

He only ran faster.

I followed against my better judgment, racing all the way to the wall, to the broken gate, and watching as he fell to his knees before it and bowed his head.

A mass of shadows had gathered in the opening. They bulged and billowed furiously, as if some beast stalked at the center, occasionally kicking and clawing and trying to fight its way free. I didn't need magical Sight to see the tumultuous energy surrounding this beast. To know that this was bad—*very bad*.

Elias never moved. Never lifted his head again, even as part of the dark mass pinched off and flew toward him, swallowing him up with a ravenous hunger. I watched, horrified, as his body disappeared. His hand reached out at the last second, his fingers stretching desperately toward me, like a drowning victim trying to flag down a savior.

But it was far too late.

He was gone.

A moment passed before the smaller mass began to churn almost as violently as the larger one behind it, swirling into the shape of a small cyclone. It roared and spun, flinging out what was left of Elias—a limp corpse drained of all life and color, which continued to shrivel and fade out of existence as I watched.

Chapter Ten

Nova

The shadowy cyclone receded, revealing the true devastation it had caused.

There was little left of Elias aside from piles of splintered bones, scattered ash, and tattered scraps of clothing.

With my pulse racing furiously, I ran toward the gruesome remains, trying to read the energy swirling around them. Trying to understand the death that had come so swiftly, so completely, so...so...

Devastatingly.

I dropped to my knees and reached a hand over the bones, desperate for answers. Maybe I could divine something with a touch. Maybe I could absorb the deadly magic still clinging to its victim, let it settle inside of me and make sense of it from within...

But the only things that settled in my gut were fear and nausea.

This realm was proving more and more brutal by the

minute. My throat felt tight. For an instant, tears threatened. I was reaching a breaking point, a horrid realization—

I never should have come here.

I was in over my head—but nevertheless, I blinked away my tears and kept my head up.

What else could I do?

Footsteps pounded close by, followed by a furious voice: "What is going on?"

I turned toward that voice, expecting to meet Aleksander's glare. He wasn't looking at me, though. He was staring at something behind me.

Glancing over my shoulder, I saw the deadly cyclone of shadows reforming, moving away from the wall and toward us once more.

I leapt to my feet and hurriedly backed away. Ribbons of smoky darkness peeled away from the main swirling mass as it thundered our direction, each strand sweeping wide and wildly about with a whip-like quickness—there would be no outrunning those dark appendages.

Aleksander's golden eyes flashed in my direction. "Chaos," he breathed, *"what the fuck is going on—"*

Ribbons of shadow clawed toward his body.

I sensed their impending strike even before I saw them, so I managed to shove him out of the way and then dance aside myself. The shadows split apart as they stretched away from the cyclone, turning into smaller spirals that swirled menacingly around Aleksander for a moment before dissipating.

He was still glaring at me like *I* had something to do with the attack. Pushing him to safety had been an automatic reaction, really—I should have just let the shadows hit the fucker.

"Do I *look* like I know what's going on?" I asked.

His eyes darted between me and the spinning cloud of dark energy. It tumbled and roared, little bursts of silvery-black occasionally exploding around it, but nothing else lashed out at us for the moment. In fact, it seemed to be retreating again, pacing back and forth at a safer distance—almost like an intelligent predator sizing up its prey.

Aleksander kept one eye on it as he knelt beside Elias's remains, lifting a pile of dust and bone fragments into his palm and letting it sift through his fingers. For a fraction of a moment, his expression looked pained. Distraught, even.

So apparently, he had other emotions aside from haughty disdain.

Who knew?

Guilt clenched my stomach as I took an uncertain step toward him. If only I'd been quick enough to catch Elias. To *stop* him, somehow…

"It happened so fast," I said, quietly.

The Light King rose slowly back to his feet. He shifted his weight from one side to the other, as if trying to redistribute the burden of this latest death upon his shoulders.

"I'm sorry. I—"

"It's over." He pointed to the cyclone, which was building in intensity, its dark clouds rolling dangerously close once more. "Focus on that."

I snapped my attention back to it. It roared louder in the same instant, a second strike of dark ribbons quickly following the sound; I lost my balance trying to avoid them.

Aleksander caught me against his chest, wrapping an arm around my waist to steady us both. And it happened again: His touch, his nearness causing a strange surge in my chest, a wild stirring of magic between us...

I ripped free of his hold, irritably trying to keep any sign of my power from erupting upon my skin—again. I didn't need another distraction right now. Didn't need the questions screaming through my head, almost as loud as the threat before us—

Why does he have this effect on me?

Why does this keep happening?

Aleksander kept his focus on the spinning storm, ignoring whatever had just passed between us as he calmly said, "I watched shadows like this erupt all around you that night at Rose Point."

"...So?"

"So maybe do something about *these* shadows?"

"It's not the same. I can't control every strand of darkness in the world any more than *you* can control every sliver of light."

A muscle ticked in his jaw. "Could you kindly do us a favor and *try?*"

The twisting mass roared again, sections of it darkening and rippling in a manner that could only be described as threatening. Like it was responding to the possibility of me *trying* anything against it. And again, I had the strange feeling that it was...*alive*.

I hurriedly took a few more steps back, trying to gain perspective. A surge of cold wind washed over me with my next breath—Phantom, returning from whatever mischief he'd been entertaining himself with. He pressed against my leg, holding me in place, his back providing a solid foundation for me to brace my hand upon.

(*I leave you alone for twenty minutes, and this is what I come back to?*)

"Spare me your judgment for once," I muttered, side-stepping a thin, wayward streak of shadow as it thrashed toward my shoulder.

Not that I would never admit it to Aleksander, but the energy lashing toward me did feel very...*familiar*. Though not in a way I could readily explain. And whether or not it was the same as what I'd channeled on the night of his demise, I couldn't say for certain; I'd never recreated those frightening, devastating claws of darkness, after all.

At least, not on purpose.

But now, memories from the night of my father's murder were flooding my mind, making it impossible to concentrate fully on anything—much less *control*. I hadn't controlled anything that night. I'd run away from it all.

In so many ways, I'd been trying to run away ever since.

Phantom whined, nudging my wrist and making my bracelets clatter together, as if to remind me they were there.

I tapped the various beads and bands, considering my options.

It had been over an hour since I'd drained that magic at the wall. It hardly felt like enough recovery time. Did I dare risk pulling even *more* strange energy into my body—the effects of which might not become truly apparent until later?

Aleksander stepped to my side, distracting me from my inner debate. "If you're going to run away, I suggest you do it now," he said, studying the orbs of light he'd just summoned to his fingertips. "So at least you'll be out of my way."

Indignant heat rushed through my body. "I'm not going anywhere, as much as I love the idea of leaving you here to die alone."

He chuckled darkly, muttering something I didn't catch—I was too busy running my fingers more purposefully along my bracelets.

Sometimes they guided me. I was used to their subtle shiverings and shiftings…but I was surprised when the black-rose bracelet was the one that began to move, its beads chattering like teeth in a blisteringly cold wind.

Then I remembered the more advanced side of projecting magic that Orin had explained to me, however many years ago now: How it was possible to send one's essence into *things* rather than into thin air—to become a possessing spirit and not merely a drifting one. I'd never managed anything close to it in the world above. But this realm was different, seemingly more conducive to my powers. I'd already witnessed a stronger ability to divine memories from objects, so maybe…

"Stay close to me, please," I whispered, quietly enough that only Phantom's ears could pick up the words. "I'm going to try something new."

(*Why do I feel as though this is going to end poorly?*)

"It's not like things can get much worse."

(*You've said that in the past. And you were wrong.*)

"Do something," Aleksander snapped, "or *move aside*."

Gritting my teeth, I firmly motioned Phantom closer. He let out another soft whine but obeyed. With his comforting weight pressing against my legs, I quickly rearranged my bracelets, shifting them so the black-rose bracelet was alone on my left wrist, allowing me to better focus on it—and the ability it channeled.

I lifted my arm and imagined a piece of myself lifting with it, separating from my body. A ghostly shade of me began to take form, glowing around my edges like a second skin preparing to shed. In the next instant, black markings spiraled over my lifted arm with sudden, powerful intensity, making my breath catch.

A good sign, I reminded myself, trying to stay calm.

The marks had always heralded stronger magic in the past, for better or worse.

A deep, settling breath, and those markings lifted from my physical arm, twisting up into the projection of it, welding the ghostly extension of me into something that felt more solid. More heavy.

Fearing it wouldn't last long, I quickly directed that fortified projection forward, aiming it at the spinning cyclone of shadows advancing toward Aleksander and me.

As my projection struck the approaching threat, I felt it in my physical body: A pressure against my hand, as though I was *actually* touching it. As though I could have grabbed hold of the swirling darkness and wrestled it into submission.

Not knowing what else to do, I tried precisely that.

I squeezed my hand into a fist as though to grab hold, and then I gave a sharp jerk of my wrist.

And a section of the winding cyclone of magic actually *moved*.

I'd managed it.

I'd possessed energy that wasn't mine.

I tried again, and this time I managed to begin peeling the churning mass apart. It didn't last long—but I unwound enough of it to glimpse what was at the heart.

What I saw nearly made me cry out in shock.

"There's a *person* in there."

"...What?"

"A woman." I stumbled several steps toward the spinning shadows, indifferent to the way they twisted with even angrier, louder, more threatening motions. "There's someone...someone is..."

Aleksander grabbed my arm, trying to hold me back. For a moment, I nearly let him. And why wouldn't I? Why would I *willingly* entomb myself in that dark cloud after witnessing what it had done to Elias?

Why? Because someone was in the center of those shadows, weaving this dark magic that looked like my own. *Controlling* it.

I'd never seen another person control magic that appeared even the least bit like mine.

So I pulled away and ran faster into the black vortex, pressing onward even as the shadows engulfed me and it felt as if they were freezing my skin into brittle sheets, threatening to shatter it right off my bones.

Each step became heavy, excruciating, sending daggers of pain shooting up my legs.

But the deeper I went, the more often I glimpsed her.

She was real.

I wasn't imagining her.

So I kept moving.

As I finally reached her, everything—my plans, my courage, my hope—left me. I blacked out one instant, and slammed unceremoniously into the woman in the next, sending us both sprawling to the ground. We tumbled through a storm of shadows and dust. The cold of her magic continued to pulse around me. As we untangled from one another and stood up, she bounced back and lifted her staff, using it to direct that cold with more precision; iciness wrapped around my limbs. My chest.

My throat.

I couldn't breathe, I *couldn't fucking breathe*—

She lifted her free hand and struck it toward me, pulling threads of darkness from the air behind her with the motion. She continued to move her staff as well, and the shadowy strings began to weave together in front of her.

I countered reflexively, projecting myself into the threads, grabbing what I could of them and pulling—*hard*. I was determined to break them before they could close her off again. I only managed to sever a few, but it was enough to catch her attention; her eyes widened as she realized what I was doing.

She went perfectly still. The shadows untangled and fell away, taking most of the cold with it, leaving the air between us hazy but relatively clear.

We stared at one another, wearing identical looks of shock.

As her magic dissipated further, I studied her closer. She was tall and muscular, her potential strength obvious even beneath the relatively loose, dark clothing she wore. Her eyes were an interesting shade of deep amethyst, and they were piercing and sharp, especially compared to the rest of her otherwise soft face. Her hair was like liquid night— waves of inky black that occasionally glistened with streaks of silver, making me think of shooting stars.

Those *stars*, I soon realized, were actually part of a delicate band fastened around her head; thin silver chains draped down from it, peeking out from under the long, obsidian strands and shimmering with even the faintest bit of light. Other, equally delicate chains crisscrossed her neck and arms in a way that seemed purposeful and precise, so that—at a glance—it all appeared to be ink permanently tattooed and shining brightly upon her brown skin.

The staff she carried remained half-raised, but as perfectly motionless as the rest of her. I kept waiting for her to move. To disappear into more shadows.

But no, she was solid.

Another being who was clearly solid, clearly real, clearly *alive* in this dead realm.

Finally, she moved. She slammed her staff into the ground and braced herself against it, and then she said something in a language I didn't understand. Paused. Tried again, her words growing more insistent. More furious.

I glanced over my shoulder at Aleksander. He looked equally stunned and confused. He started to take a step toward us—

The woman stopped him with a glare and a biting string of words that were still incomprehensible to me, yet clearly a warning.

She shifted her glare back to my face, appraising me for a long, uncomfortable moment.

And then she spoke again, this time in the common tongue of my empire, her words coming clearly but slowly: "Your magic. Possession. Necromancy. Yes?"

My heart leapt into my lungs, crowding away any chance of a normal breath. *Necromancy.* I'd heard that term used so infrequently in my life that it felt almost as if she was still speaking to me in a foreign language. As if I must have misheard her, somehow.

But I managed to nod.

"You are one of the rogue hunters, then?" she asked. "After a reward, I presume?"

I swallowed hard, hesitating, trying to decide on a safe answer. "I'm hunting...*something*. But I'm not after a reward. Not one of gold or anything, I mean."

She continued to appraise me. "You have apprehended the Light Beast, though?" Her eyes flicked toward Aleksander.

"Not exactly," I said.

"Not at all," Aleksander interjected, attempting another step forward—which the woman again put a stop to, this time with a quickly summoned javelin of dark shadows that she sent flying toward him with a swing of her staff.

Aleksander sidestepped the attack—barely.

And I liked this woman a little more, all of a sudden, despite the way she kept her other hand raised threateningly in my direction.

"I've only been traveling through this realm for a short amount of time," I told her. "I stumbled upon him without meaning to."

"He was frozen. Sleeping."

"...How did you know that?"

Instead of answering my question, she narrowed her eyes and took a step closer to me. "So you are not apprehending the Beast. You were the one who *woke* him. And now you've led him here."

"I... Well, yes, in a way I did, but—"

"And are you aware," she said, slamming the tip of her staff against my chest, "that the penalty for such a crime is *death*?"

Chapter Eleven

Nova

A DOZEN EXPLANATIONS TRIED TO TUMBLE THROUGH MY lips.

It was an accident.

I don't know how I did it.

I'd send him back into that cursed sleep, if I could.

Nothing coherent made it out.

The woman spoke again before I could utter so much as a whimper. "For seven years, we have been trying to finish him off." She dug her staff deeper into my chest. "We have kept him confined to his forest—kept him and his magic from wreaking more havoc here, at least. Who are you to have woken him up? To have freed him? To have led him *here*, so close to Erebos?"

"...Erebos? I don't even know what that—"

"*Quiet.*"

Phantom circled the two of us, snapping threateningly at the woman's heels. Her eyes darted his direction several times, but she didn't so much as flinch at the sight of his fangs, even as his body shifted and swelled into a larger size and his eyes glowed to a haunting shade of white.

He let out an otherworldly snarl that made even the hairs on the back of *my* neck stand on end. It finally, fully caught her attention; she looked as if she was considering spinning her staff around and pointing it at him instead.

Before she could move, Zayn arrived as well, along with the remaining two soldiers of our company. He exchanged a quick look with Aleksander before striding toward me without hesitation. The situation must have seemed like pure chaos to him as he blindly walked into it from afar, but he met it all with his usual, easy smile and simply said, "I suggest you point your weapon at something other than my friend. Now."

The pressure against my chest relaxed a bit as my attacker calculated her odds.

Aleksander stepped to his cousin's side, his hand balanced threateningly upon the short sword at his hip.

The woman finally relaxed her stance and let her staff drop. My breath followed the movement, a slow exhale of tension that left a pain in my chest and had me feeling lightheaded, as if I'd just had all the air stomped out of my lungs.

"Quite the traveling party," the woman remarked, her gaze sweeping over us all before returning to linger on me.

"We're not so foolish as to travel alone," Aleksander said, gripping his sword tighter, "as it seems you are."

"The shadows heed my beck and call. I am not as alone as I appear."

Despite her boast, I didn't sense any of those shadows building around her anymore. I kept this to myself, though, as I stared at her, trying to make sense of who she might be. How she had found us, and why she seemed to be so knowledgeable and concerned about me waking Aleksander. I had so many questions…

But all I kept coming back to was *what she was*.

Another necromancer.

Like me.

The words kept repeating over and over in my head: *She's like me. She's like me. She's like me…*

I was so caught up in the impossibility of it that I didn't realize, at first, how dangerously close the two separate sides were drawing to one another. Aleksander had unsheathed his sword. Zayn was staring in the direction of Elias's remains; he seemed to be piecing together all that had happened, and now he looked as if he was considering aiding his cousin in whatever bloody murder Aleksander was planning.

And as horrified as I was by what had happened to Elias, I couldn't let them attack this woman.

Not before I had a chance to truly speak with her.

I caught her attention the same way I had earlier; by calling upon the power channeled through my black-rose bracelet.

I threw a bit of my essence into her staff, this time, and it proved easier to possess an inanimate object than magic. I lifted my hand toward her, squeezed it into a fist, and I quickly felt the telltale pressure upon my palm—as if I was actually gripping the staff itself. With a twitch of my wrist, I had the weapon dipping backwards, sending her stumbling back with it.

This was already proving to be a useful new ability.

I again only managed a few seconds of control—but it

was enough to frustrate her, to make her rethink her plans and ultimately put more space between herself and my group.

Aleksander cut his eyes toward me, clearly curious about this latest trick I'd pulled.

"Just another abhorrent, abysmal, deathly chaotic thing," I said, echoing his words from back at the outpost.

I didn't wait around for his retort, already jogging after the woman.

"Let's talk for a moment," I softly called to her, once we were out of earshot of the others. "Just between you and me, perhaps?"

"Why?"

I hardened my tone. "Because I can explain things to you. Give you more information about that *Light Beast* you're so concerned about."

She threw a skeptical look over her shoulder, but—after a wary glance at the hand I'd used to conduct her weapon mere moments ago—she allowed me to catch up to her.

We made our way toward a secluded hilltop, where our only company included two skinny, brittle-looking trees and a scattering of broken stones. Phantom ran ahead of us, sniffing and scouting out the area for threats.

Zayn started to follow us as we made our way up the slope, but I quickly doubled back and cut him off.

"She used very powerful magic a few minutes ago," I told him, quietly. "We should tread carefully, I think—let me try and get on her good side."

"You think you can manage that?"

"I managed to get on *yours*, didn't I?"

He gave me a crooked grin. "Just…be careful," he said, eyes lifting toward the woman. "No one who manages to live in this hell can be trusted. They aren't natural beings. She may not even truly be *alive*."

I thought about pointing out that *we* were both here in this hell, and very much alive. But I only nodded and asked him to keep his distance along with Aleksander.

The woman's expression remained suspicious as I climbed the hill to her, her hands gripped fiercely around her staff even as I lifted my own in a gesture of peace.

"I won't let them turn their weapons against you," I told her, trying very hard to sound like someone who was actually in control of such things. "And I won't use my own magic against you anymore, either. But in exchange, I have questions."

Her mouth remained set in a hard, unflinching line, but she didn't protest. I'd *expected* her to protest. Her silence was worse; I didn't know where to start.

Phantom—who had curled up under one of the trees—lifted his head, sensing my discomfort, but I waved off his concern.

After I was quiet for too long, the woman spoke first, a sudden curiosity gleaming in her eyes that matched my own. "You controlled my shadows earlier. And then my staff."

"Briefly."

"Powerful necromancy, that."

"Is it?" I asked, realizing as the words left me that they sounded entirely too eager.

She gave me a strange look.

"It's just…it's a new skill I've recently acquired."

"A powerful and potentially dangerous one," she said, flatly. "If you don't know what you're doing."

Her point was implied.

You obviously don't know what you're doing.

I bit down my response to this, watching her as she leaned against one of the spindly trees, propping her staff in a crook of the branches and looking it over.

It was a beautiful weapon. Slightly longer than she was tall, the bulk of it carved from a dark grey wood. Some sort of silver metal wound elegantly around its tip, molded into the shape of a thorn-covered vine. It somehow looked both delicate and intimidating. Several of the thorns flashed in the low lighting—gemstones, I realized. She was inspecting each one, tapping them and occasionally whispering words in another language, both to herself and directly to the stones. Like a musician fine-tuning their instrument.

Several of the stones changed colors and luminosities as she did this, and I couldn't help staring, mesmerized into silence by the deft way her hands moved over the piece; she reminded me of Orin, the way she moved so chaotically quickly, yet expertly—tinkering, but with purpose.

My chest felt like it might cave in at the thought of my mentor.

Was he managing without me?

It had only been a little over a day, I thought, but it felt like much, much longer.

I cleared my throat, uncomfortable in the silence and the memories it made room for.

Curiosity lit the woman's gaze once more as she glanced up at me, and again, she was the one to interrupt the quiet. "The language you speak…you've spent extended time in the light."

I considered the words for a moment before their meaning sank in. "In the living world, you mean?"

Her hands stilled against the metal vine around her

weapon. She gave a single, curt nod before returning to her work.

"...I've spent *all* my time there, save for the past day or two," I admitted. There seemed no point in trying to lie about it. And maybe the truth would make me seem like less of a threat—less like someone she needed to impale with her staff. "And I've never met anyone with powers like mine in that world above."

She regarded me from under her lashes, not bothering to fully lift her head this time. "No. I would expect not. Such things don't typically last long in the light."

Twenty-five years, I wanted to tell her.

Twenty-five years I had lasted in that world, magic and all, though somedays I wasn't sure how.

Most days I wasn't sure how, if I was being honest with myself.

"Then again," she said, her gaze sliding down the hill toward Aleksander, "things like him don't typically last long in the dark, either."

"...Yet here we are," I mused.

She lowered her voice, even though the others were far in the distance and caught up in what looked to be an intense conversation of their own. "He should have succumbed immediately to the terrors of this realm," she said. "This is not a place for beings like him."

"His magic seems to have insulated him and the rest of his followers," I said. "If such a thing is possible?"

"Yes. It's possible." Her jaw tightened, and her eyes appeared to shift from frosted purple to a deeper, darker shade that brought to mind a starless night sky. "Of course, it has a cost. It's why we've been watching the Light Beast since his arrival. His initial landing unbalanced parts of this realm with catastrophic results. And every time he's woken up over the years, more calamities have ensued, lasting until he went back to sleep. The wall you crossed over was still in one piece seven years ago, for example. And we've done what we could to reinforce it with our own magic, to try and keep the destruction from spreading past it, but now…"

Now, I'd escorted that destructive *beast* right over their barriers.

Whoops.

Had his magic really unbalanced and broken down that wall, though?

What else had he destroyed over the past seven years?

The ominous chasm I'd witnessed on the way to the grove where I'd found him…the cracked ground and crumbling mountains parallel to it…had he caused all of that destruction, too?

"If he's causing such a disturbance, could you not have simply…gotten rid of him?" I wondered.

"All our attempts to kill him have been in vain. Something protects him from our strongest spells. And we keep expecting—*hoping*—the air itself will do the job for us, once he breathes it in long enough, but that hasn't happened, either."

Rather than trying to guess at the reason behind this, I said, "You said *we*. How many of you are there?"

My entire body tingled at the possibility of there being *more* necromancers hiding within the shadows of this realm. Was this why I'd never met one in the world above? Maybe they were all down here, serving the dead and keeping order among them.

It made sense, didn't it?

But then...how had *I* ended up in the living world, so far away from the rest of my kind?

And why had Orin never mentioned anything like this?

"There were many of us, once upon a time," the woman said quietly. "But not any longer."

She didn't seem to want to elaborate. I was nearly bursting with my need to know more, but instead of giving in to my curiosity, I simply asked, "What is your name?"

She jerked her gaze to mine, as if the question surprised her. As if she didn't know why I would care.

But I'd heard the loneliness in her tone just a moment ago. How her words seemed to echo with a cold, lost sort of emptiness. I knew what that felt like. And sometimes it was nice just to hear your name out loud—to remind yourself that you could still exist within the emptiness, even if everything else you loved and related to was gone.

After a bit of hesitation, she said, "...Thalia."

I offered my hand. "I'm Nova."

She stared at my hand for a moment before lightly gripping it and shaking it. "Nova of the Above. A necromancer who walks in the light, alongside the Beast and his brethren. Pleased to meet you." She didn't seem truly *pleased*, but she *did* appear more curious than hostile toward me, now.

Progress.

Still, I had to fight the urge to shrink away from her touch and her almost *too* curious gaze.

There was no way she could have known the true history I shared with the King of Light. She didn't know who I was, or what I'd done—how Aleksander had ended up in this realm after I'd channeled the shadows from it into an attack against him. How I'd apparently sent him crashing down into this place, triggering devastation in it when he landed.

And I wasn't foolish enough to tell this *Thalia* all of my secrets right away, even if I was desperate to let every truth spill out in hopes of coaxing more information out of her.

"Tell me, Nova: Where were you leading the Beast?"

I hesitated, wondering how much more I should reveal. My gaze drifted down the hill, landing on Zayn first.

I liked him well enough, but I'd only been with him and the others for a day. I had no real loyalty to any of them—and I doubted they truly felt any toward me.

Besides, I'd come for the sword, not the king. And here was a potentially better guide to take me to that sword. One with the same magic as me. One who actually *belonged* to this realm.

"I wasn't leading him anywhere," I told her. "I came in search of something else, as I mentioned earlier. I just happened to find him first. I truly didn't mean to wake him. I'm not even sure how I did it."

She clearly didn't believe me.

I wanted to insist upon the truth of what I said, to suggest we immediately leave Aleksander and the others behind without looking back.

Only one thing gave me pause.

"What *calamities* have ensued since this latest awakening of his?" I asked.

I needed to know before I risked leaving him behind.

Thalia's gaze traveled the same path mine had moments ago, studying Aleksander and the others, her eyes glazing over in thought. "None, thus far," she admitted. "But his past destructions are reason enough to be wary."

None, thus far.

My magic had woken him up, but nothing truly catastrophic had followed. Something strange was clearly happening between our powers whenever we were close to one another, however…what if it was the influence of my magic that was keeping his under control—and keeping it from wreaking havoc on this realm?

I wanted to vomit at the thought of being so intimately tied to him.

It couldn't be true.

I tried to think back on all the magical lessons Orin had given me over the years, wishing I'd paid better attention to the knowledge he'd attempted to impart. All the different laws and attributes—there had to be an explanation for what was happening between Aleksander and me.

But I'd never been one to take notes on these things.

I'd always preferred to learn by doing, however painful and messy the practical trials ended up being.

And so, I decided it was time for an experiment.

Chapter Twelve

Nova

"I need to go for a walk."

Thalia's brows rose immediately in suspicion.

"My dog is...restless."

Phantom lifted his head and cocked it briefly, curiously at me, but then he began to play the part without questioning it, hopping to his feet and spinning around in circles. He was acting, at first, until his tail actually swept across the tip of his nose—then I think he began chasing it in earnest.

I cleared my throat.

He stopped with his jaws opened wide, an instant from snapping his teeth around his tail. He read my unspoken command and then darted off down the hill.

"I'll be right back," I said, rushing after him.

I felt Thalia's stare like a physical weight against the back of my neck. But whether because of confusion, curiosity, or mere indifference, she didn't attempt to stop me.

I caught up with Phantom at the bottom of the hill. He started to slow, but I subtly encouraged him to keep running. I didn't look back to see if any of the others were watching my retreat, not wanting to see the questions on their faces; I was already dealing with too many questions of my own.

We ran for several minutes, Phantom leading the way, before I slowed to a brisk walk to catch my breath.

He circled back at an easy lope. (*Where are we going?*)

"I'm not sure." I wrapped my arms around myself, huddling against the cold, and walked faster. "Just…away. I'm testing something."

Part of me wanted to simply keep running into the depths, regardless of what became of the things I left behind. It had been easier when it was just Phantom and me on this mad, impossible journey—or maybe I'd just gotten used to it only being the two of us on all our missions.

I supposed *familiar* and *easier* felt the same, sometimes.

"I want to see what happens when my magic isn't near Aleksander, influencing whatever impact his power might have on this realm," I explained to Phantom.

I don't know how far we traveled—over a mile, at least—before something finally happened: A trembling in the ground. Faint, but unmistakable. I watched as it rattled the rocks around my boots and sent little puffs of dirt into the air.

I stopped in my tracks, the heavy truth of the situation settling over me. Though the path ahead stretched wide and empty, it felt like I'd just had a massive iron gate slammed in my face.

Phantom must have felt it, too; he skidded to a stop and spun back toward the ones we'd left behind.

Holding my breath, I turned and looked back as well.

A light was shining far in the distance, like the only star twinkling on an otherwise empty horizon—one that was growing larger and bolder with every passing second.

"Damn it," I muttered.

I tried to turn away from the sight, but I couldn't bring myself to walk any farther.

Now what?

Even without staring directly at it, the glow soon became impossible to ignore. The light flickered and expanded, flickered and expanded, over and over—now a star getting dangerously close to explosion.

Magic.

It had to be Aleksander's magic; I had yet to see anything else in this realm even come close to the brightness he created.

And I couldn't just pretend I didn't see it.

Going against nearly every instinct I possessed, I turned back toward the others and set off at a jog that quickly transitioned into a sprint.

Even running as fast as I could, Phantom kept getting far ahead and having to circle back. Finally, he shifted into a larger version of his canine self and swept in front of me, forcing me to a stop.

(*You aren't fast enough,*) he said pointedly.

I hesitated, only until I remembered how much more solid he'd become since arriving in this realm. Steeling my nerves, I grabbed a fistful of the fur around the ruff of his neck and hoisted myself onto his back.

He bolted forward, nearly flinging me off as he did.

It took effort, but after a few seconds, I managed to balance between his shoulder blades and stay there. Keeping my balance required staying low against his body, however, so I was mostly blind as we raced back across the dark landscape, my face buried in his silky, wind-swept fur.

But I didn't need to see the destruction to know we were approaching it.

I could *feel* it.

It was no longer a mere trembling, but a steady wave of power rippling through the ground, making it buckle and sway. The power was overwhelming, but the heat was worse; my lungs seemed to expand with every inhale of the searing air until they felt close to bursting.

I continued to press my face into Phantom's strong back as he unleashed a cold wave of energy. For most, that energy was a warning, a disorienting shock to their system. For me, it provided a familiar jolt of comfort—enough to bring me back to my senses. Lifting my head, I squinted in the direction where most of the heat and power seemed to be originating from.

I spotted Aleksander kneeling in the center of a storm of Light energy, his head bowed and his eyes closed.

The others were nowhere in sight.

A terrible thought clutched me—had a part of this world already broken apart and swallowed them up?

Just like the world swallowed up my father and so many others seven years ago...

It all felt so similar to the night in Rose Point—only with our roles reversed. Here Aleksander was, in a world that didn't embrace his magic, same as I'd been that night. And now the power he channeled was threatening to rip the realm apart at the seams.

But what did it all *mean*?

I didn't know what to think, or what to do. But if I didn't do *something*, then there was a very good chance neither of us would live to figure any of it out.

"Get me closer!" I told Phantom, shouting to be heard over the crackling and hissing of magic.

He hesitated for a beat before following the command, bouncing precariously over the rolling ground, dodging bolts of Light energy as they struck the shaking earth all around us. A particularly violent crack of energy lashed the dirt right in front of us and Phantom jumped straight up, his reflexes suddenly more cat-like than dog-like.

My grip on his fur slipped, sending me bouncing wildly into the air.

He managed to slide underneath me again just before I hit the ground. I rolled clumsily across his back and slid down his side, planting my feet and somehow managing to stay upright after a few stumbling steps.

Shadows swirled to life on my skin as I drew closer to Aleksander. His skin cracked and light bled through the fissures as if in answer to my power—as if that light had only been waiting for me to arrive, eager to slip free, to tangle with my darkness. And *I* felt a surge of eagerness, too. An unmistakable pull…

My shadows wanted to collide with him.

Desperately.

I didn't understand it, but I had to get to him, no matter the cost.

Phantom paced restlessly behind me, occasionally nudging me with his cold nose and trying to convince me to hop onto his back once more. But I had a sudden surge of confidence and sure-footedness—I would cross the rest of this perilous ocean on my own, and not risk my best friend as I did it.

I sprinted forward, muscles straining and balance rocking as I fought to stay upright and keep Aleksander in my line of sight. The magic grew thicker. The heat was just short of suffocating. But I was getting closer.

Twenty feet.

Ten feet.

Five feet—

I stretched out my hand.

And as soon as my fingers brushed Aleksander's arm, the world around us began to...*bloom*.

Like the forest I'd first found him in, everything around me—the withered grass, the scraggly roots of long-dead flowers, a nearby tree previously devoid of all its leaves—exploded into life, filling the air with a blinding brightness.

Once again, it all died just as quickly...but with the death came a relative calmness. The ground no longer trembled. The light stopped crackling and shooting out from Aleksander's body, leaving us in a twilight-hued silence. Not a peaceful quiet, but one heavy with the possibility of more to come, like the silent note in a symphony just before an impending crescendo. I kept waiting for it to come—the clash of cymbals, the rising notes before a bone-rattling climax...

But as I gripped Aleksander's arm more tightly, the silence stretched on and on, until finally, I trusted it would stay.

For now.

Aleksander kept his head bowed and his eyes closed. The light-filled cracks on his skin had mostly faded, save for a few on his arms, and one that ran the length of one side of his face, right through the middle of his right eye. Traces of magic still bled from those fissures, dripping down his cheeks like tears made of liquid gold.

Clinging more tightly to his arm—mostly for the sake of balance, now—I looked around.

The ground was buckled in a few places, but otherwise, no worse for the wear. A few shallow cracks remained…and there were little shoots of green sprouting up through several of them. A few of the shoots even had flower buds on them.

I was almost certain none of that had been here before.

So apparently, everything *hadn't* died as quickly as it bloomed.

Somehow, this struck me as one of the strangest things I'd seen yet: A living garden taking root in a world meant for the dead.

What the hell was going on?

Shakily—cautiously—I released my hold on Aleksander and rose to my full height. I heard voices and turned to see Zayn, Thalia, and our two remaining soldiers standing a short distance away.

They were all staring at me—except for Thalia, who was staring at the budding flowers.

Zayn moved first. He looked me over as he approached, but for once, he seemed entirely speechless. After struggling and failing to find words, he walked right past me and instead hurried to Aleksander's side. Rowen and Farren immediately followed him.

The king didn't stir at their approach, remaining in his kneeled position with his head bowed.

Was he back to sleep for another year now?

I was so busy watching him—and occasionally sweeping

another confused, disbelieving stare at the garden growing around him—that Thalia's sudden appearance at my side startled me.

"Necromancy..." she said, her gaze drifting once more over the blooming garden. "And yet, you seem to be helping him bring life, rather than death."

"But I didn't *do* anything," I said, breathlessly.

"You didn't use any spells against him?"

I vehemently shook my head. "I barely had time to think, much less summon magic."

She kept her gaze on the garden; several of the flowers were now opening, their colors brilliant and bold shades of red, orange, and yellow. All of them were golden-edged and glowing, as if catching bits of the sun—a heavenly object that didn't even truly exist in this world; there was only that strange orb of light wrapped in the shifting, cloudy energies. That orb still hadn't moved. Still, looking around, I felt the same way I did whenever I sat on the porch at Orin's and watched the sun rising over the trees.

"It's as I said before," I whispered, "I merely touched him when I woke him up, too. I swear it."

Thalia was quiet for so long that I thought she would never answer. That she would never believe me.

Finally, she said, "How...*odd*."

I held my breath, almost afraid to ask what conclusions she was coming to behind her troubled eyes.

"Your magic. His magic. They seem to have a profound effect on one another, no?"

I couldn't deny it.

"So you're..." She seemed to be searching for the correct word. "...*Together*," she settled on, tapping her fingers against one another for emphasis. "Magically bonded to one another."

I made a face. "*Bonded* is a very strong word."

She didn't offer an alternative.

My eyes slid back to the king, despite my best efforts to keep them from doing so.

Peaceful, meditative, motionless—yet he still looked utterly terrifying. Alarmingly powerful. Like he could open his eyes at any moment and send light crackling across the landscape once more, ripping it all apart faster than I could blink.

Except, it wasn't *terror* I felt whenever I looked at him.

It should have been.

But it wasn't.

I didn't know what it was. But as I stared, a memory fell, unbidden, into my mind. One of the first time we'd met—as children, when he'd found me hiding in the courtyard at my old home.

We'd been so young.

I'd been so upset—exasperated with my lessons, with my teachers who had been trying their best to teach me to crush the shadowy parts of myself away. This had been before my mother gave in to Orin's offers to tutor me. Back when she'd believed there was still a chance for me to hide my magic and live a normal life without it. Back when I had wanted nothing more than to make her happy by doing just that—when I would have given anything to just be *normal*.

Aleksander had comforted me that day; I still remembered the warmth of his magic as he summoned a show of light to distract me from my tears.

And then he'd done something unexpected: He'd asked

me to summon strands of my shadows, too, so that we might create something by weaving together both the light and the dark—something like the shadow puppets my father sometimes entertained me with at bedtime, only more elaborate.

I didn't really remember anything we'd spoken of that day. Only the stories we'd written with sunlight and shadow on the brick walls around the garden—that, and the way the flowers around us had bloomed like an eager audience coming to life at our show, and how my heart had felt truly at peace for perhaps the only time in my entire childhood.

But politics and other twisted, sharp-edged things had long since gotten in the way of whatever peace I'd felt that day. He had changed. *I* had changed. There were too many questions between us, too many plans gone astray, and I didn't want anything to do with him anymore.

Still, the evidence could not be ignored.

Our magic desperately wanted to weave together once more—to cast another story upon the walls of this world we'd found ourselves in.

And until I figured out *why*, it seemed we were bound to one another whether we liked it or not.

WE DECIDED to pitch a proper camp and rest before deciding what came next. I slept—though poorly, and only after Zayn repeatedly insisted that he would be the one to keep the first watch.

At some point, I startled awake from a nightmare, opening my eyes to a bottomless abyss.

It took me several seconds of blinking to realize I was staring at the sky. Or what passed for a *sky* in this world, anyway; I was alarmed at how deeply black it was. I hadn't realized it could get darker than the expanse I'd fallen asleep beneath. But it was as Elias had told me: there was an observable day and night cycle in this realm—and it was clearly the dead of night, now; the light I desperately wanted to call a *sun* was completely hidden behind swirls of dark clouds.

Even though I couldn't recall the nightmare that had woken me, I still felt its claws in my mind, tightening every time I tried to close my eyes again.

With a sigh, I sat up and crawled out of my bedroll—but I only made it a few inches before I froze.

Because Aleksander was right *there*, sitting with his arm draped over a bended knee, mere feet away from where I'd been sleeping. His eyes were open, bright in the dark and focused on something far in the distance.

My entire body flushed hot. Had I been tossing and turning, caught in the throes of my nightmares, while he watched?

I swallowed down my discomfort as best I could, settling back down on my knees. "You're awake," I said.

"You're observant."

"Have you just been looming threateningly over me the entire time I've been asleep?"

"I'm hardly a threat. Especially with him so close," he said, nodding to a nearby patch of shriveled-up grass where Phantom lay, resting with his head upon his shaggy paws. The dog's sides rose and fell with the slow breaths of sleep, but one ghostly blue eye occasionally cracked open, watching us.

"And I would stay much farther away from you, if I could," Aleksander added, "but the more space between us, the more restless my magic becomes. A cruel trick the universe seems to be playing on me."

On you and me both, I wanted to snap.

But I didn't, for some reason. I merely got to my feet, stretching, and muttered, "Well, glad I could help settle you down."

My attempt at a placid tone didn't fool him.

"You would leave, too, if given the choice," he said. "You were considering leaving earlier, when you went off to *talk* with that Shadow-wielding woman. I could see it in your eyes."

Lack of sleep and my growing frustration with the situation made my voice savage. "Of course I was considering it. She would likely be a far better guide than you through this realm—and she hasn't murdered anybody in my family, as far as I know. So why the hell *wouldn't* I want her help over yours?"

He shrugged. "Because we agreed to travel with one another?"

"I've traveled with you for all of one day. It was hardly a deal set in stone."

"And loyalty is for fools, eh?" He didn't sound particularly combative, for once. Tired, more like.

My laughter was still harsh. "*Loyalty*," I snorted. "I've tried my hand at loyalty over the years. It's led to more backstabbings and close-calls than I care to think about. Nearly every person I've ever dared to trust has let me down in one way or another."

"That just sounds like you're a poor judge of character."

I huffed out another bitter laugh. "Maybe so. Because here I am, close to you—again—back to travel at your side instead of finding some way to bury you and your magic out of existence, so…yes. Yes, I'd say I'm an *abhorrent* judge of character."

He met my words with a dry chuckle of his own. "I set up that particular jab against me, didn't I?"

I shrugged.

"You win that point, then. Congratulations."

"…Are we keeping score?"

"You seemed like the type who would."

I considered this, tipping my head back and pretending to mentally calculate the points we'd both accumulated thus far. "I'm ahead," I concluded.

He smirked, crossing his hands behind his head before reclining back against the ground. The movement lifted his shirt, revealing a band of firm stomach.

I forced my stare elsewhere, biting my lip as heat flushed across the back of my neck and tingled over my scalp.

Ridiculous.

But I couldn't help it; I was suddenly burning up as if I'd never seen a naked man before, even though I'd seen plenty. Too many, really—but one had to deal with loneliness somehow, didn't they? I wasn't above trading favors for supplies or information, either, though I was selective with who I engaged with; with a few of my favorite *business partners*, it was essentially a win-win for me.

It had been too long since I'd had any sort of *business* in that department, though, for any reason.

And damn it all if this beautiful specimen of a male was not reminding me of that.

The mingling of our magic didn't help, either; the buzzing his nearness caused in my power could have been the first sparks of arousal, if I allowed them to be. They felt entirely too similar.

And before I could help myself, I was wondering what sort of response—whether cataclysmic or beneficial—embracing that spark might create.

Talk about *bonded*.

Biting my lip harder, I tried to stay focused. "So, I woke you in that forest. My magic settles yours. If we continued to travel together…what's in it for me, I wonder?"

"The pleasure of my company," he replied without opening his eyes.

"Wow. I'm getting absolutely fucking *shorted* on this deal."

I thought I saw the ghost of a smile flirting with his lips, but it was gone as soon as I looked closer.

I wondered, for an instant, what his true smile looked like. Had I seen it in the living realm—maybe when we were children? I must have. So why couldn't I remember it now?

Why did I *want* to?

Against my better judgment, I kept talking, kept trying to bridge some of the uncertainty between us. "I did feel… something when I approached you earlier. A surge of strength in my own power, perhaps."

He said nothing; I wasn't even sure he was listening.

I didn't want to keep talking. Didn't want to entertain the idea that we were magically *bonded* in any way. But not understanding seemed worse than discovering an answer I didn't want.

So I said, "The shadows that appear on my skin sometimes…I used to have more control over them. They were always tied to my stronger magic use, but…soon after what happened at Rose Point, they stopped showing up. They had stopped surfacing for *years* before I found you down here. And now, they've appeared on my skin twice in the span of a day."

He finally opened his eyes, but he still didn't speak.

I swallowed. "So, your presence seems to awaken the stronger parts of my power. And my nearness settles *your* power, as you said."

"Mm. Though it's very…fastidious."

"How so?"

"When you're close but out of reach, as you are now, you just give me a dull, aching headache." He rocked up into a sitting position and inched closer to me. "It keeps things from raging out of control, yes, but the finer, more nuanced wielding of my abilities is impossible to manage. I've noticed, though…" he trailed off, stopping just short of reaching for me.

The moment stretched into one of painful uncertainty, which surprised me; I didn't think the King of Light was *capable* of showing uncertainty.

Judging by the confusion and exasperation that crossed his face, he hadn't thought himself capable of it, either.

"Never mind," he muttered. "It's strange. Let's leave it at that."

"No—explain it." I moved closer to him without really thinking about it.

He sucked in a sharp breath, as though I'd done something far more intimate than simply closing the space between us.

Intrigued by the reaction, I grew bolder, sliding closer and letting my hand come to rest on his leg.

He went perfectly still, staring at my touch with such intensity that I forgot what I was saying for a moment.

"...When I'm truly close to you like this," I finally managed to say, my voice more hushed than I intended it to be, "does it bring clarity to you and your powers?"

A pause. Then he raised his hand and his fingertips gripped my chin, lifting my gaze to his. He considered me and my question for another beat, his golden eyes burning into mine.

"Yes," he said. "For the first time in seven years, I feel like I have a true hold on my powers again." As if to demonstrate this, a jagged line of light cracked across the hand pressed to my chin. It spread up his forearm and over his bicep, and warmth poured from his skin along with the light, enveloping me.

His gaze seemed to brighten as it raked over my face again, drinking in the sight of me newly awash in the glow his magic created. "Like an anchor dropping in a storm-tossed sea," he mused, more to himself than me.

His hand moved up to cup my jaw.

I leaned into the touch before I could help myself. "I thought I was *Chaos*, not clarity," I murmured.

"It's still a fitting nickname," he replied, mirroring my low, slightly breathy tone. "It surrounds you, even if there's calm at the center." At the word *center*, his hand dropped, warm fingers trailing down my neck, splaying across the hollow of my throat.

His mouth tipped closer, his nose brushing against mine.

My eyes started to flutter shut, some deep, buried part of me actually *wanting* this, wishing his fingers would drop even lower, that his lips would find mine in the next instant—

But...*no*.

What the hell were we doing?

He seemed to ask himself the same question in the exact same instant. His brow furrowed. A combination of anger and doubt darkened his eyes. But there was also a flicker of what I would have sworn looked like *desire*.

The shadow markings on my skin leapt to life as though fueled by that desire. The power simmering beneath them was undeniable.

I pulled away, heart pounding like a drumbeat, echoing in the silence. My head was spinning. With even more questions, now...but with realizations, too. Because all of my *experiments* were yielding the very results I'd been afraid they would.

It wasn't enough to just occupy the same space as one another.

For me to summon stronger shades of my power, and for him to truly be able to control *his* power, it seemed we needed to be even closer to one another. Connected. Tangled up in one another's essence.

This just got worse and worse.

He stood and took a step away from me, lifting his eyes in the same direction they'd been staring in when I woke; there was a hazy lightness above the far horizon. Almost like the glow of a distant city, I thought, even though I knew that couldn't be what it was.

"A cruel trick of the universe, as I mentioned," Aleksander said, his tone abruptly cold. "And it makes no sense, based on all of my studies and trainings. *Like calls to like*, according to all my instructors over the years. My magic should want nothing to do with yours. We're opposites; we have nothing in common."

The words shouldn't have stung; I should have been used to not having things in common with people by this point.

So why did I suddenly care about having something in common with *him*?

We were quiet for several minutes.

Finally, I couldn't keep my thoughts to myself any longer. I said, "Do we really have nothing in common?"

He cut his gaze to me.

"It just…it reminded me of the way my magic always felt so out of place in the living world. Earlier, I mean—when I saw the light ripping out of your body, threatening to destroy everything around us."

He didn't reply, but his gaze softened a bit, urging me on.

"You've been here for seven years," I continued. "Seven years of being in a place where your magic earns you the reputation of *Beast*. And I…I know what that's like. So we have that one thing in common, at least."

Meeting his softer, more contemplative gaze was somehow even more difficult than staring into his usual intense, fiery one, so I looked instead to the distant glow on the horizon as I continued. "Because I know what it's like to not belong in a place," I said, my voice barely above a whisper, "and for your very existence to *destroy* that place. The only difference is that I actually loved what I destroyed."

He took a long time to reply. "It never recovered after what happened on the night of your birthday, I take it?"

I numbly shook my head.

"I assume my kingdom has also suffered similarly, given my abrupt disappearance—or my *death*, as I'm sure it was assumed."

I finally found the courage to look back and meet his questioning eyes.

And again, I felt a prodding to keep talking, to cross the bridge stretching between us, regardless of whatever rickety, dangerous planks might be hiding, waiting to drop our feet out from under us.

If we were stuck together, I was going to have to be honest with him about some things. There was too much strangeness at work to figure it all out on my own; keeping certain information from him could do more harm than good at this point.

My turmoil must have been obvious on my face, because his brow furrowed with concern.

"Chaos? What is it?"

"Your kingdom is fine," I told him, frowning. "Because as far as most people believe, you are still alive and ruling it."

Chapter Thirteen

Aleksander

"She could be lying," Zayn said, looking uncharacteristically flustered.

"What reason would she have to lie about something like this?"

"She could be trying to sow animosity in us, towards our kingdom and the Keepers who have been stewarding the throne since our unceremonious exit."

"…I don't think so."

"They would not have replaced you with some…*body double*," Zayn insisted, scrubbing the remains of our campfire out with his boot. "It's preposterous to even think of."

"Is it? Perhaps they panicked when I disappeared and they could think of no better alternative? Maybe they thought Elarith had already seen enough death with my parents, and the death of a third royal family member might have sent too many of them over the edge. We've talked about this ourselves over the years, haven't we?"

It was one of the fears that had haunted me most during my time stuck in this cursed hell—wondering what had become of my kingdom and its people.

My mother's death had already destabilized Elarith to an alarming degree. Father's passing had been yet another shift in the foundation of our once illustrious kingdom, and I'd barely been keeping order, honestly—which was the only reason I'd agreed to an arranged marriage with a foreign princess in the first place. A union of kingdoms to help stabilize things. That had been the plan. Eldris was supposed to have been a peaceful, easy target—one with understated power that we could mold to whatever use we needed.

I'd had a foreboding feeling about the ordeal from the start, but I'd trusted the Keepers of Light to know what was best for Elarith, just as my father had, and his father before him, and his father before *him*…

If only I'd listened to myself.

But how could I have seen any part of these past seven years coming? And my advising council replacing me with an imposter…*that* was certainly not a possibility that had ever crossed my mind.

"According to Nova, they've been building a narrative that *she* is the one responsible for her parents' demise and the dark curse surrounding Rose Point," I told Zayn. "This so-called *King of Elarith* has declared himself a steward of the Eldrisan throne. So, we've gained control of that kingdom after all—though not in the agreed-upon way."

Irritation flared hot in my veins.

But at *who*?

The imposter? The Light Keepers? Myself?

I couldn't decide who I hated more in that moment.

Zayn shook his head. "It's borderline treasonous that they would even *consider* using a puppet version of you to continue ruling."

I tried to offer a reasonable response, even as suppressed rage cut a hot, twisting path through my insides. "What would the alternative have been? *You* were next in line to the throne after me. And you disappeared that night, too, in case you forgot. Wren would be after you. Hardly a capable ruler seven years ago, was she?"

Wren was his younger sister, and she'd been scarcely a year old when we disappeared. After her, the line of succession grew considerably more blurry.

He started to argue several times, but ultimately, he merely shook his head, massaging the space between his eyes, and said, "What a godsdamn disaster this all is."

"An understatement." I used a stick to absently spread out the smoldering ashes of the fire as I considered everything. After a minute, I said, "And it seems like impossibly bad luck, doesn't it?"

Zayn tilted his head curiously, reading the unspoken implications in my tone, as he usually did; we'd always been close enough to do that. And nothing made you even closer than seven years stuck together in Hell.

"…You don't think it was all *bad luck*, do you?" he asked.

"I know the Eldrisan King had misgivings about marrying his daughter off to me. Perhaps there was fear he wouldn't go through with the arrangement."

"So you believe the Keepers arranged for someone to murder him?"

"All I know is that *I* am not the one who stabbed the king that night. But there are several members of the Light Keepers who would have liked for me to do precisely that."

I speared a chunk of burned wood, shattering it into smaller flecks of ash and embers. "I didn't see who actually wielded the blade against him. The blightdust powder that exploded on the veranda made it impossible to make out what was happening until it was too late to do anything about it."

As soon as my vision had cleared, I'd reflexively gone for the sword—*my* sword—that had somehow ended up impaled in King Eryndor's chest. And that, of course, was where my hand had been when Nova stumbled onto the scene.

Part of me wondered if *that* was intentional, too.

If someone had intended to frame me.

What had happened next, though, likely had not been part of *anybody's* plans. Meticulous, conniving, string-pulling masters they might have been, but I doubted any of the Keepers had planned on Nova ripping open a fucking portal to Hell and sending me and my closest followers crashing through it.

She had been dangerously unpredictable—*chaotic*—from the beginning.

Zayn stared into the smoke spiraling up from the charred wood I'd stabbed. He didn't seem enthusiastic about continuing this line of discussion.

I didn't blame him.

Too many things didn't add up, and there was little we could do about any of it while we were trapped down here.

"The only way to find answers is to get back to the living world," I said, "where we can confront it all for ourselves."

Zayn crossed his arms in front of his chest, tilting his head to the bruise-colored sky. He was lost in thought for several moments before he said, "Right. Which should be exceptionally easy to do—*especially* if your magic keeps flying out of control and threatening to destroy this realm and kill us all."

I ignored his sardonic tone, getting to my feet and busying myself with packing my bags, trying not to think about last night.

It was impossible *not* to think about it, though.

We'd camped a fair distance away from the worst of the destruction, but there were still thin, jagged cracks reaching toward where we now stood, reminding me of the destruction I'd caused. And *nearly* caused.

I remembered little of what had happened.

One moment, I'd been arguing with Zayn about something, while simultaneously keeping an eye on the conversation Nova and Thalia had been having on the hilltop.

Then Nova had disappeared, and all the world had seemed to grow louder in her absence—roars of thunder and clanging metal in my head, like I was in the middle of a battlefield while swords clashed and shields splintered all around me.

I remembered blinding light. Kneeling. Drawing into myself. Thinking I could keep the war inside—away from the others—if only I shut myself down tightly enough.

I remembered sudden cold. A hand on my arm. Shadows giving shape to the light. Sudden clarity…

And then I'd woken up in the middle of the night to find myself surrounded by flowers. And *grass*—lush, green grass. All of it different from the things I'd grown down here in the past; its creation had been effortless, for starters. And it all continued to live, even now, even without any help from me. It was hard to explain, but the small garden we'd created didn't look like out-of-place, glowing magic; it looked like it had always been a part of this world. Simple and unassuming. Balanced and meant to be.

The sound of laughter caught my attention. Nova was a short distance away, talking with Rowen and Farren, helping them pack up the last of our campsite. Even Rowen was smiling at whatever she was saying; I couldn't remember the last time I'd seen that grumpy old bastard smile at anything.

And laughter wasn't a sound I'd heard often throughout my time in this purgatory—maybe that was why it caught my attention. Why I couldn't seem to stop staring at her.

Zayn nudged my arm, letting out a long-suffering sigh. "At least our cheerful necromancer companion is able to settle your magic down, eh?"

She did more than merely *settle* it.

Though I wasn't ready to admit it to anyone—least of all to my assuming ass of a cousin—after this latest incident where her magic had apparently balanced mine, I'd woken up feeling…*stronger*. Undeniably stronger. And when she'd touched me last night, with purpose and poise and curiosity gleaming in her bright eyes, I'd felt…

Well, it didn't matter what *feelings* I'd had.

But the fact remained: This was a cruel fucking joke the universe seemed to be playing, and I was not at all amused.

"So, you two will just have to stay close, I guess." Zayn's tone was loaded with implications.

I shot him a withering look.

He only smiled. "It could be worse."

"It could also be better."

"You two were destined to be wed. You're trying to tell

me you never imagined what it might be like to have her close? And all to yourself?"

It irked me for some reason, hearing him talk about her as if she were little more than a political piece. "We were never actually engaged," I reminded him. "She agreed to nothing."

She also certainly hadn't agreed to being the apparent balancing act for my wayward magic—which was why I would be doing everything in my power to keep my distance from her, regardless of how desperately I might have craved the clarity and strength she seemed to bring me.

I didn't like being anybody's burden.

I never had.

I'd had roles to play throughout most of my life. I'd always known exactly what they were, and I had performed them *perfectly*. Never a foot out of line, never a word misspoken, never an extra weight added to *anyone*. All my life, I'd thought I could keep my kingdom intact if I just did what was expected of me. This idea had been driven into my head, staked into my heart, buried into the very core of my being. Strict and unflinching. For twenty years, that had been the only world I knew.

Then came Rose Point.

And this chaos surrounding me now...

I *hated* it.

"Let's stay focused on the bigger picture," I said, forcing my gaze to stay on Zayn, and to not stray to the primary conductor of the chaos herself. "Our supposed *bond* aside, the more important fact is this: She was able to get into this realm. Which means she can help us get out of it, too, hopefully."

"And *that* return will be an interesting day in our kingdom's history, hm?"

I didn't comment on this.

Interesting was not the first word that came to my mind.

I didn't know what game the Keepers of Light were playing. But I knew what they were capable of. There was a reason the Elarithian throne was as powerful as it was—why most of the Valorian Empire cowered before it.

But *I* was the head of that throne, not them.

It was the role I'd been groomed for my entire life, and the more I thought about it, the more I refused to believe they would dare put an imposter in my place.

So what was truly going on?

Zayn sauntered away, heading to join Nova and the others. I don't know what he said to her, but moments later, she was shouldering her bag and walking in my direction.

She looked pleased with herself, which—if I had to guess—was likely bad news for me.

I went back to arranging my own bags, casting her a wary glance as she stopped directly in front of me. "Your smile is entirely too cheerful, given our circumstances. What chaos have you orchestrated this time?"

She lifted her chin. "I made a deal with Thalia."

"Do tell."

"She knows of Luminor and its location."

"Right. Or she *claims* she does, at least."

She ignored my pessimistic outlook. "She's agreed to guide us to it, *if* I agree to bring you along and keep you and your magic from destroying anything else along the way. She wants us to stay close to one another, as that seems to keep our magic, well...*balanced*. And the sword is apparently being kept in a safe place that's nullifying its magic and keeping it from doing any more damage than it already has, so…"

"So she ultimately wants to lock *me* and my magic in that same place, I assume, so that I might be neutralized along with the sword? And how lucky for her that you came along to serve as a guard and escort."

"Well, she didn't *say* any of that—"

"But of course, why wouldn't I agree to such a brilliant plan that could in no way end poorly for me?"

She fumed, clearly too annoyed to reply right away. And the pout of her lips, combined with the fiery challenge in her eyes…

Fucking hell.

She was beautiful, and all of a sudden, my mind was not where it should have been in that moment.

Regardless, I kept my voice and my appearance perfectly level. Perfectly regal in its smoothness, its confidence—just the way I'd been raised to perform. "So, you essentially convinced her that you had a chain tied around my neck? That you could drag me along wherever you wished, thanks to this cursed magical *bond* we seem to have developed between us."

She shrugged. "I didn't use those exact words. But yes. *Essentially.*"

"And what happens if I break the chain?"

She fixed those impossibly bright eyes of hers on me, unflinching, and said, "I have other methods of keeping wayward beasts under control without the need for *chains*."

"Do you?" I couldn't help myself. I licked my lips and leaned in closer. "I'd love a demonstration."

"Don't tempt me."

"Don't arouse my curiosity."

"I'm not responsible for your arousal."

"That depends entirely on your definition of *responsible for*, doesn't it?"

Her breath audibly hitched at the low tone my voice had taken on. It was an unexpectedly intoxicating sound, drawing me even closer, like a sailor being drawn in by a siren's song.

Too close.

Yet, just as it had before—just as I'd explained to her last night—the closeness led to clarity. I came within an arm's-length of her, and the world seemed to still, to go silent save for the whisper of our breaths, the beating of our hearts, the hum of our magic.

She didn't pull a knife on me, this time, but I forced myself not to move any closer, regardless.

I should not have been playing this game.

Then again, how could I know what effect she *truly* had on my magic unless we experimented? The question was in my mind now, despite my best efforts to silence it—how strong could my power become if it melded more fully with hers? Strong enough to raise me from this hell? To carve a path back to the living world and confront the one sitting on my throne?

She didn't agree to be the balancing act for your magic, I reminded myself.

And yet, she wasn't moving away from me and that magic.

She looked ready to meet whatever spark I threw her way, and the thought enraptured me more than it should have. I didn't trust myself to act on it.

It wasn't a sensation I was used to feeling—that mistrust of myself. Again, all this chaos…

I fucking hated it.

"Those were her terms," she said, defiantly. "If you want her to take us to your sword, you're going to have to behave."

I couldn't help the smirk that crossed my face, knowing it would cause her lips to press into that alluring little pout once more. "I'll do my best," I told her, "but I'm not making any promises."

Chapter Fourteen

Nova

THALIA LED THE WAY ACROSS A WIDE EXPANSE OF ROCKY, flat landscape she referred to as the *Wastelands*. I trailed just behind her, while Aleksander and his company brought up the rear, with Zayn leading Uldrin—Thalia's beastly horse, who was doing us the favor of carrying most of our bags.

My gaze kept trailing toward that horse, studying his red eyes that burned like twin embers in the darkness, and his sleek black body that rippled with shadowy energy. One of the *scourge* stallions, Thalia had informed me—steeds specifically bred to withstand this realm, their bloodlines allegedly infused with magic.

Phantom spent the first several hours racing circles around the creature, memorizing it, doing his best to shift his body into an imitation of it. I encouraged the practice; if he could master the form, it would likely provide a much smoother ride than what I'd experienced on the back of his canine shape yesterday.

All morning long, we'd been walking steadily toward the glow on the distant horizon—the one Aleksander had been staring at last night. The sky was lighter, now, making the faraway shine less obvious, but I still thought it looked like the hazy halo of a city's collective lights.

I wanted to ask Thalia a thousand questions about that glow and all the areas around it. About the landscapes we were passing through. About her power—*my* power—and the magic that shaped this realm and its ghosts and its walls and everything else…

The longer we walked, though, the more my attention kept being stolen by the groups of restless dead spirits that were pressing closer and closer.

They were following us; no less than a dozen drifted along on either side. They appeared as swirling blurs of grey fog in my peripheral vision, but they took on more definite shapes whenever curiosity got the better of me and I turned to stare at them in earnest. Each time I looked, they seemed more defined, like figures being carved out by a hidden hand, released from within slabs of grey.

They felt less dangerous now that I had a group of living beings surrounding me, but they were no less unnerving.

"You seem rattled," Thalia commented, slowing to walk at my side.

"Every time I look, there seem to be more," I said. "And they seem to grow clearer to me."

"Clearer?"

"Their faces, especially."

"…Interesting."

"Is it?"

"They don't often reveal their faces to people," she said, frowning.

My heart skipped a beat as I made eye contact with one of the smaller ghosts. A child. Her body was pale, nearly translucent, and there was no color to the simple shift she wore, nor to the loose braid that swung to the middle of her back. Her eyes, though, were a bright and curious green.

I felt an immense sadness when I looked into them; a longing for something I couldn't even name.

I moved closer to Thalia, fixing my gaze straight ahead.

"They're merely shades," she informed me, her eyes darting to the clusters on either side of us, lips moving silently. Counting them, I thought. "They won't hurt us."

"They seem less…well, *dead* than I was expecting. More sentient than the ghosts one reads about in stories." I hesitated, then added, "Shortly after I first arrived in this realm, one of them chased me and got a hand on me."

Thalia gave me a long, searching look; I got the impression I'd said something wrong. Something foolish. Something one of our magical alignment should have known better than to say—though I couldn't imagine what it had been; I was only telling the truth about what I'd experienced.

"They don't see themselves as dead," Thalia explained, her tone difficult to read. "But they don't remember true life, either. They know only wandering. These are the lucky ones, I think; there are others who are more aware of the life they once lived, but still unable to truly grasp what it meant to be *alive*. They carry on in a state of neither true death nor true life, with only the vaguest impressions of memories to give them meaning—we refer to them as *wraith*s. We'll encounter them on the path ahead; to get to where we're ultimately headed requires passing through a city full of these creatures."

"So that glow ahead *is* from a city?"

"Yes." She visibly tensed. "*Erebos*. The City of Forgetting. The ones who dwell there are...well, complicated. And potentially more dangerous to us than the ghosts around us now."

The green-eyed shade girl suddenly let out a high-pitched giggle and raced in front of me, her hand outstretched as if to tag mine and initiate a game of chase. When I didn't reach back, her giggling turned to a sound more like a howling wind, and she disappeared in a swirl of grey mist and cold air.

The sorrow that had gripped me when I'd stared into her eyes was back. I stood half-frozen on the path for a moment, trying to catch my breath as the grief washed over and threatened to drown me.

"They're drawn to your magic," Thalia said. "We'll continue to gather them toward us throughout our travels, I suspect." With a grim smile, she muttered, "At least their glow gives us some extra light."

I considered her explanation as I tried to settle my nerves. "Your magic draws them too, right?"

"Not as much."

"But you're just as powerful as me, if not *more*, based on what you did to Elias back at that wall we passed through."

She shook her head. "The shadows I controlled there were not from any magic I created. The energy already existed, put into place by much stronger magic-users than me a long time ago. I merely directed some of it by way of my staff. And I directed it poorly, in all honesty; the magic of our world grows less predictable—less manageable—by the day, it seems. I didn't intend for that man to die." She glanced over her shoulder at Aleksander and the others, lowering her voice as she said, "Not that it makes any difference to those left behind."

I frowned as I, too, looked over our tense, wary group. She was right; no one in our company would be forgiving her—or truly trusting her—anytime soon. If not for my curiosity about magic and my desperate need for a more knowledgeable guide, I would have been nowhere near her myself.

We walked on in silence for a few minutes. She occasionally fidgeted with her staff, adjusting some of the gems along it, just as she'd done yesterday on the hilltop. She seemed troubled by our conversation—maybe by thoughts of Elias's death?

I didn't want to linger on that death, either, or try to make sense of the complicated feelings I had about it, so I redirected the conversation with one of the countless thoughts I had tumbling around in my head.

"You remind me of someone in the world above, the way you tinker with your weapon. He was very handy when it came to creating things that could channel magic." I lifted the wrist that held most of my bracelets and gave it a shake. "He made these to help with mine."

Slowly, she pulled her attention away from her staff. She seemed to be fighting against drawing too close to me, but in the end, her curiosity over the jewelry won, and she stepped close enough to briefly lift the black-rose bracelet from my skin and study it.

"This is powerful work," she concluded. "He must be a master craftsman, with a very keen eye for magic and how it moves."

I hesitated. It seemed foolish to be spilling too much of my life to this woman I barely knew—regardless of the things we might have had in common—but talking of Orin made me feel less alone in this upside-down world.

"Do you know of the Aetherkin?" I asked.

"Aetherkin…" she repeated, her step slowing and her voice taking on a strangely hushed tone. "It's been some time since I've heard about one of them. I thought they were all gone."

"Well, at least *one* still lives. His name is Orin."

She went back to studying my bracelets. "You draw your *own* power through these pieces he made, though, don't you? Your innate magic."

"With most of these, yes. Although this one—" I held up the leather and amethyst bracelet "—was made specifically to navigate through the magic that links the living and dead worlds."

She drew away from me and kept walking as she asked, "What happens if you lose them?"

My breath hitched at the mere thought. "I can still use my magic. It's just less…*predictable*. More wild."

"Stronger?"

"Maybe."

She considered my answer for several steps. "Like shackles, then."

The word settled uncomfortably on my chest. "…In some ways, I guess."

She nodded but said nothing else, letting the comment hang in the air. It was difficult to tell whether she thought it was a good thing or a bad thing that my magic was suppressed. I'd rarely thought of it as anything other than good. Orin had always had my best interests at heart; I had no doubt about that. And yet...

The words he'd said to me at Calista's shrine rang through my head once more—

Trust yourself. And don't be afraid of your darkness.

But I *was* afraid. Even more so now that Aleksander's magic was tangling up with mine in unpredictable ways, awakening the shadows that had laid dormant for so long.

What might those shadows do in this world if I *didn't* shackle them somehow?

The bracelets were like so many of the masks I donned in my life in order to bury my true feelings and fears, I guess. To take them off meant to expose myself to a world that couldn't handle all of me and my magic; I wasn't ready to even attempt such a thing.

"What about you?" I asked Thalia as we marched on toward the hazy lights of Erebos. "Don't you have innate magic as well?"

"Very little." She twisted her staff absently in front of her as she spoke. The shades on both sides of us crowded closer as she did, like fish drawn to the movement of a shiny lure. They dispersed quickly, however, when she tapped upon one of the staff's gems, sending a cool breeze rippling outward. "This staff helps pull out what I *do* have, but more than that, I use it to help direct the shadowy energies that exist outside of me."

I started to reply, only to be distracted by the sight of walls taking shape within the murky daylight, far in the distance.

They were massive, twisting and turning beyond where I could see. Parts of the city itself loomed even larger behind them, the spires of buildings thrusting up like swords toward the dreary sky. Pedestals full of blue fire were spaced evenly along the tops of the walls, and the flickers of more sapphire flames could be seen reflecting off the windows of the city's varied architecture.

Now I understood why I'd been able to see its glow from such a distance; the entire place seemed to be burning in some way, boldly separating it from the dark landscape all around it.

We slowed to a stop, allowing the others to catch up with us.

Zayn let out a low whistle as he approached, his gaze fixed on what appeared to be a towering trio of torch-wielding statues in front of the city's main gate. "This is a touch more intimidating than you let on," he said to Thalia.

"There is no going around it," she replied, unapologetically. "The walls stretch for miles in both directions, and at the terminus on both sides are cursed areas known as the *Grim Barrens*, which are uncrossable given our current state and supplies. We go through Erebos, or we don't go forward at all. Or *I* don't go, at least." With this declaration, she called Uldrin to her, walking the stallion a short distance away, watering and checking him over while leaving me and the others to contemplate our next move.

Zayn spoke first. "Anybody else have a terrible feeling about this city?" he asked, stretching. "Do we really *want* to go inside it?"

"As opposed to staying out here?" Aleksander asked, glancing around. "Where it's positively bright and cheerful and safe?"

"It just feels like she's not being very forthcoming with the details about this place."

No one could disagree with that.

"I want to get a closer look, at least," I said, though my voice threatened to tremble with the suggestion. It felt like a bad idea—but once again, so did turning around.

Rowen and Farren both agreed to my suggestion, giving us the majority.

We moved cautiously down the hill toward the main gate, making our way onto a great, sweeping pavilion that stretched in front of it, its polished marble floors reflecting the twisting and tumbling fires of Erebos in a way that was both enchanting and ominous. Arches of all shapes and sizes were erected across this pavilion, most with words or symbols carved into their faces; there seemed to be some organizational purpose to them, but I could only guess at what it might have been.

Stretching through one of the grandest of arches—one close to an iron-barred door to the right of the gate—a line of shades had gathered; like a queue, almost. I found myself wandering closer to it, searching for the green-eyed girl who wanted to play tag earlier, but I didn't find her.

Thalia returned to us a few minutes later, her horse's hooves clopping loudly against the shiny stone.

"There are always hordes of them waiting at the gate," she said, quietly, acknowledging the line of shades with a slight nod. "Unfortunately for them, the city opens her doors very sparingly. There simply isn't enough room for all of them inside."

"You said the wraiths inside there are worse off than the shades out here, though," I reminded her.

"In my opinion, yes." Her hand twisted and untwisted Uldrin's lead rein. "But the ones on the outside are drawn to the possibility of the city and its energy, all the same."

"So, how do *we* get inside?" Zayn wanted to know. "As

royalty, we're not really accustomed to waiting in lines, I'm afraid." He flashed Thalia a smile and a wink.

She looked entirely unimpressed by his charm. "We'll just be guests passing through," she explained. "There's a different entrance for that. It will come at a price, but it won't be impossible—you just have to know who to bargain with, and how to win him over."

"And you know these things?" Aleksander asked.

"I've passed through here often enough," she said, and then she unceremoniously dropped her horse's reins into Rowen's hands. "Mind the beast. He doesn't like this city. There's always a chance he'll try to bolt and take all your belongings with him." Without waiting for a response, she turned away and strode toward the gate.

Zayn followed, mumbling something under his breath.

Again finding myself without a better option, I started to follow as well—until I noticed Aleksander lingering behind, studying the line of shades. That line seemed to be growing longer by the minute.

I hesitated. We'd ignored each other for the better part of the day, staying just close enough to keep his magic balanced, but not close enough to actually *speak* to one another. It was much more peaceful that way.

Yet, for some reason, I couldn't help moving closer to him now.

"What's wrong?" I asked.

He cut me a sideways glance.

"Or, never mind," I muttered. "We can continue ignoring each other, if you prefer."

He looked back to the shades, seemingly eager to do just that. But I only made it a few steps away from him before he said, "The number of ghosts we've encountered today is...a lot."

What did you expect on an adventure through the underworld? I started to ask—but caught myself. Because he hadn't *expected* to be experiencing anything in this world, had he? I'd had years to prepare for my descent into Hell; he'd had mere seconds.

"It's even more jarring, I suppose, because no one speaks of the dead very often in Elarith," he explained. "We rarely even hold funerals. Our 'graveyards' consist of simple books listing the names of the deceased, whose ashes are piled into a collective urn. Anything more than that is considered grotesque."

"Really?"

He nodded. "Which is strange, I guess, but I never thought much of it until my own parents died and I was not permitted to mourn them for longer than a few days—not publicly, at least."

"A few *days*? That's absurd."

He shrugged.

"Death is a part of life."

"Not a part to dwell on, according to the Keepers of Light. It's a culture they've worked hard to instill throughout Elarith—and one they've been aiming to spread throughout the rest of the empire as well."

"But they used to be the ones in charge of sanctioning visits to this realm, didn't they?"

He nodded.

"...I always wondered why they stopped allowing them."

He looked to the torches held by those three statues near

the gate. His brow furrowed, and the reflection of fire within his golden gaze danced with a particular violence; I wondered what he was truly thinking about those Keepers, now that he knew they had placed an imposter on his throne.

"Several reasons, I've been told," he said. "It was too dangerous, for example—opening the path between the realms risked deadly energy bleeding through, much like what has apparently happened at your old home. And then you had the ones who didn't want to come back after their allotted time visiting the dead."

"I can't imagine staying here in this darkness, indefinitely," I said, suppressing a shiver at the thought.

He considered this for a long moment before answering. "People deal with loss in different ways," he finally said, turning away and starting to make his way toward Thalia and the others. "I suspect it wouldn't seem all that dark to someone who had lost what felt like everything to them."

Something in his tone drew me even closer to his side. A question danced at the tip of my tongue—*how dark does it seem to you?*

I didn't find the courage to ask. The contemplative peace between us was too enjoyable to disturb. And we were nearly to Thalia, now—close enough that I noticed she held her staff at the ready, and my attention shifted fully to her, wondering what she was about to attempt.

There was an odd pattern of different-colored bricks in the wall some distance away from the grand, main gate; she had stopped before it and, as we reached her, she lifted her staff and began to draw ribbons of some sort of foggy substance out from those bricks. Their color faded as she wound more and more ribbons around the tip of her weapon, until, eventually, there were no bricks at all.

A window had appeared.

Thalia took several steps back—nearly colliding with me—as a man slowly stepped up to this newly revealed window, rolling his shoulders and cracking his neck as though he'd been sitting stiffly for the past several hours. Even after shaking his muscles lose, his movements still seemed unnaturally stiff and twitchy. He looked as solid as us, but his skin was a pallid shade of grey. His eyes were oddly wide and blinked far too little, as though they'd adjusted poorly to the dim lighting of this realm.

"Gatemaster Atros—just our luck," Thalia said under her breath. "Let me do all the talking to this bastard, please."

Chapter Fifteen

Nova

ATROS FIXED HIS UNBLINKING GAZE ON THALIA AS SHE approached.

He worked his jaw a few times—as though loosening it up along with the rest of his body—before saying something to her in a low grumble of a voice, and in a language I didn't understand; it sounded like the same language Thalia had used when we first met.

She replied in the same language, jerking her head toward me and the rest of my party.

The gatemaster studied us for several long, uncomfortable moments before he licked his lips and continued speaking—this time in a heavily-accented version of my empire's common tongue.

"Thalia, my love," he said, his gaze sweeping between her and us, "you have five extra souls—and a couple extra, nasty-looking beasts for good measure."

Phantom protested the designation with a snarl.

The gatemaster ignored him, his strange eyes widening even further, as if resisting the urge to flutter shut for even an instant. "Surely you realize we can't simply allow you all to waltz in here and upset the balance of things."

"Spare me the show and just name your price, Atros. I know you can make things happen when you really want to."

His mouth split into an unpleasant smile, revealing unexpectedly perfect, white teeth that didn't otherwise fit his ugly appearance. "You've figured me out, haven't you?" He chuckled. "Takes a bit of the fun out of it, honestly, but all right, then—we can skip the foreplay and you can just give me what I need, I s'pose."

The glare she fixed on him was lethal, but she reached into the satchel at her hip without comment, retrieving a small bag of what sounded like coins and flinging it viciously at his face.

He snatched it easily from the air. His hand was disfigured, I noticed; several of his fingers were abnormally long and bent at crooked, painful-looking angles. He hooked the bag around one of these bent fingers and gave it a shake, listening closely to the coins clinking inside. "A nice start."

Thalia bristled. "*Start?*"

"Indeed."

"That's five times the price I paid you for my last solo passage, *with* some extra thrown in for the mutt and the horse."

"Base rate's gone up in recent days, I'm afraid. The walls at Wrathmere are failing, so we've got more refugees to contend with, as of late. Supply and demand and all that."

Thalia scowled. "We're only passing through. Not even spending more than a day. Your price is absurd."

Atros shrugged. "Reaper's orders. You know how he is. He wants what he wants, fair or not."

"Give my money back, then," she demanded.

He walked the bag between his mangled fingers, his dexterity surprisingly impressive. "There's a fee for disrupting my peace, too."

Zayn and Aleksander exchanged a look before turning away, mumbling among themselves.

My face flushed hot. I hadn't planned to intervene or get in the way, but this man reminded me entirely too much of some of the scum I'd dealt with back in the seedier areas of Eldris. The first rule to surviving my kingdom's seedy underbelly was to always act more confident than you felt—and I suspected that rule was universal.

I stepped forward. "No deal is no deal," I snapped. "The payment isn't yours to keep."

He finally, noticeably blinked—a slow, calculated fluttering of his eyelids—before flashing his odd gaze in my direction. "And who might you be?"

"No one important." I thrust out my hand. "The bag," I said, tapping my palm. "Now."

He started to smile the same oily smile he'd given Thalia—until his eyes fell upon my bracelets. The one my father had given me on my birthday had separated from the others, sliding down, dangling partially around my hand.

Atros stared at it with such a disturbing hunger that I nearly jerked my wrist back, half-expecting he might bite it off if I didn't.

But I kept still. Calm. Confident.

"The bag," I repeated.

He tossed it up and down in the air, taunting me. Daring me to try and grab it.

So I *did* jerk my wrist back, but only so I could spin my bracelets around and take hold of one of the black-rose beads. A squeeze of my fingers brought a strand of my essence to the surface, and then it whipped forward and wrapped around the bag, possessing and halting it in midair. A quick beckoning of my hand sent it hurtling toward Thalia—who managed an impressive catch, as if we'd practiced this exact routine many times before.

Atros stared.

I gave him a nasty smile before turning away. "On to alternative routes, then," I told Thalia, coolly.

Atros blustered out some response—back to his initial language, now—but I ignored him and started to walk.

Thalia caught up to me after a moment of staring at my retreating back. "There *are* no other routes, as I told you before," she said quietly.

I didn't speak until we reached the others, well out of the gatemaster's line of sight.

"Do the guards ever change?" I asked.

"Rarely. It could be days before Atros is gone."

"We don't have days' worth of supplies," Zayn pointed out.

"How's the foraging in this part of Hell?" I asked, mildly.

"Complicated," she replied—a word she was very fond of, I was noticing. "We need to get into the city sooner rather than later."

"Is there somewhere nearby where we can rest and regroup to figure this out?" Aleksander asked.

Begrudgingly, Thalia led us along the western wall,

trudging through muddy terrain for about a mile or so before we came to what looked like it had once been a grand pavilion similar to the one at the main gates, albeit smaller. The ground was cracked and uneven, littered with sticks and stones. A small building sat on the edge of it, its roof halfway caved in.

"This was one of the city's original gatehouses," she explained, "back when Erebos was much larger. It's never used anymore, now that the city has drawn more tightly into herself."

As the others scouted the area further, I turned to Thalia, replaying the tense encounter with Atros in my head. "What did Atros mean when he said *the walls at Wrathmere are failing*?"

Thalia waved away the concern in my voice. "Wrathmere is another city, some distance from this one, that's been experiencing unrest, recently. But it won't fall. He's just using the threat of its refugees as an excuse."

"How many cities are there in this world?"

"There were once lots of them."

I bit down my irritation at the frustratingly vague answer. "Why do the dead have cities at all?"

"It's as I said before: They don't see themselves as dead." For a moment, she looked as if she was considering saying more on the subject. Her eyes bored into mine, seemingly searching me for some sign that I could be trusted with her secrets.

But she ultimately revealed nothing else.

Zayn's earlier comments played in my mind.

...She's not being very forthcoming with the details about this place.

He was right. She clearly wasn't. And now she was

already turning away, hurrying off to tend to her horse—as if she could sense all of the questions building on the tip of my tongue, preparing to fire at her.

I considered following her and demanding answers. But she didn't seem like the type I could force things out of; more like the type I would need to strategically pry apart to get to the truth underneath.

In the meantime, I took in our latest ominous surroundings, looking back to what I could see of the walls and their flames through the foggy air. I didn't know how we were going to get inside of those walls. What laid within them, or what might await us on the other side of all this.

I just knew I didn't want to spend any longer than necessary in the shadows of this foreboding city.

OUR REGROUPING efforts were taking too long.

Hours later, every plan we'd come up with had ultimately been dismantled, bringing us back to where we started. I was moments away from marching straight up to the main gate of Erebos and trying my luck at scaling the damn thing.

It wouldn't have been the *worst* plan I'd ever tried to carry out, honestly.

The rest of my company, however, seemed more content with waiting, resting until we had somehow come up with a miraculous, foolproof idea. Even Phantom was asleep, snoring loudly; the combination of travel and trying to shift into new forms all day seemed to have taken a toll on him.

I was tired as well, but far past the point of sleep. Now that we'd stopped moving, I couldn't help longing for my familiar, restful routines. For something like a glass of wine and a good book—maybe a bath to enjoy them in.

The surface of a small lake could be seen in the distance, its water occasionally glistening in what little light penetrated the foggy air; Lake Nyras, Thalia had told me earlier. It was growing more tempting by the minute. Hardly the claw-footed beauty of a tub I was used to back home, but the water looked *somewhat* clearer than most of what we had encountered in this realm—perhaps because of whatever powers apparently protected and preserved the city looming nearby. Or maybe that was just wishful thinking?

Either way, baths had always been my daily salvation; Orin used to swear I was going to dissolve into the water one day, as long as I spent soaking in it.

My mind made up, I wandered back toward the others long enough to gather a clean change of clothes and a blanket to serve as a towel. Thalia and Aleksander were keeping watch while everyone else slept. I told the former where I would be, while paying no mind to the latter; Aleksander had gone back to ignoring me, and I was only too happy to let that arrangement continue.

But it wasn't long after I arrived at my chosen, secluded stretch of lake before I heard footsteps behind me. Soon after, I sensed the pulse of his magic—faint, but unmistakable. A glance out of the corner of my eye confirmed he was there, little bolts of energy lighting faintly against his skin, only visible because of how deeply the dark settled under the trees surrounding us.

I pretended not to notice him. He kept his distance, leaving his back turned while I stripped off my clothing and wrapped the blanket around myself. Determined to relax, I continued to ignore him as I made my way down to the shoreline and slipped a foot in to test the water.

I swallowed a curse at the biting cold that instantly numbed my toes. Not *exactly* the inviting pull of a bath. But at least it would be refreshing—if only I could only make myself take the initial plunge.

Which I couldn't.

Gods, how I hated the cold.

Newly annoyed at the frigid hitch in my plans, I turned my frustration toward the only other person around. "Are you stalking me?" I demanded, glancing over my shoulder in Aleksander's direction.

"No," he replied, keeping his back turned, one shoulder leaning against a tree. "Though you aren't difficult to keep track of, considering you move with all the grace and subtlety of an injured bear."

"I was purposely trying to be loud so I could scare away any predators. You know, snakes and such." That was entirely untrue—I'd actually just been loud and careless—but he didn't need to know that. "I'm petrified of snakes," I added. That part was true; I didn't trust anything with less than two legs or more than four, as a rule.

"I don't think there are any snakes in this realm," he mused.

"Ah, so it's just broody, annoying kings lurking among these waterways, then."

He laughed quietly. "Just keeping close for the sake of

our *bond*, my darling Chaos. And making sure you don't drown. The waters in this realm can prove deceptively deep, I've found; what looks shallow is very often *not*."

I considered the warning, peering into the water but trying not to let apprehension fill my voice as I said, "That's a very convoluted excuse—why not just admit you were hoping to catch a glimpse of me bathing?"

"Don't flatter yourself. I'm not that desperate."

"Are you sure?"

"Not even close."

"…Seven years you've been down here, right?"

"I was asleep for most of it," he reminded me. "And not entirely alone, if you'll recall. We've managed, I assure you."

I found myself mentally picturing all of the soldiers and others who had been at their outpost. For some reason, I didn't want to think about Aleksander *managing* himself with any of them.

"Are you projecting, Princess?" he asked.

"Projecting?"

"If you're really the pariah you claim you are in the living world, I imagine you're no stranger to dry spells yourself. Must be difficult to find men willing to sleep with a violent destroyer of kingdoms."

"Not as difficult as you might think," I said. "Some of them enjoy a little violence in the bedroom. Or dare I say, *chaos*. The things some of them have asked me to do…"

"Spare me the details."

Maybe it was my imagination—or, hell, my vanity—but his voice seemed to have taken on a sharper edge.

"Have I made you jealous?" I teased, kicking innocently at the icy water.

He didn't reply.

Wait—was he *actually* jealous? If so, that had been far too easy...which made it considerably less fun. All the same, I couldn't help turning to face him more fully, ready to see if I could rattle him further.

Heat curled through my body when I saw that he'd already turned around to stare at me, and I realized I'd... *misjudged*.

He didn't look rattled at all. He looked the opposite of jealous and bothered; he was the picture of confidence bordering on arrogance with his arms folded across his chest and one shoulder still leaning against the tree.

And suddenly *I* was the one fumbling for words, wishing the blanket around me was larger. Thicker. It barely fell to the middle of my thighs, and the thin material was growing damp in the foggy air, making it cling to my curves with a closeness that suddenly felt far too revealing.

"Why?" he asked, cocking an eyebrow. "Were you *trying* to make me jealous?"

I could tell he was attempting to fluster me, same as I'd been trying to do to him—and I refused to let him beat me at my own game.

My tone was less like flirting, more like a challenge, as I said, "Maybe it would help that bond our magic seems to have if we simply did away with all this tension and *managed* some things with one another."

He met the challenge with a smile. "What tension?"

I glared at him as he pushed away from the tree and strode toward me.

"My mistake," I mumbled. "There's clearly no tension; I must be imagining the way you're currently undressing me with your eyes."

A dark chuckle fell from his lips. "There isn't much undressing to do, to be fair."

"So you admit you're doing it?"

"I'll admit you're better to look at than the mud and dirty water surrounding you, so perhaps my eyes are drawn naturally to you."

"Such flattery."

"A useful skill for a king to possess."

"I could think of several others that would be more useful."

His gaze raked over my body. "Aren't you cold?"

"I've survived colder."

A muscle ticked in his jaw, distorting his arrogant smile for a fraction of a moment. The gleam in his eyes shifted, too, into something that looked almost like...*concern*. Something I neither wanted nor needed—least of all from him.

"Unless you and your cock are offering to warm me up, do me a favor and go away."

He seemed to consider this proposition for a moment before he shrugged and said, "An orgasm might improve your mood, if nothing else."

"It usually does," I replied, and then I couldn't help but add: "But just so we're clear? I hardly need your help for that."

"No?"

"I do have a hand. Two of them, in fact." I held one up and gave my fingers a wiggle. "These are very capable."

"Not as capable as me."

"Doubt it."

Another of those quiet, darkly amused chuckles. "If you think your own hand is a sufficient substitute, you clearly haven't been with any partners worth a damn."

I stopped wiggling my fingers long enough to flash him a rude gesture along with a charming smile.

He was undeterred. "Of course, you can use your hands to show me exactly how you like it, if you want. I'll take notes for later."

"Later?"

"Mm."

"On second thought, I think I'm going to use these hands to strangle you if you come any closer," I said, sweetly.

"That's a step up from stabbing, at least."

"Let's not rule out the possibility of a stabbing."

"So what I'm hearing is that you and your hands are into the rough stuff. Noted."

I bit my lip.

Infuriating bastard.

He took yet another step closer, stopping just shy of the water's edge—close enough to reach out and touch me, if he dared.

He didn't lay a finger on my shivering body, but the way his gaze traveled over my pebbling skin, lingering on the creases and curves where the blanket clung the closest, felt as intimate as a touch.

I felt unbalanced. Shifting my footing brought us even closer. I inhaled several deep breaths, trying to steady my heartbeat, but only ended up making it race faster as I swallowed up his scent. He smelled like earth and dew. Paired with the golden warmth of his eyes, I couldn't help but think of an early morning sunrise, when all the world still slept and the promise of the day remained untarnished. When the possibilities were endless.

And for an instant, I couldn't help wondering about the endless possibility of *us*.

But he still didn't reach for me.

Instead, he knelt down and dipped his fingertips into the water, swirling them back and forth until it became so clear I could make out every rock and twig along the lakebed.

"There," he said, straightening. "Now you'll be able to see the snakes coming. And I warmed it up a bit, even, so when you're bitten, at least you can enjoy a warm, cozy atmosphere while you drift off to your death."

"...My hero."

He gave a little bow before leaving me alone, casually shoving his hands into his pockets and making his way back up the sloped shore, vanishing into the trees.

I stared at the spot where he'd disappeared for a long moment, until I was certain he wasn't coming back, before I peeled the blanket from my body and folded it up along with my clean change of clothes. I carried the dirty clothes I'd taken off into the water to scrub them, glad to have a task to occupy my mind with and help me *not* think about how close Aleksander likely still was.

Once I'd finished cleaning them, I scanned the area, seeking a place to hang them out to dry. After draping them in the arms of a forked tree, I found myself unable to resist going back into the water for a few more minutes.

I was attempting to wash my hair when the sound of branches shifting and cracking made me freeze.

"Aleksander?"

No answer.

Another loud *craaaack*.

I sank into the water, covering myself more completely

with my arms as I looked back toward the trees he'd vanished into, waiting for him to pop out wearing that infuriatingly arrogant grin of his.

"This isn't funny, you ass."

A louder sound came from behind me—a howl of wind and a frantic rustling of bushes—and I twisted around to find that someone familiar *had* popped out to stare at me.

But it wasn't Aleksander.

Chapter Sixteen

Nova

THE GREEN-EYED SHADE GIRL WAS STANDING ON THE SHORE, staring back at me.

I looked around, expecting a horde of other shades to be accompanying her. I saw nothing—but there was still no sign of Aleksander, either. So if more ghosts *were* drifting my way, I was going to have to face them alone. While naked, apparently.

Perfect.

Well, I'd lived through worse.

I braced myself…but still, nothing else appeared.

Yet.

A minute passed before I chanced movement. Hugging my arms around myself, I waded closer, wondering if I should try talking to the girl. Thalia claimed they were aimless drifters, drawn only to magic… and yet, this one was clearly trying to get my attention for some reason. Clearly following me. And it felt like more than a mindless reaction to my magic; her eyes were too bright, too aware.

She *saw* me.

I was almost certain of it.

I took a few more steps forward, stopping a short distance away from her.

"Hello," I said, softly.

She didn't reply, lowering her gaze, suddenly shy.

"Are you following me?"

She took a step back.

"I don't mind," I said.

She paused like a tense baby deer and tilted her head, peering up at me from underneath the messy strands of hair that had slipped free from her braid.

"Really, I don't."

She opened her mouth to reply. A sound came out—not a voice, but maybe a whispered impersonation of one. Her inability to form words seemed to confuse her. And then *frighten* her. Her expression turned to one of pure panic, her eyes going impossibly wide as she looked around as though she had just noticed where she was for the first time.

"Are you okay?"

She dropped to her knees and started to claw into the ground, as if desperate to bury herself in it. Her fingers made little progress, even in the soft mud; her form was simply not solid enough to have much effect. This seemed to be a revelation to her as well—one that threw her into an even deeper panic.

I forgot about everything else—my wariness, my questions, my nakedness—as I rushed to her side, kneeling and placing a comforting hand on her shoulder.

Her body gave like clay beneath my touch, at first. But

as I continued to press against her, she seemed to take on more of a definite shape, I thought. I might have believed I was imagining it, if not for the look she fixed on me—an odd combination of surprise, hope, and terror. She trembled like a candle flame caught in a draft. Terrified, yet she leaned into me, as if testing her solidness.

As my arms cautiously circled around her, the woven, diamond-patterned bracelet on my wrist began to vibrate. A stabbing pain struck between my eyes. I tried to blink it away. Instead, I blinked another scene into my vision—something completely opposite of my current surroundings.

I saw this girl...*alive*.

She was twirling through a lush green courtyard, laughing, carrying batons with ribbons tied on the ends. Dancing, spinning those ribbons to a wild rhythm. Her hair was bright auburn, her ivory skin covered in freckles, her green eyes even more dazzling in the light of a golden red sun.

And she had an audience: An older woman who was clapping her hands and laughing along with her.

An older woman who looked like *me*.

Frantically, I pushed the girl away. I felt guilty as she looked up with confused, pleading eyes, but I couldn't bring myself to take her back into my arms.

Because I was just as frightened as she was, now.

"Who are you?" I breathed.

She tried again to speak. Again, only hushed, whimpering, unintelligible sounds made it out. A single tear trickled down her cheek.

My magic was swirling to life, suddenly, lifting from my arms like fog over a pond in early morning. Anticipating. Expectant. It wanted to wrap around the girl, and I didn't know *why*, and I didn't know what it would do—but I couldn't stop it from happening.

The shadows exploded outward, striking her and knocking her backward. She curled up as they violently swarmed around her body, wrapping so thickly that I lost track of her within the blackness.

I desperately tried to control them.

When I finally managed to pull the clawing darkness away from her, the girl's body had gone perfectly still against the muddy ground.

But that body was also *solid* and glowing faintly around the edges.

What had I done?

What the hell had I done?

Before I could work up the courage to get a closer look, the trees all around us began to shake.

Wind howled, and with it, they came like a violent, swirling river breaking through a dam—a horde of shades with hands reaching, bodies shoving, voices groaning.

I stumbled deeper into the lake, hoping against hope that the water might deter them somehow.

They hesitated only slightly as they slogged into it. Some didn't even do that; their lower halves seemed to dissolve underneath the surface, but this only made them faster. In the span of a few frantic heartbeats, dozens of them were upon me, their faces twisting in and out of focus, as if they were trying to make themselves known—to reveal themselves to me—but they were struggling to keep their shapes among the disorderly tangle of magic and all their different energies.

I fought my way free, diving underneath the water

where I knew I could move faster, trying to head in the direction of the shore where I'd last seen Aleksander.

Coming up for air, I was met by a trio of shades, their faces horribly clear: three thin, wailing women who looked similar enough to have been sisters.

I managed to dart around them and dive under the water once more. I was still far from the shore when I resurfaced, but close enough that my feet could touch the lakebed. My toes curled into the mud and silt, seeking purchase as I looked over my shoulder and tried to properly gauge the number of ghosts surrounding me.

I watched as several stopped to inspect the green-eyed girl's body before turning to me and giving chase.

Did they want the solidness I'd given her?

That glow that mimicked the brightness of life...did they think I could give it to them?

Something grabbed me underneath the water.

A fleeting hold that I easily kicked free of, but it made me panic enough that I was suddenly focused too much on what lay beneath the surface; I didn't notice the shades swirling in behind me until they were already there, surrounding me, their cold fingers clawing into my shoulders.

"Please," I gasped, thinking maybe they could understand me, connect to me as the girl had. *"Please wait—"*

But they were directionless. Mindless, as Thalia had warned. More and more swarmed in from all directions. Grabbing, clawing, washing over me like a wave threatening to drown me from existence. They couldn't put the full strength or pressure behind their attacks that a living being could have, but there were so many of them that it didn't matter; I kept being shoved off balance, shaking free of one only to have two more take its place.

My head slipped below the surface.

I fought my way back up.

More hands met me, shoving me back down.

Their shifting faces swam above, further distorted by the dark, muddied water.

They were *everywhere*.

I kicked. Twisted. Fought for clear water—but there was none to be found. Desperate to get away from the cold touch of reaching hands, I found myself rolling deeper, hitting the muddy bed, sinking in, dragging through it like an anchor.

How deep could I roll?

My arm snagged on something, jarring me to a stop.

The water around me grew warmer. Clearer. I was no longer physically sinking, but I felt like I was falling, all the same, drifting into a strange brightness—one rimmed in darkness, like the kind you saw when you clenched your eyes tightly shut. It grew more and more intense as the seconds passed, until—

My face broke through the surface.

I gasped. Choked. Cold struck me like a fist, and I cried out in misery. In fear. I wanted to go back into the warm water. Back toward the light that was too bright, too blinding to allow me to see anything else. I struggled with everything I had, trying to get back.

A voice growled into my ear, commanding me. *Keep still.*

I went rigid. And once I stopped, I didn't seem to be able to start again. Not my breaths, not my heartbeats, not my magic. I was stillness. I was death.

The same voice followed soon after, softer now. Pleading, almost. *Stay with me. Just stay with me. I've got you.*

But I didn't want to stay. I wanted to let go, to drift away in the comforting warmth.

So that was what I did.

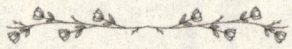

I woke from a stinging pain across my face, and the first thing—the *only* thing—I could focus on, at first, was cold.

Brutal, unforgiving cold.

Yet, a quick glance over my body told me I was no longer in the frigid water. No longer swamped by dead souls. I wasn't entirely naked, either; Aleksander had draped his coat over me. The pure, earthy scent of him clung to it, grounding me.

I was still here, still breathing, still functioning.

I situated the garment more fully around myself as I sat up, fastening the buttons from top to bottom with trembling fingers, creating a makeshift dress before I moved to take in more of my surroundings.

Aleksander was kneeling beside the green-eyed girl, looking her over.

I held my breath as I did the same. She was still solid… but the glow around her edges was rapidly fading. What would happen to her now?

Gods, what did I do to her?

Aleksander briefly glanced my way as I stumbled over and fell at his side.

"Do something," I pleaded. "Help her."

He gave me a dubious look.

I grabbed his wrist and guided his hand toward the girl.

His muscles tensed, preventing me from dragging him any farther. "I can't raise people from the dead, Nova."

"I don't think she's entirely dead. Not since I—I don't know what I did. Something is strange about her. Just...*try*. Please."

He jerked his arm from my hold.

But then a miracle occurred: *He did as I asked*.

Doubt clouded his eyes, but he reached his hand out on his own, letting it hover just above the girl's pale face. Golden light snaked along the lines of his palm, collecting at the tips of his fingers and growing thicker before falling down like drops of blood, splattering against the girl's forehead. Lines of gold raced out from the points of contact, spiderwebbing across her skin, drawing warmth into her pallid complexion, little by little.

She took a deep, gulping breath—like a fish tossed onto dry land.

I started to reach for her, but she rolled aside. She was fully convulsing an instant later, caught in the throes of Aleksander's magic, her body as lost in the flashes of light as it had been in my shadows earlier.

Aleksander hissed out a curse, drawing his hand back, abruptly getting to his feet and stepping away. "I'm making it worse. Let's just go find Thalia and see—"

I got to my feet as well, grabbing his arm and holding him still.

He stared at the grip I'd claimed on him until a sharp breath from the girl drew both our gazes back to her. She was going still once more, her body turning the color of stone as the last of Aleksander's power left her.

We should have done as he said and ran away from the scene of this strange disaster.

So why didn't I move?

Aleksander's eyes slowly shifted to me. Intense and burning and full of uncertainty. But I didn't flinch, even as the full heat of his stare settled over me—because in my mind, I saw the aftermath of our collision from yesterday: The world blooming around us. All of it dying just as quickly...*except* for those stubborn shoots of green grass and budding flowers.

A garden taking root where it shouldn't have stood a chance.

And here was that moment—that power, that connection—all over again. Except, this time, he was *awake*.

Awake and looking at me as though I was some combination of pure chaos and pure magic, something he wanted to both strangle and embrace at the same time. I felt his gaze like sunlight settling over my skin. His magic like a current of lightning building in my own body, preparing to leap to his, to weave so deeply between us that I wouldn't be able to tell where I ended and he began.

I looked to the girl, my pulse racing as I tried again to understand why she had followed me.

Who was she?

What had I divined from her body when I touched her? A memory, I assumed—but that didn't fit with the explanation Thalia had given me. This girl was a shade, devoid of consciousness, awareness...

Was there life still holding on, deep inside of her, same as there had been green grass buried in the dead soil yesterday? A buried life just waiting for *something* to pull it to the surface?

My touch slid down Aleksander's arm, my hand finding his. I interlaced our fingers. His hand felt so warm. So heavy. He shifted, angling his body more fully toward mine. Hesitation gripped me.

This is foolish.

"What are you doing?" he asked, his voice low, full of an emotion I couldn't name.

"Trust me," I replied—though I didn't know what I was even asking him to trust me about. I just didn't want him to let go of my hand. Just like he hadn't let go of me in the lake. Because it had been his voice, I realized now.

Just stay with me.

I've got you.

He'd pulled me from the water, chased away the things holding me down.

And he didn't let go, now, despite all the strange, terrifying energy building above us, below us, between us. Despite the way his magic cracked jagged fissures through his skin, sending embers of pale golden energy flying outward.

He didn't flinch, either, when bits of my magic slipped from my veins and collided with his, chasing after it like it was starving, desperate for a touch of light to balance its dark.

More magic was rising from both of us. The air was so thick with it I could hardly breathe. Questions pounded like the beating wings of birds, vibrating in the thin space separating our bodies.

What happens if we let ourselves give in?

What do we do with the mess our tangled magic becomes?

He moved to answer these questions first, the hand not holding mine reaching to trace the shadows peeking out from underneath the coat—his coat—that I wore. His fingers trailed over the swell of my chest, following the lines my shadows painted up across the hollow of my throat. Chasing away the cold of my magic, letting more of his own twist in, leaving a warm buzzing in the places where our powers wrapped around one another.

I leaned closer.

We were breathing the same air, sensing the same possibilities, tasting the same answers just on the tips of our tongues.

My lips never met his. Only his fingertips dragged over the trembling shape of my mouth. But it felt deeper than any kiss I'd ever experienced, the way his power fully dove into me, the warm tingle of his magic spreading out from underneath his touch, parting my lips, pouring down my throat.

That heat continued to circulate, sweeping down over my body—and then beyond it. The ground trembled, tickling my bare feet. The darkness dispelled around us, as if someone had pulled aside a curtain and allowed pure, full moonlight to filter into the scene. Grass shot up in the soft glow—lush, thick, all the way up to my ankles. The ground surrounding the girl's lifeless body transformed as well, and soon she was cradled by soft greenery and an assortment of colorful flowers rather than black mud.

The section of lake closest to us turned a dazzling shade of translucent turquoise, lapping gently against the increasingly flowery shoreline.

I forced my gaze away from Aleksander, taking my hand from his and walking in a slow circle so I could fully take in the sight surrounding us.

My breaths grew shallow. My hands shook. The world

tilted and spun, tilted and spun—a kaleidoscope of colors, a gentle symphony of sounds, a distant mirage of impossible images slowly coming into focus.

And the girl...

She opened her eyes. Sat up shakily. Pulled her braid over her shoulder—her bright, auburn braid—and fiddled anxiously with it.

Aleksander and I stared together, neither of us speaking. Neither of us quite believing—though there was no denying what we both saw. The girl was full of color and breath, as bright as the world around her. A world that was brilliant and breathing, teeming with new energy.

Alive.

This little section of the realm of the dead was *alive*.

And so was the girl.

Chapter Seventeen

Nova

AS ALIVE AS SHE MIGHT HAVE BEEN, THE GIRL STILL COULD not seem to speak. Nor could she walk—or even stand for very long. Her legs kept wobbling and buckling, threatening to fold up under her, again bringing to mind a baby deer.

"She's in shock, I think," Aleksander muttered. For a moment, he looked as though he was considering leaving her to her fate. A hunter allowing nature to take its course.

Then he sighed and lifted her shivering body into his arms, ribbons of light flowing from his fingertips and wrapping around her as he did. Soothing her. He didn't protest, either, when she huddled closer to him and buried her face in the folds of his shirt.

It was such a gentle, unexpected moment from him that I couldn't help but stare.

But despite his magic and other efforts, the girl still looked entirely too pale, too weak—mere moments away from returning to a ghostly shade.

"The blanket you had earlier," Aleksander said, pointing me in the direction of my piled belongings.

I quickly gathered it, along with my clean clothing. I yanked on my trousers and boots, but left Aleksander's coat on so I could donate my shirt to the girl, along with the blanket, wrapping both of these things tightly around her tiny, emaciated frame. I took care not to touch her too long, afraid of more visions popping into my head; I was still reeling from the last one. From that woman I'd seen, and the courtyard they'd been laughing and dancing in…

I finished securing the girl and hurriedly stepped away from her and Aleksander, focusing instead on our surroundings.

One inexplicable thing at a time.

The area all around us continued to thrive. Perfectly green grass, clear air, clear water…it looked like the *living* world, not the dead one.

"What have we done here?" I wondered aloud, my voice hushed as I bent to pick a flower with pale blue petals.

Aleksander studied it all for a minute before commenting: "Nothing is glowing."

"And nothing is out of control."

"Or dying."

"It just…*is*."

He frowned, pacing the area and inspecting parts of it closer before he said, "It's balanced. It looks like the living world."

I shook my head, even though I agreed. It *felt* balanced. Like it had always been here, and always would be. "But it's wrong, isn't it?" I asked, crushing the flower in my palm. "This world is not supposed to be *alive*. And…" I looked to the girl in his arms, my words catching painfully in my throat.

And neither is she.

I continued to explore, searching every tuft of grass and velvety flower petal for some sign that this was a mirage—one that would dissipate as soon as we came to our senses.

The girl seemed to have fallen asleep, but her breathing was peaceful and even, her cheeks a rosy shade of pink. Aleksander continued to hold her, his eyes scanning for threats in every direction.

After a minute, he said, "I think I hear someone coming."

"The rest of our group must have heard something, or seen our magic working…" I grimaced. "And I wonder how much attention we've drawn from the guards along the walls of Erebos?"

"Too much, knowing our luck."

Phantom bounded into sight first, racing toward me only to abruptly stop as he caught a more interesting scent; his nose lifted in Aleksander's direction, sniffing fervently, and then he cautiously trotted over to the king and poked his nose against the bundle in his arms.

(Another living being has joined you,) he said, matter-of-factly. *(She smells like apples. And dirt.)*

She should smell like nothing, I started to reply. *A ghost shouldn't have a scent.*

But, as before, my words caught in my throat. Hearing Phantom acknowledge her made it all seem much more real, somehow; I stopped trying to shake off the mirage and instead tried to think of what the hell I was going to *do* about it all.

Zayn arrived a moment later, flanked by Rowen and

Farren, and Thalia emerged from the trees soon after. Zayn stopped as abruptly as Phantom had at the sight of Aleksander and the girl, tilting his head with a mixture of amusement and bewilderment dancing in his eyes.

"Of all the trouble I expected you two to be getting into," he said, "this was definitely *not* on the list." He looked closer at the girl and the king, studying the spectacle from several different angles before he said, "But congratulations on your adoption, I guess?"

Aleksander scowled, moving toward his cousin as if to drop the child into Zayn's arms…an attempt that proved futile, as the girl woke up with the sudden movement and only clung tighter to his neck. It might have been entertaining—adorable, even—under different circumstances.

Thalia circled Aleksander cautiously, as if he held a snarling wolf rather than a feeble child. "A living girl? Where on earth did she come from?"

Aleksander and I exchanged an uncertain glance.

Thalia's gaze was insistent and borderline threatening as it fell on me; the truth once again seemed like the safest option.

"…She wasn't *living* just a few minutes ago," I said.

Thalia's face went through several different emotions—confusion, alarm, disbelief, fear—before finally settling into her usual hard, stoic expression.

I started to explain myself further, but the sound of loud voices and approaching footsteps reached us first.

Thalia immediately brought her finger to her lips, cutting me off. "Say nothing of what you did for this girl." Her eyes were a touch wild. "*Nothing*. Understood?"

"I…yes—of course."

Her gaze swept over our flourishing surroundings.

"This scene you've created is going to cause us enough trouble."

Before I could ask what kind of trouble she meant, a small host of heavily-armed men and women emerged from the darkness.

We were surrounded in seconds.

I counted them quickly—fourteen in all. Their faces were mostly covered by an assortment of scarves and masks, but what I could see of their complexions appeared unnaturally pale; not quite as gaunt as the shades, but close. They moved with a slightly inhuman twitchiness, too, and though their bodies looked more solid than the shades, their skin still took on a papery, translucent quality whenever the dim light pressed against it at certain angles. They all wore identical bandoliers, and looped onto each belt was a small, circular container rimmed in gold. Blue flames somehow burned without ceasing within these containers, similar to the fires that danced atop the walls around Erebos.

As the group closed in around us, a man strode into the middle of their circle, parting the others as he came.

He was the only one not wearing a covering on his face. A dark beard covered part of that face, split by a sharp, appraising smile that formed as his eyes passed over me and Thalia. Those eyes appeared black, two dots of shining ink against golden brown skin, and his body looked alive and perfectly solid—as solid as the pair of short scythes he had strapped against his back.

Unlike the others, he carried no flame that I could see.

Rather than acknowledging us, he whipped one of his curved blades free and swung it through a clump of tall, freshly-grown flowers, watching the severed pieces carefully as they fluttered to the ground.

I drew closer to Thalia. We both stepped in front of Aleksander, blocking the girl from view—though I didn't expect it would make much difference, should this man take an interest in her, given how outnumbered we were.

"Thalia Blackwood," the scythe-wielding man said, swiveling his head lazily in her direction. "I heard you were darkening my city's doorstep." Replacing the scythe against his back, he pressed the toe of his boot onto a pile of the severed, fallen flowers, crushing them. His gaze lingered on the mutilated petals for a long moment before he glanced up at Thalia from underneath his long lashes. "But I didn't realize you were traveling with such...*strange* company."

Thalia stood up straighter. "You know I like to keep things interesting."

"I do." He dragged his boot through the grass, his movements swift with disgust, as if he was trying to scrape something far more foul than flowers from his sole.

"And we wouldn't have been darkening your doorstep for very long," Thalia informed him. "A mere pass-through was requested, and I willingly offered the rate of a much longer stay. You would have made out handsomely on the deal."

"Is that so?"

"Atros could use a few more lessons in conducting proper business on your behalf, I believe," she said. "The fool is losing you money."

"Well, it's hard to find good help these days," said the man, tapping the last bits of colorful, crushed petals from his boots before sauntering closer.

Thalia held her ground, even as he came within an arm's reach. I mirrored her movements, drawing myself up to my full height while Phantom stalked to my side, his teeth flashing and his ears flat against his skull.

The man gave us a cursory glance before asking Thalia, "And besides, we have less and less use for *money* as the years go by, don't we?"

"All the same, you should be more selective about the ones you conduct your business with."

He chuckled at this—a low, dark sound that sent a shiver of warning down my spine. "Advice I could also offer to you." His gaze slithered over me once more, lingering this time, before darting to the rest of my company as well. "Which brings us to this little scene I've stumbled upon, doesn't it?"

Thalia remained stoic. "Does it?"

He folded his arms across his chest, stroking his beard thoughtfully as he glanced around at the scene in question. "These interesting folks you're clearly in *business* with…are they responsible for this display?"

She didn't answer right away. She seemed to be sizing up the ones accompanying him, calculating our chances of winning, should it come to a fight.

My muscles tensed at the thought. I wasn't usually one to back down from a challenge, but I had also learned, long ago, how to pick my battles, and that winning didn't always require swinging a sword.

I sized up our opponent as well—but based on his words, rather than his weapons. He might have pretended to see us as an afterthought, but he had immediately spoken in the language of the living world. He'd come to greet our party, too, when he could have just as easily left us to rot outside the walls of his city.

He clearly had an interest in us.

Which meant I had leverage.

"We aren't responsible for this scene ourselves," I lied, "but we saw the ones who *were* responsible for it."

I doubted he would believe my lie, but it didn't matter. He seemed smart enough to realize that he wouldn't get any *true* information out of us unless he first went along with my ruse.

"Grant us passage through your city," I demanded, "and we'll be happy to share what we know."

He let the full weight of his gaze fall upon me—a heavy glare of calculated precision, made all the more imposing by the way his eyes seemed to darken as the seconds passed, becoming an unsettling abyss.

"Nothing would delight me more than the chance to escort you through my city," he finally said. "Provided you do me the honor of spending the night as my guests before you carry on to wherever the next part of your journey leads you."

Thalia stiffened at my side, but she said nothing. She understood my tactics and reasoning—that we might not have another opportunity to enter the city.

We would have to take what we could get.

I lifted my chin and refused to let my fear show. "We accept."

Chapter Eighteen

Nova

AFTER PASSING BEYOND THE OUTER WALLS OF EREBOS, we were taken directly toward the center of the sprawling city. We moved swiftly through the streets. I absorbed little of what we passed; there was simply too much to take in around every corner.

What I *did* notice were more of those strange blue flames. Every shadowy being we passed seemed to be carrying their own personal fire in some way, much like the soldiers escorting us. There were statues, too, like the ones at the main gate, that held torches or cups or other vessels full of sapphire smoke and flame. A river of strangely dark water crisscrossed through the streets, under narrow footbridges, and even sections of *it* occasionally flickered with wisps of blue.

Despite calling himself our escort, the scythe-wielding man brought up the rear of our company rather than leading us. He paid us no attention as we walked, either; he was too busy scanning the dark alleyways and houses we passed, one of his blades withdrawn and hanging casually at his side. Anticipating an attack, I thought—which seemed strange if he was the sovereign of this city, as he claimed to be.

Ultimately, no one ambushed us, but we did draw the gaze of almost every wandering being we passed. As Thalia had said, they were indeed different from the shades who had haunted our steps outside the walls—more solid, their voices more clear in tone and weight, though they spoke in a language I couldn't decipher. And maybe it was my imagination, but the soldiers escorting us seemed more alive, too, now that we were inside the city.

After twisting and turning down more roads than I could keep track of, our destination suddenly loomed before us: A wide path leading to a large manor with gleaming white walls and three distinct, domed roofs. Unsurprisingly, the building was accented with blue flames. In this case, they were concentrated mainly on the corners, in lines of lamps that ran down like waterfalls, cascading into troughs of more fire that swept along the building's foundation.

As we drew nearer to the manor, the flames attached to the belts worn by our escorts seemed to glow brighter…and the bracelet my father had given me began to tremble faintly.

I had to work to steady my breathing as that trembling grew steadier. Stronger.

Aleksander cut me a curious glance, peering over the head of the revived girl, who remained in his arms; she was awake and seemingly regaining her strength, but she still had little interest in walking on her own two feet.

My bracelet continued to twitch. Now wasn't the time

to draw attention to it, however, so I picked up my pace and ignored Aleksander's questioning gaze as we made our way into the towering residence before us.

Inside, the air was thick with the palpable weight of things lost and left to rot. Grand hallways led to opulent yet decaying rooms full of furniture upholstered in dust-covered velvet. Faded murals lined the walls, depicting a myriad of scenes, many of which were set in places that reminded me of spots in the world above. I wondered if they were the memories of the dead who had taken up residence here, and if the dead themselves had painted them.

Did they still possess the kind of knowledge and awareness needed to create such things?

As we passed into a narrower, more private-feeling corridor, we were immediately met by a small army of servants dressed in dark robes, their faces entirely covered by deep purple veils, save for a strip revealing their eyes. All of these eyes gleamed in similar shades of blue, but with varying levels of brightness—as though their color had been leaching away at different rates over time.

They ushered our group to the second floor, where we were each assigned a private room to rest and recover in. Even the young girl received her own quarters. I nearly intervened as she was pried from Aleksander's arms and shown toward those quarters—she looked terrified at the thought of being separated from us—but the servants ultimately moved too fast for me to stop them.

All of this was moving alarmingly fast, and suddenly, Phantom and I stood alone at the end of the hallway, facing the door to our own room.

(*They seem eager to get us alone and separate from one another,*) Phantom said, voicing my concerns.

I tried to reassure him with a scratch between his ears, even as I was scanning the area for potential escape routes.

A metal sculpture caught my eye—one of a tall, fierce-looking woman carrying a shield in one hand and a torch in the other. Her torch was empty, missing the blue flames I'd come to anticipate everywhere in this city. She was balanced on a pedestal at the end of the hall, and in the reflection of her raised shield, I watched our host saying something to one of his servants before he turned and glanced toward me with a smile.

"One moment," he called.

I turned slowly to face him.

"We haven't truly introduced ourselves, have we?" he asked.

"We haven't." I smiled, still determined not to show any of the fear I felt, and I stepped forward, offering my hand to him first. "Bellanova Halestorm. Or just Nova, rather."

He squeezed my hand. His skin felt even more calloused and rough than it appeared. Up close, I couldn't help but notice how he seemed much older than I'd initially thought; there were patches of peppery grey within his dark beard, and his face was as rough as his hands, his features hardened in that particular way that came from a lifetime of making difficult decisions.

"Kaelen Drakmere," he said. "I've earned the nickname *Reaper* around these parts, you might have heard—but it's very much a misnomer, I assure you. Death is not my focus these days; I'm far more interested in the bits of life we've managed to hold on to here in Erebos. I apologize for speaking so roughly to you all before; it was merely part of the act I usually put on while outside the safety of this manor."

Phantom drew closer, sniffing at the weapon Kaelen still held casually at his side, his hackles lifting.

I introduced the two of them as well. The sovereign of Erebos sheathed his weapon and tousled the fur between Phantom's ears, placating him for the moment as he said, "You'll find the rooms well-appointed, I trust. But if there's anything else you need, don't hesitate to ask."

His eyes lingered on me for several seconds, as if there was more he intended to say. But then he left with no more than a polite bow, drawing all but two of the servants with him. These two took up residence on either side of the shield-and-torch-bearing statue. Presumably waiting to retrieve anything else we might have needed—though they felt less like maids and more like spies ready to report our every movement back to Kaelen.

I avoided eye contact with them as I stepped into the room I'd been granted.

It *was* well-appointed. Stocked with all the basic comforts of home that I'd missed, albeit lacking any of the charm Orin's place possessed. Plain in decor—but then again, I couldn't think of why Kaelen would need charming guest quarters.

Or *any* guest quarters, for that matter.

What had he meant by *the bits of life we've managed to hold on to*?

And all the blue flames we'd passed on our way here, carried by all those strange beings who were more alive than the shades, yet clearly still ghosts…what exactly was the purpose of this city, and how did its citizens end up here, rather than outside of its walls?

The questions swirled in my head as I circled the room. But I was so thrilled to have a proper bath and clean linens that I eventually forgot most of those questions—if only for a little while. Long enough to properly wash up, to organize my things, and to take a short nap on the bed, even though its mattress was astoundingly lumpy.

That nap was soon interrupted, though, by a fresh barrage of anxious thoughts. Remembering the terrified expression I'd seen on the green-eyed girl's face, I slipped my boots back on and went to check on her.

She wasn't in her room.

With the help of Phantom's nose, I managed to track her down; she'd made her way to the backyard of the manor—a rolling expanse of space covered in grey dirt and dead grass.

She'd finally found someone to participate in her game of tag, too: Zayn. The Lord of the North Reaches was looking rather undignified with his shirt untucked and his cheeks red and flaming as he huffed and puffed for breath.

I took a seat on a stone bench at the yard's edge, observing them through drooping eyelids, wishing I'd managed to get more sleep.

Within minutes, silent servants appeared and dropped trays of food and drink beside me. They bowed and left again without a word. I stared at the things they'd brought. Like the room I'd been granted, it all felt almost too normal —too good to be true.

Which made it feel dangerous.

Nevertheless, Phantom braced his paws against the bench and helped himself to the tray, sniffing each item upon it before taking some sort of thinly sliced cheese delicately between his teeth, tossing it into the air and catching it in his mouth.

"Are you sure that's safe to eat?"

(*It's cheese,*) he informed me. (*It's worth the risk of poisoning.*)

"Debatable," I said, my smile crooked.

He responded by wolfing down the rest of the stack.

I reached for a glass bottle of crystal-clear water myself, cautiously pouring it into a cup and taking a few small sips. When I didn't immediately expire from the drink, I couldn't help draining the rest of it in a few gulps. I was alarmingly thirsty, all of a sudden.

Not as thirsty as Zayn, though, judging by the way he was bent over with his hands on his knees, heaving for breath. The girl showed no mercy, despite his position; she launched herself onto his back. He tumbled to the ground —mostly for show, I assumed, given that she couldn't have weighed more than fifty pounds. He pulled a handkerchief from the pocket of his coat, waving it like a flag of surrender.

Biting back laughter, I called, "Come drink something before you pass out. Both of you."

Zayn rolled over and pushed himself up, jogging toward me with a playful smile.

The girl started to follow, but stumbled to a stop when she caught sight of Phantom. Her green eyes went wide. Her hands clenched together, shaking, until—at my prompting—Phantom shifted into a puppy-like size and gave a happy *yip*.

Her eyes never leaving him, she took the drink I offered and gulped it down, missing her mouth with most of it. Then she was off again, giggling as Phantom gave chase.

While she continued to roll around in the dusty grass with the dog, Zayn collapsed at my feet and stretched out on his back with an exaggerated sigh.

"Children are exhausting," he said, yawning and closing his eyes.

"So I've heard." I mirrored his yawn. "Partly why I'm more of a dog person, myself."

He cracked one eye open. "All of the courtiers who had started planning for an abundance of heirs to the Elarithian throne would have been disappointed to hear that."

My cheeks flamed at the thought. But I refused to dwell on what might have been had my arranged marriage ever taken place. "She seems to like you, though," I said, nodding at the girl, who was now busy trying to teach Phantom how to offer his paw for shaking—a trick he was pretending to be entirely ignorant about.

Zayn shrugged. "Well, children are easy to impress and entertain. Much easier than the grumpy asshole of a cousin I've spent most of the past seven years with."

My smile brightened, though my stomach twisted at the mention of Aleksander; I'd hoped I might run into the grumpy king in question, but I hadn't seen him since watching him disappear into his room hours ago.

We needed to talk about what had happened. I should have tracked *him* down rather than this girl, maybe, but I hadn't been able to bring myself to willingly seek him out.

The girl was equally confusing, but she felt less dangerous than the Light King, at least.

"Still no words from her, I'm guessing?"

"Not a single one." Zayn's face scrunched in concern. "Poor thing. Can't even get a name out of her. I've just been calling her *Red* because of her hair."

"Very creative."

"I'm a simple man with simple tastes." He gave me his usual easy grin, but I couldn't help noticing how it didn't light up his eyes the way it normally did. He went back to staring at Red, his expression clouded over in thought…and longing, maybe.

"That wistful look on your face…she reminds you of someone, doesn't she?" I guessed.

"I have a little sister, back in Elarith," he said, after a pause. "She was only a year old last time I was there."

"…So she'd be around the same age as our mysterious *Red*, now."

The pain that flickered in his eyes was brief, but obvious. "Yeah. I guess she would be."

"What was—*is*—her name?" It was so easy to speak of the ones in the living world in the past tense; even after only such a short time down here, it felt as if my very existence had flipped. Like everything above was now dead and gone, while this strange world around me was my only existence.

"Wren," he said.

"Like the songbird."

He nodded, the motion heavy—with regret and memories, I assumed.

I tried to make my smile encouraging. "Hopefully, you'll get to see her again soon."

"Hopefully. Though she won't remember me, of course." The words seemed to tumble from his mouth before he could stop their fall. He hurried on, as if trying to escape them. "What about you? You don't have any siblings, as I recall."

I hesitated. "I did have one, actually. A twin. He died when we were just babies."

He tried—and failed—to cover up his shock. "Oh. I… I'm sorry."

I waved the words away; I never knew what to do with

apologies about Bastian. I couldn't even remember my brother. The loss of him was just a part of my identity, as simple as the raven-wing color of my hair, or the way I was left-handed; I rarely gave it much thought.

I wondered if it was the same way for Zayn when it came to his sister. Seven years of time he'd lost with her—but he hadn't really ever *had* her. There was an absence there, same as my loss of Bastian, but how did one grieve something they'd hardly known?

"Although, apparently *death* isn't as permanent as we might have thought," Zayn mused, his gaze trailing back to Red. "Not sure if that makes it any less painful to experience. But…it's interesting to think about, no?"

I hugged my arms tightly around myself, trying to fight off the sudden sense of disorientation I felt.

"No idea how you two did it, huh?" he asked.

I shook my head. "Before—when she was still a shade—she came to me alone. Following me, I thought. She seemed upset, so I tried to comfort her, and I saw something when I touched her. A vision."

"A vision?"

"Divination is a skill some necromancers possess. I've never been very good at it, myself, but the power seems to be awakening more and more since I've been in this realm."

"So what did you see?"

I tried to explain it in as much detail as I could—which wasn't much; it felt like trying to describe a dream that had fled from my thoughts the moment I'd woken up.

"You didn't recognize the woman or the location?" he asked.

"Not truly, no. Though I swear that woman looked like

she could have been an older version of me. But I've never heard of a necromancer divining the future; only the past. And the girl appeared to be the same age as she is now."

Zayn was quiet for a long time before he said, "Have I ever told you you're a very strange person?"

I gave him a wry smile. "Yes. You've mentioned that."

We fell silent, contemplating, picking at the tray of refreshments the servants had brought.

My turquoise bracelet was stirring again. Not the subtle shivering of earlier, but a tightening—occasionally clenching so fiercely to my wrist that it cut off my circulation and left my fingertips numb. I did my best to ignore it; I didn't want to talk about my *strangeness* any more just then.

"What are the chances at least *some* of this food is poisoned or otherwise cursed, I wonder?" Zayn asked, lifting a small cake and giving it a dubious nibble. "Or, at the very least, not meant for real, *living* human consumption?"

"Kaelen seems as alive as we are. I assume that's why they have this food and water with actual substance to it—though who knows where it comes from. And I wonder if the wraiths eat anything similar?"

He shrugged, his eyes clouding over in thought once more.

"...I don't think our host wants to poison us, either way," I said. "He could have killed us outside the city if that was his game. He wants something else from us." I frowned as I thought about the way his eyes had lingered on me in the hallway earlier. "Something from me."

Zayn nodded. "He likely wants to figure out your magic —and how he can use it for his own gain."

"Something I'd like to figure out for myself," I muttered.

The comment hung in the air until I couldn't take it any longer; I wasn't solving anything, sitting here eating cakes.

I forced myself to stand. "I need to talk to Aleksander. Do you know where he is?"

"Off brooding somewhere, if I had to guess," Zayn said, back to his usual, teasing expression of bright eyes and an easy grin.

"Not helpful."

"I know he wasn't in his room when I checked an hour ago, if that helps."

I thanked him, drained the last of the water I'd poured, and then set off. I thought about using Phantom to help track Aleksander down, but Red seemed more at ease now that she had him to play with, so I insisted he stay beside her.

Part of me wanted to explore the house on my own, anyway. To wander through at my own pace, trying to make sense of its existence in this realm, while simultaneously trying to prepare myself for the talk I needed to have with the Light King.

I wandered up and down all three stories of the manor, taking in its haunting beauty. Though it was dulled by dust and darkness, its grandness couldn't be denied. More metal sculptures lined the hallways—more figures whose identities I could only guess at. After studying their faces more closely, though, I concluded that they all seemed to favor one another. Several of the peeling and faded murals appeared to feature similar people, too. So this was a house built by—or for—one family. Like a mausoleum, I supposed. Except, there didn't seem to be any truly *dead* bodies anywhere…

and there were far too many things that no ghost would have any use for.

The longer I spent walking through it all, the more confused I felt.

I wanted to keep exploring. But eventually, I heard familiar voices I couldn't ignore—Thalia and Kaelen were nearby, having what sounded like a heated conversation. I cautiously drifted closer to the sound, which brought me to a balcony above a wild, overgrown garden. They stood alone on one of its cobblestone paths, their bodies half-hidden by thorny vines and shriveled flowers.

The balcony was massive, protruding out from an airy, open room, with multiple doorways leading onto it. I was cautiously creeping along it, searching for a way to get closer to Thalia without being seen, when I spotted Aleksander.

He was leaning against a column of the balcony, his gaze narrowed intently on the garden below. A tattered curtain hung overhead, casting him in shadows and further hiding him from view; we'd had the same idea of eavesdropping, apparently.

I carefully made my way toward him.

Chapter Nineteen

Nova

"Chaos," he greeted me, his voice low.

"Asshole," I replied.

He arched a brow.

"...It occurs to me, now, that I never really came up with a fitting nickname for you," I said.

"Most just call me *Aleks* for short."

"I can do better than that, I think. Just give me time."

"Right." He turned his attention back to Thalia and Kaelen. "Happy creating, then."

I smiled a bit at his dry tone before settling into the shadows beside him. Closer than I wanted to be, but it was a necessary evil to stay out of sight of the pair we were spying on.

I did my best to ignore him. To not breathe in his crisp, earthy scent too deeply. To avoid getting too caught up in the changing rhythms of his heartbeat.

And yet, my magic shifted with the awareness of him

and his power, shadows moving over my skin despite my best efforts to control them; I soon gave up trying to stop those shadows and simply allowed a few tendrils to break the surface and swirl around us, further cloaking us in darkness.

We could hear occasional bits of the conversation in the garden below, but it didn't matter—they weren't speaking any language either of us knew. I watched carefully, all the same, trying to interpret what I could from their expressions and body language.

They both proved difficult to read in this way, too. I got the impression this was not the first time the two of them had sparred with one another, and that each one was trying to outdo the other when it came to not giving any outward sign of distress—or any emotion at all, for that matter.

Finally, their argument seemed to reach a climax; Thalia whipped a knife from somewhere, its blade gleaming in the light of the blue-flame lanterns dotted throughout the garden. Her movements were still perfectly precise, cold and controlled. She pointed the blade at the throat of Kaelen—who didn't move—and said something in a low hiss of a voice before turning on her heel and storming away.

I leaned closer to the balcony railing, watching the Erebosian leader for any emotion he might betray now that Thalia wasn't there to see it.

He started to glance upward at the exact moment Aleksander wrapped an arm around my waist and smoothly, silently pulled me out of sight.

I again did my best to ignore his closeness, calmly pushing away from his touch—but keeping well within the shelter of shadows—before glancing toward the garden and asking, "What do you think that was about?"

"No idea." He frowned. "But the sooner we get out of this city, the better, I believe."

"We agree on something, for once."

"It's a day of miracles, clearly," he said, heading back inside.

I fell into step beside him, slowly gathering my courage enough to say: "Speaking of miracles…"

"…The incident at the lake?"

I nodded.

He sighed. "We should discuss that, I suppose."

We made our way over to a corner of the room, into a space that felt less open and exposed, and that was far out of view of the nearest doors and windows. Aleksander reclined against the wall while I perched on the armrest of a chair, but didn't truly sit in it; I was far too anxious to relax into its weathered cushions.

Neither of us seemed to know where to start.

He held his hand in front of him, tracing his magic as it faintly lit up the lines of his palm, before he finally said, "That girl, and the area that came to life around her…I've never seen magic like that before."

"Me neither."

"Granted, I don't know much about your type of magic, aside from what I was taught by my tutors."

"Teachings that were almost certainly biased."

He didn't comment on this—but he didn't disagree, either. "But regarding my own magic," he went on, "I've brought things to life before, but those things typically only live so long as I continue to feed them with my power; they never take root the way they did near that lake. I cut off my magic entirely back there, yet everything continued to flourish."

"...And something tells me if we went back to it now, it would *still* be flourishing," I said. "It seems impossible. I've managed to loosen death's hold on things in the past, but that effect never lasts, either. Phantom is the closest I've come to reviving something, and it certainly wasn't as permanent a spell as what we seem to have done with that girl. He was the only instance where I've managed such a thing, too, and I still don't know how I pulled it off, aside from desperation."

"So what is it about us—*together*—that makes this realm and its beings come back to life?"

Come back to life.

The words struck me as impossible, even as I closed my eyes and pictured—with perfect clarity—all the *impossible* things we'd done together. My balance teetered. I gripped the armrest I sat on so tightly I was likely leaving permanent indentions in its worn upholstery.

This was not why I had come to the Underworld.

I was here because I wanted to return my mother and my kingdom to life—not revive whatever ghosts decided to follow me around down here. I didn't have time to solve the mystery of this city and its flames, either, or the mystery of the man standing before me.

And yet, what we'd done...it all felt too incredible, too consequential, to ignore.

Someone coughed in the distance, snapping our attention toward the sound. Several long shadows shifted over the floor, stretching out from one of the doors on the opposite side of the room.

No one ever stepped over the threshold, but it was

several minutes before we heard footsteps moving away from us—as if they'd lingered by the door, hoping to overhear our conversation.

"...Let's see if we can find somewhere more private," Aleksander suggested, stepping toward me as I rose from the chair.

Pressing a hand to the small of my back, he guided me toward a staircase in the corner of the room. We climbed the spiraling, creaking stairs into a small, lofted area hidden from the space below by banners hanging from the ceiling.

A grime-covered skylight stretched across the middle of the sloped ceiling, offering a glimpse of the tumultuous, hellfire sky and casting the space in a warm, ambient glow. Our footsteps stirred up dust that shimmered like flecks of gold, lending a magical sort of feel to the otherwise dark and eerie space. Most of the beams of light were concentrated toward a raised platform in the loft's center, where an ornate bench with clawed feet and gold-embroidered cushions stood.

It all reminded me of a fancy viewing box in the theatre my mother and I used to attend in Luscerna—and I was again struck with the thought that it was a strange thing to exist in a city of the dead; who was meant to sit in this place?

And what sort of show might they watch whenever the banners across the ceiling parted?

Aleksander didn't take his hand away from my back even as we stepped deeper into the loft, well out of sight of anyone below. I didn't try to move away from him; I was too intrigued by the way I could feel warm magic pulsing through his fingertips. It seemed less wild and intimidating, confined within this more intimate space and fixed to a single point against me.

He finally drew his hand away, drifting back toward the stairs and peering over the curved railing, making certain we weren't being followed.

"There are eavesdroppers everywhere in this manor, including ones I'm sure we can't see," he muttered, casting his gaze about the loft, as though expecting more potential offenders to be hiding even among the dust and cobwebs. "Be careful of what you say."

I nodded.

I didn't feel the need to *speak* just then, anyway; all of my questions had quieted, lost in the curious pulse of his magic. I could still feel it against my skin in spite of the space he'd put between us.

He stepped closer again, as though drawn back by that same pulsing—as if he had left a piece of himself in me and he couldn't stop himself from returning to claim it.

My breath hitched at the thought.

His head tilted curiously in response to the sound. The movement brought half of his face into the light, painting it in rich strokes of red that made his golden eyes seem to burn from within. He didn't speak. He merely reached an arm around my waist, dragging his fingers across my back, letting them linger on the spot where his magic was starting to leave what felt like a permanent mark.

"It isn't just me, is it?" My voice was so low that he had to lean closer to hear me, which only made my words come out softer as I said, "You feel what your touch does…" I lifted a hand and pressed it against his chest, watching the shadows moving around my wrist, noticing the way they darkened as soon as my fingers met his body.

"...And you see what our closeness seems to trigger, don't you?"

He looked reluctant to admit it, but he eventually nodded. "I keep expecting the reaction to ease."

I swallowed hard, trying to manage rational thoughts and explanations despite the disorienting flush spreading over my skin. "Seven years' worth of magic has been building up in your body, released only during your occasional, erratic wakings," I pointed out. "A lot of pent-up energy needs to be unleashed before it can have any chance to truly settle, maybe."

He nodded, though his eyes stayed distant and troubled, unsatisfied with the explanation.

I wasn't entirely satisfied with it, either. Because it felt deeper—like more than a mere itch that needed scratching, or a dam needing a routine release.

"At least it seems to be a *good* thing when we combine, for whatever reason," I said.

"The question is, can that combined power be controlled in some way?" he asked. "Summoned at will?" His fingers tapped thoughtfully against my back. Each tap sent another vibration of warm power skating along my spine, and soon, I was losing the battle to keep my thoughts steady and rational. Every breath I took sent his warmth deeper, flooding all the way to the tips of my toes, curling them inside my boots.

I lifted my eyes away from the hand I had against his chest. He watched me closely, staring with the same quietly confident gaze he'd fixed on me at the edge of Lake Nyras, as he said, "And would the craving subside if we indulged it, I wonder?"

Craving.

The word settled like an invitation between us.

I kept waiting for him to take it back.

He didn't.

I licked away the dryness on my lips, and then I heard myself say: "Let's try it and see."

Something hungry yet hesitant flashed in his eyes. His heart raced beneath my touch, and mine skipped several beats, trying to catch up.

"This could end poorly," he warned. "Or dangerously."

"I'm sure I've survived worse than whatever *dangerous* things we might awaken."

"As have I. But still." He drew his hand away from my back. For a moment, he appeared to be at war with himself—an instant away from turning and rushing back down the stairs.

Then he reached toward my face, letting his knuckles graze my jawline. His thumb traced my lips, and his own lips parted as if in anticipation. "But still…we should go slowly. Carefully. So we can better pinpoint our exact…"

His hand slipped lower, trailing across the hollow of my throat, and I forgot to breathe for a moment.

"…Reactions to things," he finished in a low, tense voice.

I took a step back so I could collect myself enough to calmly agree with this plan. I regretted the space the instant I put it between us; it only seemed to make the heat in my blood worse. The air all around us was suddenly charged with energy, the pressure of our rising power growing more intense—more undeniable—with every passing second.

He was the one to close the distance between us again, circling me as he came, studying the cold shadows I could feel moving across my skin. He twisted a hand through my hair, moving a section of it over my shoulder so he could watch the darkness creeping its way along the back of my neck.

"This is as dark as I've seen these markings," he commented.

"Maybe it's the terrible lighting in here."

"Maybe."

A flutter went through me as he traced the shifting markings with a thoughtful touch. I kept my eyes straight ahead, focused on the ornate bench, studying the faded shimmer of its teal and gold cushions.

"But every brush of contact seems to stir them up even more." He seemed to lose himself in the act of mapping out my skin and stirring things up; testing the way the shadows reacted to his touch; memorizing the patterns they followed; gently pushing the collar of my shirt aside so he could better study the branches of black reaching toward the space between my shoulder blades...

Eventually, he pulled his hand away and replaced his physical touch with one of magic, summoning tiny spears of light that pressed against my skin like branding irons. Everywhere the light burned in, my power followed, cooling it. Calming it. Making it feel...*balanced*. When he stopped summoning and let his light tumble freely through the space, the opposite proved true as well; his magic naturally gravitated toward mine.

For several minutes, we watched it all dance among the dust, Shadow and Light circling and occasionally twisting together with fleeting, iridescent glints of something more powerful.

The space began to glow with hints of that greater power. Nothing grew among the wood and plaster, of course, yet it all still felt more *alive*. The floorboards shivered. The light siphoning in from above seemed purer. The quiet was no longer eerie, but warm and expectant—like the excited hush before a theatre performance, bristling with promise and possibility. I would have sworn I heard the whispers and quiet laughter of a jubilant, just barely contained crowd.

And every time the shades of our magic collided, I felt it twisting along my body as if Aleksander was physically touching me again—as if his fingers were raking across bundles of exposed nerve endings. The sensation was so intense I found myself drifting closer and closer to him, wanting to see what might happen if he *actually* touched me.

Could this high I was experiencing possibly spiral even higher?

The line between my magic and desire steadily blurred. A ribbon of his light wove around my legs, its warmth caressing the apex of my thighs, and a soft sigh of pleasure fell from my lips before I could catch it. My eyes had fluttered shut, but I could sense Aleksander's gaze settling more intentionally on me at the sound.

His warning from before whispered through my thoughts.

This *did* feel dangerous.

But maybe not in the way he'd meant.

And maybe not in the way I'd been prepared for.

I forced myself to turn and take a step away, trying once again to stay focused on experimenting with *magic* and nothing else.

But Aleksander followed as if it was part of the dance we'd recklessly, foolishly started, hooking an arm around my waist from behind, just barely letting its weight rest against me. His fingers caged lightly against my hip. Just enough pressure to hold me in place.

I fought the desire to shift more completely into his arms, but I couldn't keep my hands from reaching for the light that was peeling off him in gossamer strands. It settled briefly between my fingers, its weight palpable, but as soft and delicate as spider-webs.

His face pressed against my hair, warm breath drifting through the dark strands and tingling over my scalp as he whispered, "I want to touch you."

I swallowed hard. "You *are* touching me."

"Not the way I want to." The words slipped out, low and rough with reluctance. Almost like a confession.

"The way your magic wants to, you mean."

"Yes," he ground out. "That."

I leaned a little more fully into his embrace. Such a small movement, but it felt like tipping my weight forward instead of backward—like *hurtling* forward onto a precarious, crumbling ledge that was seconds away from giving out beneath me.

Chapter Twenty

Nova

"Nova..." My name on his lips somehow sounded like both a plea and a command rolled into one. Like a king not accustomed to asking permission for the things he wanted; unsure of how it was done, yet willing—at least in this moment—to try groveling for it.

For *me*.

He nuzzled his face more fully into my hair. Another warm breath, and then I was nodding, giving him permission, desperate for the tingling across my scalp to overtake the rest of my body.

His feather-light touch was abruptly gone, replaced by a far more possessive grip against my hip. He pulled my back flush against his chest as his fingers dug in, pinning me in place while his other hand traveled along my curves, delicious heat spreading from beneath his large palm as he grasped and fumbled at my clothing.

I felt a stirring low in my stomach, a tightness coiling

without mercy. An anticipation, an ache, a need…or, no—it was the word he'd used earlier: *A craving.* The only real name for this insatiable feeling building between us.

Part of me still hated it. Hated *him*, even as I gave in and allowed his fingers to continue to explore, to slip beneath the hem of my shirt.

This was wrong, so *breathtakingly* wrong, and so against everything I had believed for *years*.

But I wanted his hands to keep roaming across my stomach. To continue inching higher, finding their way to my breasts. I *needed* him to do more than just chase shadows and drip light over my skin. I needed his fingers to find all my other places. Hidden places. Deeper places.

My balance swayed at the thought, and a quiet laugh rumbled in his chest before he said, "You could survive whatever dangerous magic we might summon, you claimed, yet you can't even properly stand."

"It's been a long couple days of walking, in my defense."

"Well, allow me to help steady you," he said, pulling me even more fully to him, his lips brushing against the shell of my ear with the words. He kept his mouth close to that sensitive spot as his hand roved over my hip, moving toward my inner thigh. My body arched automatically, trying to pull his hand closer to my center. He sucked in a breath at the motion, shifting his weight from foot to foot, trying to balance.

"You don't feel particularly steady yourself," I teased, the words breathless and faint.

He raked a hand into my hair, the bite of his grip just shy of hurting. "An infuriating effect you seem to have on me."

"Another cruel trick the universe is playing?"

"The cruelest yet." He used the grip in my hair to tilt my head toward him, exposing my neck to his ravenous mouth.

Stars danced in my vision as he kissed and sucked against my throbbing pulse. I felt like I was falling—another slip of balance. Mine, or his, or both of ours, I didn't know. But we eventually backed together toward stability, toward the raised platform and the bench centered upon it.

He sank onto the discolored cushions, dragging me down into his lap as he went. His hand smoothed across my body, encouraging me to stretch it out against his. I reached back as I did, hooking my arms around his neck. The pose felt wonderfully, terrifyingly intimate and vulnerable, even with my back to him, even with both of us remaining entirely clothed.

His lips were again pressed to the side of my neck an instant later. His leg wedged between mine, spreading them apart, leaving more room for his hand to cup the space between. He moved slowly, just as he'd said we should, applying pressure to my aching center with teasing strokes, yet leaving a barrier of clothing between us.

"And darker, still," he murmured after a moment, the fingertips of his other hand trailing along my arm.

I blinked the stars from my eyes, focusing long enough to see what he meant; the markings upon my skin were so black they looked less like shadows and more like shining ink. His magic continued to build as well, the threads of it occasionally diving into my darkness, weaving us together in a heady combination of power and pleasure.

Magic.

We were supposed to be trying to see if we could

connect more deeply, to access the hidden reserves of our power. To purposely control it. This was an experiment.

Magic.

Nothing more.

So when I moved my hips against him, I was thinking only of drawing out *power*, not pulling out his groans that vibrated so pleasantly against the back of my neck. I was not focused on the way his hand roamed under my shirt and uncovered the bare curves of my breasts. Not the way that hand traced and pinched the velvety tip of one into a perfectly erect point, either—or the way his other hand continued to work between my legs, finally sliding beneath my clothes and finding the dampness awaiting him. And I was certainly *not* focused on the way his breath audibly caught at the feel of that dampness and his touch became rougher, less restrained.

The room seemed more alive than ever—bright and shivering with a power that heightened all my senses, almost to the point of ecstasy. The air felt less heavy, somehow. The banners hanging above us started to sway and flutter as if stirred by a gentle breeze.

The hand teasing my breasts stilled, and Aleksander pulled the other one from between my legs. I started to protest only to be silenced by his fingers slipping into my mouth. I was so aroused by this that my first instinct was to try and pull them in more fully, more deeply—a move that had his cock twitching against my backside.

"*Fuck,*" he growled.

I pulled my mouth away from his fingers, dragging my lips over them as I went. "I would be willing, but I don't think that would count as *going slowly.*"

He let out something between a harsh laugh and a curse.

I pressed harder against him, rolling my hips a bit.

He responded to my taunting by slipping his hand back between my legs and plunging two wet fingers inside of me.

I cried out from a combination of shock and pleasure, and he moved the hand from my chest to instead cover my mouth.

"We're trying not to be overheard, if you'll recall," he said as his hand moved away from my mouth and down across my body once more, skimming over my stomach, joining the other in worshipping my sex. While that hand stretched me further to accommodate him, his fingers slid in and out of me at a torturously slow pace, thrusting deeper each time, pressing and curling against my inside walls until I was biting back a moan.

I kept one arm looped around his neck for balance, but with the other I reached down to grip the hand with its fingers inside of me, urging him even deeper.

Aleksander pressed his face closer to mine, his voice low as he said, "Eager to use your hands again tonight, I see."

I blushed, remembering our conversation from the shore of Nyras. "I'm very good with them, if you'll recall."

With a low, dark laugh, he said, "It's still no substitute for what I could do for you, if you'd like me to."

Those last five words succeeded in turning what remained of my rational thoughts into a useless pile of mush.

"So we've given up on *going slowly*, have we?" I purred.

His lips trailed along my jawline, nipping at my earlobe. "Say the word, and I'll stop."

I swallowed hard, as if to clear a path for such a word.

But I couldn't say it. I couldn't seem to say *anything* while he was kissing my face, my neck, my hair so hungrily; while his fingers continued to fill me, to move against me with such perfect, expert strokes.

If you'd like me to.

There were far too many things I would have *liked* him to do in that moment.

He shifted beneath me, sitting up slightly, angling himself so his fingers could penetrate more fully.

My head tipped back. Both my arms dropped to my sides, hands grappling for the edge of the bench, searching for something else to steady myself against.

As soon as I gripped the wood, a vision flooded my mind.

The chatter of the crowd I'd heard earlier returned in a deafening rush, violently jerking me out of my rapture. I blinked, and the scenery flickered; suddenly, there were other benches below the platform I sat upon, all of them filled with smartly dressed people, their jewels glittering in the light of countless chandeliers.

Another blink, and those chandeliers burned much lower; a performance was underway on a stage in the room below—a tragedy, judging by the distraught faces around me, and by the sudden rush of anguish that overtook me.

I leapt from Aleksander's lap so quickly I tripped. I would have slammed head-first into the floor if not for the way he reflexively hooked an arm around me, slowing my fall. He tumbled with me off the bench, and we were a mess of tangled limbs and breathless, confused cursing for a moment before we managed to pull apart and face one another.

"What's wrong?" he asked.

All of this, hissed a scathing, terrified voice in the back of my mind. But I couldn't speak; I was still breathing too hard, my thoughts racing too wildly from my latest strange vision.

It had reminded me, again, of my mother. Of the plays we used to attend in our royal city. Of the world I'd once belonged to, and how thoroughly ruined it all was. How I'd *thought* I knew how to fix it all, just days ago. But now…

I slowly rose to my feet. The floorboards continued to shiver and sigh underneath us. The twisting remnants of our combined magic filled the air. As I stared at a particularly dark and curling strand, I was transported all the way back to the beginning of this—to the night of my birthday. The sight of the shadows channeling violently through my body. The breaking ground. The bodies falling. The screams echoing.

Aleksander's touch might have distracted me more than it should have, and our magic might have created balance and life where it shouldn't have existed, but some things still hadn't changed.

I still couldn't trust him. Our kingdoms were still enemies. And this realm we stood within was still Hell. I would be a fool to forget any of that, regardless of the shiny veil our magic might have draped over it all.

"Nova?"

Three times.

He'd now used my actual name three times today. And this was twice, now, that he'd caught me as I tumbled off balance—first in the waves of Lake Nyras, and now in the waves of memory and the strange haunting visions that kept popping up at the worst possible times.

What's wrong? he'd asked.

And the concern in his eyes…

Why was it so much harder to endure that concern than it was to deal with his insults and cruel taunts? Why did it frighten me even more than all my haunting visions combined?

"It's this," I whispered, watching him closely as he got to his feet as well. "All of this." Taking a deep, steadying breath, I said, "I lost everything the night your sword *somehow* ended up in my father's chest."

"I didn't—"

"I *know*. I heard you before, when you claimed innocence. But I have spent seven years believing you were my enemy—that there was a path to redemption and healing if I could just find that cursed sword of yours and then confront the one who sits on the Elarithian throne. But now I'm here, and nothing in this realm is like I expected it to be, and you…" I took a step back, clenching and unclenching my fists, trying to settle my frustration enough to keep talking. "None of it makes any sense."

He settled back on the bench, clasping his hands behind his head and tilting his face to the ceiling. Even though the pose suggested exasperation, he still managed to appear calm—perfectly poised and regal—and I hated him all over again for it.

"I don't understand it." I wanted to scream. Instead, my voice came out hoarse, just shy of cracking as I said, "I don't understand *any* of it."

After a weighted pause, he said, "I want answers, too. And you are the last person I wanted to search for them with. But here we are." He looked down and met my eyes —truly met them—and he shifted one of the hands behind his head, as though he was considering reaching it out to me. The beginnings of a truce, however feeble.

I couldn't bring myself to encourage that truce along. Maybe it was stubbornness. Or fear. Or maybe it was because I had wrapped myself so tightly in plans for revenge for so long, that now I couldn't even imagine what else could possibly grow between us.

Nothing else felt real.

Nothing else felt safe.

So I simply shoved the mess of my feelings down for the moment. Pushed it all down. Pushed it all back. Buried it all, just like I always did, as if that would kill off these feelings and make them into something I could control.

I had a terrible feeling, though, that whatever was building between Aleksander and me would not be so easily laid to rest.

"I need to go find Thalia," I told him, evenly. "We need to make a plan to get out of this city as quickly as possible, as we said earlier. I'm sorry I got carried away a moment ago. Let's…" I forced a cordial smile. "Let's just pretend it never happened."

He stood, an unreadable mask falling over his face. He didn't agree or disagree with my plan to pretend, nor did he try to close the distance between us as I thought he might.

I didn't give him the satisfaction of seeing my growing confusion and irritation; I headed for the stairs and started down without another word. I was moving so fast by the time I reached the bottom that I nearly collided with the person starting to climb them—Kaelen.

He caught my arm in a strong grip, steadying me. "Sorry to startle you. I hope I'm not interrupting anything?"

I threw a glance over my shoulder.

Aleksander now sat on the top step, elbows propped on his knees, chin resting on his hands. Perfectly composed once more. As if he'd been sitting there all afternoon, drinking in the room and all its tarnished and dusty splendor, contemplating it.

"Nothing at all," I said to Kaelen, all my lingering frustrations making my voice cold as ice.

"Good. Because I've been looking for you," he said, drawing my gaze back to him.

"...Have you?"

He nodded. "I was wondering if you would care for a proper tour of the city?" He didn't explicitly state it, but it was clear enough by the way his eyes focused on me and only me: He intended for this to be a private tour.

Aleksander's stare was like a tangible blade carving into my back, suddenly.

Desire curled through me before I could guard against it.

We weren't finished with what we'd started, regardless of how quickly I'd made my escape.

And for a brief moment, I wanted him to stop me. To show concern. To challenge the sovereign of Erebos on my behalf. To drag me off somewhere so we could *finish* things.

For an *instant*, I thought perhaps we could be more than a pair of wayward souls caught in this strange hell, forced together by confusing, unfortunate circumstances.

But the King of Light didn't move from his place at the top of the steps. He'd redirected his glare to the ceiling, his face betraying no hint of concern for anything below it. Certainly not for *me*. Our experimenting for the day was over, and, clearly, he didn't care what I planned to do next.

Kaelen cleared his throat, expectant.

I shouldn't have answered that expectation. I knew this man—this so-called *Reaper*—before me was not someone I could trust. But more than any of that, I wanted *answers*. Even if it meant taking a risk to get them. It wouldn't have been the first time I'd danced along the edge of a wolf's mouth to get what I needed.

So I calmly turned to Kaelen and said, "Lead the way."

Chapter Twenty-One

Nova

THE CITY FELT EVEN MORE MASSIVE AND DIFFICULT TO comprehend as Kaelen and I took our time walking through it.

We wound through streets paved with shadowy stones that glistened as if wet—even though there had been no rain, as far as I knew.

Did it *ever* rain in this realm?

I looked to what I could see of the violent-colored clouds above, pondering the question. But any expanse of sky was difficult to see, given the city's jagged roofline, its towering black spires, and the banners hanging from many of the houses. Almost all of those banners featured the same thing: A golden stag with a torch burning between its vine-wrapped antlers.

We eventually came to a corner where stalls were set up, strange wares on display for the countless wandering wraiths making their way through the area.

I stared the longest at a table containing neat rows of diamond-shaped containers, each with a swirling mass of some sort of cloudy grey substance inside. The merchant who stood behind this table had eyes that danced restlessly between shades of orange and red, like the flickering flames of candles. They fixed in my direction, and he beckoned me over with a curl of his long fingers—but Kaelen placed a hand on my shoulder before I could even consider taking a step.

"Memories of our living world," he explained, nodding at the diamond-shaped containers. "You break them and breathe in the mist, and it's like being back there for a bit."

I gaped, barely resisting the urge to run over and grab one to try for myself.

Kaelen's grip on my shoulder tightened, as if he could sense my desire. Annoying, at first, but the more I thought about it, the more I realized he was probably right to protect me from myself; dropping into a clear memory of the living world right now would do nothing to settle the vexation I felt after everything that had happened today. I was working hard to bury the part of me that wanted to abandon my mission and run back to the world above; tempting myself with visions of that world would be foolish.

My gaze fell instead to the table beside the memories, where small vials in several different sizes and colors were lined up in equally orderly rows.

"And those are strong emotions, bottled up for consumption," Kaelen said under his breath, his tone suggesting he didn't fully agree with them being displayed so prominently.

"How?" I asked. "And why?"

"The *how* is by way of relatively simple magic. The

why…" He hesitated. "It's easy to forget the sensations these spells create, even here in the protective walls of my city. I see to it that my citizens never have to *fully* forget. Some get more addicted to the spells than others, though, and would ruin themselves chasing down an emotion if they could—so it's an important commodity, but one that must be regulated."

My curiosity fully piqued, I watched the colorful fluids shining, bubbling, rising up and tumbling down in their vials. It was likely similar to what Orin would have called *parlor-trick* magic—generic spells that anyone with the right ingredients and a bit of knowledge could pull off. Nothing that would leave any lasting impact, in other words.

I wanted to experiment with these things, anyway—to experience what such common magic tricks might be like in this realm. But I also had no money to buy any of said tricks; coins had not been on the list of things I'd thought I would need for the Underworld, after all.

There didn't seem to be much exchanging of money or goods going on, anyway. Although, one transaction did catch my eye: A squat little woman with pale violet hair was holding up her wrist to one of the merchants across from the memory dealer, affording him a good look at the caged flame dangling from her bracelet. They were speaking in quick, hushed tones; the lady seemed distraught about something.

My eyes jumped from the flame around her wrist to another one around the wrist of the merchant assisting her, and then to all the other fires on all the other beings around us.

They were *everywhere*.

I hadn't imagined it during my initial walk through this

city—all of the citizens of Erebos carried flames on them in some manner. Some hung from bandoliers, others were fashioned into necklaces or rings, while a few simply carried them in small metal lanterns.

"What are all these blue fires for?" I asked Kaelen.

"*Vivaris* flames," he replied. "They draw from the greater concentrations of similar fires you might have noticed scattered around the city."

I nodded, remembering the sapphire wisps gathered along the base of his manor and elsewhere. "What do they do?"

"It's…rather difficult to explain."

"Thalia said the ones in this city are more alive than the shades outside of its walls," I pressed, refusing to accept his evasive answer.

"She's right."

"Do these flames have something to do with that?" I asked. "I can sense magic in them." My hand absently went to the bracelet of turquoise beads my father had given me. It kept happening whenever we drew close to a concentrated pool of fire—or even just a large group of flame-carrying wraiths—the vibrations, the humming.

But I still had no idea what any of it *meant*.

"It's very old magic," Kaelen confirmed, "put in place by powerful beings back when this city first became what it is today. I'm a descendant of those beings—the only one left after all this time. I've been tending to the flames and the wraiths here since I was ten years old."

Powerful beings…

More necromancers, like the ones who had built up the barrier where we'd first encountered Thalia?

"You're the only living being within these city walls, normally?"

"Yes."

"And you've been here since you were a child…so you've aged and changed, while I assume the wraiths stay the same?" It was a theory I'd been piecing together while trying to understand the vision I'd had when I'd touched Red; if she hadn't changed since her death, then perhaps the woman I'd seen—the one who looked like me—was merely a distant ancestor of mine who had known the child when she was alive. Maybe that's why she'd been drawn to me; because she thought I was someone else.

"Correct," said Kaelen. "Typically, only the ones with Shadowblood in their veins can survive in this realm these days. Though, we are aging at a more rapid rate than before, and our magic is becoming less and less potent."

"Shadowblood…" The term struck me as somewhat familiar.

He read the curious look on my face, and he moved to answer it with a demonstration; he rolled up his sleeve and reached out a hand toward a nearby concentration of vivaris fire—a gathering of it inside a large metal bowl held by a regal-looking man carved from marbled stone.

I watched as the veins on Kaelen's arm darkened. As the twisting strands of fire within the bowl did, too, the mass of them turning almost black before he began to pull some of that darkness out, siphoning it into his own body.

Once he was finished, the flames held by the statue were a much brighter blue than before, though the size of their collective mass had decreased.

Several of the meandering souls around us began to move

with more purpose, funneling toward the brightened flames. They took the personal fires they carried and held them closer to the metal bowl, and one by one, those personal lights flickered and briefly burned with more intensity than before.

My turquoise bracelet shivered. I clenched it tightly as I studied the man beside me more closely, realization settling over me. "The way you drew that darkness in...you're a necromancer. Like Thalia. Like me."

His eyes returned to the road ahead, and he trudged onward through his city, guiding me underneath an arching black-iron gate as he said, "Yes. For whatever that's worth anymore."

"So, all of those with our blood can move freely through this dead realm."

"That's right—though the ones traveling with you seem to be managing it, too, Thalia tells me. The Light King's magic must be very powerful and protective, indeed, for them to have lived and aged relatively normally in the seven years they've spent here."

I nearly stumbled to a stop.

What *else* had Thalia told him? And why? She'd seemed furious with him earlier...why trust him with any of our secrets? What sort of relationship did the two of them truly share?

The longer I spent in this city, the more questions I seemed to have.

I tried not to let my nervousness show, attempting to steer the conversation away from myself and the ones I traveled with, as I said, "You tend to the flames here, then?"

"With some help from the more sentient wraiths that I can guide with my magic."

A chilling prospect occurred to me. "What happens

when you're gone, if you're the last living Keeper of Erebos? What becomes of the flames—and the ones they give sentience to—if there's no one left to tend them?"

He didn't answer.

"Why are you keeping them to begin with?"

Again—no answer. The silence stretched into a heavy, crushing thing, settling over us and slowing our steps.

Finally, he said, "The explanation for that isn't covered on this introductory tour, I'm afraid."

The dismissive reply sent a rush of indignant heat through me. My magic stirred dangerously in response. I considered letting it loose, using my shadows to intimidate him into giving me an *actual* answer.

But then I glanced around at all the hooded eyes watching us pass by—all the wraiths that he apparently controlled in some way.

The numbers were not in my favor.

I held my tongue.

I continued trying to sort through all the other questions in my head as we walked on, eventually coming to a center square. Here, a series of metal bowls stood like a strange art display, each one tipped at a different angle. The centermost bowl was enormous, yet the flame within it was puny in comparison.

Had fire filled the entire thing at some point?

There were seven other bowls scattered around the large one; nothing burned within them, now, but I had a feeling that hadn't always been the case.

Curiosity getting the better of me, I ran my fingertips over the rim of the one closest to me.

As expected, my woven-diamond bracelet twitched as soon as I touched the cold metal, and a blinding vision of blue flames struck through my mind—a vision of the past, when such flames burned brightly.

Blinking, I stumbled back, bumping into Kaelen.

He hardly seemed to notice me; he was too busy staring into the largest bowl, his eyes haunted and distant as they reflected what remained of the fire.

"The people of Erebos are survivors," he told me, his voice low, as if he didn't want any of those people to overhear. "But the magic—the fire—that once protected them fades more and more by the day. Many other cities like ours have already fallen. And their citizens have been...*erased*."

"Survivors?"

"The word is unexpected to you?"

"I expected nothing but death in this realm. I was *prepared* to face death. Not...this."

His expression was grim. "And for the most part, death is what you will find if you continue to journey outside of the safety of our fair city."

"But that's not what's here."

"Not yet."

I hugged my arms around myself, overtaken by a sudden surge of cold. "Can the flames be rekindled?"

The silence grew heavy once more. Burdened—like the kind that came before bad news. A buzz of warning skittered through me as I recalled my conversation with Zayn from earlier.

I fixed Kaelen with a hard stare. "Why did you truly bring me into this city?"

He didn't take his eyes off the dwindling fire as he said, "To give you a tour of it, as I told you earlier. To help you understand it."

"Is that really all?"

"Is that not the hospitable thing to do? They do such things in the living world you call home, too, if I'm not mistaken."

"In my experience, people are more forthcoming with their *hospitality* when they need something in return."

His teeth bared in a not-quite-smile. His fist clenched, and I would have sworn the flame in the bowl flickered, as if suffocated by his closing hand.

He still didn't look at me as he said, "So maybe I do have a favor to ask of you."

Chapter Twenty-Two

Nova

I braced myself.

"You clearly carry an enormous amount of magic."

"Yes, but it's not predictable or always entirely *useful* magic."

"And yet, you brought an entire section of our dead realm to life."

"I told you: I didn't do that."

It was a flimsy attempt at a lie, and it didn't stick in the slightest.

"Come now, Nova. We both know you were lying."

A group of wraiths wandered closer to us. Uncomfortably close. My turquoise bracelet again reacted to the concentration of their flames, coming to life with a fluttering that made my wrist itch. I gripped it as casually as I could, trying not to draw attention to it, while also trying to settle it. "It's not entirely a lie," I told Kaelen. "I did cause some things to bloom, yes. But I didn't do it on purpose. And I didn't do it..."

I trailed off, fixing my eyes on a distant, rippling banner to avoid Kaelen's expectant stare.

Alone.

That was what I'd nearly said.

But something had caught my tongue, and something continued to hold it now. Despite the frustration and uncertainty I felt toward the King of Light—and the way I'd hurried away from him earlier—some part of me didn't want to betray him.

It wasn't just about protecting him, and it had *nothing* to do with the lingering ache that came when I thought of what we'd done in that loft. Or what we *could* have done, had my vision not interrupted us.

We were simply safer if I didn't speak of our full abilities.

The Keeper of Erebos didn't realize how powerful Aleksander and I were together. He didn't realize we'd brought that girl—our mysterious *Red*—back to life. He only had suspicions about me and my own powers. Nothing else.

And I wasn't foolish enough to give him any more than that.

"Nevertheless, you clearly have magic we haven't seen in this city in some time."

I remained silent.

"You don't deny that your magic could potentially help us, do you?"

I gritted my teeth. "It isn't really a *favor* if you guilt me into it, now is it?"

He held up his hands in a gesture of peace. "I won't

force you into anything. Just…consider it. All the potential of it."

We walked on in uncomfortable silence, slowly weaving our way back toward the manor. The sharp cold from earlier persisted, snapping at our heels, urging us to keep moving, lest we end up as frozen statues. My skin felt tight, as if it was already halfway to a statuesque state, and my feet ached with a numbness I couldn't shake off.

More than once, I had the sensation of drifting out of control, my boots not truly touching the ground, my body belonging to someone else—and I didn't think it was solely due to the cold.

Was it something about the air in this city?

Something about drinking its water, or staring too long into its flames?

I chanced a glance at Kaelen, who seemed to be trying to avoid my gaze. His brow was deeply furrowed in thought. The expression highlighted the dark circles beneath his eyes and a puckered scar above his cheek. A man who had clearly seen his share of battles. Horrors and sorrows, too—and had likely inflicted his share of such things.

Despite this, he didn't really strike me as a *bad* man. More like a desperate one. But the desperate ones were far more dangerous, I'd long ago learned.

Because you could predict what a bad man would do.

That wasn't always true of a desperate one.

And worse: I *wanted* to help his city. I wanted to rekindle all the fires, to go back to the market and find that distraught-looking woman and see how I might be able to aid her. It was a familiar compulsion of mine, the need to fix things. A role I'd gravitated toward throughout most of my life—that of the helper.

Often to my own detriment, as Orin frequently chastised.

But like so much of what I'd encountered in this realm thus far, so many things about Erebos simply didn't add up. I had the same feeling with Kaelen as I did with Thalia: That he was leaving parts of the narrative out. So how could I possibly *help*? It would be like trying to steer a carriage that was missing one of its wheels.

The mansion came back into view, its whitewashed exterior burning orange in the light of the strange sky—a lighting that I was beginning to associate with late evening. Whether that was accurate or not, I didn't know; I just needed to label it in order to give myself a sense of time and meaning.

Rather than walking straight to the main residence, we veered onto a more narrow side trail, twisting our way past overgrown hedges and dead clumps of prickly bushes, following a path of red bricks that soon gave way to mere dirt. There were curved metal troughs lining our way; scorch marks in their interiors suggested they, too, had once held flames—but now they were empty, just like the metal bowls in the center of the city.

The manor remained in my peripheral vision, but that wasn't where Kaelen led me. Instead, we made our way to a smaller building off to the right, where a sizable host of wraiths milled about in a fenced section of yard. Most of them were carrying more shallow versions of the metal bowls I'd seen on display in the city, each with a small, dying flame in its center. Like starving people wandering, preparing to beg for food that I feared didn't exist.

"What is this place?" I asked softly.

Kaelen's expression was solemn. His voice, low. Pained. "An infirmary, of sorts. A holding place for the ones whose flames are going out."

Ones like that distraught woman in the marketplace?

"Sometimes they find a way to rekindle their fires, however briefly. Other times..."

"They're *erased*?" I asked, recalling the word he'd used earlier.

"You've seen the shades outside of this city. They're the cursed ones, the fallen ones—the ones who aren't strong enough to keep themselves burning, so to speak."

I couldn't help my morbid curiosity; I stepped closer, studying the gaunt figures who stood before me. The beings were caught somewhere between the drifting shades and the sentient wraiths, as Kaelen suggested. Their bodies were still well-defined, solid aside from the occasional wispy edges. But they moved slowly, as if each step took a massive effort. It was haunting to watch them struggle. Like I was watching the living embodiment of dying hope.

"You say you can't control your magic," came Kaelen's voice, cold and distant, "but *something* must trigger it. The question is...what?"

He seemed to be speaking more to himself than me. Regardless, I had no definite answers to give him. Lots of things seemed to trigger it. Fear, pain, arousal...any powerful emotion.

And the strongest waves, unfortunately, were undeniably kindled during my interactions with the King of Light.

Another fact I had no intention of sharing with Kaelen.

As I continued to watch the fading wraiths, a sudden, sharp pain ripped across my shoulder and down my arm, followed by a blossoming warmth. It happened so abruptly it took several seconds longer than it should have for me to register what that warmth actually was—

Blood.

It rushed over my arm, soaking my sleeve and gathering at my fingertips, a few drops dripping down to the dusty, grey ground.

Fear and confusion tangled together, tearing a violent path through me. My shadows leapt to the surface, ready to defend against whatever threats were causing me pain. Their movement triggered a reaction amongst the fading wraiths—they surged toward me so violently, I nearly fell backwards. Clearly drawn to the energy I'd unleashed, to the scent of blood and magic swirling in the air.

"As I suspected," came Kaelen's still-musing voice, from somewhere far behind me.

I realized quickly what he'd done: He'd answered his own question, pulling my magic to the surface on purpose, throwing me like a scrap of meat to a pack of dogs just to see what would happen.

One of my shadowy scraps drifted into the faint flame carried by one of the wraiths, and to my surprise—and horror—that flame *instantly* grew brighter.

The one holding it slowly lifted his gaze to mine. His eyes seemed to grow more aware, more *alive*, even as I stared into them.

Again, I found myself bringing life and light into this world, rather than the death and darkness I was used to.

But at what cost?

Dozens of hungry stares lifted in my direction.

My bleeding shoulder burned and ached. Panic clawed at me, but I forced it back long enough to assess the situation. The wraiths were circling closer, their forms becoming more defined in the haze of the dim evening light. Their eyes glowed faintly, like the embers of the dying fires they carried, yet they focused intently on me.

One of the wraiths lunged forward, faster than I expected, its form flickering like smoke. I tried—and initially failed—to possess it with magic, to drive my will into its fading essence. The black-rose bracelet rattled with the effort, shaking so intensely I thought it might break, but I held my arm steady until I felt a cold, foreign energy stabbing through my arm. I clenched my hand into a fist, trying to grab that energy as I'd grabbed other things by using this possessing power. But it felt different against my palm, this time; like trying to grasp mud—solid one moment, squeezing through my fingers the next.

Nevertheless, I managed to bend the will of the wraith enough to throw it off balance, sending it tumbling away from me.

Countless more moved to follow its attack.

The group was not as listless as it had first appeared. Now that I'd drawn their attention—their hunger—they swarmed with purpose, their movements swift and synchronized. But they were also smart enough to stop and consider their tactics when I lifted my palm threateningly in their direction, ready to throw more aside as I'd done with the first.

One of them stepped out beyond the others, raising a hand and gesturing to them, issuing commands. A leader. As he spoke to the other wraiths in a harsh, booming voice, I spun furiously back toward Kaelen.

The sovereign of Erebos was watching me with a strange, slightly mad gleam in his eyes, one of his scythes in hand. His gaze drifted between the streak of my blood staining the blade, to the drops of scarlet that had splattered the ground.

"They've been aware of your magic since I brought you into my home," he said. "Hungering for it."

"You *bastard*." I took a furious step toward him, shadows flying around me as I did. "You said you wouldn't force me into anything!"

He sheathed his weapon with a slow, deliberate motion, as if indifferent to the growing chaos around us. "*I* am not forcing anything. But the citizens of Erebos grow desperate, and I am bound as their leader to toss them a bit of hope every now and then." He motioned to the trail of my blood.

His idea of *hope*.

This man was beyond desperate.

"What they do with you is up to them," he said.

My gaze darted frantically around, seeking escape routes but finding none; the wraiths were closing in from every direction. Too many of them.

Far, *far* too many.

"Or perhaps you can figure out a different plan?" Kaelen continued, his voice flat. "Go ahead: Tell them you have nothing to give, despite all the evidence to the contrary. Maybe they'll leave you in peace. Maybe you can continue on your way, ignoring the plight of my citizens."

I glared at him, my fury building. "You're out of your fucking mind."

"I've made my case and asked my favor." His eyes stared past me, focused on nothing in particular, like an executioner resigned to his duty. Whatever doubts he might have had about my sentencing, he lifted his hand and signaled for the carnage to continue.

The motion was chillingly casual.

The crowd of wraiths needed only this slight wave of Kaelen's hand to surge forward once more, into a blur of shadows and hunger and fading, flickering flames.

I immediately lost sight of Kaelen within the mayhem. I could do nothing except try to push my way through the swarm, fighting for breath, for balance, for some way out of the madness.

Occasionally, I managed to grab hold of one of the wraiths with my magic, shoving it aside and clearing a path. But for every one I threw back, three more converged, cutting off my path just as quickly.

Horrific memories of Lake Nyras flashed in my mind. I felt the weight of those ghostly shades pressing me underwater all over again—except these ghosts were much heavier, much more violent. Much more hungry.

And Aleksander wasn't here to save me this time.

A cold hand clawed into the wound on my shoulder. I screamed, and with it, more ribbons of darkness exploded outward—an automatic defense mechanism that only led to more of my shadows finding their way into the flames the wraiths carried.

One after the other, those flames burned brighter, hotter, higher.

My turquoise bracelet rattled again. I gripped the beads tightly, tucking my head toward my chest, trying to keep from vomiting in response to the pain radiating through my shoulder.

The swarm of starving dead around me swayed and

groaned, a sea of insatiable hunger. Until suddenly…it parted.

I found myself in the middle of two rows as their leader emerged once more, approaching me. The blue flame he carried was the brightest I'd seen yet. His eyes had already been more intelligent than most of the others; in the light of the fire, they were…different. Uncanny. His entire face was, really—slightly off and unsettling, as if he'd been revived but had yet to remember how to mold his features into proper human placements.

He watched intently as one of my wayward shadows fell into the nearest flame. And just as before, the fire grew as it devoured the dark ribbon, turning the fuel of my magic into a bolder, brighter light to live by.

As it burned, the wraith leader shouted another command.

His voice was like rocks scraping against glass, making me cringe. The words were foreign, but the meaning in his disturbingly-expressive face was clear…so terribly clear that I could almost feel the weight of it pressing down on my chest, making my heart stutter in fear—

Bleed her dry.

Chapter Twenty-Three

Aleksander

IT HAD BEEN NEARLY AN HOUR SINCE THE MOMENT IN THE loft, and Nova still had not returned from her alleged *tour* with Kaelen.

Not that I was counting the minutes.

But something didn't feel right.

"Why don't we just go look for her?" Zayn suggested. Again. And again, Rowen and Farren agreed with him.

Still, I didn't move.

"She's capable of taking care of herself," I said, my voice low so as to avoid waking Red, who had curled up against my side minutes ago and promptly fallen asleep. I had no idea why this child insisted on clinging to me, but it was the least of my concerns. At least she was being calm and quiet.

"We don't have any idea what the princess is *really* capable of, though, do we?" Rowen pointed out.

"I believe she's capable enough to deal with the likes of Kaelen, should he attempt anything," I replied.

And yet, I couldn't stop thinking of the moment last night, when I'd spotted her sinking below the dark water of Lake Nyras. The panic that had gripped me, and the...*fear*.

I'd actually been afraid.

Not an emotion I often experienced. Especially not for the sake of someone else.

But of course I was afraid to lose her; she was my shield against the deadly energies of this realm, *and* our potential ticket out of this hell. When I considered her usefulness to me, I had to admit that Zayn and the others had a point: She'd been gone too long. We were playing with fire, letting her out of our sight. What if she was off with Kaelen concocting some elaborate plan to leave us behind to fend for ourselves?

I was still weighing the pros and cons of tracking her down when Thalia stepped into the courtyard where we sat. Her expression was distracted. Her hands fiddled restlessly with the gems adorning her staff, and she startled as she drew near to us, as though she'd just noticed us sitting there.

"...Where is Nova?" she asked.

"The question of the hour, it seems," Zayn replied with a yawn. "But from what I've gathered, this dumbass made her mad—" he jerked his head toward me "—and she retaliated by running away with Kaelen so they could start a new life together that didn't involve arrogant kings and other annoying things."

"That's not exactly how it happened," I said dryly.

Thalia gripped her staff more tightly. "She's with Kaelen?"

"We assume," said Rowen.

The necromancer woman rarely showed any sort of strong emotion; I liked that about her, generally speaking. But it was frustrating to not be able to get a read on her now. What did she know about this Kaelen character that she wasn't telling us?

I decided to be blunt. "I overheard you arguing with him earlier. What was that about?"

She fixed her still-unreadable gaze on me, and simply said, "Nova."

The hairs on the back of my neck stood on end. "What about her?"

A pause, and then she averted her eyes as she finally said, "She's more than she seems. I had my suspicions about her, but nothing definite in my mind until I saw what the two of you did at Lake Nyras. And even now, there are still a lot of questions…"

"What do you mean by *suspicions*?" I asked. "And why haven't you mentioned anything about them before now?"

She didn't reply, instead returning to her task of assessing and adjusting her staff's gems.

Farren and Rowen tensed and sat up straighter, their fingers dancing over the hilts of their sheathed swords.

Zayn rose from the chair he'd been carelessly lounging in. He was still smiling as he stepped toward Thalia, as per usual, but this was the sharp, slightly feral smile that usually came before he pounced on an unsuspecting victim. "I think we've all had enough of your half-truths and evasive answers to things."

"I'm taking you to better answers," she insisted, leveling a glare on him. "But there were things I needed to arrange, first—and none of those things can be spoken of in any detail as long as we're here." She lifted her chin. "If it makes you feel any better, *that's* what Kaelen and I were arguing about as well—my *half-truths and evasive answers*. I wouldn't tell him everything he wanted to know. Which is why I'm sure he plans to keep Nova here as long as he can, to bleed what truths he can from her." She fixed me with a hard stare. "And you shouldn't have let her out of your sight."

"I am not her bodyguard," I growled, despite the uneasiness the words caused me.

I *wasn't* responsible for her.

But I couldn't deny the regret and concern settling heavily in my chest.

I shouldn't have let her go.

I stood, carefully slipping out of my coat and sliding it underneath Red's head to keep her from waking. Pacing the yard, I tried to come up with a rational next move. It had been a well-honed skill of mine, once upon a time—the ability to make plans in the face of any disruption or danger. But now…

I felt unbalanced.

Even when she wasn't close to me, her infuriating chaos persisted.

Farren started to offer up a plan, only to be interrupted by a low growl as Nova's ghostly dog rose to his feet. The beast sniffed the air, his body rippling with dark energy, the solid form underneath growing more and more fluid. The distress rolling off him was palpable. The heaviness in my chest grew worse as I watched him, wishing I shared Nova's ability to hear his thoughts.

He stayed in his dog-like form but grew larger, his chest rumbling with another restless growl. His pale eyes shifted in my direction, staring without blinking, as if trying to force whatever he needed to say directly into my mind.

"...Something's happened to her, hasn't it?"

He let out a low whine.

In the same moment, the flames in the torches along the manor's face began to flicker, to dance and fluctuate and eventually flare brighter.

Thalia stared at the flames, wincing at their brightness, her face finally betraying a hint of emotion—*fear*.

"What does that mean?" I demanded.

She took a deep breath, as though preparing to plunge into deep water. "It means go grab your things. Quickly. We need to find Nova and get away from this place. *Now*."

WHILE ROWEN and Farren collected our belongings and followed Thalia out of the city, Zayn and I made our way through the manor's grounds, scrambling to keep up with Phantom as he tracked his master down.

Thalia had taken Red with her, instructing us to meet them at the northern gate of the city. She'd given us hasty directions, an even more hastily-drawn map, and we'd parted ways before anybody could second-guess our escape plans.

The sky was the color of dark rust. The air smelled like the smoke wafting off the blue flames all around us, and it seemed to sizzle with something volatile. I pressed against a rough stone wall of the manor's dead gardens, watching shadows flicker and warp in the light of the shifting fires—

fires that were suddenly brighter, just as they had been in the courtyard.

"Is it just me," I began as Zayn caught up to me, "or does every damn day in this realm somehow end up worse than the last?"

"We've made our way through more dire things than this, surely," he said.

Ever the fucking optimist.

"Have we, though?"

"All this sneaking around actually reminds me a bit of home."

"How could it *possibly* make you think of home?"

"The countless times I snuck my way out of whatever boring duties they tried to saddle me with…this labyrinth around us reminds me a bit of the gardens in the Graystone District, even. Don't you recall any of our late-night escapades into the seedier sections of Solaryn?"

"You forget: I didn't accompany you on most of your clandestine adventures in the royal city."

"Ah, that's right—you were the grumpy, boring one who stayed home."

"I was the *responsible* one," I corrected, "with a hundred eyes on me at any given time. Your house was much easier to sneak out of."

"Well, that's true enough, I suppose."

"But I'm glad I could keep all the attention on me so you could live your life of debauchery to the fullest."

"Many thanks for that, by the way," he said, grinning.

"Don't mention it."

He continued to quietly reminiscence about the life he'd left behind. I only half-listened—just enough to distract myself from the fears trying to rise in me. It wasn't that I'd had no taste for questionable adventures and breaking rules back home; it had merely been impossible for me to partake without severe consequences—the reality of being the heir to a throne held by a king and queen not expected to live to see their only son grow into adulthood.

As far as anyone knew, my mother had perished in a riding accident, and my father had taken his life soon after. That was the story long ago decided upon, scripted, and eventually performed to perfection.

The truth was far more complicated. But, in short, they had been sick for a long time before their deaths. So I had been raised with the expectation that I would have to take over the rule of my kingdom at any time—and the Keepers of Light had been cruel, strict masters while preparing me for that inevitable rule.

Or what I'd *thought* was an inevitable rule, at least.

Clearly, plans had changed.

Phantom let out a sharp bark, urging us toward him. I gave my head a determined shake. None of our memories or plans would matter for much longer if we didn't find Nova and get the hell out of this place.

Her dog continued to lead the way. I followed closely, even as he radiated waves of cold, unsettling energy; I was getting more used to the chill of Nova's magic—and to her beast's magic by extension, I supposed.

I needed to keep close, too, because the farther we ventured through the dead gardens, the thicker the smoke in the air became. A strange fog was settling as well, making matters even worse. Every now and then, we'd catch a glimpse of blue among the smog—a flame flickering. Sometimes stationary. Other times, carried by wraiths careening wildly past us, racing recklessly toward some unknown target.

They all seemed to be converging in the same general direction we were traveling in, and soon, we stumbled upon an entire, organized line of them.

Phantom tore directly forward, the billowing, ghastly cold energy rushing out from him and causing a brief panic, creating an opening as the wraiths scattered.

And there, on the other side of their broken line, we finally spotted Nova.

She was eerily still, standing with her head bowed, shadows coiling and snapping around her body like living, protective snakes. Several limp wraiths were scattered across the ground at her feet. The ones who remained upright kept a wide berth, even as they calmed and fell back into a somewhat organized line. They watched her intently, hungrily, but didn't dare approach.

I didn't blame them.

I had no idea what Nova had done to the lifeless beings on the ground, but looking at her now…

My heart skipped several beats.

She was terrifyingly brilliant, her shadows sharp and shining with energy and casting her in an unearthly glow, making her look every bit like a goddess of chaos and death.

Except she was also…*bleeding*.

A reminder of her mortality pooled heavily beside her. Her sleeve was soaked in the same crimson dampness. And as I drew closer, I noticed her face was even more pale than usual; she was so obviously drained of energy that I had no idea how she was still managing to stand up.

A strange heat shot through my gut, incinerating the

fear I'd felt, leaving space for something far darker to rise up. Something far more violent. My gaze swept around the area, searching for the one who had done this to her.

Where was Kaelen?

Where the fuck was Kaelen?

"This doesn't look good," muttered Zayn, unnecessarily.

While he stared at the blood-soaked ground, I rushed forward—

Only to slow just out of Nova's reach, remembering the last time I'd charged at her while those solid shadows were snaking around her body. I wondered, briefly, if there was an even deeper hell than the one we currently stood in. If her shadows might send me crashing down into it if I made another wrong move.

But then she let out a small gasp—one laced with pain —and I no longer thought of the danger I might have been putting myself in. I raced forward without hesitation, placing my hands on her hips, steadying her.

Her shadows rattled with renewed awareness, and cold enveloped us both. Reflexively, I summoned light to my hands to counter the chill—just enough warmth to create balance.

She blinked. Lifted her head. Blinked again, trying to focus on my face. A flicker of recognition brightened her eyes after a brief struggle. Relief washed over her, the tension slipping from her shoulders…but without that tension, she didn't seem to be able to keep upright any longer, and her legs crumpled underneath her.

I caught her as she fell, doing my best to avoid the wound on her shoulder. It looked deep.

How much blood had she already lost?

Carefully, I picked her up. Her shadows shifted into less solid versions, easing away as if they somehow realized I meant her no harm. She was still blinking rapidly, drifting in and out of awareness, as she tilted her gaze toward mine. "You're here." Disbelief clung to the words. "You...you came for me. Again."

I gathered her more completely against my chest, my eyes still searching for Kaelen as I said, "Yes. We're stuck together, I'm afraid."

I glanced down just long enough to see the beginning of a wry smile twitching her lips. She faded again before it could fully take hold, burying her face against me. Shaking her and calling her name failed to wake her.

Muttering curses, I steadied myself under her weight and turned back toward the line of wraiths I'd crashed through a moment ago.

They were moving toward Nova without fear, now that her shadows had eased into less solid versions. They seemed *drawn* to those safer, wispier versions of her power, in fact.

A particularly large one shoved its way to the front, rushing to within mere feet of me before stopping. His lips parted, revealing a black abyss of a mouth that contorted gruesomely as he hissed, "*Give her back to us.*"

"No."

"*She belongs to us.*"

"The fuck she does."

His hiss was unintelligible, this time, as he lifted a small metal lantern toward me. A blue flame burned within, and I watched as it seemed to suck in the wisps of Nova's shadows and grow brighter with the effort.

So it wasn't merely blood loss; they were draining her of her magic, too.

Fury brought my hand forward. Jagged cracks of light glowed down my arm before lifting from my skin, gathering into a swift dagger of energy that knocked the lantern from the wraith's hand. He fell to the ground, chasing after it. I aimed another javelin of light into his back. The air crackled with a scent similar to rotting and burning flesh as he writhed about in pure, obvious agony.

It made little difference—several more simply appeared to take his place.

I shifted Nova's weight in my arms as I dodged clawing hands and knocked away more receptacles full of flames.

Phantom bounded to my side, a frigid burst of energy accompanying his approach, driving several of the wraiths backward.

I felt a surge of warmth behind me and twisted around to see Zayn stepping between me and another line of the approaching fiends. Light magic sparked around him, feeding off what I'd already summoned. He'd withdrawn his sword as well. As one of the wraiths charged, he swung, gathering light to the sword in the same motion. It sliced cleanly through the wraith's neck, severing its head and sending it flying.

"Still solid enough to lose their heads, as it turns out," he said to me, while flashing a taunting smile at the other wraiths, who were now hesitating. "I've been wanting to test that theory."

"Keep gathering evidence for that theory, why don't you?" I said, twisting to avoid an attempted sneak attack.

Zayn gave me a little bow, accepting the challenge in

one instant and spinning to slice his sword through my attacker's neck in the very next.

Phantom took up the challenge as well, slashing and ripping his way through the swarming wraiths for several minutes, trying to clear a path so I could carry Nova away from them. But it was hopeless; there were simply too many.

"We need a different plan," I growled, catching a wrist as yet another fist swung my way, and finishing my counter-attack with a burst of blinding Light magic that sent the wraith stumbling backward, shrieking as it went.

I wasn't certain Phantom could understand me the way he could understand Nova, but in the next moment, he was shifting his form.

When he finished, he resembled the beastly stallion Thalia rode—aside from his head, which was more dragon-shaped than equine-shaped. He snapped that head toward me, his gaze burning and expectant.

Understanding, I carried Nova toward him, hoisting her onto his back as he kneeled down.

She woke enough to clutch at the dark strands of his mane, but her grip was feeble, her balance still off; I had no choice but to swing up behind her to continue to steady her —a move that earned me a haughty snort from Phantom. He seemed to understand the necessity of it, though, and managed to refrain from tossing me to the ground.

I hesitated, glancing over my shoulder in search of my cousin.

Our eyes met through a haze of smoke and magic just as he finished beheading another wraith. He seemed to be enjoying himself entirely too much, given the circumstances.

"I'll catch up!" he assured me.

Before I could protest, Phantom's muscles coiled with power and he lunged forward, knocking several bodies aside as he went. It cleared a wide enough path for Zayn to follow, at least—though I worried he wouldn't be able to keep up.

We moved too fast for me to look back again, either way.

The city blurred around us. I kept one hand tightly woven into Phantom's mane, while my other arm circled Nova's waist. I tried to keep her from being jostled too much, though this was mostly in vain; every rough step or sharp turn drew whimpers of pain from her. The sound of them undid me in ways I wasn't prepared for—ways I wouldn't take the time to wonder about now.

Rowen and Farren met us at the northern gate, as planned. Rowen held the reins of Uldrin, Thalia's stallion. Red was clinging to the back of that massive beast, wide-eyed and trembling.

Despite myself, I exhaled a small sigh of relief to see her safe.

Nova seemed aware enough to keep her balance for a moment, so I slipped from Phantom's back and strode toward my soldiers.

"Where is Thalia?" I demanded.

"We're not sure," Farren informed me with an uncertain frown. "She disappeared shortly after bringing us here and speaking with the guards at the gate."

I sized up that gate, wondering how the hell we were going to get through it.

Not that I was leaving yet—not without my foolish cousin.

I was a moment away from racing back into the city to

find him when, finally, he appeared, racing down the street with his usual foolish, cocky grin on his face.

He wasn't alone.

No less than two dozen wraiths were chasing him. He was well ahead of them, but they were closing the distance at an alarming rate.

My hand gripped the hilt of my sword, but I didn't draw it out. How many more enemies would follow? We couldn't behead the entire city. We were outnumbered, with no time to keep up this aimless butchering.

Phantom was pacing restlessly, sizing up the gate as I had done, looking as if he was considering trying to jump over it.

He understood as well as I did: Nova needed treatment. She needed out of this city.

Jagged lines of light split across my skin once more, as if in response to this thinking. I still had no real plan, but I embraced my magic and the thoughts that had summoned it. Thoughts of healing her. Protecting her. The light expanded, the bolts of it crackling out toward the approaching mob of wraiths just as Zayn raced to relative safety behind me.

Before I realized what I was doing, I was following the path of those bolts, walking directly toward our enemies.

Though she remained barely conscious, Nova's shadows lifted and chased after me, the threads of her magic weaving around mine and giving it more weight. My steps, too, felt heavier, more purposeful.

I inhaled, breathing in the greater power building in the air all around me. But before I could wield a single scrap of that power, Thalia seemed to appear out of nowhere, grabbing my arm and roughly jerking me to a stop. "*Don't.*"

I shot her a furious look, but stayed my hand and my magic—for the moment. "What do you mean, *don't*?"

"If you two summon any sort of magic like you did on Lake Nyras's shore, it will draw the entire city down upon us. Every wraith in here will come to try and take it for themselves—you can't unleash something so powerful, something you have so little control of, within this desperate place. It will lead to pandemonium."

"Then what are we—"

She shoved me back toward Nova. "Just take her and run. I'll be right behind you, along with your soldiers. There's help waiting on the other side of this city."

"Help?"

"I told you: I've been arranging things."

Skepticism flooded through me, rooting me to the spot.

But then, what was our alternative?

I looked back to Nova. Her shadows were still drifting, circling around her with what seemed like a conscious anticipation; she was upright and balanced, yet her eyes were closed, her head bowed just as it had been when I'd found her earlier.

"I've already paid off the guards, too," Thalia urged, waving me toward Nova. "Go before they decide to cheat us out of our exit. Run straight for the gate and trust that it will open. *Now!*"

Zayn was already swinging himself into the saddle of Thalia's horse and securing Red in front of him.

Seeing no better options, I backed quickly toward Phantom and followed Zayn's lead, hoisting myself up and pulling Nova against me once more.

My pulse pounded against her back as I threw one last glance over my shoulder. It all felt…*unfinished*. Too many questions unanswered. Too much magic lingering in the air. Too many possibilities unmet. But my mind was made up; I had no intention of dying here.

The gates creaked open.

We raced through without hesitation, the city and its monsters howling at our backs, all its blue flames flickering desperately against the deepening night.

Chapter Twenty-Four

Aleksander

THERE'S HELP WAITING ON THE OTHER SIDE.

I repeated Thalia's words over and over to myself as we galloped into the darkness.

There's help waiting on the other side.

I didn't believe her.

I had never been one to believe in help from others, regardless of where it came from. I didn't expect it to find me in this realm, or in any other—I'd had such foolish notions beaten out of me at a young age. Accepting help was always a dangerous endeavor, anyway. It led to debts. And the rule of the Light King was meant to be *debt-free*, as the head of my council and the master of my studies, Lord Ithar, used to say.

We made it perhaps a mile before slowing and circling back toward Erebos, hoping to spot the rest of our party gaining on us. But no one was behind us, nor ahead of us, and the landscape was even more desolate and daunting on this side of the city.

If not for the fact that she'd given Zayn her horse, I would have been entirely convinced that Thalia had tricked us and had no intention of ever seeing us again.

"What now?" Zayn called from Uldrin's back, while struggling to keep the steed still.

I didn't know how to answer him. I wasn't sure what plans Thalia had for catching up with us, I just knew we couldn't leave Rowen and Farren solely in her hands—but we *also* couldn't effectively fight our way back to them, given our current cargo.

"Nova."

She mumbled something in response to my voice, but she didn't open her eyes.

Could I force her awake?

Should I?

No; it wasn't even a question, really. Fresh blood continued to seep from her shoulder, even now, despite my attempts to staunch its flow with my coat—I couldn't leave her to go back for the others.

"The chaos never fucking ends with you, does it?" I mumbled, partly in an attempt to get a rise out of her. I needed to hear her voice, even if it was simply her telling me to fuck off.

But before I could rouse her enough to speak, Zayn interrupted us by shouting my name.

"Company!" he informed me, pointing at a line of riders taking shape in the distance. The blue flames affixed to their horses' gear suggested wraiths.

Of course.

We could outrun them, perhaps, but it would mean

leaving the others behind indefinitely. The others who *also* had most of our supplies.

In the short time we spent debating, the wraith riders drew close enough to count, and I realized just how outnumbered we were.

From bad to worse, over and over and over.

"Seven years of surviving against the odds down here," Zayn said, pulling Uldrin up beside Phantom. "It was inevitable that death would eventually catch us in this place, I suppose."

"We must have set some sort of record for the amount of time we *did* last," I replied, matching his morbidly amused tone.

"What are the chances we could extend that record?"

I circled my gaze, seeking some miraculous key to victory that I might have missed, even though I knew I wouldn't find one. "Not good, I'd wager."

He joined me in my pointless searching.

Red was huddled against him—offering no comment, as expected—her face hidden from view by a thick riding blanket. I felt a stab of something like guilt, watching her shake beneath that blanket, thinking of how we'd brought her back to life, only for her to meet a gruesome end.

I was considering a last, desperate effort to somehow send her away with Nova and Phantom, when Zayn suddenly said, "Perhaps *they* can help us shatter our previous record?"

I blinked, following his gaze toward an astounding, unexpected sight: A herd of scourge stallions like Uldrin charging out of the darkness, rushing toward us.

There were no less than twenty of them. The ground shook underneath their pounding hooves, and the air rippled with a strange, quivering tension, as though the world itself was holding its breath at their approach. The soldiers who rode upon their backs were silent, dressed in leather armor that made them blend in with their surroundings. This made their true number difficult to count, as did the way they moved so astoundingly *fast*—so fast that they were galloping past us in no time at all, colliding with the wave of approaching wraiths.

I watched them moving up close for only a moment before I came to a startling realization: They were as alive as I was. *All* of them, however impossible that was. The blades they carried were solid and real, too, gleaming and swishing with weight and purpose through the air. Each of their swings tore into the wraiths with terrifying precision, hacking the creatures to pieces with brutal efficiency.

Phantom danced nervously at the edge of the battle. I urged him away from the worst of it, but stayed close enough to continue observing.

One of the newly-arrived riders soon stood out—the only one who didn't wear a helmet or any other protection over his head. His black hair flowed loosely as he twisted back and forth, twin blades flashing as he cut down enemy after enemy. He was the main one shouting directions at the other shadow-clad soldiers, and his horse's regalia suggested importance as well, from the silver-embroidered reins to the saddle cloth adorned with an emblem that featured a tree with dark red blossoms. That tree kept catching my gaze. It was hardly the time to worry about such things, yet something about it seemed strangely familiar.

As the carnage grew wilder and louder, Nova stirred against me, fighting to lift her head. Her eyes opened. She stared blankly for a long moment, and then a single word fell from her cracked lips: "*Stop.*"

"...What?"

"Tell them to stop."

"They—"

"It isn't a fair battle," she said, gritting her teeth as obvious waves of pain rocked through her. "The wraiths will fade outside their city, anyway, there's no need to *massacre* them like this."

"They're desperate for our magic," I told her. "They won't stop unless someone stops them."

"They're desperate because they want to *live*."

I couldn't deny it; I just didn't understand why she was making this argument, all of a sudden.

What had happened to her in that garden back in Erebos? What had she seen—what had she endured—before I reached her?

She averted her eyes as one of the soldiers severed a head and sent it flying dangerously close to us.

"It's not a crime to want to live," she whispered.

I didn't know what to say to this.

The quick *thwack* and wet, bloody squelch of metal cleaving its way through flesh reached us, followed by another *thump* of some sort of body part hitting the ground nearby. Nova grimaced, and a strange instinct to cover her ears—to protect her—overcame me, but I fought against it. I merely kept my arm around her, tightening my grip as her body shook against me.

A moment later, I realized…

She wasn't shaking with fear or disgust, but with *power*. Power that was soon taking on a tangible form—her shadows lashing into the air.

Before I could stop her, she somehow found the strength to pull away from me, leaping from Phantom's back and trudging headlong into the mayhem.

I sat in shock for an instant before sliding down to the ground myself. Even then, I hesitated, one hand braced against Phantom's side as I watched Nova and the magic building around her, still trying to understand why she wanted to protect these beings who had only just recently tried to devour her.

We could have been using this opportunity to run.

So what the fuck was she doing?

Phantom stomped his hooves anxiously, giving me a vicious nudge with his sharp snout, urging me after her.

I needed no real encouragement from him; in the next beat I was already running, picking my way carefully through slashing weapons and rearing horses, darting wildly to avoid falling bodies, all while fighting to not let Nova out of my sight.

The shadows whipped more frantically around her, drawing the eyes of every wraith she passed. She didn't seem to notice, or care, even as several peeled away from the soldiers they were battling and instead converged toward her.

I broke into a sprint.

Drawing my sword, I cut a path to her side, felling three wraiths along the way.

Nova turned as I reached her, still moving as if in a trance. Her brow furrowed. She clearly saw the other wraiths closing in on either side of us, but she didn't flinch as they pressed closer. She kept her eyes on mine and stepped to meet me, reaching out her hand.

I stared at it. At her. I still didn't know what this foolish woman was doing. This chaotic, infuriating, fucking beautiful, *foolish* woman.

She didn't speak, but I could hear her voice in my memory, whispering while we stood by the frigid waters of Nyras.

Trust me.

I had. Somehow, I had, and then we'd brought the world to life around us. It was hard to think of *life* at the moment, though. Hard to think beyond the suffocating fiends pressing in around us, choking away what little bit of light and air existed in this hell.

It felt ridiculous to think of life after all the death we'd witnessed today.

But I put away my sword.

And I reached back.

As our fingers brushed one another's, it happened again: The same rush of energy that had overtaken us at Lake Nyras. The same spark of power that felt unlike anything I'd ever known. All the background seemed to fade for a moment, the world condensing to the single point of touch between us.

From that point, a greater magic began to pulse.

Not fully Shadow magic, nor entirely Light, but a combination of both—a shimmering blanket of silvery-white power that rose up like a wave, rolling higher and wider before crashing down over everything around us, sweeping life and color over all that it touched.

The air hummed. The world rattled and shuddered, a deep tremor coursing under the ground. I felt every movement in my bones, as if some primal part of me was now irreversibly connected to the earth.

I felt the moment our magic approached its limits, too

—like a bowstring drawing back as far as it could go before it snapped with a sudden *crack!* that reverberated through the ether, ripping Nova's hand from mine and sending us both staggering backward.

I immediately started to race toward her again, but stopped in my tracks as I realized…it was done. The spell was already finished. There was little else left to do but stare and try to make sense of the aftermath. To try and catch my breath and find my footing underneath the exhaustion settling like a leaden weight upon my shoulders.

As I was beginning to expect, we'd left a scene of vibrant growth all around us—swaying grass, shimmering flowers and shining, fluttering insects.

But far more interesting, this time, was what had become of the army of wraiths.

The dead did not stir from where they'd fallen. But the ones who still stood were changing, just as Red had changed that night at Nyras; color returning to their complexions; emotions filling their eyes; their edges growing sharper, more defined.

Astonished whispers filled the air, soon followed by sobs and laughter.

The closest noise to me—a combination of sobbing and laughing—came from a woman who was crawling across the ground, blood trailing down her arm. It was dried, and mostly black, as I'd noticed wraith blood tended to be. She'd been wounded, but had stayed in one piece, and now…she was alive.

Alive.

I staggered toward her despite my dizziness, helping her stand, mainly so I could look more closely into her face and confirm what still seemed impossible. The flush of her cheeks. The feel of her breath. The blood on her arm, which was now turning to a brighter, more *alive* shade of crimson. She looked thrilled about that fresher, brighter blood. As the trail of it oozed against my steadying hand, I abruptly let her go and stumbled back.

Turning around, I spotted Nova again. She was kneeling among several more of the newly-revived. Her body was visibly heavy with exhaustion, but her eyes were alert as she surveyed the scene.

The black-haired man who'd caught my attention earlier strode into my peripheral vision, studying the scene as well. His calm voice filled the air a moment later, somehow perfectly clear even over the astonished chatter building around us.

"Secure her before she does irreversible damage to herself," he said. "And let's get away from here before we draw more attention."

It took a moment for his words to register. For my eyes to focus enough to realize what was happening—to see the people moving toward Nova, preparing to grab her. Without another thought, I was drawing my sword, ready to cut them down as swiftly as I'd cut down the wraiths minutes ago.

But just as she had at the city gates, Thalia seemed to materialize from nowhere just in time to step into my path and cut me off.

"Let them be," she urged. "They won't hurt her. Watch and see."

I was inclined, once again, to not believe her. Not until she pointed, drawing my attention to what was now happening around the rest of the crowd.

All of the fighting had ceased. The revitalized wraiths

and the soldiers, alike…all of them had gone perfectly still, and they were all watching Nova as two men helped her to her feet and held her upright.

She drew her shoulders back, her eyes straining, fighting for awareness. Fighting to take in the face of every person now looking in her direction.

And as she stared at them, they all bowed before her.

Chapter Twenty-Five

Nova

I woke to the sound of birdsong outside my window and warm sunlight washing over my face. The scent of honey and woodsmoke tickled my nose. My body was cocooned in soft blankets, and my clothing was equally soft, a flowing tunic and trousers that were pure luxury against my skin—and they felt *clean*.

No more blood.

My eyes remained tightly shut. Because for a moment, I wanted to believe I was home. This warmth, this cleanliness…it was all real. Orin was just downstairs, preparing me a cup of tea. I had never truly left the safety of our home. The nightmare wasn't real—it never had been.

And now, it was over.

I could wake up.

I could go *home*.

Minutes passed in this fantasy before I forced myself to open my eyes and stare at an unfamiliar ceiling. Tears streaked silently down my face as I tried to collect myself, to gather the courage to face whatever awaited me next.

Slowly, I sat up, my muscles protesting every inch of movement, aching as though I'd spent an entire winter in hibernation.

After several blinks to shed the last of my tears—and to further adjust to the unexpected brightness—I noticed that Aleksander was asleep on the other side of the room, stretched out on a cushioned bench in front of a large window that was covered by heavy curtains. It didn't look nearly as comfortable as the bed I was resting upon, but he had blankets and pillows piled around him to help make up the difference; so wherever we had ended up after this latest misadventure of ours, at least it was cozy.

I rose shakily to my feet, trying to grasp at more scraps of my shredded optimism. The space was more than cozy; it was beautiful. Teeming with so much light and energy that, even now that I was fully awake, I could still pretend I was back home—or somewhere in the living world, at least.

My gaze drifted back to Aleksander.

Was it our combined magic that had created this place?

With my eyes on him, I didn't see the shaggy throw rug until it was too late; I stumbled over it, sucking in a sharp breath as pain radiated from my jostled, injured shoulder.

"Still smarts, huh?"

I twisted toward the gentle, unfamiliar voice—wincing as the movement caused *more* pain—and I found a squat little woman watching me from the doorway. Her hair looked brittle and white with age, but her face didn't appear much older than mine. Her dark blue eyes were kind—another unexpected sight after days of darkness and desperate battles for survival.

What *was* this place?

Was I even still in the Underworld?

"We have things that will help with the pain," the woman said, stepping inside, "but I wanted you conscious before I administered any of it." She looked me over from head to toe, as though trying to decide if I truly *was* conscious.

I wasn't entirely sure myself; this room was so bright and warm that I still felt like I was in a strange fever dream.

I looked closer at the different parts of it, trying to ground myself further in the details.

Beside the bed, a nightstand carved from dark mahogany held a crystal goblet filled with fresh wildflowers. A small chandelier hung from the ceiling, its crystals sparkling, catching the sunlight slipping through the curtains and casting intricate patterns on the walls. The walls themselves were covered in silk paper in a soft, pretty shade of green. There was at least one bookshelf against each of these walls, each bursting with leather-bound tomes. In the far corner, a fireplace of shining marble reached up to the ceiling, the centerpiece of its mantle a metal shield featuring a tree with red blooms, intricate filigree around its border, and a word I couldn't decipher curving across the bottom.

So many emblems of royalty and wealth…

All of which only served to disorient me further.

As I studied it all, a thought popped into my head before I could stop it: This scene could have been from another version of my life, if only my path had veered differently. A palace filled with light and splendor, and me waking up to the sight of Aleksander sleeping nearby…

I was staring at him again, I realized, when the white-haired woman let out the sort of soft *hmm* my mother used to make when she wanted to pry, but manners dictated silence.

I swallowed hard, redirecting my thoughts and keeping my voice businesslike as I asked, "He's injured?"

"Exhaustion, mostly. We tried to take him to a room of his own to rest, but he refused." She picked innocently at the wide sleeves of her colorfully embroidered tunic, peering at me from under her lashes as she said, "Hasn't left your side since you arrived—I think he's convinced we're going to steal you away from him for good if he leaves us alone with you."

I again forced down the complicated feelings I had toward the King of Light as I asked, "How long have I been asleep?"

She shrugged, as though time meant little to her. "Two days, give or take."

I walked to the window on the other side of the room, peering through the partially-drawn curtains and into an outside world as lush and beautiful as the room I stood in. I was on the second floor, and the grass spreading out below was thick, rolling in a gentle breeze. The branches and leaves of flowering trees swayed in that same breeze, creating a swirling rain of white and pink petals.

The sky above it all was a pale, powdery blue, and there appeared to be an actual *sun* hanging in it—perhaps the most disorienting thing I'd seen yet.

"What is this place?" I asked, glancing back at the woman. "Are we still in the Underworld?"

"Oh, Love." She fixed me with a look that was part pity, part concern. "I don't think I'm the one to answer that for you—or to answer *any* of the many questions I'm sure you have." She hesitated before taking a step closer. For a moment, she looked as if she wanted to wrap her arms around me and not let go.

Instead, she clasped her hands together in front of her, anxiously rubbing and continuously readjusting her grip as she said, "But there *are* answers here, if you have the courage to go looking for them."

The strange words rendered me speechless for a long moment.

"Rest up some more if you need to, first," she added, forcing her hands to her sides and a kind smile back to her face. "I'll send food and bring back something for the pain after you've eaten. And my name is Aveline, by the way."

She was gone before I could find my voice.

I stared after her, thinking over all she'd said.

Courage.

It would be a while before I finished gathering that, I feared.

In the meantime, I wandered closer to Aleksander. He looked utterly spent, as Aveline had suggested; he hadn't stirred an inch during my entire conversation with her.

There was an empty vial on the small table beside the window seat. Something he'd taken to help him sleep? He was shirtless, his arms and a section of his abdomen wrapped in bandages. Minor injuries, from the looks of it— but none of this was what caught my eye.

It was the evidence of past injuries that had me drawing toward him for a better look.

There were faded scars covering his chest, shining faintly in the muted light passing through the curtains. I couldn't tell what had made them, but it had been something wicked and wielded by a purposeful hand, judging by the precise pattern and the depth of each mark. I carefully felt my way around to his back, and my fingers quickly found evidence of more scars between his shoulder blades. These felt deeper, and perhaps more erratic than the ones on his chest. Perhaps more...*violent.*

Who had done this?

And why?

A rush of anger and sadness washed over me, leaving me feeling unbearably heavy. I settled down beside him, trying to focus on his face instead of his scars.

He looked so different while he was sleeping soundly like this, his features relaxed, free of their usual tension. His dimples were more prominent, for one thing—a feature I'd rarely gotten to witness during this latest reunion of ours, as he'd spent so much of the last few days scowling at me, or otherwise disapproving of the *chaos* I'd brought him.

Sighing, I tentatively pressed the back of my hand against his cheek. When he didn't wake, my touch trailed higher, my fingers weaving through the pale waves of his hair.

His head shifted, rolling from the pillow onto my leg. He started to raise up. I held my breath, but he was merely repositioning himself; his head quickly settled back into my lap, and he returned to the peaceful breathing and soft unawareness of before.

My heart thundered at the more intimate position, but I managed to keep still, even as the reality of the situation—of how far off track my plans had veered—hit me like a punch to the gut.

A week ago, I would have given anything to introduce my dagger to the head currently resting in my lap.

Now, I was scarcely breathing, afraid of causing any movement or discomfort that might interrupt his rest.

After a few minutes of sitting there, studying him, I realized something odd: Despite the powerful surge of my emotions coupled with his nearness, our magic wasn't rising at all.

I still sensed it moving inside me when I focused on it, but it was strangely calm, with none of the desperate reaching and fighting for balance that I'd come to expect. Maybe because everything about this moment already felt balanced—and again, like I'd somehow stumbled into a life I'd anticipated living before my world had broken apart all those years ago.

But…no. This was not normal. And they were not real, these feelings stirring in my chest. We were not married, as we might have been, and we were not at home in his kingdom. We were in Hell, and we had the fresh scars to prove the things we'd been through, however bright our current surroundings might have been.

I heard a familiar, distant bark, and I barely kept myself from jumping at the sound.

Carefully, I slipped out from under Aleksander, tucking pillows under his head and pulling a blanket up over him before leaving him to his rest.

Crossing to the opposite window and peering out of it once more, I spotted Phantom and Red racing through the yard. They were tumbling through the abundance of petals, Red occasionally stopping to gather them and toss them up for Phantom to catch.

Relief warmed my chest, seeing the two of them safe.

But where was I supposed to lead them from here?

I had to figure out where we were, and what came next—and I couldn't do that while sitting in this room.

With or without courage, I had to keep moving.

With slightly trembling hands, I washed my face with the bowl of rose-scented water that had been left on the vanity in the corner of the room. I braided the front of my hair and pulled it back, securing it in its familiar half-updo that made me feel more like myself—which seemed silly, but also important in this peculiar, unpredictable place.

After finding my boots tucked away behind a changing screen, I yanked them on, along with a luxurious coat I discovered hanging nearby, and then I cautiously slipped into the expansive hall outside.

The brightness and beauty of my dreamlike room persisted into this new space. This was a proper palace—that much was made more and more evident by the minute, thanks to the tall windows and soaring ceilings; the shining, pearlescent grey floors; the countless works of art lining the walls; and the halls that seemed to go on for miles.

And it was a *functioning* palace, at that. There were actual, living people scurrying about in most of the rooms I passed.

They avoided me. Or, failing that, they let out a panicked gasp and gave a deep bow before scrambling away. More than once, I looked back to see heads peeking out from around doorways and corners, trying to catch a glimpse after I'd safely passed.

I couldn't make sense of this, either, so I stayed focused on my goal of reaching my destination, heading in what I believed to be the general direction of the petal-strewn courtyard I'd seen.

Eventually, I heard a few more barks that allowed me to pinpoint my target.

Phantom's ears perked up as soon as I stepped outside, and he immediately abandoned whatever game he and Red had been playing so he could dash to my side.

(*You slept an awfully long time,*) he informed me.

I smiled down at him, scratching between his ears. "Almost dying is exhausting, it turns out. You of all beings should know that."

He let out a soft whimper, nuzzling his head against my leg, his tail swishing slowly through the grass.

"But I'm fine, now. Really." It was a lie, of course, but one I told often enough that I didn't stutter as I delivered the line.

Phantom let out another soft, knowing whimper, but I settled him with a few more intense ear and chin scratches, even dropping to my knees so I could rake my fingers more thoroughly through his cold fur. It was a level of affection he didn't always tolerate, but he was reveling in it, now—proof of how worried he'd been, even if he wouldn't admit it.

Red watched from a distance. I smiled at her, and she gave me a shy little wave before plopping down in a pile of fallen petals. She hummed softly to herself as she sorted those petals into lighter and darker heaps, then proceeded to demolish those heaps, laughing as she swept her hands through them.

Phantom's ears twitched and his tail thumped as he glanced over his shoulder, watching the petals rise and fall.

"Go on," I encouraged.

As he streaked toward her, snapping at the drifting flower bits, I slowly rose back to my feet, hugging my arms around myself. My smile remained despite a nagging sense of...*something* building in the back of my mind.

The whole scene was like something from a dream I'd once had. Not the feverish fantasy of earlier, but something that stirred a hazy sense of familiarity in my heart. Maybe it was simply the warm air, or the sunlight filtering through the swaying trees, reminding me again of the home I'd left behind.

I was strolling around the yard, absently taking it all in, when the truth finally struck me.

This was the same courtyard I'd seen in my vision, back when I'd first touched Red—*that's* why it felt familiar.

I froze, a mixture of shock and yet more confusion icing my blood.

"Bellanova, isn't it?" came a sudden voice.

I tilted my head to see a man approaching me.

His hair was similar to my own, both in its raven-wing shade and in the unruliness of the waves, though his waves stopped just past his chin. His grey eyes were serious as they fixed upon me, his lips drawn into an even line—but both looked as though they could, and often did, easily give way to laughter.

I vaguely remembered seeing his tall figure on the fields outside of Erebos before I'd collapsed from pain and exhaustion—though most of what had happened on that battlefield remained a blur to me.

"It's just Nova," I corrected, barely managing to stammer the words out as my thoughts raced with my latest realization.

Before we could say much more, Red caught sight of the man and raced toward him, spinning cartwheels and skipping as she came. It was the most animated I'd ever seen her, and she showed no fear toward this man as he opened his arms to her, allowing her to leap into them.

To my surprise, Phantom didn't show any discomfort toward the man, either; he watched us intently, but continued to lounge beneath one of the trees on the bed of flowers Red had made for him.

The man embraced Red for a moment before setting her back down, kneeling so they were face-to-face. He spoke to her in a foreign language, but I didn't need to decipher the words to understand that he'd asked her to return to her games while the grown-ups spoke in private.

"You know her," I said as she raced away.

He kept his eyes on her as he said, "She lived here, once upon a time."

"Before she ended up in the dead areas outside of this place?"

He nodded.

"But how could she *live* here? I don't understand what *here* is, and I've not been able to get her to speak about any of it, besides."

"That doesn't surprise me; she stopped speaking well before she ran away into the Deadlands." He looked to the sky, thinking. "Precisely two weeks after her mother died, as I recall."

"Her mother lived in this palace, too?"

"She was a dear friend of my own mother."

Something about the way his gaze flickered toward me when he mentioned his mother, only to quickly return to watching Red... I couldn't explain it, but it made me uneasy.

I studied him closer, trying to make sense of him. His features were a strange mixture of powerful yet gentle. A calm, quiet strength seemed to radiate from every move he made. He wore a plain but finely-tailored shirt, the sleeves of it rolled up to his elbows, and…

And there were strange, gnarled dark scars running up the centers of both his arms, disappearing underneath his clothing.

A cold sweat washed over me, along with more confusion. More questions. More potential realizations.

Softly, I asked, "Who are you?"

He finally looked at me, but he didn't answer the question.

I took several steps back, even though I wasn't entirely sure why. This man didn't *feel* threatening. Phantom still had not stirred, either, which was usually a reliable sign that there was no immediate danger.

Yet it still took everything in my power not to run away.

"Nova…" He gestured to a nearby bench. "I think maybe you should sit down."

"I don't want to sit down. I want you to tell me what this place is, and why it's so different from everything around it."

"Because it's protected."

"Like Erebos?"

"With far stronger magic than that city, or any of the others throughout Rivenholt."

"Rivenholt?"

"That's the name of this kingdom."

"Kingdom?" I realized I was doing nothing except stupidly repeating everything he said in a breathless tone, and I tried—desperately tried—to figure out something more intelligent to say. "The world of the dead doesn't have kingdoms; I've never heard of such a thing."

I had researched this realm for years before descending into it, after all. I had planned it all out so rigorously. I'd mapped it out in painstaking detail. I'd known what to expect...

And it all turned out to be completely different, whispered a small voice in the back of my mind.

I stared at the ground, suddenly unable to deny all the strangeness—the *wrongness*—I'd encountered any longer. There was no making sense of it all within the framework I *wanted* it to make sense within.

So I had no choice but to keep silent as he said, "This is not the world of the dead."

I shook my head, but he didn't stop talking.

"This palace was once the center of a thriving, *living* empire," he said, "one that lived in peaceful tandem with the empires of the Above. And the beings you've encountered over the past days are not dead. They're cursed. A curse our mother hoped we might someday break, which is why we were sent to the Above over twenty-five years ago."

I forced myself to lift my gaze to his.

He smiled sadly at me, his eyes shining with an emotion that was impossible to name. "Welcome back to your true world, Nova."

Chapter Twenty-Six

Nova

IT FELT AS IF THE GROUND BENEATH ME HAD VANISHED AND I was falling, tumbling, careening through nothingness.

I might have fallen forever if not for the steady hand that gripped my shoulder. Slowly, my gaze traveled upward, over the odd scar that split through the inside of his arm—a charred black line of rough, ruined skin. The scar on the opposite arm was identical. I couldn't see his abdomen, but I wondered...did he have a mark splitting up the center of it, too?

These were the sort of scars that had destroyed my brother's skin, according to the ones who had found him dead in his crib over twenty-four years ago.

Ripped apart by his own magic, they'd claimed.

I choked on a breath.

None of this made sense.

Those scars should have been smaller. More faded with time. And yet...the longer I stared at them, the more convinced I became that they *had* been left behind by magic, whether it had torn through him twenty-four years ago or otherwise. The gnarled twists of black clearly weren't normal. I could sense something brooding beneath the surface of them, too—the energy of something far more powerful than any common blade or other weapon.

"Sit down," the man suggested again, nodding toward the nearby bench.

I listened, this time, just barely making it to that bench before my knees gave out completely.

He hesitated a moment before sitting down beside me. We were silent for a long moment. I clenched my hands together in front of me to keep them from shaking.

"Who are you?" I asked, again, my voice cracking.

"My name is Bastian."

I gripped my hands more tightly together. "No, it isn't. It *can't* be."

I could feel him watching me closely, but I kept my eyes straight ahead, fixed on Phantom. The dog was still staring at us with interest, his ears fully perked and his head occasionally tilting, silently questioning if I needed him.

"Bastian is *dead*," I whispered. "He died when we were just infants."

"...I didn't die that night," he said, after a long pause. "Though I came close, I'm told. Our adoptive parents and Orin ended up sending me back here, in hopes that the magic around this palace would help bring me to full health once more. Somewhat ironically, since they'd originally sent us to the Above to *protect* us from being overwhelmed by the very same magic."

Orin.

The name was a lifeline, something familiar to grab

hold of, tossed out into the sea of impossible revelations raging around me. And yet…now I felt as if the truth of my beloved mentor was in danger of slipping through my fingers, too.

Though I was afraid of his answer, I asked, "You knew Orin, as well?"

"Only by name, really. I was too young to remember the journeys he apparently escorted me on. He hasn't been back here in nearly twenty-four years; it isn't easy to cross between the realms, as I'm sure you're aware."

"So he knew the truth about what happened to you…"

"Yes."

I squeezed my hands so tightly together I'm surprised I didn't snap any bones. "No," I said. "*No*. You're *lying*. He wouldn't have kept such an enormous secret from me."

His voice was astoundingly level—especially compared to mine—as he said, "I imagine he kept a *lot* of things from you, in hopes of keeping you safe for as long as possible, and keeping you away from this realm until you were ready to come home to it."

"This isn't my home," I said, getting back to my feet.

Bastian stayed on the bench. "But it's where you were born. Where we *both* were born into royalty. And you came into this world with the mark of the Vaelora in your palm… the last hope of this lost world that's been decaying for centuries now."

"The Vaelora…" I tried my hardest to match his even tone. "What are you even *talking* about?"

He pinched the bridge of his nose, massaging away some of the distress beginning to creep into his expression. I couldn't help noticing how much that nose looked like mine. Narrow, gently sloped, a smattering of faint freckles across the bridge...

"It's hard to imagine how thoroughly the truth has been scrubbed from the world above," he said. "But it's a plot centuries in the making, so...it makes sense that you wouldn't be aware of any of it, I guess."

"*What has been a plot centuries in the making*? Give me the plain truth, or I swear—this conversation is *over*." I looked to the door of the palace, thinking of running back inside, either way.

I didn't move, in the end, mainly because Phantom chose that moment to trot to my side and lean against it, nudging his head under my hand, urging pets. The solid weight of him held me in place as it had so many times in the past.

(*Do you want me to bite his legs off?*)

I numbly shook my head, but gave him a few extra ear scratches for the offer.

Red was dozing under a tree in the distance. I watched the tree's flowers shaking loose above her, swirling down in the arms of the strange, warm wind that seemed a constant in this yard. It was tempting to follow each drifting petal, to let my mind drift with them and escape my current reality.

The man who claimed to be my brother took a deep breath and said, "This is how it used to be, for several millennia: Two worlds. One in the above, one here in the below. Soltaris and Noctaris, respectively—both of them fueled by the magic of the *Aetherstone* that rests between them. In the beginning, they existed in tandem, the Stone granting life and power to both. But over time, its magic failed to the point that only one world could be sustained. Bitter and bloody wars were fought over which world would live and which would die, until finally, the two most powerful magic users from each side stepped forward and made a deal."

"A deal?"

He stood, moving closer to me, his gaze lifting toward the sky. The clear, perfectly calm, perfectly blue sky. It still sent a shiver down my spine to look at it. To think of how *alive* it looked—how all of this realm had supposedly looked, once upon a time.

"Yes, a deal," Bastian said. "One that involved a ritualistic, periodic shifting of the Aetherstone's magic, so that it concentrated on one world for a set period of time before shifting to the other. In every generation, a being known as a Vaelora was born within each world, and eventually, they were destined to meet and wield their powers together to turn the stone. *Aequinoctium*—or Equinox Day—it was called, when this turning took place."

"I've never heard of *any* of those things."

He lowered his gaze to mine, his voice turning solemn as he said, "Yes, because at some point in the past, the agreement was broken. The Stone didn't turn toward Noctaris when it should have, and the Light Keepers and their minions have been working for centuries to *keep* the magic shining over their world, alone, and to scrub the Above of all knowledge of this world that lies below it. It's a…complicated story."

"It seems like an impossible story," I said, frowning. "Especially considering there's no knowledge of it that I can recall. I was well-read enough as a child and beyond—surely, I would have come across *something* about all of this in my twenty-five years."

He mirrored my frown. "You'd be surprised how

quickly knowledge can erode when the wrong people manage to put themselves in charge."

I bit my lip, unable to bring myself to speak. My thoughts were racing too quickly to settle on words.

The Light Keepers...

Those were the dangerously powerful beings who essentially ran Aleksander's kingdom. So did he know about any of this history? Again, it seemed impossible that they could have hidden the truth so thoroughly...

But they'd put an imposter on his throne, and he claimed he hadn't seen that coming, either. So, maybe it wasn't improbable that he was oblivious to whatever grander schemes those Keepers were concocting.

"It's a lot to take in, I understand," said Bastian, gently. "But you were always meant to come back here. You were a princess here before you were adopted by the King and Queen of Eldris—two rare, Above-world allies to our cause. Your true crown has been kept safe, deep inside this palace, ever since you left."

I was staring at his nose again. And then his eyes—they had the same deep-set look as mine. His high cheekbones, his bow-shaped lips, the particular way of tilting his head and arching his brows. Such silly, small things we had in common. And yet...

"You really are...*him*, aren't you?"

He gave me another sad smile. A slow, yet certain nod. The weight of all our lost years seemed to settle between us, crushing down all the things I wanted to say. It seemed unfair to be forced to make sense of him—of *us*—and all our broken pieces while *also* facing the earth-shattering revelations he'd just dropped at my feet. If all he was telling me was true...

Where was I supposed to start when it came to making sense of it all?

He rolled some of the tense weight from his shoulders. He seemed to be bracing himself, as though he'd only just skimmed the surface and he was preparing to dive deeper.

I couldn't bear the thought.

"I have to go."

"Nova, wait just a moment—"

I didn't wait. I *couldn't* wait. The gravity of the situation hit me, all at once, and I wanted to crumble underneath it —but I also didn't want an audience for that particular breakdown. I called Phantom to my heel and headed inside.

But as soon as we stepped through the massive wooden door, we found ourselves facing another obstacle: Thalia.

Phantom bristled at the sight of her, a low, uncertain growl escaping him.

She darted a gaze toward the dog, but ultimately seemed unbothered by him. "You're finally awake," she said, her eyes sweeping over me, assessing. "That's a relief."

She *did* look relieved, but I wasn't in the mood for niceties. My confusion was swiftly turning to anger that made my voice sharp. "Why did you bring me here?"

She seemed taken aback by my tone, but recovered quickly. "Because you asked me to bring you to Luminor."

Luminor. Of course—the whole reason I'd descended into this dark world to begin with. With everything else that had happened, it had slipped my mind.

I gave her a skeptical look. "…It's here?"

She nodded curtly.

It wasn't enough to assuage my anger. "So you truly did

know where it was, but you *also* knew the truth about this realm all along."

She didn't deny it. I hadn't expected her to; I was getting used to her unapologetic attitude.

"Why didn't you tell me?" I demanded.

She lifted her chin. "I had to make certain you weren't working for the Keepers of Light. You *or* your companions. Those Keepers of the Above believe this world is entirely dead—and it's imperative that they *continue* believing that, if we want to keep it safe long enough to carry out our plan to save it. A plan that we fully intended to involve you in, once you proved yourself trustworthy."

"What kind of plan?"

She didn't seem prepared to elaborate just yet, which did nothing to quell my irritation. Our silent standoff lasted long enough to allow my brother time to catch up.

"What *plan* do you have to save this world?" I asked, again, alternating my glare between the two of them.

Thalia folded her arms across her chest, and her expression darkened and closed down, as though she wasn't entirely convinced I was trustworthy, even now.

Bastian laid a hand on her arm. I was surprised when she didn't shrug it off; his relentless calm seemed to soothe even her prickly nature.

"There are several parts to that plan," he told me. "And now that you're here, you and your magic can help—"

"My magic is dangerously unpredictable."

"Maybe. But we've seen what you can do. What you did for the wraiths outside of Erebos. And even before that, Thalia tells me."

"I didn't do any of it alone. My magic—my *unpredictable*

magic—is affected by Aleksander's, and we still don't truly understand the nature of how it all combines."

"...So I've heard." His expression remained soft, but there was an undercurrent of urgency that made my own pulse race faster in response. "Nevertheless, you clearly carry the mark of the Vaelora, and the magic that comes with that. Magic that could be enough to turn the Aetherstone's life-giving power in our world's favor. Maybe with the Light King's help, maybe not; there are things we need to work out, certainly. A lot of questions that still need answering."

I took a deep breath, shaking my head. "Why do you need *me* for whatever your plan is? You have magic, too, don't you?"

"Yes, but it's nowhere near as strong as yours. I don't carry the Vaelora's mark. The only reason it's as strong as it is, the palace scholars believe, is because I once shared a womb with you and absorbed some things. I've done what I could with what I had, helping to build up the protections and wardings of cities like Erebos. But I'm not the one who *created* any of those things. I've never managed to truly bring life back to this world, either, or..." He trailed off, a shadow crossing his features.

Silence settled. They both stared at me like they'd truly been waiting a lifetime for something—an answer, a sign—and here I was. Even Thalia's usual hard features eventually softened, a flicker of something like hope in her eyes.

I could only shake my head again, my heart pounding with a mixture of disbelief and fear. "You've made a mistake. I'm not the savior you think I am."

I started to back away. Thalia moved as if to stop me, but Bastian caught her arm again, his grip firm yet gentle.

She shot him a sharp look, something unreadable passing between them. Her jaw clenched, and for the first time since I'd known her, I saw a flicker of something like uncertainty in her pale purple eyes.

Her mouth opened as if to argue, but Bastian spoke before she could, his voice low but full of a king-like authority: "Let her go."

What he said beyond that, I didn't hear.

Because I was already walking away.

Chapter Twenty-Seven

Nova

EVEN MORE EYES FOLLOWED ME AS I MADE MY WAY through the palace this time.

Still, no one spoke to me or approached me. Oddly enough, it felt like I was back in Rose Point as a child, merely existing in a world of splendor and intrigue, surrounded by endless chatter, fascinating lives, and unfolding stories...yet somehow entirely set apart from it all.

Phantom followed closely at my side, but even he eventually abandoned me—distracted, as he so often was, by the scent of food. He was gone the instant I took my eyes off him, darting into what appeared to be a pantry of some kind. Just before the swinging doors settled shut behind him, I caught a glimpse of several servants frozen from a combination of fear and curiosity at his approach.

My stomach growled, urging me to follow him. But my heart resisted; it didn't want to be forced into awkward small talk with any of these palace dwellers who were working so hard to avoid me.

Instead, I carried on alone—the way I was used to doing—and eventually flung open the door to the room I'd woken up in earlier, slamming it shut behind me. I was so caught up in trying to escape everyone outside that I forgot, for a moment, who was waiting for me *inside*.

Aleksander was awake and shrugging into a clean shirt when I turned away from locking the door. He eyed me curiously, but otherwise continued to button up the shirt—as if it was a common thing between us, this coming and going into the same space. Like we shared a room all the time.

I kept my head up and tried to pretend everything else was normal, too, ignoring the way my insides felt like they were unraveling, twisting and turning and trying to put themselves back together in a way that felt right.

I wasn't sure anything would ever feel *right* again.

Nevertheless, on the outside I smiled my usual optimistic greeting, hoping it would be enough to fool him until I was alone again and I could crumble in peace.

We had clearly been spending too much time together, though, because he glanced up at me while rolling up his sleeves and asked, "What's wrong?"

I ignored the question, making my way over to a silver tray centered on a desk, piled high with the food Aveline had promised earlier. Rich, delicious-looking food—bright fruits, thinly-sliced meats, buttery bread and some sort of spice-sprinkled spread to go with it. I wasn't sure I could truly stomach any of it at the moment, but I pretended to be deciding on a feast for myself so I could avoid answering Aleksander as he stepped closer.

"Nova?"

I picked up a bright red berry and proceeded to study it, counting every seed visible in its shiny skin. "Nothing is wrong."

"Liar."

I breathed in deeply through my nose.

A corner of his mouth inched upward. "And here I thought raising the dead together would have brought us close enough to share a secret or two."

I tried to mirror his smirk with the same confidence he carried, but my attempt fell flat.

He watched me expectantly for a moment, but when I didn't answer, he focused his attention on the platter of food as well. Seeing an opportunity to distract him, I quickly handed him a plate and insisted he eat something.

He accepted the plate and carefully, neatly filled it, but didn't take a single bite of anything he'd grabbed.

It was a habit of his, I'd noticed—being more concerned with putting his food into perfectly neat, even piles than with anything else. He never ate all that was before him, was slow to eat what he did, and he had a tendency to silently re-count and size it all up after he swallowed down each bite—like he was preparing to ration and hoard it. It seemed like a strange mannerism for a prince who had undoubtedly had more food than he knew what to do with, growing up in the Elarithian Palace.

"Well?" he prompted, glancing up at me. "Are you going to tell me what's wrong, or not?"

His voice made my heart skip a few beats; he sounded genuinely concerned. Not the *strangest* thing I'd heard today…but it was high on the list. And it pulled the truth out of me.

"The ones we raised weren't truly dead," I blurted out, voice trembling a bit despite my best efforts to keep it from doing so.

"...What are you talking about?"

I placed my fruit back onto the tray. I was hungry—starving, really—but I strongly suspected anything I ate was only going to come right back up.

"The ones we revived weren't really deceased," I told him. "They were..." I shook my head. Tried again. Failed again. After several false starts, I managed to repeat a condensed version of the information my brother had given me.

When I'd finished, breathless and still trembling slightly, Aleksander took a seat on the edge of the bed, resting his elbows on his knees as his head bowed in thought.

A minute later, the sound of voices outside reached us. His eyes narrowed on the door. We both tensed, likely wondering the same thing—were we truly safe here?

"Do you think they're telling you the truth?" he asked, once the hall had gone silent again.

"I don't know. Maybe."

His brow furrowed.

"Though I think I'll be more inclined to believe them once they show me to Luminor," I said. "Thalia claims it's here. If she can keep her promise about leading us to it, then maybe..."

His eyes flashed with renewed interest at the mention of his sword, and I recoiled slightly, remembering for an instant how we had started this journey: As *enemies*.

What a strange, twisting path we'd taken to get to this point.

And if what my brother said was true, it was only going to get more twisted. Because Aleksander and I were from two entirely separate worlds—worlds that were not able to exist in tandem. So what happened to the Above if the Below was successfully revived?

What happened to the world I knew best, and to Aleksander and his kingdom?

To *us*?

More importantly, why the hell was I thinking of *us* as a collective entity?

Gods, I needed to stomach some food somehow; I was clearly getting lightheaded and delusional.

"I'll believe they actually have the sword when I can hold it again, and not before," Aleksander said, snapping me back into awareness.

"Agreed," I said, pacing the room. "And this is what I came to this world for; I'm not sure why I'm hiding in here, now, instead of marching myself down to whatever place the sword is being kept in."

He muttered a simple explanation, his eyes glazing over in thought once more: "Because this is not how you imagined the end of your quest would go. It's gotten more complicated than expected, hasn't it?"

I didn't want to admit he was right—*how did he know me so well, all of a sudden?*—but I couldn't deny his words.

Quietly, I said, "I don't want to be a savior of this world. I don't want any crown this palace has to offer. I've *never* really wanted any of those things, even in the Above."

"You were always royalty, even in Eldris," he reminded me.

"Yes, but it never really *felt* that way. My mother was the queen, but I was just…" I swallowed down the emotion trying to rise up, shaking my head. "Just a shadow that no one really wanted."

He blinked, his intense gaze shifting, focusing more fully on me. I fought the urge to squirm, wishing I'd just kept my mouth shut about that last part.

Even if it was irrevocably, painfully true.

Deep down, I think one reason I'd been so desperate to brave the depths of what I'd believed was Hell was so that my kingdom might remember me as something *other* than a nuisance. I wanted to prove myself worthy of being seen. Of existing as something more than a mere shadow blocking the light of my parents' reign. And then I could have died here, even, and maybe left a legacy worth something. Yes; a very real part of me had been willing—maybe even *ready*—to die here.

Now I was being asked to *live*, instead, and to bring life to an entire dying world?

A much scarier prospect, somehow.

Aleksander's usual grumpy expression had melted into something softer—but clearly uncertain. He didn't respond to my painful admission, though he looked like he was searching for a way to do so; I half-expected him to offer me an awkward pat on the head and wish me good luck with my feelings.

Praise the gods, he did neither of these things—he merely watched me with that uncertain concern for a long moment before he cleared his throat and said, "You're bleeding."

"Hm?"

"Your shoulder."

"Oh." I looked, and he was right; the bandages wrapped around it were soiled, dampened enough that the blood had started to leach through the sleeves of my shirt. I tried to wave it off, but he stubbornly beckoned for me to follow him over to the vanity, where a fresh bowl of water had been left by someone, along with healing supplies; Aveline had intended to redress this wound in addition to bringing food, it seemed.

I didn't particularly want *either* of them to tend to my wounds, but I wasn't in the mood to argue for once. So, I let Aleksander work while I fixed my eyes on the bit of courtyard I could see through the half-drawn curtains.

I tried not to think about his touch.

But it was impossible not to.

It was light. Precise. Perfectly clinical. But as he shifted my shirt out of his way to better assess the bandaged wound underneath, I couldn't block out the flood of vivid memories—images of the last time he'd skimmed his fingertips along my skin. The moments spent together in that loft in Erebos. The way his touch had explored me so hungrily, so confidently. The heat and magic that had risen between us...

I was holding my breath, I realized—and for a moment, so was he.

Was he remembering it all, too?

How...*unfinished* we'd left things?

It had felt wrong in Erebos. But now, everything had changed. Again. His touch felt familiar, and yet altogether new, the connection between us relentlessly shifting, forever threatening to knock me off my feet...but suddenly, there was a part of me that didn't completely hate the idea of being swept off balance by him. At least he was an enemy I *knew*.

And, at the moment, he didn't feel like an enemy at all.

"They told me you didn't leave my side the entire time I was unconscious," I said, quietly, as he snapped out of the stillness that had overtaken us and went back to his precise re-bandaging efforts.

"...It's a large palace. It seemed simpler to stay put." His voice was frustratingly flat. Guarded.

"Simpler?"

"Yes."

I huffed out a laugh. "Nothing about us is *simple*, Aleks."

He didn't reply. He finished redressing my wound in complete silence, and then he crossed to the other side of the room, gathering up his coat that was draped over a velvet-trimmed settee. His gaze was distant; I could only guess at what he was thinking.

I shouldn't have wanted to know.

I had plenty of my own thoughts to worry about.

"You came back for me in Erebos," I heard myself say.

"And?"

"You followed me into the battle outside of it."

He tilted his head toward me. "I did."

Even at an angle, his stare was intimidating. Even at a distance, I felt like I might catch fire if he kept his eyes on me for much longer.

Curiosity seemed to grip him, turning him further toward me rather than toward the door. He debated a moment before indulging that curiosity, closing the space between us once more. His gaze skimmed over the work he'd done on my shoulder, then flashed up to my face, questioning. Expectant. "Your point?"

"My point is that I..."

I'd had a point when he was on the other side of the room; where had it gone?

He stepped closer. Only half an inch closer, at most—not even touching—yet it felt like he was pinning me in place by the sheer force of his presence.

I still couldn't remember what I'd been trying to say.

"You what?" he prompted, a hint of a smile curving his mouth—just enough to make his dimples more pronounced.

I don't understand why you keep saving me.

Was it merely because he needed me and my magic to survive in this world?

Or was it something else?

Fate seemed to have drawn us together. Our magic had tangled us up more completely. But my magic was perfectly calm at the moment, as it had been since I'd woken up in this protected palace. It wasn't blindly edging me toward him, this time.

I was fully aware of what I was doing.

Too aware of the heat and need spiraling through me, of the choice I made to stretch onto my tiptoes, to cup his strong jaw in my hand…

His lips parted, a hint of shock registering in his golden eyes. But he didn't pull away. He leaned forward, branding me with the faintest of kisses, one filled with equal parts anticipation and electricity. Static skipped over my skin—the warning before the lightning strike.

"Chaos," he whispered against my lips. "This isn't going to make us any simpler."

"No. It isn't," I agreed. And yet, I was angling my mouth more fully over his, desperate to plunge deeper into this mess we were making, fully aware it could all end in disaster.

As I cradled his face between both my hands, he grabbed my hips and jerked me closer. I gasped at the violence of the motion, and, at the sound, his hands moved on top of mine, pressing against them, pulling my mouth even closer to his.

Then he was kissing me like I'd never been kissed before, the force of it causing me to stumble back against the wall. His fingers wrapped around my wrists, pulling my hands away from his face and pinning them above me instead.

His strength was breathtaking. His tongue was commanding, relentless as it pushed deeper into my mouth. His lips were warm, pulsing with the faintest hints of his magic. I wanted that magic to explode. To surround me. To drive into my body, my blood, my soul.

I wanted it to swallow me whole.

He pulled away far, far too soon, leaving me panting and shaking.

His gaze fell immediately to my mouth, eyes burning with unmet lust—but he didn't move.

My lips tingled with a similar lust. Yet, I kept as still as him, forcing a slightly dazed, crooked smile. "Is this revenge for leaving you unsatisfied back in that loft in Erebos?"

I tried to make my voice sound unaffected.

I don't think I succeeded.

He chuckled humorlessly. "No. I can be a vengeful bastard, it's true. But leaving me was the right thing to do back then. If you hadn't, I would have…" He trailed off, shaking his head.

Every nerve ending in my body was suddenly alight

again, aware of his every breath—of every twitch of unspoken emotion—and desperate for him to finish his sentence.

I wanted to know what he would have done to me in that loft, had we not been interrupted by my vision.

He let out a small cough. "I'm curious, though, about what truly interrupted us that evening. You pulled away from me as though you'd seen a ghost. And then we were distracted before we had a chance to talk about any of it."

I averted my eyes; it made it easier to stop thinking about what might have been. "I…I had a vision. My unpredictable magic at work."

He nodded slowly, knowingly. "…I suspected that might have been it. Zayn told me you saw something when you touched Red, too."

"In the case of the loft, it was some sort of performance that I believe took place in Kaelen's manor at some point in the past. Which I guess lends credibility to what Bastian claimed—that Erebos was once a thriving city in this kingdom called Rivenholt."

He pulled on his jacket, fastening its buttons with elegant precision despite his thoughtfully distracted gaze. "So many unanswered questions," he said, more to himself than me. "We're going to have to stay here until we figure all of this out, aren't we?"

"It looks that way."

I absently reached for my shoulder. It ached dully, but not as badly as before. Some balm he had put on the scars —or maybe some faint show of his magic at work? I'd heard that some wielders of Light magic could use it for healing, though I'd never witnessed him or anyone else doing it; it was a very advanced facet of such power, allegedly.

"Thank you, by the way," I said.

"There's no need," he replied.

"There is—for saving me in Erebos. And for…for the bandaging and everything."

He acquiesced with a wave of his hand. "I don't know the answers to any of the things your brother said, or about where we go from here. But I know how to tend to wounds; I've had plenty of practice at that, at least."

"Because of your experience tending to the ones on your back and chest?"

He went very still.

"I…I'm sorry," I said, quickly. "I didn't mean to see them, I just…I was checking on you, and…" I swallowed hard. "To be fair, you were half naked in my window when I woke up. It was difficult *not* to stare and…um, to see."

He shrugged, trying and failing to roll away the obvious discomfort he felt. "I ran out of energy to finish changing."

"…You did seem exhausted."

A muscle ticked in his jaw, a flex from holding back whatever he'd started to say.

He headed toward the door. I assumed he wasn't going to say any more on the subject, or otherwise acknowledge it at all.

But then he drifted toward one of the room's two ornate, standing mirrors, pausing to study his reflection in it, pulling his jacket and shirt down so he could more clearly see the highest of the marks on his chest.

He noticed me staring. Without taking his eyes off his reflection, he said, "When I was six years old, I came down with an illness that nearly killed me. A spell or some rare poison snuck into my food by some enemy court, we suspected—we never truly figured it out. The doctors tried everything to oust the sickness from my body. The only thing that seemed to have any effect at all was bloodletting. That's where the first row of these scars came from."

"...And the rest of them?"

"I carved them myself, after being left alone for too long. I woke in a feverish panic and grabbed one of the ceremonial knives on display in the hall outside my room, I'm told. I don't remember any of it, but I likely would have bled to death that night, had some of the servants not found me as quickly as they did."

That explained why the ones on his back were messier; he hadn't been able to reach there as easily.

"A bright light alerted them to my alarming state, they claimed, though I don't really remember that, either."

"A light...your magic?"

He nodded. "I assume. After this incident is when it first emerged."

"You weren't born showing signs of it, you mean?"

He shook his head.

"...But you're an innate magic wielder, I've always heard. A legendary one, at that."

"That's what everyone in my kingdom was told, too. And perhaps it's the truth; maybe it was always inside me, only waiting for something like that infection and fever to trigger it. I'm not sure. I just know something strange happened that night." He ran his fingers through his pale hair, magic softly lighting his palm and making the strands shimmer like frost in the moonlight. "I still have nightmares, sometimes," he said. "Shapes I can't make sense of.

Blood covering my chest and back. A voice calling my name until I wake up."

"That sounds...horrifying." I stepped closer, until our reflections were side-by-side.

He glanced my way for half an instant before fixing a determined stare back on the mirror. "They're only nightmares. I know they aren't real."

I could hear the thinly-veiled fear in his voice in spite of his obvious efforts to hide it. I wanted to know more about his nightmares and all the other scars he'd collected as a child, but I didn't want to force him to relive those things— or to admit, out loud, that I was curious about any of it.

"...I should go find my cousin," he said. "It's never a good idea to leave him unsupervised for too long."

I couldn't think of an excuse quickly enough to keep him. And he was probably right, besides; the gods only knew what sort of trouble Zayn was getting into.

Aleks hesitated one last time before stepping away from the mirror. His expression was difficult to read, hinting at a thousand different things he might have said. But he only nodded toward my shoulder and told me, "Be careful with that. The wound is deep."

"I'll be fine."

He was gone a moment later.

Gingerly, I touched the bandage again. The ache underneath was almost completely gone. I was more convinced than ever that he'd soothed it with his magic. Something that must have been exceptionally difficult to do given his exhaustion, especially under the weight of whatever protective spells surrounded this palace.

Two days, Aveline had said. Two days I'd been asleep.

Two days he'd been in here, comforting and watching over me. And now he'd tried to heal me, too.

But that was inside of this room.

Outside, the pressures of our separate worlds awaited, and I could already feel their weight threatening to crush the fragile truce we'd started to build.

Chapter Twenty-Eight

Nova

"THERE ARE TWO SWORDS, ACTUALLY," MY BROTHER SAID AS he led me, Aleksander, Zayn, and Thalia down a narrow corridor with a set of double steel doors at its end. Phantom perched on my shoulder, shifted into the form of a small dragon with a lanky body, sharp claws, and feathery wings. Red had stayed behind in the parlor on the other side of the palace, where she was being doted upon by Aveline, who seemed thrilled to have a willing taste-tester for the copious amounts of baked goods she'd originally, unsuccessfully tried to foist off on me.

"Luminor has a counterpart—*Grimnor*," Bastian continued, stopping before the doors and running his fingers along the swirling designs etched into them. "Both swords were made by the same divine hand. Both once belonged to the first Vaelora of their respective worlds. The swords channel all sorts of magic, but the most important facet of their power is their ability to guide the Aetherstone on the

Equinox—though accounts differ as to precisely *how* they help control its power."

"A power that isn't enough to support both worlds, you claim," Zayn said.

"And hasn't been for many millennia. A growing population and an increasing reliance on magic were the original culprits, and then, even as these things stabilized, it never fully recovered."

"Perhaps because the turning weakened it further?" Zayn mused, speaking in his usual easygoing tone despite the tense mood hanging over the rest of us. "That's what they get for trying to share, eh? One of the worlds should have just been greedy from the beginning, and then we wouldn't be dealing with this mess, now."

Bastian didn't comment on this, keeping his focus on running his hands over the doors before us, working to break what was apparently an elaborate sealing spell. The tension thickened with his silence, settling over us like a heavy, itchy blanket.

Despite their connections to the Light Keepers, my brother had tentatively agreed to allow both Zayn and Aleksander to accompany us and learn more about the swords and the legends surrounding them—mostly at my insistence.

Thalia, however, seemed less enthusiastic about their presence. Not one to bother with hiding her true feelings, she'd been staring daggers at the two of them for most of our walk. Zayn appeared oblivious to this; Aleksander had been glaring right back at her.

"How many of these turnings have been missed?" I asked.

"According to most records we've deciphered, it's been

five-hundred and ninety-six years since that fateful moment when the Aetherstone's magic didn't turn toward us as it should have," said Thalia, stepping closer to my brother, positioning herself as if to shield the movements of his hands from Zayn and Aleksander's sight.

Finally, the etchings Bastian had been tracing and tapping began to shine with a faint silver glow.

My turquoise bracelet shivered as they did. I was distracted before I could wonder too long about the reaction, however, as the doors pulled apart, revealing a large room on the other side.

Phantom bounced anxiously back and forth between my shoulders, occasionally stretching his long neck out, taking a cautious sniff of the air only to quickly draw back. I clamped a hand onto his wriggling body, holding him still as I gathered my courage and stepped inside along with the others.

The room was cold enough that I was surprised I couldn't see my breath. Its walls were paneled in dark wood; its floor was smooth, reflective stone; and in the center of the space, suspended in mid-air above a pedestal of polished metal, were two swords.

I drew as close to them as I dared, coming to a stop some ten feet away. Nothing was holding them up, that I could see—they were simply floating, being slowly spun by some unseen hand.

Phantom curled more closely to me, wrapping his scaly body against my neck. His talons caught in the waves of my hair, but I was indifferent to the painful pulling his tangling caused.

All I could think about—all I could see and feel and hear—were those two swords before me. They hummed with a faint, ancient power, whispering against my skin like a brush of wind over water, sending ripples of awe radiating through me.

Luminor was as beautiful as I remembered. In the low light of the room, it seemed particularly radiant, its broad blade faintly pulsing with a glow that shifted between shades of pale gold and soft blue. The hilt was polished moonstone, with a guard that was simple, yet elegant, its intertwining spindles of gold like protective beams of shielding light. Delicate, but strong—the sort of weapon that I imagined would feel like a weightless extension of one's arm.

Grimnor hung with a more obvious weight. Its beauty was of a different sort—haunting, heavy, unyielding. Where Luminor gave off light, Grimnor seemed to absorb it, staining its more narrow blade in a deep, velvety shade of black that occasionally tumbled with a smoky-white energy. The hilt appeared crafted from obsidian, inlaid with veins of a red gemstone that sparkled whenever Luminor's light shifted over it. The guard was minimal, a jagged flaring of polished black metal that made me think of dragon wings.

"They're both here." My voice was hushed. I couldn't fully explain the sense of reverence rising in my chest, but it felt as if I was looking upon the faces of gods.

"Yes," said Thalia. "Luminor fell into our possession seven years ago, thanks, however inadvertently, to you—a bit of good luck that this realm was sorely overdue for. Grimnor, meanwhile, has been here ever since Calista's passing, centuries ago."

"...Calista?" I was immediately, mentally transported back to the shrine where I'd last stood with Orin. "Argoth's wife and queen, you mean?"

"They were never truly wed," Thalia informed me. "And she was never a queen."

"Though they were in love," Bastian added.

Zayn settled down on the crimson cushions of a bench against the wall, propping himself up on the armrest with the air of a king settling in to watch a performance.

Aleksander gave him a wry look.

I arched a brow, waiting for the Elarithian lord to summon food and drink to enjoy along with his show.

But Zayn only shrugged and said, "There's clearly a long story here." He waved a hand toward my brother, urging him on.

Bastian slowly nodded, looking back to the floating swords as he began. "Calista was the last Vaelora born into Noctaris until Nova came along hundreds of years later. Her counterpart was Lorien Blackvale, one of the most powerful wielders of Light magic to ever walk in Soltaris. Some say Lorien was more than a human, even, and was in fact the offspring of a mortal and a god. His heart was human enough, however—because it fell in love with Calista.

"Prior to these two, the Vaelora were always celibate beings. They were bound only to their duty, both by tradition and by the magical pact put in place between the first Vaelora and the old gods themselves. They were raised with strict objectives: Make it to adulthood without bonding to anyone else, master their magic, and be prepared to work with their counterpart to carry out the Equinoctial Turning through the use of magic and their respective swords. After the Turning, the expectation was sacrifice."

"Sacrifice?" The word felt heavy on my tongue.

"Another duty of Luminor and Grimnor," said Bastian.

"Once the Vaelora ritualistically impaled themselves upon the blades, the magic they carried would leave their bodies and eventually find its way into the souls of the next pair of them to be born, and thus the cycle continued."

"You said *prior to these two*," Aleksander said. "So I'm guessing Calista and Lorien didn't follow expectations?"

"That's putting it mildly," Thalia said.

Bastian nodded, his expression solemn. "Lorien was the first to suggest they abandon the traditional Turning. He claimed he wanted to seek a way to bring balance back to *both* worlds once more—but truthfully, it was an attempt to avoid death and keep Calista alive for his own selfish desires."

"And Calista pretended to go along with this plan," Thalia said, "because she didn't want to turn the Aetherstone's magic either. Her reluctance had nothing to do with any love for *Lorien*, though—even though she led him to believe that was the case."

"It was her love for Argoth, wasn't it?" Zayn guessed.

Perhaps it was my imagination, but the room seemed to darken at the words, both swords shifting, wobbling in their suspended places. Luminor, in particular, appeared restless, its blade continuing to shiver and shimmer for several moments after Zayn spoke.

"...Yes," Thalia said, watching Luminor out of the corner of her eye as her head tilted toward Zayn. "She loved that mortal, magicless king so much that she refused to turn the Aetherstone's power to Noctaris because it would mean the end of their relationship."

"What happens to the worlds when the Stone is turned away from it?" I wanted to know. "When things were still functioning as intended, I mean."

"A death-like slumber would overtake every living thing in those worlds," Bastian said. "A...*hibernation*, of sorts. Some of the souls in it were preserved and would revive as soon as the magic shifted and the time to reawaken came; others would perish in the time between; and a chosen few were believed to be immediately transferred into the opposite world, to be given an opportunity to live in it as well… it's an interesting thing to study, really, if you wanted to—"

"Interesting, but not a subject we have time for at the moment," Thalia interrupted.

Bastian gave her a sheepish look. I got the impression it wasn't the first time she'd stopped my brother from launching into a tangent of fact and figure reciting. Despite her hasty silencing, however, there seemed to be a rare glimmer of affection in her amethyst eyes—as though she admired his enthusiasm, even if we didn't have time for it.

I wondered briefly at their relationship—at *all* the relationships my brother had with everyone but me. All I'd missed. My heart beat unsteadily in my chest, still unsure of how to feel about him and the idea of making up for all our lost time.

"Anyway," Thalia continued, "when Lorien discovered Calista's love for the mortal king, he tried to murder her in a fit of jealous rage. She was badly wounded, but she escaped and fled to this palace. Here, she poured the last of her magic out, creating a protective ward around this area. She died soon after.

"With her death, the already delayed Turning was more… *permanently* delayed—but the spells she laid in place here carried on, and they've allowed the palace and the royal city south of it to continue to exist in a relatively normal state. The Below outside of this, however, has been withering away ever since—though nothing truly *dies*. You've seen the shades, the wraiths, the cities full of flames…all of it shadows of what once was. All of it has been sustained by Calista's desperate last spells, and occasionally bolstered by the weaker magic of the ones who served her, in hopes that one day it could all be truly restored."

"*Can* it be restored?" Zayn asked.

"The people here were beginning to doubt it," said Bastian."Generations went by before any Noctarisan child was born with a Vaeloran mark—until Nova was born here twenty-five years ago."

"What took so long, I wonder?" Zayn mused.

"Most of the population of this world is currently in a frozen, undead state," Aleksander pointed out. "So there haven't been many opportunities for such a child to be born, have there?"

"That's true. But…" Bastian hesitated, as if preparing to speak of something cursed and evil—something wicked that might gain a foothold just by hearing its name in the air. "There are many who believe Lorien Blackvale might have influenced this, too. That he's still out there, still doing all he can to make certain Noctaris *never* wakes again—thus vengefully ensuring that Calista and the world she came from suffer eternally for lying to him and rejecting him."

"So he's immortal, then?" I asked.

"In a sense," my brother said. "The Vaelora were always granted longer lifespans, as were the ones who served them and their cause—the ones I believe you know as the *Aetherkin*."

"The Aetherkin…like Orin?"

"Yes. Like him," Thalia said, her tone oddly strained all of a sudden.

"Lorien's longevity is believed to have far surpassed any of them, however," said Bastian, placing a hand on Thalia's arm and giving it a little squeeze, "thanks to an ability he stole from Calista during the attempted murder. Luminor bled magic from her when it pierced her body; a corruption of the sacrifice the blade was meant to perform after the Turning. Her ability to possess other beings and objects ended up settling in Lorien, among other magical talents. And, coupled with his own magic, this allegedly makes him able to possess other people with a lasting hold.

"We believe he's been jumping from one body to the next for centuries, avoiding death. And his servants continue as well, doing all they can to aid him in his quest to rise the Above higher while our Below is crushed further down."

"His servants…the Keepers of Light, you mean?" I asked, recalling our conversation in the courtyard earlier.

He nodded. "They started as Aetherkin, meant only to aid the Vaelora as the ancient agreements decreed. But he's somehow made them stronger over the years, and now… well, now it's hard to say exactly how much power they truly hold."

"If they're in league with this immortal demon, as you claim, then they've done an exceptional job of hiding it," said Zayn, skepticism lacing the words.

Aleksander looked more troubled by the possibility, but he said nothing.

No one else said anything for several moments, either. The swords continued to hum and spin, while Thalia and my brother circled the platform below them, as if inspecting for damage. Zayn closed his eyes, leaning back against the bench. Aleksander watched the blades with a look of fierce consideration, scarcely blinking even as Luminor's glow shifted over his hard features.

Phantom wiggled where he perched on my shoulder, pressing closer to my neck. His mouth full of tiny, needle-sharp teeth found my ear, affectionately nipping me out of the overwhelmed stupor I was falling into.

After some thought, I settled on a question among the countless number of them tumbling through my head, and I interrupted the silence: "Argoth…what became of him?"

To my surprise, it was Zayn who answered first, his eyes popping open as he said, "He lived. Married, too, and had at least one child."

"Lorien didn't kill him?"

"It was a worse punishment to live without Calista, I'd imagine," Zayn said with a shrug.

"But how do you know he lived?"

"Because I'm his descendant," Aleksander said quietly. "Though we didn't speak of him often back home—for reasons that are becoming somewhat clearer, if all this messy history is true."

I considered the words, the implications of it all. "So he married someone other than the one he loved…"

"Queen Elowen, if my memory serves," said Zayn. "And their son was called Arius." He flashed me one of his roguish grins. "Though I didn't really pay attention during most of my history lectures, so don't quote me on any of that."

"…An heir out of necessity, I guess," I mused. "Because all of the stories that circulate through Eldris only speak of Calista and his great love for *her*. There are poems and songs written about that love, even, and the roads that were built into this world…weren't they for her as well?"

"Yes," Bastian confirmed. "He built them in an attempt to recover Calista's body, and to do what he could to save her world—but his efforts were ultimately hindered by the politics of needing to marry and produce an heir for his kingdom, and said efforts eroded even further after his death. Over time, the true story of their love and the paths it created was twisted and rewritten by his enemies."

"And eventually, the Keepers of Light started to refer to this world as Hell, and so Hell it became," Thalia added. "It was easy enough to convince the dwellers of the Above that Noctaris was a place only of darkness and demise, given the powers of the Vaelora and the Aetherkin who hailed from here."

"In reality, necromancy is no more evil than luxmancy —the Light magic—that the Above is known for," said Bastian. "Both shades of magic have a capacity for great good and for great evil. They're merely *different* in order to balance the worlds. But the Light Keepers, and the one they serve, aren't concerned with balance. They needed to demonize Noctaris and its magic in order to properly bury it, so that was what they did. The roads Argoth created became known as roads to death, and, eventually, all belief that the Below was anything but a place for lost souls faded into history, then into legend, and, finally, into a barely-believed myth."

Dizzy with the weight of all this new knowledge, I wandered over and sat down beside Zayn. Phantom dropped into my lap, burrowing underneath my crossed arms so he could press his face against my chest. Zayn placed a hand on my knee, offering a comforting squeeze.

"It took *years* for me to find a way to enter one of those roads to death," I said, turning my attention back to my brother. "I still don't understand why I was taken away from this world in the first place. Earlier, you said it was to protect us, but…"

"Yes. Because when you were born, your magic initially caused more harm than good—it was simply too much to contain within this small section of our world. It was drawing in all manner of wraiths and shades, and far worse creatures, who essentially lost their minds trying to feed off it. So, Orin took you Above, vowing to keep you safe until your magic stabilized enough to come back here to reclaim your sword and crown."

I gripped the bracelets Orin had made for me, lifting my eyes toward the sword in question. Would Grimnor help stabilize and channel my powers further?

My brother's gaze followed mine, settling on the dark blade for a long moment before he tilted his face to me and said, "You are meant to wield it. And through it, to turn magic in our favor once more."

It looked incredibly heavy. And yet, at least in that moment, it was impossible not to imagine wielding it. Impossible not to wonder about what would happen if I wrapped my hands around its beautiful, sparkling hilt…

Before I realized what I was doing, I found myself rising to my feet, making my way to the swords and kneeling at the pedestal they floated above. Phantom latched onto my shoulder, peering nervously up at the blades while the bulk of his body hung against my back.

There were words etched into the face of the pedestal. I ran my fingers over them, feeling out a message in a language I couldn't read, and I soon realized…

Some of the symbols here were the same as the ones painted on my turquoise bracelet.

And that bracelet had started to tremble gently against my wrist.

"What makes you think she'll be able to use the sword to save this world?" Zayn asked, getting to his feet as well. "She doesn't have the greatest history when it comes to keeping her magic under any sort of precise control." Clearing his throat, he added, "No offense, Princess."

"None taken," I said, distractedly, my fingers still tracing the pedestal's strange words.

"And what would she be attempting to wield it against, truly?" Aleksander asked. "You claim the Keepers of Light are in league with this Lorien figure; I imagine they won't make reaching the Aetherstone easy, even if she can figure out how to work the sword and magic needed to manipulate it."

"Yes." Bastian's voice seemed laden with a thousand unspoken concerns, yet he doggedly continued on: "The Keepers are, in fact, guarding it fiercely, and have been for centuries—presumably under Lorien's orders. It's the other part of the battle we face, unfortunately. We can't breach their protective lines. Or we couldn't, at least, until Nova came along and gave us a chance at resurrecting a proper army."

I could sense his gaze shifting, pressing against me, heavy with hope. With expectations. I closed my eyes against the doubt trying to flood through me, keeping my hand braced against the pedestal. Something about the feel of the words beneath my fingertips—even if I couldn't decipher them—kept me calm. It quickly settled the shivering in my bracelet, too. Almost as if whatever power slept in its beads had only been waiting for me to reunite it with the power at the center of this chamber.

"What you did outside of Erebos was nothing short of astounding," Bastian continued. "You're bringing *life* back to this world. Not to all of it, no, but your power will be enough to help us raise an army capable of taking on the forces that have kept us from entering Nerithys—the domain where the Aetherstone resides—for all these centuries."

"She didn't raise those beings from the dead on her own," Zayn reminded them.

"And there were always two of the Vaelora, didn't you say?" Aleksander added. "But is there another aside from Nova, now?"

Thalia's reply was stiff. "None that we're aware of."

"So who will wield Luminor? Don't you need both to adequately control the Stone?"

This time, Thalia didn't reply; the questions hung like a storm cloud in the air, charged and heavy and waiting to break.

An invisible, yet very clear fence seemed to be rising between us. I stood slowly, glancing over my shoulder and studying the faces on each side.

Aleksander was staring at his sword, his eyes glowing a brilliant shade of gold in its light, as he said, "This blade was a gift to me as a child. I know its weight, its magic, and *I* could potentially wield it…but why would I help her—or *you*—when to do so would likely mean the end of my world and my kingdom's rule?"

The cold calculation in his words stung. But I couldn't deny that he had a point; I'd asked myself the same question, earlier. Despite all the progress we'd made toward *not* wanting to murder one another, it seemed we were destined to remain enemies, whether we liked it or not.

"Whatever power she's been borrowing from you, we will teach her to do without it," Thalia said, cooly. "She won't need you once she's had a chance to properly practice her powers with the other magic users that share her same alignment."

"You think she can turn the Stone by herself?" Zayn asked.

"With an army at her back, yes. The old ways are long dead, the pacts broken, the laws forgotten—and we intend to make that work in our favor, now."

Both Zayn and Aleksander started to protest, but my brother cut them off.

"I hardly think I need to point this out," came his voice, low and filled with warning, "but the two of you are vastly outnumbered in this palace. So whether or not you intend to help us willingly is rather irrelevant."

At this, the conversation collapsed into nothing but arguments.

I looked back to the swords, blocking out the noise behind me as best I could.

As I stared at Grimnor, watching the way it sparkled whenever Luminor rotated closer to it, a solution quietly, nervously snuck into my thoughts. One that seemed obvious, albeit fraught with uncertainty. It took me several moments to work up the courage to say it out loud.

Raising my voice above the bickering, I said, "Isn't it possible that we could...*balance* the two worlds, as Lorien claimed he wanted to do?"

The arguments slowed to a stop, silence settling like a

blanket of snow over the room, creating a quiet so deep it was almost eerie.

"What would happen if we truly tried to do such a thing?" I said into the chilly silence, studying my reflection in Grimnor's dark blade. "Could the worlds both exist together, as they once did?"

I could hear the frown in my brother's voice as he said, "It's been thousands of years since they existed that way."

"Yes, but Aleksander and I have managed to weave our power together to balance things around us over this past week, and to bring life...*together*. And without even really trying." I braced myself before letting my gaze trail toward the Light King. He was watching me with an expression that was equal parts doubtful and curious.

I steeled myself and kept going. "That has to mean something, doesn't it? So much about this legend of the Vaelora and everything concerning them has been skewed and rewritten...so maybe it's just another lie, the claim that only one world can survive at a time."

"Noctaris is a breath away from eternal death and damnation," Thalia said, as though I needed reminding. "Now is not the time to experiment."

Gritting my teeth, I swallowed down my response. Our words seemed destined to chase circles around each other. I had half a mind to move to action instead—to grab the swords and storm out of the room. But as I started to reach toward them, a cold wave of pressure rippled over me, raising the hair along my arm and clenching my muscles into stillness.

"There's a shield protecting them and suppressing their power," my brother explained. "We need to make sure you're ready to handle the full effect Grimnor will have on your magic before you draw it out; otherwise, we may end up in the same dangerous situation that followed your birth."

So much power to potentially change *everything*...yet it still remained out of reach, even after I'd come so far. Frustrated, I looked around—though what other answers I was hoping to find, I wasn't sure.

There were guards at the door, I noticed.

Likely in case Aleksander and Zayn decided to try anything to get to Luminor—but I couldn't help feeling as if they were there to cage me in, too. I felt trapped. Backed into a corner with a strange mixture of power and despair swirling around me.

"Once you step fully into your magic, Grimnor is yours for the taking," my brother assured me, "along with a crown, and the loyalty of the ones in this palace and all who fight for it."

"How long do I have to prepare to take it?"

"The next Equinox is in just under four weeks, according to our calculations," Thalia said. "This will be the easiest time to both reach and manipulate the Aetherstone—perhaps the *only* time—and likely our last chance."

Four weeks.

I bowed my head, fighting the urge to sink to my knees.

"Less than four weeks to prepare to change the fate of an entire lost world," Zayn said with a disbelieving little chuckle. "No pressure, though."

Phantom nudged his snout under my chin, urging me to lift my head and see the shadows that had started to swirl around Grimnor's blade. They looked remarkably similar to the ones that often rose from my skin.

I watched them circle around Luminor, the light blade

glowing brighter in the same breath, ribbons of its magic taking on a more solid shape. I expected the air to rumble as those ribbons collided with Grimnor's shadows, but no violence came of it—they merely weaved in and out in a dance of clearly powerful yet peaceful precision.

Balanced.

As if responding to the plan I'd spoken of minutes ago. Light and dark, dark and light…I might have been born of this lower realm, and I'd never truly belonged to the one above…

But I still didn't want to see anything happen to *either* realm.

"I will do what I can to fix the Stone and its wayward power," I said, quietly but firmly, "but I am not saving one world at the expense of another. I will fight for both, or I will not fight at all."

Thalia and Bastian exchanged a worried look.

Zayn appeared mildly amused.

I paid the three of them little mind, my eyes automatically trailing toward Aleksander.

He was watching the same twisting of light and dark that I'd been watching. Like we were kids once more, enjoying the show of shadow puppets on the walls looming so impossibly high before us.

Slowly, his gaze fell to me.

The cold calculations continued behind his eyes, but deep in their golden depths there was a hint of the boy who had comforted me all those years ago. He was still in there, despite how fiercely everything seemed to be trying to rip us apart.

He tilted his head, studying me, and the world seemed to tilt with it as he said, "And I will fight with her."

Chapter Twenty-Nine

Aleksander

"The air in this place makes me want to peel my skin off," Zayn muttered.

"That seems like a rather dramatic solution," I replied, offhandedly, as I concentrated on directing a current of magic into the cracks of the wall running around the perimeter of the palace's northern yard. Ivy covered this wall, dotted with withered white flowers. As my light sank deeper into the cracks and pulsed through the stone, the wall shimmered with golden energy, bringing those white blooms to life, doubling their size and making them glow around the edges.

Zayn stretched out on top of the low wall, like a cat sunning himself, as he continued to lament our situation.

I didn't respond to anything he said—but I didn't disagree with his sentiments, either.

It had now been five days since our arrival to Rivenholt Palace, and the protective magic here—meant to deter

Lorien Blackvale and all who served him—remained oppressive, no matter how much practice our lungs had at breathing it in. Our bones seemed to creak under its weight, as if the very air was working against us, sinking into our muscles and dragging us down.

We'd spent the past several mornings practicing to better acclimate our magic; hours of trying to manage even the simplest of spells. It was uncomfortable to work within the suffocating conditions, but the alternative—not being able to summon any useful magic in what was essentially an enemy court—was far worse.

"At least Rowen and Farren seem to be enjoying themselves," Zayn said. He'd rolled onto his side and was looking toward the edge of the yard, to where our two loyal soldiers were reclining on a grassy knoll. They looked perfectly relaxed, even in spite of the intimidating palace rising behind them with its glistening dark spires gleaming like the teeth of dragons. Farren even appeared to be fully absorbed in reading a book.

"Let them," I mumbled, my focus quickly returning to my magic. I pulled a knife from my belt and started to push Light energy into the blade, then used it to trace patterns in the air. It was an old method of practicing concentration—one of the most basic tricks I'd mastered as a child. "It's been too long since we've relaxed in a proper palace, hasn't it?"

Zayn rocked up into a sitting position. "...I'm still having a hard time believing this *is* a proper palace. I ventured into Tarnath—their royal city—yesterday evening, you know, and people were truly going about their business as if it was any city in the Above. It's very strange; it almost feels like we're back home, until you remember the dead things pressing in along the edges of it all."

"Not truly dead," I reminded him.

"Close enough."

"For now, anyway."

He averted his eyes, crossing his arms and tapping his fingers against the thorny vine tattoo encircling his right bicep, clearly debating whether or not this was worth arguing about. He typically chose to let things go—arguing got in the way of having a good time, as he frequently reminded me. This time, however, his brow remained furrowed with concern.

I fixed my gaze on his, questioning.

"…There's the small matter of two worlds, unable to exist at the same time," he said.

"Unless we find a way to balance them both."

Another hesitation. Then, "Let's assume we *don't* find a way to do that…what then?"

I traced my thumb along my knife, injecting more energy into the blade. The air crackled with it—enough to make my skin tingle and the hairs on my arms stand on end, even with the suffocating air closing in around it.

"If it comes down to our world or theirs, who do you think she's going to choose?" Zayn pressed.

"She won't choose between them. She's already stated as much."

"I'm afraid they'll force her to," he said. "She's as outnumbered as we are, truthfully. They have their plan in their minds already—they've had it for *years*, and I doubt she'll sway them from it, ultimately. Have you seen the way they look at her? They want to make her into their little puppet."

I bristled at the thought, and the magic surrounding me sizzled. It had crossed my mind several times since we started uncovering truths in this palace, and it was why I'd taken Nova's side while we'd stood in the shadows of Luminor and Grimnor. Why I had vowed to fight alongside her instead of against her. Why I hadn't tried to steal the Sword of Light and make a run for it, yet—even though the idea was tempting.

True, it had partly been self-preservation.

But there was more to it than that.

I didn't trust this brother of hers—or any of the ones who answered to him—to not betray her. And the thought of her fending for herself against them…

"They won't make her into anything without her consent," I told Zayn.

"No?"

"I won't let them."

The words seemed to echo in the stifling air. Zayn started to reply several times, only to press his lips back together every time, eventually settling on a quiet "*Hmm*."

I gave him a sharp look. "What?"

"This is a first."

"*What* is a first?"

"You feel protective of her, don't you?"

The statement nearly made me drop my knife. "I do not. At least, not beyond taking care of a crucial cog in our own plans. We lose our connection to her, we lose our best chance of making it out of this world alive. And if they gain complete control over her and her magic…well, it's only going to end poorly for us and the rest of our world."

"Not like you to get so attached," he commented, as though I hadn't spoken. "Not like you at all."

"I'm not attached. On the contrary, I find her infuriating. But also a necessary evil, I'm afraid."

His grin was slight. "Well, that's often how it starts, isn't it?"

I didn't bother to answer this, choosing instead to walk beside the wall he sat upon, studying the sections still shimmering with the light I'd summoned. It was lasting a little longer than my previous attempts, at least.

"For what it's worth, I like her too," Zayn said. "But there are greater things at stake. And I trust her more than any of the other necromancers here, but she still has deeper ties to Shadow magic, and to this world, than to anything in the Above—even if she isn't ready to embrace those ties yet."

"I know that."

He hopped down from the wall, stretching. "There are no easy answers, I guess. But you know I've had your best interests at heart for nearly twenty-seven years now."

"Yes; it's why I tolerate you."

"And, as your most *tolerated* advisor and friend, I have to insist that you think twice before getting any closer to her. You have a duty to your kingdom and its people—to the whole world of the Above. And I foresee her clouding your judgment about that."

"You severely underestimate my ability to judge."

"Just be careful."

"No problem."

"None?"

"At all."

He flashed me a full, crooked grin. "Well, here comes an opportunity to prove it."

I followed his gaze, spotting Nova approaching us from the direction of the palace.

I tried not to stare, but it was impossible not to.

Whereas the air around here was proving detrimental to Zayn and me, it was having the opposite effect on her. Her shadows moved more freely—and calmly—than I'd ever seen them. Even now, faint hints of her power flowed around her like an extension of the loose-fitting trousers and sleeveless tunic she wore, as if a skilled tailor had designed them to flow in perfect harmony with her movements. Her eyes seemed even brighter than usual. There was something in her step, too—a decisiveness that hadn't been there before.

She might not have been embracing the crown of this kingdom yet, but she still looked like its queen.

Zayn clapped a hand on my shoulder, making me jump slightly; I didn't realize how still I'd gone.

"Good luck," he said, with a sound that was part laughter, part sigh.

He made his exit quickly. I instantly wondered if I should have followed him out, but it was too late, by this point; Nova was somehow already in front of me.

She wore her usual, cheerful smile—that wasn't strange. What *was* strange was how that smile seemed to be directed at me...I still wasn't used to her regarding me with anything other than disdain.

She carried a large basket, which she promptly placed on the wall Zayn had just been sitting on. Without a word, she started to unpack it, setting an excessive amount of food along the still-shimmering stone. There were fruits of every shape and color, their skins glistening in the warm light of my magic; pastries with perfectly-browned crusts; a platter of various cheeses; bottles of drink fastened with corks and ribbons.

"What's all this?" I asked.

"This would be what's known as *food*."

"Yes, but why is it here?"

Why are you here? was what I truly wanted to ask. She had been working separately with Thalia and the others all morning, I knew—and, now that she was close, I could tell she was tired. Though her eyes were brighter, dark circles underneath betrayed the depth of her exhaustion. There were odd, bruise-colored smudges along her arms, too, as if the shadows that flowed so freely around her now had been considerably more violent when exiting her body.

She should have been resting.

Not that I cared.

"It's here because someone told me you hadn't eaten all morning," she said with a shrug.

"Aveline?" That head maid was notoriously good at pushing her way into other's business, I'd noticed.

Nova gave another shrug. "Just someone."

"Why are you concerned about whether or not I've eaten?"

Instead of answering me, she finished unloading her basket and then walked along the wall, her eyes widening with interest as she traced her fingers over the ivy creeping over the stone, plucking one of the glowing flowers from it. "You did this?"

I nodded.

"Your magic continues to impress, even here." She made her way back to the food, hoisting herself onto the wall and reaching for an apple with pinkish-gold skin. "I wondered how that would go."

"...It's getting more acclimated to the stifling protections that surround this palace, I suppose. But it's still much more difficult to summon here than it was outside of it."

She considered this, slowly chewing the fruit as her brow furrowed in concentration. "The air in here feels unnatural, doesn't it?"

"It does. I wasn't sure if you would notice it, given your magical alignment."

"It's not a...*bad* feeling, to me. But it's overwhelming, almost. What's happening inside here—what Calista did to protect this area—isn't natural or sustainable, according to the laws of our worlds." Her eyes glazed over as she stared at a distant wall of black stone, which separated the palace grounds from the dark, cursed lands outside of it. A few more bites of apple, and then she said, "My brother believes that the reason you and I have been able to bring things to life outside of this area—and to *sustain* that life—is because it's traditionally required both necromancy and luxmancy to rebalance the realms. To turn the Stone, to activate the magic to wake the worlds, and then to maintain them in a way that feels normal."

I frowned, not sure I agreed with this theory. "Such magic always came from the Vaelora; I carry no mark of those beings."

"I no longer have a visible mark, either—though I remember having a strange, star-shaped scar on my forearm, some time ago." She shrugged. "I just thought it was a regular birthmark that faded with time." She studied her arm, as if expecting the mark in question to make a reappearance.

When it didn't, she lifted her gaze to mine and asked, "Do you think it's possible you had something like that as well—something you've forgotten about—that your court and Keepers hid from you?"

Before the events of the past week, I would have answered with a quick and emphatic *no*; I'd been so certain of it all, what seemed like such a short time ago.

Now, I simply remained silent.

Nova sighed. "Whether you carry such a mark is irrelevant, I guess; Bastian seems to think—or at least wants to believe—that I can revive Noctaris on my own."

"...You don't believe there's a way to do so?"

"I think there's a reason a Vaelora was always born into *each* world. Both kinds of magic matter. Even he admits that. They're meant to work together; anything else feels like going against the nature of...well, *everything*."

"Yes, but you don't need *me* specifically for my magic."

"Don't I?"

"I'm sure your brother and his followers are busy scheming other ways of getting the Light magic they need; perhaps siphoning it from Luminor, or otherwise. I'm only another vessel for such magic, after all." *Vessel* was a word the Keepers had often used to refer to me; I'd never thought much of it.

But Nova set her jaw, and her eyes looked troubled. "You're more than a mere *vessel*, you idiot."

I stared at her, unsure of how to reply.

The more often we talked, it seemed, the more often I found myself speechless like this.

She was so...*different* from the cutthroat members of my life and court back in Elarith. Nobody spoke of working together and striving for balance in the world I grew up in—only of how they could tip the balance in their favor.

Death Maiden, some of them used to call the Princess of

Eldris. Or *Death Witch*, if they were feeling particularly cruel. And they had said it in hushed tones, often with a mixture of fear and barely-masked disgust. When our impending arranged marriage was announced, countless courtiers had tried to talk me out of it.

Yet, for all the shadows surrounding her, *death* was not the word that came to mind when I looked at her now.

"You're more than a vessel," she repeated, as if it were a simple fact, "and they'll understand that before the end."

"Your optimism continues to impress, even here."

She exhaled a breathy little laugh, and her voice was perfectly flat as she said, "It's a bad habit I can't seem to shake—this sunshiny disposition of mine."

Fighting a smile, I hopped onto the wall as well, mirroring her pose with one leg tucked underneath me and the other hanging over the side.

She gestured toward the spread of food, her expression expectant.

I hesitated to reach for any of it, only doing so once her gaze became more of a glare; I knew she would keep glaring at me until I gave in—it wasn't the first time we'd performed this particular routine over the past week.

As I picked at the food with precise movements, I soon forgot she was even there, busying myself with my usual ritual of separating the bread from the fruit, the cheese from the meat—making sure everything had its own place, and that it was all laid out in an even, acceptable way. Some for now, some set aside for later, some—

"Why do you do that?" she asked, suddenly.

My fingers stilled against the bread I'd just reached for. "Do what?"

"Count and organize your food, as if you expect it to go

missing if you don't inventory it properly. Was there really a need for rationing things in the plentiful halls of your old home?"

"Do you just blurt out every question that comes into that head of yours?" Memories of the uncomfortable conversation we'd had about my scars flashed in my mind.

"I…well, yes. Sometimes." She blushed. Silence stretched between us. The color deepened in her cheeks, and it was impossible not to notice how that flush of pink made her all the more attractive—to not immediately start thinking of other ways I could make her blush.

Fucking hell.

Zayn might have been on to something after all.

I rolled the tension from my shoulders and fixed my eyes on hers, keeping my tone as nonchalant as possible. "Did you not receive etiquette lessons as a child?"

"They were lost on me."

"Of course. Why am I not surprised?"

"It's one thing to be taught rules and manners from a stern-faced tutor," she insisted. "It's another thing to live it, to practice it, and I…I guess you could say I didn't have a lot of conversations during which I could practice. People avoided me, as I believe I've told you before."

"After you left Rose Point, even?"

"I had Orin—not exactly the picture of *etiquette*, that lovable but crass old man—and I had the occasional accomplice who helped me with some of my more complicated…*adventures*. But, no. No one I ever trusted enough to have prolonged conversations with, really."

It caused a strange ache in my chest to picture her alone with no one to talk to.

I cleared my throat. And just as before, when we'd

spoken of scars and nightmares in her room, I felt a compulsion to answer her questions...even about the things I usually did my damnedest to keep to myself.

Quietly, I said, "There was certainly no shortage of food in Duskhaven—my palace—but there were still a lot of days I went without."

"Why?"

"It was a tactic often employed by my teachers. A punishment for failing at lessons. Fifteen days was my record, I think. I reached it more than once." She looked horrified, but I had detached myself from it all enough, by this point, that I numbly kept speaking. "At some point, I guess I developed a...compulsion surrounding it. A need to control food whenever I did have plenty of it in my possession. A desire to organize and hide things, as necessary. Some for eating now, some for later."

When her horrified silence stretched on, I hurriedly added, "I know it's strange."

She shook her head. "It's not strange." Her voice was firm. "People do what they need to do to survive."

"Maybe. Though...I never really saw myself as trying to *survive* any of it," I said. "More like simply meeting expectations, whatever it took."

She was quiet for a long beat before she said, "Well, I think sometimes traumatic things look different from the inside, when you're trying to endure them."

The words lingered in the air between us. I had a strange desire to reach for her and pull her to my chest. Different from the lust I'd started bracing myself for whenever she was near; it wasn't her body I craved in that moment. It was...*her*. All of her. I wanted her closer simply so I could feel her heartbeat against me.

I shifted where I sat, trying to find a better sense of balance.

"These are the same bastards who wouldn't let you properly mourn your parents," she commented.

"They were…strict."

"They were monsters—*are* monsters. Why didn't your parents intervene in their punishments when they were still alive?" she asked. "Didn't you have anyone to protect you?"

I didn't need protecting, I nearly snapped.

But for some reason, I swallowed down this typical, defensive response and told her the truth instead. "My parents were sick for most of my childhood. We lived in the same palace, but I might as well have been raised in a different kingdom, for all I saw of them; the Keepers claimed it was for the best, so that I wouldn't be a burden on the king and queen in addition to all their other obligations and ailments."

"A *burden*?"

I shrugged.

She looked as though she might combust from the effort of trying to bite her tongue on the matter. Her cheeks were bright again—a furious, bristling shade of red.

So much anger on my behalf.

It was…strange. Even stranger than her smiling at me and bringing me food.

"It's just how things were," I insisted. "From the time I was born, I never really knew anything else."

She took several deep breaths through her nose. "Well, these Keeper assholes seem like the controlling type, don't they? The type who would put an imposter on the throne if it served their plans. And maybe the type to not tell you of your true magic and power, too."

I couldn't deny she had a point, even if I couldn't bring myself to admit it out loud.

"One more thing we need to sort out," she said, as if she were making a casual to-do list.

I shouldn't have been surprised by her nonchalant tone, I supposed—this was also the woman who had put *descend into Hell* on her fucking to-do list.

Such a chaotic, beautiful little beast.

She didn't try to force me to eat any more. We passed some time talking of theories and future plans, letting our past ghosts linger on the edges of our conversation but no longer inviting them in.

After an hour or so, we went our separate ways.

But when I returned to my room some time later, I found a pile of food neatly packaged up on a tray, waiting for me. She'd taken the time to leave notes, too, in slightly messy handwriting; one pile was labeled *For Now*, while the other was labeled *For Later*.

I stared at the tray for a long moment before slowly taking a piece of bread, carrying it over and sinking down onto the edge of the bed. I ate all of it while staring at the royal crest of Rivenholt that hung over the door, trying to remind myself of the warnings Zayn had given me earlier.

Think twice before getting any closer to her.

Easier said than done.

Chapter Thirty

Aleksander

Two more days passed in the Rivenholt Palace.

On the third, I dozed off late in the afternoon only to wake up with a start, sweat dripping from my skin, echoes of a nightmare pounding through my skull—the same, recurring one I'd told Nova about days ago. It had been a long time since it had visited me, and the haunting images seemed to be trying to make up for lost time, clawing through my thoughts with much more sharpness and clarity than usual.

These nightmares always affected me the same way: I staggered from the bed feeling completely drained of life, my magic roused, but scattered and weak, as though it had tried to fight off the dark dreams on my behalf.

I made my way to the washroom across the hall. As per usual, the violent stirrings of my mind and magic had left temporary cracks in my skin—though the golden energy glowing within them was fainter within the walls of this palace and its protections.

These nightmares had once been the only thing that caused such cracks…until Nova came along.

Why she had the same effect on me as my nightmares, I could only guess at.

Just one more piece of our relationship that I couldn't make sense of.

Splashing cold water over my skin helped settle the exterior cracks, but my insides still felt as if they'd been wrung dry, all the life in me squeezed out.

I was determined not to let weakness win—especially not in this foreign court, where any wrong move might prove fatal—so I set off for the palace training grounds, where I could deal with things the way I often did: by battling my way through until I was too numb to think of pain or confusion or anything else.

Bastian had offered this training space to me freely, along with access to the armory next to it—a show of hospitality I suspected Nova had encouraged him to give. His desire to win her affection seemed to be greater than whatever suspicions he held toward me, and I planned to use that to my advantage for as long as I could get away with.

I grabbed a sword from the armory—a heavy claymore that required both hands to wield. Not my usual choice of weapon, but I needed something that would require focus rather than familiarity. Something to better distract myself with.

Without any hesitation, I set about carving up the practice dummies lining one end of the field. Occasionally, I tried fusing magic into the blade as well. It was such a broad, thick piece of steel that it required every ounce of my focus to pull off this trick. My nightmares were soon forgotten, lost among my growing exhaustion, as I'd hoped they would be—though the pounding headache I soon developed wasn't much of an improvement.

I'd thought my cousin was being dramatic the other day, suggesting peeling the skin from his bones to rid himself of the cursed weight caused by the protective air in this palace. The longer I worked through my motions, though, the heavier and hotter my body seemed to become. Discarding my shirt and jacket helped somewhat, but I was still breathing harder than I should have been, and making far too many mistakes for my liking.

The open-air grounds were lined with burning torches, situated between the armory and a wing of the palace that had once been reserved for less prominent guests. The bedrooms in that wing had sat empty for ages, I'd been told, but the central parlor was still in regular use.

A small crowd of palace dwellers soon gathered on the balcony of this parlor, giving them a bird's-eye view of the training area. Judging by their chatter and raucous laughter, they were thoroughly enjoying a round of after-dinner drinks.

I paid them little mind until some time had passed—until a hush fell over them, followed by a chorus of excited whispers.

Nova had just arrived, I realized. She ignored the whispering, pointing crowd—and me—taking up a spot on the opposite side of the training field. All of her attention was on readying the bow she had slung over her shoulder.

I watched her out of the corner of my eye for only a

moment before returning to my own practice. She seemed focused—in need of some kind of disciplined distraction, same as I was—so I let her be. We merely existed in the same space for the better part of an hour. Day eased fully into night as we went through our motions, little sound between us save for the hacking and swishing of my blade and magic, occasionally punctuated by the echoing thud of her arrows hitting a target.

But I could *feel* her, even when I couldn't see her or hear her.

Or, more specifically, I could feel her magic. For every spark of light that escaped me, I sensed one of her shadows rising, as if in answer.

Like everything else, it was different within the protective shell surrounding this area—more muted. Almost as if our powers were sentient enough to realize that there was no need for balancing or revival here, and so my magic's desperate, clawing desire to get to hers was absent for the moment.

I still found myself drifting closer and closer to her side of the grounds.

A particularly bright surge of light rolled from my veins toward my sword. Cold shot through me a moment later as Nova's shadows shifted in response. The back of my neck prickled, and I tilted my gaze in her direction to find her staring at me as she fought to catch her breath. Shadows framed her body, flaring out in shapes almost reminiscent of wings.

"It's rude to stare," I called to her.

She snorted at this, averting her eyes. "I told you before: My etiquette lessons were pointless. I'm afraid I'm destined to be hopelessly rude."

A smile tugged at my lips as I sauntered closer, stopping a few feet away from her.

She still didn't look at me as she said, "I *do* think there might be some social rules against parading around half-naked as a visitor in a foreign court, though."

"Am I *parading*?"

"You've drawn spectators," she said drily, nodding toward the balcony above us—to where the crowd of onlookers had nearly doubled in size.

I lowered my gaze back to Nova. "Maybe they're here to watch you?"

"Doubt it."

Another glance from me caused a series of giggles to break out, followed by a shuffling of bodies as they all jostled for better positioning. The commotion seemed to fluster Nova, drawing a disgruntled noise from deep in her throat, and I couldn't help the arrogance that curved my lips into a more complete smile.

"Do their stares make you jealous?"

"No." The reply was quick, but her blush had been even quicker.

I beckoned her toward me. "Come here. Come practice magic with me."

She hesitated.

"I bet we can make *them* jealous," I said, dropping my voice to a low, conspiratorial tone.

"I don't care about making other women jealous."

"No? Manipulating emotions is at the center of all court life and politics. A useful skill for a future queen, in other words."

"How noble."

I chuckled. "Let me guess: You didn't pay attention in your political classes, either."

"Do they teach this sort of thing in classes?"

"It's the underlying message in *all* the lessons where I'm from."

"That's concerning," she said. But she was stepping closer, all the same, her gaze obviously fighting to stay fixed on mine and not trail lower.

"I can put my shirt back on if it helps you concentrate," I offered.

"Don't flatter yourself; I'm not that flustered by your bare chest."

"I'll have to find some other way to fluster you, then."

"Keep talking," she deadpanned, "and I'm sure it will happen. It usually does."

I chuckled at this as she slipped off her cloak and tossed it next to my shirt and coat, revealing light, form-fitting leather armor underneath, before redoing the braid that hung nearly to her waist.

I looked her over as she went through these motions; I was searching for more bruises like the ones I'd noticed during our impromptu picnic the other day…but my gaze got caught on her throat—on a shadowy thread that encircled it before dipping lower, caressing the curves of her breasts.

"Staring is rude," she informed me with a smirk.

"It is." I returned her smirk. "You're a fast learner."

"One of the many things I pride myself on. Also? It's good to know you *are* flustered by a mere chest."

"*Flustered* is a strong word."

"Shall I keep removing articles of clothing and see if we can get you there?"

"Are we going to practice magic or bedroom antics?"

"I don't need practice in the latter," she said.

"It never hurts to learn new skills."

"That's true. And there's plenty I could teach you, I'm sure."

"I'd relish the opportunity," I said, with a wink that caused another rush of color to spread across her cheeks.

She coughed. "Let's stick to magic, for the moment."

"If you insist."

"I do," she said under her breath—as if muttering a reminder to herself. With a wave of her hand, the shadowy threads around her dissipated. She walked to a nearby bench and laid her bow and quiver against it; I did the same with my sword.

"I've been speaking with some of the scholars in this palace, trying to make better sense of both our respective magics," she said.

"And?"

"And a lot of our discussions have centered on how luxmancy is the opposite of necromancy—the opposite of what this realm thrives on. It's why your magic proved so destructive here, before it met the balancing weight of mine. The area around us now is already somewhat stable, however, so I thought perhaps we could more safely experiment with our powers. Yours, in particular."

"Experiment?"

She nodded. "I've been trying to better determine what the opposite of each of my own specific powers might be— what you might *truly* be capable of doing. Because something tells me you weren't reaching the full potential of your magic back in Elarith. Who knows what parts of it those controlling Keeper bastards were hiding from you?" Her fists clenched and her face turned to the star-streaked sky, as if she was considering storming back into the Above and confronting those Keepers that very moment.

If anyone could have managed such a thing, I was beginning to think it would have been her.

She took a deep breath and continued more calmly: "It will take all facets of both our powers, I think, if we're going to find a way to bring balance to both realms."

I had my doubts, but still I said, "Go on. What sort of *specifics* did you have in mind?"

"Well, for example, I can possess things—overtake objects, magic…and even living beings, in theory. It involves projecting a small part of my soul and magic into a target and using it to control it. I wonder…can you do whatever the opposite of that would be? Maybe…*un*possess something? Pull the pieces of me back out of a given object?"

The idea was intriguing, if nothing else. "I can try."

She took a small knife from the sheath hanging from her belt, quickly getting to work before either of us could second-guess her plan. She tossed the knife to the dirt and stretched her hand out over it. I caught a glimpse of what looked like a faint tendril of one of her shadows lifting from her palm and darting into the knife; it happened so quickly I would have missed it if I'd blinked.

She raised her hand, and the knife rose with it.

"I usually feel it like an extra hand grabbing hold of whatever I'm trying to possess," she said. "I don't know if thinking of that will be helpful to you, but…"

I circled her, examining the floating knife from all angles. Tentatively, I reached toward it. I could feel her essence twisting within the blade, and I focused on this—on its chill, its heaviness—as I let my own magic bleed forth and directed it, imagining it wrapping around her soul like a fist. When our two energies were indistinguishable from one another, I beckoned my fingers. The blade darkened—a glimpse of the shadowy power possessing it.

I beckoned again.

The knife dipped slightly.

Nova drew in a sharp breath.

But it was over just as quickly, my grasp on her essence slipping before I could truly catch hold of it.

Nova frowned, opening her mouth several times to speak but ultimately finding no words.

I attempted to mimic some of her usual optimism. "...That felt like the start of something, at least. Something that might have been stronger outside of this protected palace."

"Maybe," she agreed, distractedly, as she guided the floating knife back to the ground. "I wonder what else we could try?" She paced as she contemplated, her fingers tapping and twisting the multitude of bracelets running up her arm.

"You often reach for those bracelets when summoning magic, I've noticed."

She paused mid-step. "They were made by Orin, the first at my parents' insistence—they help channel my different powers."

"Do you ever take them off?"

"It's dangerous to take them off. I had a much harder time sorting out the chaotic energies inside of me—and keeping those things under control—before I started wearing the bracelets."

"So...never, then?"

She shook her head.

Though she obviously tried to mask it, I'd seen the fear that flashed in her eyes at the question, and I realized...she was afraid of her own power.

Reasonable enough, given what that power had done on the night of her eighteenth birthday. And I could only guess at what sort of chaos she'd endured before that.

But it still bothered me, for some reason, that her caretakers had opted to bind her powers rather than embrace them. Maybe she'd had her share of controlling keepers, too—they were simply nicer than the ones I'd grown up with.

I didn't say any of this out loud. But, as I watched her possess the knife and effortlessly pull it up into the air again, directing it toward the bench where our other weapons rested, I found myself wondering what sort of queen she might ultimately become, and where the true edge of her power lay.

"So, they all channel different strands of your magic?" I asked.

"Yes," she said, considering each of the bracelets in turn before focusing on one woven from an assortment of colorful threads, tugging it away from her wrist for me to see. "This is the one that reacts whenever I have visions of the past. And if I can see the past, I wonder..."

"If I can see the opposite—the future?"

"It would be incredibly useful, wouldn't it?"

"It would. Unfortunately, I've never experienced anything like that before."

"And I'm still not particularly good at seeing the past," she admitted—but her expression remained determined. "Maybe something simple, though. Maybe the knife again?

I've seen glimpses of past things I've cut with it whenever I grasp it. So perhaps if you touch it…"

After a moment of deliberation, I walked to the bench and cautiously reached for the object in question. I wasn't entirely sure I *wanted* to see any part of what the future held for us—so it was almost a relief when nothing happened, regardless of how hard I squeezed the weapon.

"Nothing?"

I shrugged. "Afraid not."

She looked defeated for half an instant before moving on. "Well, maybe we should work on perfecting what we've already had some success at." With this, she pointed toward the knife and pulled it back into her command with a quick bit of concentration and a flourish of her wrist. "Take away my hold on it if you can," she challenged.

I stepped forward to meet her.

Again and again, we practiced—her shadows sliding into the blade, taking control of it; my light following, attempting to draw the darkness back out, to break its hold.

The crowd above continued to watch, silently but intently, holding their breath as if waiting for something to go wrong. Nova occasionally threw them a haughty glance, but otherwise remained focused on the task at hand.

And, slowly, but surely, we began to see progress. She grew more confident, more swift in her movements. I nearly pulled her hold loose more than once—though she always managed to get control back. It felt like a representation of the time we'd spent together in this realm, in a way; a constant push and pull, the occasional breathless exchange of power and trust followed by frustration.

A long time passed before she showed signs of needing to stop—a hesitation, a sharp intake of air as her expression grew pained. Concern gripped me for an instant. The distraction proved costly; a slip of concentration from both of us, and the blade shot toward me, slicing my forearm as it came.

Nova let out a gasp. "Ah—sorry."

"Don't be. It's nothing." I wrapped a hand around my arm to staunch the flow of blood while the crowd above grew restless, their whispers getting louder and louder.

Nova didn't spare them another glance, but a muscle in her jaw twitched with what might have been a mixture of worry and irritation. "We should go inside and clean this up."

"You want to get me away from my admirers and into a more private room, hm?"

"Keep talking," she said, eyes narrowing, "and I will give you a matching scar on your other arm."

I smiled at her threat, and her tone softened a bit as she added, "Actually, I just want to return your favor from the other day." She ran a hand along her shoulder, which had made a full recovery since the incident in Erebos.

I hadn't done much to aid in that recovery, aside from sending a weak bit of warm, soothing energy into the wound—not really a favor.

She was insistent, though. She walked to the pile of our clothing, slipping her own cloak back on before picking up my shirt and coat and tossing them to me. "You should probably cover up, anyway, before your *admirers* hurt themselves trying to get down here to treat your injuries."

Chuckling, I pulled the loose shirt over my head, gingerly rolling up the sleeves, trying to avoid smearing it with blood. As soon as that was settled, Nova took hold of my hand and dragged me inside.

"You dragging me away like this looks very scandalous to my admirers, I'd imagine," I said.

"It won't be the first time people have started talking about me behind my back," she replied, matter-of-factly.

We ended up in the washroom across from her bedchambers. In truth, there were very few eyes to witness our *scandal*; the palace was quiet, its lights burning low—it was much later than I'd realized. Somewhere in the waves of shared power and magic between us, I'd lost track of time.

"This brings back fond memories," I commented, settling onto the counter beside the sink and holding up my arm, allowing her to wash away the blood as she insisted on doing.

"Does it?"

"Of the time you stabbed me in the wrist after violently disturbing me from my cursed sleep."

"Oh. Right. That… We got off to a rough start in this world, didn't we?"

"Some might argue things are *still* a bit rough between us."

She sighed. "It's certainly more complicated than any relationship I've had with any man in the past."

"…Relationship?"

She stiffened a bit, but she didn't retract the statement. "What else do we call it, now that we've taken turns cleaning blood off one another?"

I stared at the ceiling, fighting the urge to wince as she wrapped a bandage around my arm. "We seem to have skipped over the more fun parts of a typical *relationship*."

"What are you suggesting?"

"Nothing at all."

She made an unconvinced noise deep in her throat.

"Is there something you would *like* me to suggest?" I asked.

Her hands grew clumsy. She chewed on her bottom lip as her eyes narrowed on the knot she was working on, clearly trying to stay focused on her task.

I leaned forward. "Because I have plenty of suggestions to make, if you'd like to hear them."

She regarded me from underneath her lashes. "Is this an example of those courtly skills you spoke of earlier? Are you trying to manipulate my emotions right now?"

I smiled, taking her hand and drawing her in until she was wedged between my knees, her mouth tantalizingly close to mine.

"It's a useful skill, as I said," I replied, breathing warmth onto her lips with the words, sending a shiver racing through her that triggered one in me as well. "I'm merely doing my best to teach you."

"Is that so?"

"Yes."

I realized it in the exact moment I said it: I was lying.

It would have been the easier thing—the better thing—for this to all be just another courtly game we were playing. A lesson with a clear beginning and ending.

But that's not what this was.

Her gaze fell to my lips. "Keep manipulating me, then."

The confident purr of her voice sent a shock of desire straight through me. Desire that was treading entirely too close to *need*.

"Those are dangerous words," I told her, cupping her jaw and tilting her lips closer to mine.

"I'm aware. And I don't care."

I traced the shell of her ear with my thumb. "Chaotically wicked, reckless thing," I muttered.

"My nickname has gotten more elaborate, I see. No longer simply *Chaos*."

"And I'm holding myself back. I have a few other choice words I could use, if I wanted."

Her reply came in a fluttering whisper. "Go on. Use them."

I trailed my hand lower. Across her neck, her throat, the swell of her breasts. Down, and further down, taking a possessive hold on one of her hips. "Impetuous. Foolish. Infuriating."

She leaned even closer. "Keep going."

"Impossible." I pressed a slow, lingering kiss to her lips. "Beautiful," I said, dragging my mouth away.

The last word drew a smile from her. She backed up, and I moved as if attached to her by an invisible string, following her toward the hallway, stopping several times to catch her in my arms and crush my lips to hers once more.

We stumbled and kissed our way through the room, pressing up against walls and cabinets, knocking over baskets of linens, bottles of soaps and perfumes and other toiletries as we went.

The hallway seemed darker, narrower when we finally re-emerged, still caught up in each other, and stumbled toward her bedroom door. I stopped just short of throwing open that door and ravaging her across the threshold, instead pinning her against the wall beside it.

My lips hovered inches from hers. "You're incredibly tempting, do you know that?"

"Is *flustered* still too strong of a word for what you feel when you look at me?"

"We're well past flustered," I braced one arm against the wall, hooking the other around her and pulling her hips flush with mine. She inhaled sharply as my hardened cock pressed between her legs, and I dropped my voice lower, bringing my mouth to her ear, as I asked, "See what you've done?"

She caught her breath. Her eyes burned into mine as I drew back just enough to better see her face. "Would you like me to apologize?" she asked.

"I think we both know it would be insincere."

I leaned in to kiss the smirk from her lips in the same moment that loud, relatively close voices caught our attention.

She tried to act as though she didn't hear them, but I saw the flicker of doubt in her eyes. I did my best to ignore it—because I *wanted* her.

I wanted her so fucking badly it was nearly driving me feral.

But I was also thinking of what came next. And I'd been listening to the chatter throughout the halls these past days. To the gossip. The questions. The doubts. Most of that doubt had nothing to do with her, and everything to do with *me*. Her people didn't trust our closeness. And I knew how hard she was working to gain the trust and respect of the people in this palace, which made every kiss I stole from her feel like sabotage.

Reluctantly, I took a small step back.

The voices in the distance persisted. Nova's gaze was on the door to her room. Slowly, she tilted her face to me, her bright eyes shining, her lips parting for words she couldn't seem to get out.

Her meaning was obvious enough, even if she couldn't find her voice.

Come inside with me.

Her tongue slid over her lips, and the temptation became a painful, physical thing. A beast ready to devour us whole.

There would be no coming back from giving into it.

If we walked through that door, I would lock it behind us. I would forget every person outside of it. Every kingdom in the Above and Below, every pact, every law. It would be my Chaos and no one else, and I would fuck her, claim her, fill her in every way possible. The depth of our magics' bond was nothing compared to how deeply I wanted to bury myself inside of her. How badly I wanted my name on her lips, and her taste on mine.

She was breathing hard as she stared at me, awaiting my answer, shadows rolling like smoke across her skin.

The voices in the distance were close enough that I could make out some of their conversation, now.

But the voice in my head was far louder.

You have a duty to your kingdom and its people—to the whole world of the Above. Think twice before getting any closer to her.

There was no justifying it; getting closer would ruin at least one of us.

Probably both of us.

Utilizing every ounce of restraint I possessed, I planted a chaste kiss on her cheek and whispered, "Good night, Nova."

A swirl of emotions crossed her face—frustration, disappointment, hints of regret. But, as she was so skilled at doing, she quickly slipped a cheerful mask on, covering every trace of whatever true feelings she might have been experiencing.

"Good night, Aleks." She disappeared into her room without a backwards glance.

I stood like a fool outside of her closed door for far too long before I managed to make myself walk away.

Chapter Thirty-One

Nova

I couldn't stop thinking about last night.

I hated Aleksander for invading my thoughts so thoroughly. I wanted him out of my head. Wanted to be able to focus on my magic, alone, to pretend nothing had happened between me and him, to never think about his smirking face; or his bare, sculpted abdomen; or his stupid, beautiful laugh ever, *ever* again.

And yet, I *also* hated that he hadn't been beside me when I woke up.

The conflicting emotions had been waging a war through me all morning long. My head ached. My stomach twisted. My steps had grown increasingly clumsy as the hours went on.

"You seem distracted, Highness."

Stop calling me that, I almost snarled.

But I bit my tongue, knowing it would do no good; the young man before me insisted on referring to me as his queen, even though I'd yet to officially pick up the crown of this kingdom.

Eamon Ashmore was his name, and he was the older brother of Red. He was a talented magic user—even moreso than Thalia. We'd spent the past several mornings together, and the time had been surprisingly pleasant in spite of the challenging trainings; his positive demeanor was a refreshing change from Thalia's near-permanent scowl.

"I'm fine," I assured him, attempting to smooth some of the sharpness from my tone. He wasn't the one I was truly frustrated with, after all. "Let's go again. I need as much practice as I can get at this."

We were focusing on the same thing we'd been focused on every morning before this one: On more precisely forming, and better controlling, the shadows within me.

Shadows that I'd cursed and feared for most of my life. Shadows that were made of the very same kind of power and energy that made up this twilight world I was allegedly meant to save. I was Noctaris. Noctaris was me. This was what it meant to be one of the Vaelora. And my potential power was as vast as the world itself—

Or so Eamon claimed, anyway.

As for him, he was similar to Thalia in his abilities: able to pull from and manipulate existing magical energies, but not conjure anything into existence. One of the *feyth*—beings who were apparently a step below the Aetherkin like Orin, power-wise. The term *necromancer*, I had learned, was a collective one that encompassed all these different tiers of beings who could in some way channel the dark energies of Noctaris.

The luxmancers were on the opposite side of the spectrum, able to forge Light magic from the energy of Soltaris. They had different levels of beings as well, but I still couldn't figure out precisely where Aleks fell on this ladder. How he was able to conjure up such powerful magic, despite being in this world where there was so little of its aligned energy to work with. Or how—

No.

No, it didn't matter; I wasn't thinking about him right now. I had magic of my own to worry about.

I drew my shoulders back and fixed Eamon with a determined look.

"Again," he agreed with his good-natured smile. "As you wish."

It was deceptive—that smile of his—given the amount of power and dangerous skill hiding within his lanky frame. He could pull shadows from nearly everything around him, it seemed, and control them with an astounding amount of precision and force. During our first training session, I'd been entirely caught off guard by his youthful, easygoing appearance—and had promptly gotten knocked on my ass, over and over again, because of it.

I set my stance, determined not to let that happen again.

Closing my eyes, I continued to inhale and exhale as calmly as I could while picturing the darkness flowing through my veins. Trying not to fear that darkness, but to give shape to it. To call upon it.

When I opened my eyes, multiple shadowy ropes twisted around me like serpents ready to do my bidding. Already, I had made some progress during these sessions—the threads of my shadows didn't lash out quite as wildly as they once had, even here in this space where Calista's lingering magic fed into their power.

I took another deep breath.

With small movements of my hands and twitches of my fingers—following the techniques Eamon had shown me—I started to work. We'd set up targets across the training ground, and, one after the other, I unraveled my pack of shadowy serpents and sent them curling up, over, and through these targets.

It was excruciatingly difficult, even with the progress I'd made. They were more contained compared to the past, but the darkness still resisted being directed; it felt like trying to adjust a dozen different sails at once, all while battling a storm-tossed sea. My balance swayed and my arms ached. Sweat dotted my forehead, dripping into my eyes.

Red—whose true name was Brynn, I'd learned from Eamon—watched from the edge of the training yard, one hand absently rubbing Phantom's belly. Her gaze was wide as it followed me and the shadows, little gasps escaping her every time I managed to successfully hit a target. Her brother regarded me with a similar, reverent kind of interest. I tried to soak up their enthusiasm, letting it chase away some of my foul, frustrated mood.

Stop thinking about Aleksander, I commanded myself fiercely. *You have bigger problems*.

If I was going to raise an army worthy of marching into Nerithys and dealing with the Aetherstone, I had to be able to direct these shadows as if they were an extension of my own body. This was the first part of the grander plan we were working on: Guiding my magic—the very lifeblood of Noctaris—into a ghostly army of shades with a precise hand. Reviving those shades. Then, there was the matter of sustaining their revival. Bastian, Thalia, and a few others were working on siphoning and refining some of Luminor's power into a smaller weapon, creating something that I could safely wield. Searching, as Aleksander had predicted, for some way to balance out my powers without relying on him.

Stop thinking about Aleksander, I ordered myself.

Again.

Giving my head a hard shake, I sent the last strand of my shadows into the final remaining target. They all hovered above their respective marks, darkening the light filtering down from a glowing, periwinkle sky.

"To me," Eamon commanded.

I brought the separated strands back together into one churning mass. Widening my stance, bracing myself, I stretched my fingers forward, sending the mass firing toward Eamon with the motion.

He halted it in mid-air with rapid, exact gestures of his hands, twisting it a few times above him and studying the billowing black cloud before lowering his gaze to me.

"Now," he said with an encouraging smile and a challenging gleam in his bright eyes, "bring it back into you."

My heart skipped several beats. This was always the most difficult part—trying to settle the shadows back inside after they'd been given a taste of the world at large.

I beckoned. The tumbling ball rolled quickly toward me. *Too* quickly. It slammed into my chest like a pouncing beast, and the collected shadows threatened to unravel. They always felt like they were at their most sentient during this part of the training—resisting my command to return, trying to assert their dominance over me.

It was violent and messy, but I ultimately managed to draw them in with only a few new bruises on my arms and chest to show for it.

As they settled back inside of me, my weight felt like it was doubling. I staggered for a few steps before dropping to one knee. My balance teetered further. I was on my back before I even realized I was falling, pain shooting down my spine and dots dancing in my vision. The sky rushed overhead, a canvas that someone had recklessly dumped paint onto—a messy swirl of purples and blues and whites.

Eamon was leaning over me a moment later. "You were brilliant, Highness."

I felt like I was cracking into a thousand pieces, but I forced a smile as I sat up, trying to catch my breath and stay upright despite my dizziness. "If you say so."

(*I thought you were astoundingly average,*) Phantom informed me from his place at Brynn's side.

"Thank you for that," I muttered, knowing that his sensitive hearing would still be able to pick up my words, even from a distance.

He responded with a yawn, and then burrowed himself into Brynn's arms, nibbling on the buttons of her dress and making her giggle.

Eamon beamed at me for a moment more before walking over and grabbing a drink from the canteen he'd left beside his sister. A thoughtful expression settled onto his boyish face as he drank, wiping the sweat from his forehead and surveying the targets across the grounds. They were still mostly intact—evidence that I was getting better; my first attempts had resulted in my over-eager shadows obliterating several of them.

Despite all my progress, however, it still didn't feel like

enough. The days were moving too fast. The amount of hopeful eyes watching me increased by the hour, the weight of their growing expectations piling onto my shoulders. And targets were one thing, but the shades—the *people*—were another. If my shadows moved too recklessly against them...

Eamon strode back to me, offering me my own canteen, and asked, "Shall we go once more?"

I stood on wobbly legs, taking the water and sipping it slowly, trying not to think about the chance of my darkness doing more harm than good. Images of the damage I'd done on the night of my birthday continued to haunt me, even now. And in spite of how desperately I needed practice, I didn't think my mind was going to cooperate.

"...I might need a break," I admitted, reluctantly.

Eamon looked as though he was considering sweeping me off my feet and carrying me to safety before my dizziness could get the better of me. But before he had a chance to do anything of the sort, I stiffly made my way over to a bench on the edge of the yard.

He followed dutifully. "May I take you to lunch?"

"I'm not really hungry at the moment, but thank you."

His grin never faltered. "Next time, then. I'll be looking forward to it." He gathered up his things and turned toward his sister. Glancing over his shoulder at me, he added, "And you truly *were* brilliant—an honor to practice alongside. We'll be moving on to practicing with Grimnor, and the full expanse of your power, in no time at all, I'm certain."

I tried for another polite smile, even as my heart sank at the thought of that sword of legend. It remained in its chamber, alongside Luminor. Safe. Protected. And it was so incredibly tempting to *keep* it there.

My brother had assured me I could take it out and practice with it whenever I was ready to do so. But, despite his insistence and Eamon's endless votes of confidence, I didn't feel anywhere near ready.

I wasn't sure I ever would.

Eamon went to his little sister and swooped her up in his arms. They looked incredibly similar; the same stunningly green eyes; the lean, bordering on lanky, frame; the same slightly lopsided grin. His hair was more blond than red, but just as unruly. Brynn gave me one of her shy waves, and Eamon mirrored her, offering one last smile before turning away for good.

As they left, Brynn happily perched on her brother's shoulders, Phantom trotted over to me, settling down at my feet. (*He likes you a lot, doesn't he?*)

"He's merely grateful to me for bringing his sister back, he's said."

(*It seems like more than that.*)

"He's not really my type. Much too cheerful—even for me."

(*You prefer grumpy types?*)

"Yes; it's why I'm so fond of you," I replied, patting him on the head.

He growled, yet nuzzled his head more completely into my palm. (*How many times has he asked you to lunch, now?*)

I exhaled a slow breath. Eamon seemed sweet. Harmless enough, too—his dangerously impressive command of dark energies aside. But I wasn't interested; I was still too busy trying to get a certain Light King out of my mind.

My jaw clenched, my hand stilled, and Phantom cocked

his head to the side and asked, (*Do you want me to bite his legs off?*)

I snorted. "What is it with you and wanting to bite the legs off of the people in this palace?"

(*I don't know,*) he replied, dropping to his stomach and rolling back and forth in the dirt. (*I'm getting bored here.*)

"Would you like to venture back out into the unprotected Deadlands instead?"

He whined at the suggestion.

"Exactly. Personally, I think we're overdue for a little boredom in our lives."

He didn't disagree.

"Although, somehow, I don't think we're going to get it," I added—and, right on cue, I noticed Thalia approaching us.

We'd worked together enough over the last few days that I felt as though she was starting to warm up to me—as much as I'd seen her warm up to anybody, anyway. Her scowl was less intimidating, somehow, and there was even a hint of concern in her eyes as she looked me over.

"Still in one piece?" she asked.

"Despite Eamon's best efforts to ensure otherwise."

The comment made the corners of her mouth twitch, maybe with the beginnings of a smile. "Good," she said. "Because I have a plan for us this afternoon, if you're up for it."

I sat up a little straighter on the bench, trying not to reveal my true exhaustion to her.

"Your brother suggested I show you more of our kingdom," she told me. "There's one place in particular I wanted to take you—one that we'll have to navigate on the day of Equinox and…well, it will be easier to explain at the location itself."

Despite my tiredness, I couldn't help but perk up at the thought of learning more about the world I was apparently destined to save. So, I agreed, heading to my room to change and otherwise clean myself up.

When I opened the door, Aveline was there, busily directing servants to change linens, dust furniture, and fluff pillows. Everything had already seemed perfectly clean when I'd left this morning, but I'd learned not to question her about these things.

She wrapped me in a bone-crushing hug. I didn't mind; her embraces always felt genuine. She smelled like a comforting blend of rosewater and freshly-pressed linens, with an occasional hint of spice and sugar if she'd been baking—which was the case today. Warmth radiated from her soft, plump body, and I felt as if I could have melted into her and been entirely safe…like I'd known her for much longer than a week.

As soon as I told her of my plans for the afternoon, she helped me change, conjuring up a beautiful outfit consisting of a knee-length, dark blue dress made of the softest fabric imaginable, paired with a gold-trimmed coat and comfortable walking boots. It was a far different kind of magic than anything I possessed, this ability of hers to always put me in such perfect, flattering attire.

"Have a seat," she said, gesturing to the stool before the mirrored vanity.

I was eager to get back to Thalia, but I still sat.

Before arriving at this palace, it had been some time since I'd been fussed over like this. I'd never admitted it to Aveline or anyone else—and likely never would—but a part of me had missed my days of extravagant dresses and hairstyles, even though I hadn't been overly fond of such things when I was younger. I guess it was true that you didn't often realize what you had until it was gone.

"You have your mother's hair," Aveline commented under her breath as she tugged and twisted at the strands, attempting to braid them. "Beautiful but wild."

I tensed, gripping the plush cushion beneath me. She clearly meant my real mother—but the word *mother* still made me think of the Queen of Eldris.

Another thing I'd taken for granted for so many years.

It was difficult to imagine that there had ever been another in her place, but curiosity made me ask, "What happened to that real mother of mine?"

Aveline didn't answer right away. I watched her in the mirror, her eyes scrunching and her lips pursing as she struggled to find words. "Most who give birth to one of the Vaelora don't live to tell the tale. Your mother was no exception."

"And my father?"

Another long pause, during which her hands became uncharacteristically clumsy as they continued to comb through my dark, wild locks.

"Aveline?"

"...I don't know. The King of Rivenholt died long before you were born. No one knows who laid with Queen Isolde after him; she never revealed his identity—not even on her deathbed."

My fists clenched tighter into the velvet cushion.

"If you had a father who loved you in the Above, as I understand you did, then I'd consider him your true parent and not worry about the rest."

I *did* consider him my true father, even now that he'd been gone for years. Even knowing he shared no blood with me. He was still the one who had raised me, doing everything he could to protect me.

And he'd ended up dead because of it.

The mysterious circumstances surrounding his murder still needed solving, but one fact now seemed clear and undeniable: If he hadn't been harboring me in his palace, he wouldn't have ended up on the wrong end of Luminor's blade.

The one I considered my true mother would not be frozen in that palace, either, a victim of my out-of-control power. Because Orin had clearly lied about this, too—he'd tried to convince me that all the things that had happened on the night of my birthday were not my fault.

But so much of it *was*.

I had ripped open the earth. The darkness from Below had surged into the Above world because it was trying to get to *me*.

And now the only way to save the one I called Mother was for me to somehow balance and breathe life into Noctaris once more. Bastian was convinced that doing so would settle those restless shadows at Rose Point, allowing the victims there to break free of their curse.

But what if I couldn't do it?

A numbness overtook my body. Aveline seemed to notice; her head came to rest on top of mine, her arms encircling me in a gentle embrace. Pulling back a moment later, she carefully stroked my hair, pinning it away from my face with a golden, orchid-shaped pin.

"You look beautiful, my lady."

I managed a small smile despite the aching pain in my heart. "Thank you."

My vision was blurry. I couldn't make out my reflection through the emotion swelling my eyes, but I didn't *feel* beautiful. I felt like a monster who brought death and darkness wherever I roamed—one who had done so from the second I'd been born, apparently.

Had my true mother even had a chance to know my face before my shadows swallowed her up? What about my brother's? Had she heard my voice? Or his? Was she the one who had given us our names?

What if I ended up responsible for the deaths of *both* my mothers?

They were heavy questions. And I understood why Orin had tried to protect me from their weight. But that didn't make me any less angry about it.

All those years spent feeling like I didn't belong in the Above, and nobody had bothered to tell me *why*. I hadn't understood my magic, so I had grown to fear it.

And now I wasn't sure how to shake the grip of that fear from my heart.

More desperate than ever for answers, I hugged Aveline goodbye and hurried back to Thalia, who had stayed behind at the training grounds. Phantom was curled up under the bench, snoring loudly. I nudged him with my boot. He woke with a disgruntled little growl, but quickly shook off his irritation and grew excited at the chance to stretch his legs and run somewhere outside of the palace.

While Thalia went to the stables to collect Uldrin, I took Phantom up on his offer to shift into his horse-like form and carry me; I felt safer on his back than I would on any other mount.

We rode for what felt like close to an hour. Far beyond the palace grounds, through the glittering royal city of Tarnath, back into the unprotected Deadlands beyond it all. The farther we traveled from Tarnath, the darker the sky became. The trees grew more and more bare; the ground, more dusty. The air became thick with the acrid stench of sulfur, mixed with the faint, metallic tang of something like blood.

Even knowing the truth about what this place was, it still felt like descending into Hell all over again.

"My kingdom," I whispered under my breath, over and over—a reminder. "*My kingdom…*"

This was my kingdom, and I could still save it.

Chapter Thirty-Two

Nova

A chill began to overtake us, sneaking its way into my bones and settling there. I pressed closer to Phantom's back, to the heat radiating from him, and kept a watchful, determined eye on our surroundings.

The sky eventually began to lighten again, shifting to a bruised shade of violet rather than black—but its light was different from the one that hung over Tarnath and the palace. Not the light of a proper world's sun, but a veiled shine with no source that I could pinpoint. One that felt threatening despite its softness.

We came to the head of a narrow, sandy grey path, marked by two columns wrapped in thorny vines. Thalia finally slowed to a stop and dismounted, unsheathing her staff from the special sling attached to Uldrin's saddle.

"We won't linger here long," she said, "because it isn't safe to do so. You and your power will eventually attract the attention of any shades that might be nearby. But generally, this is an area that those shades avoid. So we should have a few minutes to work with—a *very* few minutes, as your brother stressed to me, over and over and over."

I couldn't help noticing, again, how fond and familiar her tone was when the subject of my brother came up.

"So, you've known him for over twenty-four years," I said, hopping down from Phantom's back.

"Give or take."

"The two of you seem close."

I had so many questions about him, I hardly knew where to start. I'd had precious little time with Bastian since my arrival—he was a popular man, it turned out. He called himself Regent, but most everyone else referred to him as *King*, and he served in the role with what seemed like an endless amount of patience and resolve—though more out of obligation than any real desire for power, based on my limited observations.

I was the older twin, and, by their laws, apparently, I was the one meant to rule Noctaris's central kingdom of Rivenholt. This most powerful crown of the Below was mine…if only I wanted to wear it. Yet, despite the significant opportunity it presented, the whole idea felt like an afterthought to me.

Because if I couldn't master my magic, and ready my sword and army, then there would be no kingdoms left to rule over.

"We've come to rely on one another over the years," Thalia replied, her tone lacking some of its usual, frigid confidence. "But that isn't important right now." She gestured to the path of grey sand that lay through the columns. "This is. Come on."

"What about Uldrin?"

"He's not a fan of the place we're headed," she said, already starting to walk, "so he'll want to stay behind. Don't worry; he won't go anywhere."

I cast an uncertain glance toward the scourge stallion—but he'd already started pawing at the ground in a bored manner, uncovering sprigs of grass and lazily chomping them.

He was large and terrifying enough that nothing would trouble him while we were gone, I supposed.

I jogged to catch up with Thalia's long-legged strides. Phantom shifted into his dog form and loped ahead of us, sniffing at clumps of withered flowers and snapping at the floating specks of purplish-blue light in the air. Those specks grew more numerous the farther we walked. I thought they were fireflies at first, until some of them began to dart about in a strange manner, occasionally forming a glowing outline of a larger creature—spectral, winged beasts that were there one instant, gone the next. I started to slow to a stop, watching one of them more closely, but Thalia urged me on.

"We need to hurry," she reminded me, gaze darting toward the distance, where the darkness was absolute. Her hand gripped her staff so tightly her knuckles turned white.

I did my best to ignore the strange glowing creatures as we walked on—even though they seemed to be curiously, timidly following us.

At the end of the path, we came to a small area where the ground was covered in silver grass. The trees here had actual leaves still on them, iridescent and papery-thin, their edges shimmering like dragonfly wings caught in a wash of moonlight. A fine mist drifted over everything, adding to the shimmering effect—and to the cold sinking into my bones. The air was heavy with the scent of earth and moss, and filled with a soft rustling, like the brush of unseen wings —or perhaps the whispers of unseen spirits.

In the center of it all, a stone archway curved over a freestanding door made of dark wood. The wood gleamed as if lit from the inside, casting intricate patterns of light and shadow over the various symbols carved into it. I walked a wide circle around it all; there was nothing noteworthy on the back side—just another stretch of grey sand, and a smooth wall of stone where I'd expected the back of the wooden door to be.

It all felt...*ancient*. Timeless. As though it had been here long before any living creature, and it would remain long after all of them had perished.

"What is this place?" My voice came out hushed.

"The *Nerithys Gate*."

"Nerithys...as in the realm where the Aetherstone resides?"

She nodded.

"So you can access that realm by passing through here?"

"In theory, yes. Though the gate doesn't yield to just anybody."

I cautiously stepped forward, studying the stone arch and its doorway more closely. Brushing aside a small bit of moss, I noticed that the bottom of the arch on either side of the door had a small footing jutting outward, each with an opening sliced into the stone. "Two openings...for two blades?"

"Exactly."

"Grimnor and Luminor."

"Yes."

Still uncertain about my ability to wield the infamous Sword of Shadows, I asked, "Is it possible to open it without those two blades?"

Thalia seemed to be caught off guard by the question. "It would take exceptionally powerful magic to do so, but... maybe? The swords are undoubtedly the easiest method, though. The intended method."

"Has anyone tried to open it lately?"

"Not lately. We have records of prior openings, warnings from our kind about the dangerous place Nerithys was becoming. Of the Light Keepers who patrol the realm on behalf of Lorien Blackvale, but..."

"But things have likely changed since the last time anyone went through it, I take it? We don't *truly* know what we'll be facing once we pass through this door?"

"I'm afraid not," she said.

And the weight of the upcoming Equinox grew heavier, still.

Wrapping my coat more tightly around myself, I walked away from the door, trying to slow my racing thoughts.

The trees in the area were sparse, and after a short walk, they gave way to rolling hills covered in more silver grass—grass that was gleaming from the light of the creatures floating above it. More of them were taking on larger, more definite shapes, now, and I was certain I wasn't imagining what I saw; they were foxlike, almost, with sharp faces and bushy tails—but they also had small, sleek wings.

"*Vaekin*," Thalia informed me.

A realization occurred to me as I watched the creatures soar, tumble, and swoop over the landscape. "I've seen very few animals in this world."

"Many have perished, with our world's limited, remaining energy being channeled elsewhere and focused on saving as many *people* as possible. There's a sanctuary in the South District of Tarnath, however, preserving all different sorts of creatures. And a few other such sanctuaries are still holding on in cities like Erebos. So, when our world is righted once more… hopefully we'll be able to rebuild populations of things."

I watched Phantom run in circles, trying and failing to catch one of the glowing creatures. He would come close to snapping a tail between his jaws, only for the vaekin to shift back into a mere speck of light with a high-pitched noise that sounded eerily similar to laughter.

"These aren't typical fauna, though. The more intelligent of these creatures serve as occasional messengers between the realms," Thalia said, "and they gather here because this is the point where the veil between the worlds is at its thinnest. The gate is here, but several of Argoth's roads are also nearby."

"How did Argoth build those roads?" I asked—a question that had been nagging at me for some time. "He wasn't capable of any powerful magic, was he?"

"He didn't build them, truly; they were already here, from back when the two worlds coexisted alongside one another. He merely found ways to open them up again. There's quite a bit of debate as to *how*. Ask your brother about it, if you ever have a spare five hours to kill." Her smile was slight. "He'll give you all the details about it, whether you like it or not."

I smiled a bit, as well, thinking about how nice it would have been to have the sort of time to just sit in one of the palace's cozy studies, curled up by a roaring fire reading books or listening to my brother regale me with stories of history and magic.

I held out my hand to one of the vaekin that seemed particularly curious. It cautiously sniffed my palm several times, and then its body twisted around my arm with a fluid grace before it snorted into my ear and shot off toward the sky.

"They can travel freely in both worlds?" I asked, rubbing my ear.

"They're more stable in this one, but yes, they're capable of going into the Above. One of the few creatures we know of that can. Much like your dog."

"...My dog?"

"Phantom is a vae*hound*. Like the vaekin, his kind are born of the energy of this world, and the first of their species was personally shaped by a Vaelora's hand and infused with their magic. They don't live and die in a natural way; their energy is more fluid, capable of something like reincarnation—much like the magic of the Vaelora themselves. Which is why you were able to keep him from dying, I suspect, even without your fully-realized powers. And why he regained even more of his form once he returned to this world. Because even though he's able to find form and power in both worlds, this world is his true home." Her voice softened a bit as she added, "You two sort of have that in common."

The dog in question was currently on his back, paws in the air, feigning surrender. Trying to lure the vaekin in with a false sense of security—I'd seen him use the same tactic with the birds back in Orin's yard. It coaxed another small smile from me, despite the battles and uncertainties piling up around us.

"Your brother sent him to you, you know. There are a few wild packs of these dogs that roam close to Tarnath; he found your Phantom abandoned by one of them. A dangerous thing to take in, but…" She shook her head, a reluctant fondness in her expression. "The regent has done far more dangerous things, I guess."

I should have been flooded with gratitude, maybe. Because Phantom had saved my life more than once, and in more ways than one.

All I could think about, though, was how strange it was that I'd received such an enormous gift from this other world—this other life—and yet the truth had *still* been kept from me.

"Yet another thing I've spent years being clueless about," I muttered.

Thalia tilted her face toward me, a rare shimmer of sympathy in her eyes.

"I just…I don't understand how Orin could have kept so much from me."

"He's not a particularly good man," she said flatly. "Though he serves his purpose for us well enough, I suppose." Despite her measured tone, there was obvious hurt simmering in her expression—I'd noticed it a few times, now, whenever the subject of Orin came up.

Curiosity got the better of me, this time, and I couldn't help but ask, "How well do you know him?"

"Not as well as I would have liked to."

"What does that mean?"

She exhaled a slow, exasperated breath. "It means he abandoned me twenty-five years ago, shortly after you were born."

"Abandoned…so he lived in this kingdom?"

"Yes."

I stared at her, an uncomfortable possibility pressing into my thoughts. *Her eyes.* That strange amethyst shade... I'd seen similar eyes in only one other person. "Was he...is he related to you?"

A muscle ticked in her jaw. "My father."

The words stole the breath from my lungs.

How many times was it going to happen—this feeling of being punched in the gut with knowledge?

How many more things was I clueless about?

"He chose to leave this palace so he could look after you, once the decision was made that your magic would overwhelm you if you stayed here," she said. "And aside from a brief trip to bring your brother back to us, he hasn't returned."

Her cold, aloof attitude toward me suddenly made some sense—because it must have seemed like I'd stolen her father away from her. Another monstrous thing I'd inadvertently done.

Feeling sick to my stomach, I sank into a crouch, absently reaching for the vaekin that had started trying to unravel the laces of my boots.

"His duty as one of the Aethers always came first," Thalia continued. "I don't have many clear memories of our time together—I was only six when he left to protect you instead—but I do remember the distance he kept even before you came along. The distracted look that was always in his eyes, and how quick he was to race off to practice magic whenever he could.

"My magic is relatively weak, and so, I think...I think I was a disappointment to him. I don't believe he even loved my mother, either; she was merely a servant in the palace, and—as you know—the Aetherkin live unnaturally long lives, and so I doubt she was his first or last love. She died years ago. We almost never talked about him, but…" She trailed off with a shrug.

I didn't know what to say.

What could I possibly have said?

I had plenty of memories of him as a very different sort of man than the one she was describing. People were complex, after all—paintings made up of all different shades, strokes of light and dark that created depth on a canvas. But I kept this thought to myself. Somehow, I doubted she was ready to hear any heartwarming stories about the lighter shades of her father—especially not from me.

Instead, I rose slowly back to my full height, looking over my shoulder at the gateway in the distance, and I tried to keep the conversation focused on learning more about the realms and the tasks before me. "He traveled freely between the different worlds, then?"

"Relatively speaking. It takes a lot of magic to manage it—it's not something anyone can do on a regular basis anymore, aside from a Vaelora with fully realized powers."

"Could he have come with me this last time, though?"

"Maybe. But we need a presence in the Above, and it was agreed upon that he would stay there. They've been discussing it for some time, via messengers like the vaekin."

My cheeks burned from a combination of anger and embarrassment over my lack of knowledge. "So my coming here, and you finding me and bringing me to the palace…it was all orchestrated?"

"Only some parts. We didn't know how your magic would react once you returned to Noctaris, so we could only plan so much. Orin purposely guided you to a point far from the Rivenholt Palace—where the energy of this world was weaker—so your powers would have more time to acclimate before you made your way to us. We thought you would be quicker, though; your magic should have led you directly here. But you veered from the shortest path, for whatever reason, and toward Aleksander instead—we certainly didn't expect you to find the Light King and drag him along with you into our royal city."

"That wasn't in my plans, either," I muttered.

We were quiet for several minutes. I continued studying our surroundings while trying to balance under the weight of everything Thalia had said. She stood by the gate, her hands occasionally smoothing over the stone arch. She paused several times with her palm against that arch and her head bowed, as if praying. Maybe to the ones who had made the gate, whoever—or whatever—they might have been.

I didn't want to keep poking her wounds, but I couldn't help the curiosity still burning inside me. "I didn't think the Aetherkin ever had children," I said. "I assumed they remained celibate, like the Vaelora were expected to."

"It's true that it wasn't typical for them to have children. But almost all of the ones who served Calista eventually did. Desperation became a factor when no Vaelora reappeared in Noctaris, even centuries after Calista's death… and once they realized their children were almost always able to learn how to draw out and manipulate the magic of our world, even if it was to a lesser extent than their parents."

"…The feyth," I realized, piecing this together with my lessons from Eamon.

She nodded but averted her eyes. "Sometimes, I think he wanted to have me merely out of a misguided sense of duty—because this world needed more beings who could control its fading magic and keep it going until a more permanent solution was found. And I don't think I'm the only one who came about because of this. There are a few of us within the palace."

"Like Eamon, you mean?"

"Yes. Though he doesn't like to talk about it; both of his parents were Aetherkin, actually. They died sacrificing themselves to fuel the vivaris flames of Erebos."

"Sacrificing themselves?"

"Yes—in order to carry out a ritualistic pouring of their magic into those flames. That city burns to this day because of them. Kaelen is Eamon and Brynn's uncle, though Brynn had never met him before our encounter. He is Aetherkin as well, and the last remaining Keeper of the vivaris. He continues to tend to the fires partly in memory of his sister and her sacrifice."

I shook off the uncomfortable feeling creeping through me. I didn't want to think of Kaelen, or wonder what had become of him after our dramatic encounter.

Instead, I wondered at yet another unexpected revelation surrounding his niece; I hadn't witnessed Brynn controlling any Shadow magic—but she'd managed to find and follow mine. She'd truly *seen* me, even as a shade. Was it because of some latent power that had reached automatically for mine?

I thought about puzzling this over with Thalia, but her gaze had become distant. Walled off.

"We should probably head back toward the palace," she said without looking at me.

I didn't argue and, as we walked, I decided it was time to change the subject. "The glow of the vaekin reminds me of a festival I once attended back in my old kingdom," I commented. "The Moonweaver Festival. The city was full of lanterns that night, all of them glowing with a similar bluish-purple light."

She angled her gaze my way to show she was listening. We fell into a friendly enough conversation, despite the questions still lingering in the air.

The night of that festival was one of my clearest memories...perhaps because it was the only time I recalled Orin ever truly getting *mad* at me.

Two years ago, the King of Elarith—or the one posing as him, I supposed—had descended upon my kingdom with the goal of gaining even more favor among the subjects of Eldris. He'd taken one of our oldest traditions and put his own hands on it, sparing no expense to create a celebration that the people of Eldris still talked about, even to this day. The glitz and glamor had won over even some of his staunchest opposers.

Only a few had seen it as the propaganda it truly was.

I remembered every detail. The sky thick with stars overhead; the floating lanterns tethered to colorful strings; the dancers spinning in their dazzling, gem-studded costumes; the firework cannons igniting, exploding high in the air and showering the laughing, applauding crowds with smoke and sparks.

I'd worn a dress the color of blood and shadows—fully prepared to end up with both on my hands before the night was over with—and I'd stolen one of those cannons and aimed it at the king as he paraded down the street.

I was one of several rebels who caused chaos that night.

But I was the only one who had aimed directly for the king.

The only one who had still been standing in front of him when the smoke cleared, a clear message easy to read on my lips: *Leave.*

A reckless challenge, I could admit. Especially all these years later. And it felt even more dubious, after all I'd recently learned—that it wasn't even the actual King of Elarith that I'd been aiming for. His face had been covered by an elaborate mask, with most of his ceremonial motions taking place while heavily surrounded and shielded by his Keepers, and now I understood why.

I still didn't regret anything I'd done that night.

Because something had awakened in me the moment I fired my cannon. Something that had grown even stronger during the ensuing pandemonium.

I'd ruined the party. Had been branded an outcast and a menace more loudly than ever before. And so it was that night when I realized—or maybe *admitted*—I'd entirely lost any claim to my kingdom. That my subjects were blinded by a foreign king's light, his riches, by the celebrations he could conjure to cover up his atrocities, and they always *would* be, unless I could come up with a better way to show them the truth.

Standing alone with the smoke and screams settling around me, I'd fully committed myself to my desperate plan of traveling into the Underworld to retrieve the sword that had ruined my life and kingdom.

Two years since that fateful decision.

It had all led to this—to the waves of impossible revelations and impending revolutions rising around me now.

All from a single strike of a cannon's fuse.

The memory of igniting that cannon rekindled my sense of urgency. As interesting as my conversations with Thalia had been, I was eager to get back to the palace, to a relatively safer place where I could sit and make sense of all these new things before they slipped through my fingers.

And, as annoying as it was, Aleks was the only person I could imagine talking through all of these difficult things with.

I didn't have a chance to track him down, though; we returned to the palace to find it abuzz with activity when we stepped inside, and we were immediately surrounded by a swarm of hurried servants and panicked guards.

"What's going on?" Thalia demanded.

Before any of the guards could answer, my brother strode toward us, parting the crowd as he came. He breathed a sigh of relief at the sight of us, the tension in his features loosening for an instant.

"Bastian?" Thalia pressed.

He took a step closer, his eyes flicking over me as if searching for any signs of injury, before he took a deep breath and said, "Someone tried to break into the chamber where the swords are being kept, and they killed two of our guards in the process."

Chapter Thirty-Three

Nova

The blood on the walls was dry by the time we reached the entrance to the swords' chamber.

The doors to that chamber remained sealed. A handful of guards were examining the splatters of blood along with a section of one of the doors that appeared to have been burned; Bastian went to speak with them while I stood numbly, taking it all in, and Thalia mumbled curses to herself as she examined the bloody footprint closest to us. Phantom, in the form of a smaller-than-usual dog, darted between the guards and the walls, sniffing the bloodstains, his ears twitching with unease.

After a few minutes of discussion, Bastian opened the chamber doors at my request—just so I could see for myself that both swords were still in their proper places.

I exhaled a slow, relieved breath as their power rippled over me. I had no idea who would have tried to take them, but the thought of their power falling into the wrong hands numbed me straight to my core.

They had been safe in this chamber for *years*. We'd only needed them to stay safe for a short time longer—long enough for me to prepare to properly wield Grimnor. I'd already felt as if I didn't have enough time to manage it.

Now, it seemed our time was even shorter, and the situation even more precarious, than we'd feared.

"How could this happen?" I asked. "*When* did this happen?"

"It could have been hours ago," my brother said. "The dead were only discovered when the next round of guards came to relieve them of duty."

Hours ago.

Had they purposely waited until I was gone from the palace to attempt their heist?

"Somebody in this palace knows *something*," Thalia said. "As secluded as this corner is, there are still plenty of curious eyes falling upon it every day. However sly the assassin and would-be thief was, unless they were invisible…"

An uncomfortable, uncertain silence fell over us, lasting for several minutes, until my brother grumbled something in the Noctarisan language and ushered us out of the chamber; too many curious servants and other palace dwellers were pressing too close, trying to peer inside.

We sealed the room shut once more. My brother ordered everyone else away from the hall, but he, Thalia, Phantom and I lingered in the space, still trying to make sense of it. There was a particularly large splatter of blood near the center of one of the doors; I couldn't take my eyes off it.

"Where is the Light King?" Bastian asked, after a moment.

"I haven't seen him this morning," I said, offhandedly. I was so busy studying the blood that it took a moment for the meaning behind his words to sink in. My gaze shifted to him. "…Why do you ask?"

He didn't reply, but the concerned look in his tired eyes said enough.

"Aleks wouldn't have done this."

He cleared his throat. "…You know I'll have to question him, all the same. Along with the ones who travel with him."

My stomach clenched at the thought. "I'll talk to him myself."

"I don't know if that's a good idea." He took a step toward me, as if planning to prevent me from leaving.

But I was tired of other people speaking on my behalf. Tired of not seeing things for myself, of having others make decisions for me. It was becoming more and more clear that entirely too much of my life had been orchestrated by hands other than my own.

I couldn't—*wouldn't*—let that trend continue.

I backed away from my brother and started briskly down the hallway, only to slow as he called after me: "I'm only trying to keep you safe."

I paused, glancing over my shoulder to see him hesitating with a pained look in his eyes.

"It's all I've ever done," he said, "even when I didn't realize I was doing it."

"…What are you talking about?"

"The magic that you thought killed me when we were younger," he explained, closing some of the space between us, "it wasn't some random manifestation of my power—it was a defensive response. We were attacked that night. There was evidence of other magic used against us, according to both Orin and the King and Queen of Eldris. Evidence of *Light magic*. It nearly killed us both. My power protected you, according to the ones who witnessed it—but only just. It was a massive amount of power used against us."

"That doesn't mean all luxmancers are bad. And it's certainly not proof that Aleksander would do something like this."

"The Keepers of Light are our *enemies*, Nova."

"He doesn't work for them."

"He spent twenty years being indoctrinated by them."

I opened my mouth only to snap it shut in frustration; I couldn't refute this fact. I didn't know the full extent of what had happened to him in his kingdom, but I knew enough that it made my skin crawl to think about it. There was no telling what sorts of things they'd done to him. What beliefs they'd branded into him through abusive, horrendous methods.

Bastian breathed in deep, collecting himself. "You survived the Above for twenty-five years, and you've made it all the way back here. Our world is counting on you. *I'm* counting on you. So just…just don't throw it all away. That's all I'm asking."

"I'm not throwing anything away. I know Aleks didn't do this."

My brother's silence was heavy. Suffocating. His tone was equal parts concerned and exhausted when he finally said, "You trust him? Truly?"

My heart whispered *yes*.

My mind screamed *you shouldn't.*

It was funny how the whisper seemed louder in that moment. More insistent—as though no amount of noise could drown out the feelings stirring in my heart.

"He wouldn't have done this," I repeated, fully aware that I sounded like a stubborn fool.

Bastian clenched and unclenched his hand. He seemed to be fighting the urge to reach for me. "You've made up your mind about this."

I somehow steadied myself enough to calmly reply: "Yes."

"…Speak to him, then." I was the older twin, but he suddenly looked ten years my senior as his gaze shifted between me and the blood all around us. "Just…please be careful, Nova. I don't want to lose you again after all this time."

I didn't know what to say to this, so I simply nodded. "I'll be careful."

Phantom caught up to me, weaving between my legs and sitting down on one of my boots, as if trying to anchor me in place. I hesitated a moment longer, kneeling to give him a reassuring scratch between the ears.

"Stay here and see if you and your nose can help figure some things out."

(*I don't smell anything unusual,*) he informed me.

"Keep searching. I'll be back soon."

He cocked his head from side to side, clearly uneasy, but he obeyed, staying in place as I turned and hurried away.

Thalia immediately went to my brother and started arguing against his decision to let me go; their heated discussion echoed behind me as I picked up my pace. I half-expected one of them to come charging after me, but they didn't.

I checked the training grounds first, where Aleks typically was at this time. Only Eamon was there, and he informed me that he hadn't seen the Light King all day. I got a similar answer from every person I encountered during my swift march through the palace: No one had seen him in hours.

With every step I took, fear coiled more tightly in my stomach. Everything I'd spent the morning learning—everything I'd so desperately wanted to talk to Aleks about—rose around me like water, until it felt as if I was just barely keeping my head above the surface.

Was I fooling myself, thinking he was the one to tell everything to? Had I only dreamed the possibility of us being on the same side?

Did my brother have a point?

By the time I reached the hallway where Aleksander's room was, I was practically running. With effort, I slowed to a jog, trying to catch my breath, gathering at least some composure before I pounded on his door.

He answered almost immediately, as if he'd somehow sensed me coming. He took one look at my face, and then he was moving toward me with concern, his gaze narrowing, searching the hall behind me as if expecting to see someone chasing me down.

"Nova? What's wrong?"

"Where were you earlier today?"

His eyes settled on my face, questioning.

"Just answer me."

"What the hell is going on?" he asked.

"Where. Were. You?"

"...*Why?*" Tension sparked in the air between us—and for an instant, it was as though all the trust we'd started to build was in danger of unraveling. As if it had been held together by a single thread.

"Because someone attempted to break into the chamber where Luminor and Grimnor are being kept," I said, as calmly as I could, "and they killed everyone standing in their way."

His expression changed abruptly. Confusion overtook it first. A hint of panic followed, but that was gone in an instant, replaced by his usual hard, fierce gaze.

Breathlessly, I said, "My brother thinks you—or one of your companions—could be responsible."

"I don't know anything about this."

My throat ached and burned, like I'd swallowed a mouthful of sand. I couldn't just take his word for things, could I? No one had seen him all day. No one had proof of where he'd been.

"I swear I don't know anything, Nova."

Just like he swore he didn't know who killed my father.

I still didn't have conclusive evidence of *that*, either—though I realized, in that horrible instant, how I might be able to obtain it.

I could have gone back to the chamber with the swords.

I could have placed my hand on Luminor's blade, allowed myself to see what I could of its torrid past—whatever the truth and its consequences ended up being. I was getting better at reading the histories of objects. And there was a chance, too, that I could read something useful from the chamber door itself. Maybe my magic would reveal who had bloodied it, burned it, attempted to force their way through it...

I hadn't thought of this while examining the scene, and I doubted the idea had crossed Thalia or Bastian's minds, either; this power wasn't unheard of, but it wasn't a common manifestation of necromancy—and it wasn't something I'd been practicing in the presence of anyone other than myself and Aleks.

It seemed like an obvious way to find the truth.

But did I *want* to find it?

I immediately knew the answer to that question: *No.* I felt like a coward...but I wasn't sure my heart could take being wrong about the feelings I'd started to develop for the man standing before me.

My pulse pounded as I braced a hand against the doorframe.

You trust him?

Truly?

"Come inside," Aleksander said. "Let's talk about this. Please."

I shook my head. I wanted to run. I wanted to stay. I couldn't get my feet to move in either direction.

"Let's talk elsewhere, then. Wherever you want to go, I'll go."

"What should we talk about?" I asked, voice wavering a little. "The way nothing between us makes sense? The way we've both been manipulated so badly that we have no hope of knowing who or what to trust?" I managed a step into his room. Probably against my better judgment...but the hall seemed too open, too exposed for all the things I needed to say. "How about the way you would never—*could never*—choose me over your duty to your own kingdom?"

"You don't think I would choose you?" he asked, quietly.

"Everyone here would disagree with that choice, even if you did. This entire palace has done nothing except warn me about you since we arrived. And Zayn has done the same to you, right? I've seen the way he looks at me when he thinks I'm not paying attention. He doesn't trust *me* any more than my palace trusts *you*."

He didn't deny it.

"And maybe they all have a point. We're wrong for each other. All wrong. What hope is there for balance, honestly? With every new thing I learn about our worlds and their history, it feels all the more impossible. You feel impossible. *We* feel impossible."

Again, he said nothing in his defense.

We stood without speaking for a long moment. That thread binding us together seemed to shake with uncertainty, keeping rhythm with my unsteady heart, twisting and tightening one moment, starting to fray in the next.

Please don't break, I thought, desperately.

All the things I'd wanted to tell him, all the important, world-shattering, war-related things I *needed* to talk to him about…none of those things mattered to me just then.

Because, suddenly, all I could think about was *him*.

All I needed to know was where we went from here—how we could possibly bridge the valleys of hurt and mistrust between us to keep going, to keep bringing life to places where none had any right to bloom.

I could handle things on my own. I knew how to be alone; I'd spent my entire life doing it. But, for perhaps the first time in my life, I didn't *want* to face the future alone.

I wanted to face it with him.

I just didn't see how I could.

Voice breaking a little more, I said, "You let me go last night. You left me alone."

"I did."

"Because it was for the best."

"Yes. It was."

I steeled myself for another rejection.

"But I regret it," he said.

My breath hitched. I was certain I'd misheard him. Then he said it again, in a voice clenched tight with emotion—

"I regret it. I swear to the gods, *I regret it.*"

Before I could reply, he was grabbing the front of my coat, yanking me deeper into his room, pulling me nearly flush with his body. And like a floodgate opening, the confessions began falling from his lips, his growl of a voice sending shivers racing over my skin.

"I haven't stopped thinking about it for a second," he said, his grip on me shifting, his hands slipping underneath my coat, taking hold of my hips. "I've barely eaten. Or slept. All I've really done is think about how badly I wanted to follow you into your room last night and make you forget everything outside of it. How badly I wanted to make you forget *everything* except me, to bury myself so deeply inside of you that my name would be the only thing left for you to gasp out. To fall asleep, still inside of you, and then wake up and do it all over again."

I was breathing too hard, my heart pounding too fast, to properly reply.

"I'm tired of fighting with you, Nova. *I want you*. More than I should, more than makes sense, more than any godsdamn sword or kingdom or anything else."

"That doesn't change the fact that we're on two separate sides of a war. I don't see how we both win—"

"I don't care about winning." His lips crashed against mine, pressing so completely they sealed away any chance of properly breathing. I was dizzy when he finally pulled away and whispered, "I concede defeat."

The walls spun around me.

He cupped his hands against my face, steadying me as he kissed me again, slower this time.

"I don't know what's going on outside of this room," he said against my lips, his voice low and ragged, "but…stay. Just stay here. Don't make me beg."

I closed my eyes against the spinning, leaning my forehead into his shoulder. His arms wrapped around me, enveloping me in the scent of him and his soap; a bright burst of citrus—fresh, tangy, clean. Underneath it lay his more familiar earthy scent, grounding the brightness. Warmth overtook me as I breathed it in—a warmth unlike anything I'd ever felt. The bright blaze of lust was there, gods help me it was *always* there, but something else had started smoldering underneath it. Something more like a steady, constant glow that I could settle into.

Something that made me think of home.

"Do you even know how to beg, Light King?" I murmured against him.

He laughed softly. "For you, I would manage it."

I lifted my head. He brushed a hand across my cheek. Threaded his fingers into my hair. His eyes burned into mine, their golden color even more mesmerizing than usual—because I knew he saw nothing else but me in that moment.

He *wanted* nothing else.

"Stay," he repeated. "Please stay. And we can figure out the rest later."

I'd already made up my mind.

I walked back to the door. Closed it. Locked it. Every inch of me was trembling. I didn't know what happened next. I just knew I didn't want us to be interrupted—that I wouldn't *survive* another interruption.

I turned back around, and the sight of him expectant and waiting for me took my breath away all over again.

He held out his hand. I stepped forward and took it, letting him pull me in. My palm came to rest flat on his chest. His free hand slid around to my backside, cupping my curves, bringing my body firmly to his once more.

I gazed up at him. "You concede defeat."

"Yes."

"I win."

He brushed a hand across my cheek. "You do."

"And what have I won, exactly?"

The smile that crossed his face was nearly my complete, instant undoing.

Wordlessly, he led me over to the long, cushioned bench that stood at the foot of his bed. Pausing here, his hands roamed over my body, removing my coat, undoing the belt cinching my dress, deftly unfastening the buttons at the back of that dress so he could slide it down.

My head tipped back. My eyes closed as he trailed kisses along my bared shoulders before moving lower, taking hold of my dress as he did, rolling it down along with the supportive binding underneath. The fabric bunched up beneath my breasts, pushing them up to meet his eager mouth. He curved a hand around each breast in turn, gripping them possessively, while rough strokes of his tongue turned their satiny tips into stiff peaks.

A soft moan escaped me.

He paused.

My eyes flashed open.

He nodded toward the bench. "Sit," he ordered.

I sat.

Kneeling before me, he ran his hands down my legs, leaving a trail of little bumps in the wake of his touch. Slowly, he pulled off one boot, then the other. Stockings and the sheathed knife at my left ankle came next—disarming me, in more ways than one.

He cradled my leg as his lips brushed my calf. My knee. The inside of my thigh. His hand smoothed its way upward at the same time, stopping just short of my center before skimming back down to my knee. He teased me this way several times before finally letting his fingers travel all the way up, where they caressed the thin, dampened fabric between my thighs, applying pressure but not quite penetrating.

His touch was unhurried—savoring.

Gently, he pulled aside the last bit of cloth that separated us, his fingers slipping through the evidence of my arousal, mapping their way over the soft folds trembling with need. That trembling soon overtook my entire body, until even the faintest touches from him threatened to send me over the edge.

He swept another series of kisses along my inner thighs, and then his eyes sought mine as he gave a low, rough command: "Lift your hips for me, Chaos."

I did, enabling him to roll my dress up over them, further exposing me. He slid the garments underneath off, tossing them onto my boots. His own shirt followed. I settled back down onto the bench, admiring his firm body...and that was when it struck me—

This was actually happening.

Stripping our clothes away felt like peeling away the outer world, like all the dust and doubts of every kingdom were being tossed aside, leaving only the two of us. Nothing else mattered as he kneeled before me once more. As his head dipped between my thighs, pressing a kiss to the needy ache in my center, following it with a few slow, tantalizing swipes of his tongue.

Bracing a hand against the edge of the bed, he leaned up, hovering over me. His mouth found mine, his tongue pushing its way through my lips as his hand settled between my legs.

After a moment of gentle massaging, one finger slipped inside of me. A second soon followed. He dragged his lips away from mine so he could study my face, watching my every reaction to his every touch. Memorizing every gasp and twitch and moan, finding the precise way to draw out more of these things.

While his fingers pushed deeper, curling and coaxing against my inner walls, his thumb found my clit and began to tease it, just barely tapping and circling against its sensitive nerve endings until I was begging for more.

He answered my pleas with heavier, more wicked pressure and movement from his thumb. I lifted my hips again, rocking against his hand with an eagerness that drew a low, dark laugh from him.

He slipped his free hand underneath the small of my back, helping me rock higher, pressing us even more fully, more deeply together. A third finger tapped against my entrance, the tip of it slipping inside. It burned in a delicious, devastating way as he prodded and stretched.

I didn't want him to stop, yet I heard myself gasp out something that sounded like *can't*.

"You can," he encouraged, his hand moving from my back, instead collaring my throat as he pressed closer and claimed my lips in a deep, hungry kiss, "and you will."

He moved more slowly, more deliberately, tracing his finger along the edges of me before sinking it all the way in. The sudden fullness pulled a moan from my throat. He silenced it with a kiss and then moved his mouth to the curve of my neck, lips sucking and tongue darting against my pulse as he pressed his fingers farther inside.

"Gods," he breathed against my skin, "I can't wait to bury my cock in this tightness."

The mere thought was enough to send me spiraling toward release. My back arched. Deeper and deeper his fingers plunged, relentlessly pounding in and out of me until I was crying out with pleasure, unable to hold back the orgasm that shattered through me.

As the last cry of release echoed from my throat, he brought his mouth back to my neck and murmured, "What a beautiful fucking sound that was."

The low-burning chandelier danced above me. I felt as if I was floating in the ceiling alongside its flickering candles. Closing my eyes, I whispered, "You were right about what you said that night at Lake Nyras."

"...About?"

"Your hands being more *capable* than mine."

He laughed quietly, his fingertips delicately tracing the still-throbbing space between my thighs, sending ripples of ecstasy rolling through me. "Is this you conceding defeat as well?" he asked.

"At least about this."

"So what do *I* win?"

"What sort of prize did you have in mind?" I opened my eyes to find him watching me as closely as he had earlier, the hunger still burning brightly, beautifully in his eyes. Pleasant shivers cascaded through me as he considered my question for several beats, his hand smoothing its way up my stomach, across my bare chest, pinching my still hard nipples.

He didn't answer right away, so I let my gaze drift out of focus, thinking only of the way his hands felt as they explored my body.

"For my prize…" he finally answered, his touch trailing back between my thighs, fingers circling through the dampness, "…I want to taste you. To *truly* taste you, and show you that my hands are not nearly as capable as my mouth."

I'd thought I was finished, utterly spent and satisfied from what he'd already done—but his words sent a fresh shock of desire through me. My heart immediately began to race again. My breaths grew ragged and shallow.

Before I could find the words to reply, his strong hands closed around my hips. He lifted me onto the edge of the bed, slightly higher than the bench that he then kneeled on, perfectly aligning his mouth between my legs.

His tongue was gentle at first, wide and flat, the measured strokes interspersed with puffs of warm air as he carefully teased my sensitive places back into arousal. Those places still pulsed with the blissful feeling that walked the narrow line between pleasure and pain. He was patient, easing up when I whimpered, but never waiting long before returning with a slow, rapturous lick.

As soon as my sounds became more pleasure than pain, his hunger truly revealed itself. He became insatiable, hooking his arms around my thighs, gripping them in a dominant hold that he used to pry my legs farther apart so he could properly feast between them.

"So fucking sweet," he panted, coming up briefly for air. His low voice vibrated over my skin. "So fucking delicious. You taste like the first orgasm I gave you. Which is perfect," he added, in between quick, torturous lashes from the tip of his tongue, "because it means you taste like *mine*."

Because I am, I wanted to reply. *I'm yours, I'm yours, I'm yours*—

But before I could speak, he had buried his face completely between my legs once more...and I could no longer form words.

I could only gasp as his hands reached high along my inner thighs and pressed my legs more firmly into the mattress, opening me more fully for him to devour.

I writhed beneath him as he ate, the waves of my second orgasm building quickly to crescendo. His strength was uncompromising as I rocked within those waves, holding me hostage until his mouth had sucked every last ounce of satisfaction from me.

The bed felt like it was shifting. My body tingled everywhere, floating in a state of perfect bliss. Yet, I was aware of him moving between my legs, positioning himself above me, sliding his pants lower and letting his cock spring free. Then my hands were moving, too, circling around the hard, impressive thickness of him. Feeling it throb beneath my grip as he drew close, so close—

His head tipped back. With a low, rumbling cry, he reached his climax, painting my chest with hot cum, the feel of it dripping over my tingling skin drawing out one last aftershock of my own orgasm.

As the last drops of his release trickled over me, he leaned down, his body still shaking slightly, and pressed a soft kiss to my forehead.

I used a throw blanket draped nearby to clean myself off. Then, exhausted, I curled onto my side and closed my eyes. They didn't stay shut for long, though; as soon as I felt him moving again, I was wide awake once more, tracking his every motion as he went about cleaning himself up. Entirely, undeniably aware of him. I felt like a foolish, lovesick girl, but I just wanted to keep *looking* at him.

He came back to bed and laid down on his side, facing me. My hand found his, holding tightly to it until the room stopped whirling around us.

I don't know how long we laid there.

I think I drifted off at some point, only stirring when I felt him shifting, his body nudging closer to mine.

"I don't want to leave this room," I whispered. "I don't want to face the people outside."

He slid an arm around my waist and rolled onto his back, pulling me against his bare chest, and said, "I'll keep them away for as long as you want me to."

It was what I wanted to hear. That was why he'd said it. And I also knew it was impossible—nothing would keep the monsters we faced away forever. He might have been willing to protect me from all of the questions and dangers pressing toward us, but he couldn't slow the passage of time. And he couldn't change the complicated history of us and our respective worlds, or the battles that had started raging long before we came into being.

Nevertheless, I let myself rest in our comforting lie for a few more minutes, listening to the quick pounding of his heart, imagining a very different sort of life for us both.

But then I slipped from his embrace and sat up slowly, taking deep, steadying breaths as I started to put myself back together.

He reluctantly followed my lead, rolling from the bed and going to the linen cabinet, returning and offering me a towel from it.

I cleaned myself more thoroughly. Put my dress, and everything underneath, back on properly. Pulled on my stockings and boots. Redid my braids.

Aleks watched me without speaking, without moving to put himself back together. His shirt remained in a crumpled heap on the floor. His pants still hung low on his hips. He ran a hand through his hair, smoothing it somewhat, but most of it still fell in disheveled waves around his face. A thin sheen of sweat glossed his chest, and all his edges were aglow from the bit of daylight creeping through the drawn curtains…or maybe from his own magic, stirring beneath his skin; it was hard to tell him apart from the sun in that moment.

I wanted to pull him back into the bed with me.

As much as he'd accomplished with his hands and tongue, I could only imagine what *other* parts of him could do.

But there were other things we had to focus on, so I swallowed hard and said, "Hand me my knife, please."

He picked it up from the floor. It had nearly slipped free

of its casing, and as his fingers pressed against the bit of exposed steel, he froze, his gaze briefly glazing over.

"...Are you okay?"

He blinked, smiling softly at me, as though he'd just woken up. "I'm fine," he said, handing me the blade.

Odd, I thought. But I was too focused on what awaited me outside the room to think about much else.

I finished securing the knife back in its embroidered leather sheath, then forced myself to make my way to the door—though I stopped short of reaching for the handle.

Aleksander followed, wrapping his arms around me from behind, pressing his face into my hair and breathing comforting warmth over the curve of my neck. "We'll figure everything out," he promised.

I somehow managed a nod.

It was only after I'd left and started making my way down the hallway that the strangeness of his moment with the knife truly struck me—along with a potential explanation for it.

He hadn't been able to see anything when we'd tried working our magic on this very same knife yesterday. But if I knew anything about this man, he'd likely spent the whole night trying to perfect this spell that had eluded him. Likely the whole morning, too.

Had he managed to uncover a glimpse of the future in that knife?

It was the only explanation I could think of for that horrified look that had briefly crossed his face.

But what had he seen?

Chapter Thirty-Four

Nova

I didn't make it far before I heard a scream.

It was such a sharp contrast to the blissful quiet and peace I'd experienced in Aleksander's bedroom that it took my mind a moment to accept what it was hearing, to jolt me entirely back into the reality of the world and wars I was now a part of.

Following the scream—and the rising babel of other voices that followed it—led me to the bedrooms where Rowen and Farren had been staying, which stood across from one another in the hallway running perpendicular to Aleksander's chambers.

The doors to both rooms were open. Servants and guards rushed back and forth between them, hurriedly exchanging words and harried looks. I caught a glimpse of a bloody blanket wrapped in the arms of one of the servants. Another left a trail of scarlet footprints in her wake.

Chaos further enveloped the space as I stepped into it, my arrival drawing multiple gazes. Heads bowed. Bodies shrank away in uncertainty. Most voices dropped to a whisper, but they were joined by the voices of more arriving onlookers, and so the overall clamor in the narrow hall grew louder still.

The frantic march between the rooms continued. Several people were soon calling for someone to fetch my brother, their voices booming to be heard over the panicked chatter.

There was so much noise that I didn't realize Aleksander had joined me until I felt his hand press against the small of my back. I knew it was him, even without turning around, as there was magic in his touch—a warm burst of comforting light amidst the mayhem. It sank into my skin, briefly transporting me back to the moment where I'd rested in his bed, wrapped in the warmth of his arms.

Had that really only been minutes ago?

The warmth didn't last.

Before I could find my voice and demand answers from any of the people before me, Zayn strode furiously from one of the rooms, his hand tightly gripping the sword hanging from his belt. He looked as though he was considering unsheathing it and silencing everyone around us with a few precise swings.

I'd never seen him look so upset.

Aleksander stepped away from me, cutting his cousin off before he could do anything drastic. He held tightly to Zayn's arm, speaking in a low voice, trying to calm him down; it took several moments before Zayn seemed to realize he was even there.

While the two of them discussed something in the

language of their own kingdom, I gathered my courage and walked numbly toward one of the open rooms.

Worried expressions followed my every movement, but no one tried to stop me.

The room was dark, lit only by a lamp in the connecting washroom that spilled a weak glow into the space. Two candelabras were lying on the floor, along with an assortment of other objects that looked to have been knocked from the top of a dresser. The room smelled of wax and smoke…

And blood.

Making my way around to the other side of the bed, I quickly found the source of that sharp, metallic scent: a body. Its throat had been slashed wide open. The face was horribly mangled, but after a moment of staring, I managed to make out a familiar pair of eyes, wide open with the haunting, unseeing gaze of the dead.

Rowen.

Something told me Farren was sprawled out in an identical scene across the hallway.

"Fuck…" Aleksander muttered, coming up behind me.

A crowd had gathered at the door. Now that I was present, they all seemed to be halting there, waiting on me to give them orders. But I still didn't know what to say. I couldn't even speak. I could only stare. First the guards murdered at the swords' chamber, and now, this.

What next?

Aleksander managed to move before I did. Carefully, he picked his way over splattered blood and the scattered objects from the desk, kneeling at his soldier's side. My gaze followed his as he examined a chunk of flesh on the floor beside Rowen's head…

"That…that's his tongue, isn't it?" I whispered in horror, moving toward the dresser, fumbling to grab onto its edge as my balance swayed.

Aleks averted his eyes, his breaths growing shaky and uneven, his usual stoic demeanor starting to crack.

Zayn pushed his way through the crowd at the door. Fury radiated from his body. Even in the low lighting, I could see it—the twitch in his jaw; the fire in his eyes; the tense coil of his muscles, ready to snap. His voice was sharp, each word cutting through the air like a blade, as he said, "Someone clearly didn't want them to be able to talk. They must have seen something they shouldn't have."

I gripped the dresser more tightly, my head throbbing with the implications of this latest bloodshed.

"Yes," said Aleks. "The question is, *what*?"

FIVE MORE DAYS PASSED.

Every corner of the palace was searched, every person in it questioned, but the investigation yielded no answers. The murders and the attempted break-in remained a mystery.

When I wasn't helping with that investigation, I spent every second I could trying to master more of my magic, or else mentally preparing myself for balancing the weight of Grimnor in my hands.

After most training sessions, I collapsed in exhaustion on my bed, not moving until one of the servants tempted me with food or a warm bath—or, more and more often, I sank into Aleksander's bed and all the different temptations of *him*.

He relaxed me, more than anything else this palace could offer. It wasn't merely about physical release, either. Somehow, when I hadn't been paying attention, he'd gone from a source of white-hot irritation to one of undeniable comfort.

The evening of the fifth day found me alone in my bedroom with my face buried in a pillow, wishing Aleks was much closer than he was. Phantom was sprawled out beside me, hogging the majority of the bed, one errant movement away from knocking me onto the floor.

Aveline trundled in soon after my head hit the pillow, her arms laden with trays of food. I could smell her cinnamon cookies—one of my favorites—but I was too tired to show much interest beyond rolling toward her.

Phantom, on the other hand, was up in an instant, clambering off the bed and sitting expectantly at her feet.

"Nothing here for you, little scamp," she said, shooing him away.

He slipped under the table and proceeded to lay down and sulk, settling his head on his paws with a loud huff.

"I expected you'd be in the Light King's room, but no one answered his door," she said, ignoring the pouting dog and turning to me.

"He's still at the training grounds," I informed her.

Zayn had insisted they keep going, even after I'd stopped. I'd wanted to stay as well, but my body had fought against every attempt I made to prove I could keep practicing magic, turning me into an embarrassing, stumbling mess—until both men had insisted I needed to go lay down.

Aveline considered me for a moment. And then, in her

blunt, matter-of-fact tone, she said, "Well, that gives me a chance to talk to you about this in private, at least." She held up a small glass bottle full of a pale blue liquid with herbs swimming in it.

"And what is *that*?"

"Something to prevent *accidents*, if you two are going to insist on messing around every chance you get."

I sat up, cheeks burning slightly. "We haven't done anything that would warrant the need for such a tonic, thank you very much."

She looked skeptical.

"It's true," I insisted.

And it was. Though, not for lack of desire. Something always held me back. Fear, I guessed; I'd never been one to consider sex particularly sacred, but things felt...*different* with him. And it terrified me, the thought of giving myself so completely to him, knowing all the things waiting in the wings, ready to rip us apart.

Besides, he had proven very...*creative*, and more than capable of using other methods to help me relax.

"Well, it's only a matter of time before you do," Aveline said, unfazed. "Anyone who's spent more than a minute in the presence of you two can see that much."

"I have a few larger concerns than who I'm sleeping with, and to what extent," I mumbled, flopping back against the pillow.

"No disagreements there," she said with a sympathetic click of her tongue. But she plopped the bottle down on my nightstand all the same.

I sleepily watched the herbs rising and falling in that bottle while Aveline hummed to herself as she laid out my dinner on the nearby table. The scents that wafted over to me were a strange combination of nauseating and enticing.

"Eat, my love," Aveline encouraged, rubbing my back for a moment before dismissing herself. She tossed a handful of cheese slices to Phantom on her way out, putting an end to his pouting session.

I rolled from my bed and stomached what I could—which wasn't much. A couple morsels of cheese, a bit of peppered turkey, a few crumbs of those cinnamon cookies that I normally devoured by the dozen. But I couldn't even find the energy to bathe after eating, as I normally would. Sleep proved elusive, as well.

Eventually, I staggered out of my room and went in search of Aleksander. Phantom stayed behind, happy to have my bed all to himself—and to polish off all the food I'd left on my plate.

As I made my way through the halls, I kept my thoughts only on Aleksander; everything else was too exhausting to think about. My mind soon filled with images from the previous night, when the two of us had relaxed together in the massive tub that stood in the center of his washroom, sipping on sweet wine. Thoughts of repeating this activity proved more enticing than cinnamon cookies, even, and somehow my tired feet kept moving.

But he still wasn't in his room, unfortunately. And he was no longer at the training grounds, either—nor anywhere else I looked.

It wasn't Aleksander I ultimately found, but Zayn. I rounded a corner and nearly collided with the Elarithian lord; he was standing beneath a portrait of Calista, studying it with a frown and a pensive gaze.

Since our arrival in this palace, we hadn't seen much of one another outside of occasional shared training sessions. I'd seen even less of him since the murders of a few days ago—and we almost never found ourselves alone together. I suspected he was avoiding me. That he disagreed with how close Aleksander and I were becoming, but he wasn't one to argue if he could help it...so he was simply trying to pretend I didn't exist, instead.

Nevertheless, he greeted me warmly, this time—maybe because it was too late to get away. We stood together for several minutes, engaging in a pleasant enough, if shallow, conversation.

As that conversation trailed off, his gaze shifted between me and the portrait he'd been studying.

"You favor her a bit," he informed me. "Of course, they say that all the Vaelora of a given affinity favor one another, even though there's no blood between them."

I favored Queen Isolde, as well; there were several paintings of her hanging in the hall outside of my room. I had to pass them every day, and every day the weight of her eyes seemed to grow. And I couldn't help but think of how my own eyes were the same color as the Queen of Eldris's, too, even though we apparently shared no real blood.

All these powerful women with personal ties to me...

Why did I feel so weak, so uncertain, so small within their shadows?

I gave Zayn a half-hearted smile before fixing my eyes on the painting of Calista. Though she had never been a true queen, she was the very picture of regal grace. Her eyes were dark green, a stunning compliment to her raven-black hair. Her gaze was intelligent. The slight tilt of her head conveyed a sense of quiet dignity, while her lips were curved into a slight, mysterious smile, as if she was well aware of her own power and waiting for someone to dare to challenge it.

As I stared up at her, my turquoise bracelet tightened slightly against my wrist. I slipped my fingers between it and my skin, trying to relieve the pressure without taking my gaze from Calista's.

"I don't see the resemblance, I'm afraid."

"Maybe you will once you take up your sword?" Zayn offered.

The words flooded me with a myriad of confusing feelings—and questions.

Did he *want* me to take up that sword, knowing it would only make the relationship between all of us that much more complicated?

The last hints of warmth between us seemed to flee as the seconds ticked by in silence. I realized how much I missed the relationship we'd been building before the complications we'd found in this palace, and a question escaped me before I could stop it: "You told Aleks to be careful of me and that sword, didn't you?"

"I tell Aleks to be careful of everyone. He's a notoriously bad judge of risk—thinks he's invincible, that one."

"Be serious, Zayn."

He was quiet for a minute, back to studying the portrait. His chest rose and fell with a deep sigh. "It was quite the tragedy, wasn't it? The story of Calista and Argoth, I mean." He tilted his face toward me. He wore his usual, carefree smile—close to the one I'd been missing—but it didn't reach his eyes. "I guess I've just never been one for tragedies."

"...I suppose I'm not, either," I said, quietly. My lungs

felt like they were shriveling up, preventing me from taking a proper breath no matter how hard I tried.

Silence threatened once more, but Zayn broke it with a brighter, more determined smile. "I *am* a fan of evening strolls through the gardens, though."

It felt like a peace offering, so I couldn't help but take it, even though I was still curious about where Aleksander had gotten to. Zayn didn't seem to know the answer to that question, either—but I was soon able to put it out of my mind as we slipped back into a comfortable rhythm of conversation, the heaviness between us easing a little more with every passing minute.

We walked together for an hour, at least, through rows of rose-dotted hedges, over weathered brick paths, along a babbling stream. The air was crisp, filled with the invigorating scent of citrus and jasmine.

My tiredness was eventually forgotten, and I was in relatively good spirits when we returned to the front of the palace to find my brother standing with one shoulder leaning against a column, gazing into the distance as if watching for something. He was merely standing there, yet there was a gravity surrounding him that I couldn't explain; one that put all my nerves right back on edge.

"He always appears so serious," Zayn whispered, a crooked smile flirting with the words. "I feel like I'm in trouble every time he looks my way."

"We very well might be in trouble," I whispered back, trying to keep my tone light.

"I'll distract him if you want to run," he offered. "I provided that favor to Aleks a few times when we were growing up."

"That won't be necessary," I said, returning the smile he

gave me. I looked back to my brother to find his watchful gaze now fixed on me. With a sigh, I added, "Thank you for the company and conversation, but it seems I'm due back to the *serious* business of saving the world and such."

He chuckled and gave a little bow, bidding me good night and offering my brother a curt nod as he made his way inside.

Despite the laughter we'd shared, as I watched Zayn go, I found myself thinking, again, of the troubled expression he'd worn as we spoke in the hallway earlier, and of the long shadows cast by Calista and all the others who had shaped my life.

I've just never been one for tragedies.

I took a deep breath, trying to convince myself I wasn't walking toward a tragedy as I climbed the steps to my brother.

"I've been looking for you," Bastian said. "We need to talk." He sat on the top step and gestured for me to take the space beside him.

I sat, hooking my arms around my legs and drawing them up against my chest, trying to ignore the restless fluttering in my stomach.

"I've been discussing your training progress with Eamon and Thalia," my brother continued, "and we all agree that it's time you took up your sword—at least for a trial run."

"A trial run?"

His gaze lifted to the distant horizon once more. "There's an army that needs reviving, as we previously discussed. The soldiers we have at the palace and in Tarnath are limited in number; we won't last long on the other side of the Nerithys Gate without reinforcements."

"You have specific targets in mind for this revival, I assume?"

He nodded. "Tomorrow, if you're willing, we can follow the road that leads east out of the city. A relatively short ride will bring us to Graykeep and its barracks, a place historically used for the staging and training of our kingdom's finest warriors. The shades there are...*different* than the ones in other places."

I realized now that this was what he was looking toward—those distant barracks.

A distant possibility of hope.

"How are they different?" I asked.

"Though most of the people who have turned to shades now drift aimlessly through the Deadlands, the ones who were at Graykeep when they began to fade have yet to leave that fortress behind. They were marked by Calista well before her death, given an extra blessing and protection from her magic—as were the grounds of Graykeep itself. It seems this shared blessing has tied the warriors to that place. Fated them to remain loyal, even now...and we're hoping this will make them easier for you to awaken. That their loyalty might transfer to you."

I sat up straighter as I tried to picture it: An army at my back as I opened the Nerithys Gate and stepped through to whatever fate waited on the other side.

The vision was still blurry, but the outline was there. Maybe it would all grow clearer once I had my sword in my hand, as Zayn had suggested.

Bastian was watching me carefully. Expectantly. I was struggling to put my thoughts into words—a recurring problem over these past few days.

"We have very little time to work with," he said, "but if you're at all uncertain, then maybe…"

"No," I said quickly, before doubt could sink its claws into me. "I'm not uncertain. I can do this."

I *had* to do this.

The cost of failure was too difficult to even think about.

He exhaled a held breath, his smile relieved—though his eyes were a bit pained, as though he ached to think about how we'd come to such a desperate place.

After a bit of quiet deliberation, he stood, decisively, and offered me a hand up. "You should first learn how to access the chamber of the swords, then. Someone aside from me should know how to do this, anyway, just in case something happens to me."

He said those last few words like an afterthought as he turned and started into the palace, but I couldn't shake the foreboding feeling that settled over me as I hurried to catch up with him.

We made our way to the chamber doors. Two guards stood outside of it, their bodies so still they might have been statues. I wondered what was going through their minds every time they heard anyone approaching their station—how often they had thought of the murders that had taken place right where they stood, mere days ago.

The walls, floors, and the doors themselves were all spotless once more. Yet, everywhere I looked, I thought I saw blood at first—at least until I blinked, making it disappear every time. The scent of it lingered, however, no matter how I tried to make it go away. Whether memory or reality, I couldn't say for sure.

The guards bowed to my brother and me, stepping aside

without a word. As they took up a new position a short ways up the hall, I wandered closer to the doors. The bracelet my father had given me began to shake, just as it had the last time we'd visited this chamber. I'd been too distracted to pay much attention to it before, but now, its buzzing seemed to echo in the quiet air—loud enough that Bastian tilted his head toward the sound. I held it up for him to see.

"It's reacting to the doors?" He stepped closer, fixing a curious gaze on the jewelry.

"It did this before, too."

"...Reacting to the magic that seals this chamber shut, I suspect—as it's pure Vaeloran magic. In fact, you can likely follow its promptings and figure out how to break the sealing spell yourself. Go ahead; try it and see."

Tentatively, I reached my hand toward the doors. The bracelet rattled more violently as I did so, but, other than this, nothing happened right away.

I closed my eyes, blocking out all sensation except the movement of my bracelet. I soon felt an odd pressure in my chest, like someone taking hold of my heart and squeezing it. A sudden, rapt awareness of my body followed—like I could feel every individual drop of blood in my veins, every whisper of breath in my lungs. I was hyper-aware of every bump of gooseflesh on my skin, too...and what felt like ghostly fingertips lightly brushing my arm.

Those fingertips trailed down the length of my arm, collecting into a greater pressure at my hand. Then it was like someone else taking that hand and guiding it—showing it which symbols to trace on the doors. Which ones to avoid. Where to press, and how hard or soft to make my touch.

My eyes opened to see nothing more than a hint of

darkness swirling beneath the surface of my skin, so faint I wondered if I was imagining it. Yet, the pressure in my hand continued to build, the ghostly guidance heavy and insistent.

I did my best to let this apparent new facet of my powers lead me, but I almost panicked at the bizarre sensation more than once.

Bastian steadied my hand every time it started to drop, guiding it along with my magic. Within moments, the etchings in the steel were glowing—as they had the last time we'd been here—and the doors swung open.

My bracelet continued to shiver as we stepped inside. I clenched my hand around it, breathing hard. I'd been trying to channel some sort of power through this bracelet for *years*.

But now that I'd done it, all I felt was...*strange*.

The hyper-vigilant state it had induced persisted, making me entirely too aware of my every labored breath and twitching nerve, to the point that it made me feel almost paranoid.

My brother seemed to pick up on my discomfort. "Your ties to Vaeloran magic are what will allow you to wield your sword properly as well," he said, encouragingly. "You'll get used to the sensation; the bracelet should keep it from becoming too overwhelming, in the meantime."

I tried to take slower, calmer breaths. "I've been clueless about what this piece does for years now; it's only reacted to a few things since I've had it, and I could never pinpoint *what* it was reacting to, or what sort of magic it was encouraging me to do." I absently spun the beads of it around, thinking. "It seemed to wake in Erebos, too, when it got close to the vivaris flames."

My brother didn't seem surprised by this. "Those flames were originally created by a Vaelora," he said. "Not Calista, but one of the Shadow Vaelora who came before her. There have been sacrifices from Aetherkin and the like to keep them going over the years, but those blue fires were originally born of a higher, purer magic."

I turned this over in my head a few times before settling on a theory. "…So, whenever it reacts, there's likely powerful, pure Vaeloran magic at work nearby?"

He nodded, gingerly taking my hand and lifting it so he could better examine the bracelet. "That would be my guess."

"…What do you think would happen if I took it off?" I don't know what made me choose that moment to ask him such a thing—except that it was a question that had always lingered in the back of my mind, but it had been getting louder and louder over the last few days.

Bastian's expression was equal parts curious and troubled as he considered his reply. It was a long moment before he said, "You are part of a long line of Vaelora, and, in a way, all of the past manifestations of them are a part of you. As your powers have awakened with age, so too have your connections to them and all the magic they laid upon this world. Without anything subduing it all, I imagine your journey through Noctaris would have been even more dangerously overwhelming. But there will come a time for taking the constraints off, I suspect."

I shoved down the pessimistic, intrusive response I had to this—*what if that time never comes?*

What if I fail before we reach that point?

My brother turned the beads around a few times, situating them so all the symbols were facing him. "The letters on it are an ancient script; in our modern tongue it would be pronounced *avelian*. It's an old Noctarisan word that means something like *kindred spirits*, or *souls that are bound to one another*."

While he turned his attention to the floating swords, I clenched and unclenched my fist, trying to think of the magic that had guided my hand as something kin to me—reminding myself that I was not a stranger in this strange land any longer, even if I still felt like one.

A thrum of power radiated from the center of the room, drawing my eyes to the swords.

My gaze fell first on Luminor. The idea of touching it—of reading the memories contained in its glimmering blade—struck me again. Yet, even now, as close as I stood to it, I couldn't bring myself to reach for it. I knew what I wanted the truth to be. But I was still afraid of being wrong.

So, instead, I focused on Grimnor. It looked as heavy and daunting as ever, its velvety dark blade shining dully, like a blackened mirror that only occasionally caught the light.

"Kindred spirits who have all wielded this sword at one point or another…" I thought aloud.

The look Bastian gave me bordered on proud. "Exactly."

Another stab of pressure struck my hand. It didn't frighten me as much, this time. I tried to imagine all my predecessors within that pressure point, each laying their hand upon it, and I took a step toward the pedestal in the center of the room.

Grimnor stilled in the air as I drew near, its slow, subtle movements coming to a stop with its grip lined up almost perfectly with my hand. As if inviting me to grab it.

Part of me still expected resistance when I reached for it.

But there was none; before I knew it, my fingers were already closing around the obsidian hilt. Drawing it away from the pedestal felt like pulling a heavy tree limb from a muddy river. Once I took a step back, though, its weight seemed much more bearable.

The turquoise bracelet rattled once more. I closed my eyes, briefly, and let the ghostly pressures take over my wrist, leading me into a series of swipes and thrusts.

For several minutes, I went through the motions like I would have during any practice session, while my brother watched with a contemplative look on his face. It felt oddly mundane—like I'd done it a hundred times before—in one moment, but breathtakingly momentous in the next. Like a mountain beneath a deep sea, only the tip of the sword's true strength was obvious—but so much more lay hidden underneath the surface.

Once I felt relatively comfortable with the weight and feel of the weapon, I slowly walked it back to the center of the room. I didn't want to let the sword go; it felt like leaving behind an old friend. Yet, it also felt safer—smarter—to leave it here until I was ready to truly use it.

My hand slipped from the grip, and the sword took it from there, lifting on its own to float back into its suspended spot above the pedestal. I marveled at it for a minute longer before my eyes were drawn once more to its counterpart, and a troubling question reared its head.

"I can wield Grimnor, but what about Luminor?"

Bastian avoided answering me, instead making his way over to a small chest in the corner of the chamber. It sat on a pedestal similar to the one the swords hovered above.

Another spot protected by the same kind of magic?

"Aleksander wielded that sword in the Above," I pressed, following him across the room. "He's been training as hard as I have these past weeks to get his magic acclimated to this palace and everything around it. And every time I've revived any of the shades, he's been right there. We should consider what he might be able to do alongside me, with the Sword of Light in his hand. I've told you this from the beginning."

"A lot has happened since then," he insisted.

It was true—four dead bodies, and an ever-growing sense of desperation and mistrust. Still, I stubbornly said: "True revival requires balance. You've told me that yourself. And I know you've been trying to create some other source of Light magic, but—"

"And we've done it."

"...You have?"

His fingers worked deftly over the lock on the chest for a moment, and then he opened it and pulled out a necklace —a thick cord with a long, shimmering pendant attached to it. Walking back and offering it to me, he said, "We've been working on this for some time. A potent jewel made from a piece of Luminor's blade, honed into something any skilled magic user should be able to use with little difficulty."

I took the necklace, unable to stave off my curiosity. It hummed softly in my palm. A marvel, I knew—the end result of dozens of scholars and magic-users working tirelessly for a solution to their dying world.

But it was nothing compared to the warmth and power of Aleksander's magic. And holding it brought none of the certainty I'd felt when holding Grimnor.

I gazed up at my brother, fighting the urge to crush the jewel in my fist. "You're never going to trust him, are you?"

He took the pendant again, fastening it around my neck. "This is the safer route. The more predictable one."

"Safer doesn't always mean better," I argued. "And how can you expect to win any war for this world if you aren't willing to take any risks?" My tone came out harsher than I meant for it to, but I didn't take my words back.

He fixed me with a hard look, a rare glimmer of anger simmering in his grey eyes. "Almost everything I have done for *decades* has been a risk. To survive in this world is a risk in and of itself."

I shuffled my weight from side to side but held my tongue. Furious—yet freshly reminded of the things he'd had to bear without me for so long.

He exhaled deeply through his nose. "Let's just see what happens tomorrow."

My heart was ready to go to war with my thoughts, but I somehow managed to silence them both and continue to hold my tongue.

Perhaps I owed it to my kingdom to try and follow through with this task without questioning it. To put its needs first. To protect it from the complications of tying myself to Aleksander—and, by extension, to his dangerous kingdom and its Keepers.

No matter how badly I wanted something else to be true, there were two sides in this war.

And I could not fight for both.

Chapter Thirty-Five

Aleksander

THE FIRST DAWN OF OUR THIRD WEEK AT THE RIVENHOLT Palace arrived, heralded by a blood-red sunrise sneaking through my window and the sounds of eager preparations being made outside my door.

Twelve days remained until the Equinox.

Time was running out. The air was thick with a growing sense of fear and unease. To counter it, the would-be saviors of this world had an ambitious goal for today: Reviving an army that could give them a fighting chance once they opened the gate to Nerithys.

And Nova would be leading the way.

She'd informed me of the plan late last night; it had been well past midnight when she crept into my room, unable to sleep. I'm not sure she ever *did* end up sleeping. But I'd dozed off with her in my arms at some point, only to be nudged awake to find her watching me with a haunted expression and a quiet plea on her lips—

Promise you'll come with me.

And despite all my lingering questions about us, our separate worlds, and the duty I owed to my own kingdom, I'd promised.

I couldn't let her go alone.

So, shortly after waking, I was securing saddlebags and adjusting tack while ignoring the questioning, concerned stares of the soldiers who would also be accompanying Nova during the day's mission.

"You'd think *we* were the ones who had personally cursed their world, based on the way they stare," Zayn said under his breath, before swinging onto his horse's back. "Also? Given the recent murders of our own allies, we should be staring right back, shouldn't we?"

I didn't comment on this as I hoisted myself onto my own horse. I didn't want to think of those murders; I'd only just managed to stop seeing Rowen's severed tongue every time I closed my eyes.

After an hour of riding, we found ourselves atop a hill covered in grey dust and pebbles, overlooking a large clearing wedged between columns of dark forest.

The trees of that forest were strange, their trunks charred black, as if a fire had roared through but somehow left them otherwise perfectly intact—intact, tall, and strong, swaying and creaking in the slight breeze. Ash-colored dust swirled across the hillside, and the air had an undercurrent of smokiness in it, too.

In the center of the clearing were several rows of barracks flanked by walls of black stone. There were waves of white moving between these walls, and filing in and out of the buildings. Like a swirling ocean of fog from a distance, but as we rode closer, I was able to pick out individual bodies, occasional faces—*shades*.

More than I'd ever seen gathered in one place.

They moved with slightly more precision than the ones we'd encountered in the past. Regimented, almost. Most of them carried a small sword, as well, clinging to it as if it were the last weight anchoring them to life. And perhaps it *was*; the blades of those swords occasionally flashed a pale, greenish blue—part of the blessing Calista was said to have laid over these soldiers in life, maybe.

Their surroundings occasionally seemed to pulse with a similar-colored glow, as well, though it could have been a trick of the poor lighting; whatever magic Calista had laid over this area, it didn't extend to the sky. The frozen "sun" was a pale coin, lost in a sea of grey, its feeble glow struggling to pierce the heavy canopy of clouds.

I watched the soldiers for a long moment, transfixed by their quiet, relentless repetition. They marched endlessly back and forth through the bleak barracks, their feet making no sound against the earth, their motions synchronized like clockwork.

It was somewhat unnerving, to think of them potentially spending an eternity going through these same motions, all preparing for…*what*? Their minds were likely too faded to even realize what they were doing, or why they were doing it. It wasn't *loyalty* that kept them marching this way; it was magic. Magic that might have felt like a blessing in the beginning, but now looked more like a curse.

We dismounted, tying our horses to the most intact stretch of fencing we could find, a safe distance away from the area Nova would be targeting.

We moved silently toward that area—myself, Zayn, Nova, Thalia, and Bastian. Phantom, who had just shifted from a horse-like creature into a dog-like one, was immediately distracted by something in the distant forest; he gave chase despite Nova's protesting. A dozen soldiers from the palace accompanied us as well, led by Eamon, the young man who had been responsible for much of Nova's training these past weeks.

Nova and I remained side-by-side as the others walked the perimeter of Graykeep's grounds, discussing their strategy.

The two of us didn't speak right away. Nova's gaze was set, her hand tight on the grip of Grimnor, which hung in an ornate sheath at her hip.

I could sense the sword's power, a deceptively soft humming that felt poised to erupt at any moment. I could sense *her* power as well, though the feel of it was closely intertwined with Grimnor's. Being amplified by that sword, clearly. As the seconds ticked by, and her focus increased, it became harder and harder to tell their two separate energies apart.

There would be no talking her out of what she was about to attempt, I knew—though I had a sudden urge to try.

Her brother beckoned her toward him.

"Wish me luck," she said, somewhat faintly.

Luck won't keep you safe among those ghostly fiends, was my immediate, anxious thought. But I held my tongue in a way I wouldn't have weeks ago. For her, I could feign optimism, knowing she needed that more than she needed anything else just then.

"You don't need luck," I told her. "You'll be fine."

She gave me a small smile, but the confident mask she usually hid her emotions behind didn't fully settle back into place before she made her way over to her brother. They spoke for several minutes, sizing up targets and reciting plans, and then she turned and started down the hill.

It was an automatic reaction, the way my body turned to follow her; I only just managed to stop myself. But the few steps I took after her didn't go unnoticed by Thalia and Eamon, who had just moved closer to me.

"She can do it on her own," Thalia told me, her gaze fixed on Nova as she spoke. "You don't need to worry." Her words somehow sounded like both a reassurance and a threat…a reminder not to intervene.

But it seemed foolish, not to worry—and *on her own* was not entirely correct, either. They had created another tool for her to wield alongside Grimnor. A jewel hung from her neck, one that was at least partially comprised of elements stolen from Luminor.

I was, of course, skeptical of its power.

And afraid it might lure her into a false sense of security, or otherwise unbalance her and end up doing more harm than good.

Thalia and Eamon kept perfectly still, as did Zayn. Bastian paced restlessly after making his way back to us. I was somewhere in between, managing to remain calm until I felt the magic around Nova fluctuate, at which point I would have to force myself to breathe slowly, to keep still, to just keep watching the scene unfolding below.

Nova stopped right outside the main gate to the barracks. Without a second of hesitation, she pulled her sword from its sheath, pointing its tip at the barrier of ivory and twisted metal. The blade was as black as the charred trees flanking the area, and the sword brought to mind fire, as well—maybe because of the red veins of gemstone inlaid in its dark hilt, flashing like embers in the muted lighting.

Even from a distance, the sight was arresting.

Nova handled the sword as though she'd trained with it her entire life. Like it was an extension of her. Shadows soon began to bleed from its blade, and then from her arms, intertwining with precision and elegance, creating a solid wave that flowed over all the ghostly figures she was drawing toward her.

Those shadows within her and her blade were made of the same energy, I'd been told—the same energy that also made up the very world we stood in. Which meant it could be channeled into a pulse that gave the shades life. And the pendant of Light magic Nova carried would help balance the shadows, preventing the force of them from overwhelming the ones being brought back to consciousness.

Simple enough, in concept.

Nova made it look simple in execution, too—like a perfectly choreographed dance. Her shining blade and dark magic alike swept through the air with a fluid grace, each movement flowing seamlessly into the next.

She was…incredible.

There was no other word for it.

And, one by one, the spectral soldiers began to awaken, shedding their grey, muted appearances like snakes slipping free of their dead skins.

They shook the stiffness from their limbs, stumbling for a few moments before stepping into their renewed strength —into an awareness that was obvious even from a distance. Their swords glinted in the hazy daylight as they lifted them with reborn dexterity, twisting them this way and that. A swell of voices rose and fell—from confused whispers, to an excited clamor, then back to an awed hush.

One of them pointed his blade toward the sky, as if in salute. Others followed his lead. All of their gazes remained fixed on Nova; soon, she was surrounded entirely by them, nearly lost in a forest of lifted, shining swords.

Her brother and the rest of his circle moved closer, dividing up, preparing to help organize their waking army.

I stayed in place beside Zayn, a sudden heaviness in my limbs making it hard to think about moving. "It's... working."

"Seems like it." I could hear the frown in Zayn's voice; I didn't take my eyes off Nova.

I had two very different, conflicting feelings about her success.

Relief, because it meant she was still safe where she stood among that shifting army.

Dread, to think of what it meant for everything that came next.

"And so they'll move to the next part of their plans," Zayn said, quietly enough that only I could hear him. "Which means we might need to reconsider our options. Back to our original idea, maybe."

The thought cracked through me like lightning splitting a tree, leaving a dead, aching hollowness inside.

Because the original idea, of course, had been to leave her behind. To collect Luminor and use it to help carve a path back to the Above, no matter the cost to her and this world I'd found myself trapped in—because I hadn't cared about those things, weeks ago.

"She knows how to access the chamber, now, according

to the whispers I heard in the palace this morning," Zayn pointed out.

I cut my eyes toward him.

"So it should be easier than ever to get to Luminor."

"You're suggesting I use her to get into that chamber?"

"I'm suggesting survival," he said, even more quietly. "Because surely you realize: If the rulers of this realm have no need for your magic, we have no leverage here."

"So we return to our world and see how this impending war plays out…meet her on the opposite side of the battlefield and hope for the best? That's your suggestion?"

He gave me a tired look. "Not my favorite plan I've ever come up with, admittedly." He was quiet for a few beats before adding, "But you're only going to make things more difficult for her by staying."

This last point was the only thing that gave me pause.

I wasn't worried about what might happen to me. *Survival* was not a concern of mine; I'd been surviving my whole life. I doubted there was much this realm and its rulers could do to me that I couldn't endure.

But Nova had the eyes and expectations of an entire realm upon her now. I couldn't exactly ask her to turn her back on these things, or to put her future at risk for my sake.

So maybe it *would* be easier to part ways before we were forced into a much messier ending.

I could see the logic in Zayn's reasoning, yet I couldn't bring myself to answer his expectant stare. Instead, I turned my gaze back to the waking army and its commander.

Still an incredible sight to behold.

But the longer Nova worked her magic, the more often

I felt it fluctuating, like the ebb and flow of a tide losing its rhythm.

There were too many soldiers who still retained their ghostly forms, flickering with an unsettling instability. The sea of them was relentless; no matter how many she revived, more still flooded in, wave after wave thrashing against the nets of her power, demanding more from her.

Bastian and the others had stopped midway down the hill, where they balanced hesitantly, apparently not wanting to interrupt the process so long as Nova still remained on her feet making any progress at all—even if that progress was slowing.

Nova continued to spin and sweep her sword through the air, dauntless and unwavering, but a sick feeling started to take root in my gut as I watched her.

"I still think they're asking too much of her, too soon," Zayn muttered, voicing my own concerns.

I tried to veil the uncertainty in my tone. "She agreed to this," I said, "knowing their time is running out."

We continued to watch, but only a few more minutes passed before I couldn't take it any longer; it seemed like the horror I'd witnessed in Erebos, developing all over again. I'd nearly taken too long to get to her side that day.

I couldn't let it come that close again.

I walked quickly toward her brother. Another ripple of magic emanated from Nova, overtaking the wave of shades nearest to her—but her steps seemed to be getting more sloppy, the weight of Grimnor dragging her a little farther toward the ground every time she swung it.

"Stop her." I didn't realize I'd said the words out loud until Bastian shifted his gaze to me, tension crackling like a palpable thing in the air between us.

"She's nearly finished," Bastian said.

"She's done enough."

"A moment more—"

"*She's going to hurt herself.*"

He took a deep breath. A frustratingly calm, deep breath. I could see the concern in his eyes…yet he didn't move.

"Stop her," I growled, "or I will do it myself."

He seemed to be debating his options—but he was debating them far too slowly.

Magic rose from my skin before he could make any decisions. Jagged light flashed through the air along with a hiss, a crackling—a *warning*.

He shielded his eyes from the growing brightness with one hand while the other made a sharp, diagonal cut through the air. A signal. In my peripheral vision, I saw both Eamon and Thalia move, along with several others.

As powerful as the light building around me felt, I knew my magic was at a disadvantage in this realm. I was outnumbered, too, and fighting them all would waste time.

I didn't think beyond this.

I simply abandoned my magic and swung my fist instead.

The punch crashed into Bastian's face, sending him stumbling back in surprise, clutching his nose.

While he was distracted by the blood streaming from his nose, I moved past him without another word. Soldiers swarmed after me, trying to cut me off. But I was looking far beyond them, all my focus on one singular point in the distance.

Nova had collapsed on the ground.

Her body was quickly disappearing within the relentlessly swarming shades.

I withdrew my sword, prepared to do more than simply punch the soldiers trying to stop me. Several of them drew weapons, as well, forming a half circle before me.

"Let him go," came Bastian's sharp voice, before any of us could take a single swing.

They hesitated, but ultimately obeyed, exchanging uncertain looks as they stepped aside.

I sheathed my sword and broke into a run. Though I tried to suppress it, magic once again rose around me as I drew closer to Nova. Bands of golden light streamed toward her, wrapping tightly around her body, as if seeking to comfort her fallen form until I could reach it. Those bands became almost solid, lifting her from the cold ground and rolling her into my arms as I dropped down beside her.

Dozens of the revived soldiers crowded around us, many of them still dazed-looking, leaning on one another for support. Despite their shocked state, they seemed to be trying to shield Nova from the waves of shades still attempting to push their way toward her magic.

My eyes fixed on Nova's face. There were more of those bruise-like shadows covering it—the same kind she'd gained throughout her trainings these past weeks. They looked much more disturbing out here under the pallid, dead sky. I carefully shifted her more fully into my lap, brushing a strand of hair away from the darkest of those bruises.

"Open your eyes," I whispered.

She didn't.

The pendant of Light magic lay shattered on the ground beside her, I noticed.

I curled one arm around Nova, holding her more

securely against me while reaching with the other and running my hands through what remained of the pendant. They had been fools to assume such a trinket would be enough. Fools to risk her this way. And as my fingers trailed through the sharp dust, feeling the faint, useless hints of magic clinging to it, a burning fury unfurled in my chest.

I knew the plans Zayn and I had made. I knew the mess I was headed toward, should I choose to go the other way.

But I would let *both* worlds fall to ruin before I left Nova here alone.

Another surge of magic coursed through me. I didn't bother trying to suppress it, this time. It rolled from my body, bolt after bolt of light lashing out, spinning and pulling Nova's scattered shadows toward it.

I watched, still holding Nova tightly against me, as our power collided and tangled together, twisting up into a column that nearly brushed the corpse-grey sky before collapsing back toward the dusty earth. It stretched wider as it fell, creating a vast, fluttering veil of magic that was neither fully light nor shadow—one that settled over more of the shades surrounding us, wrapping them in its embrace, bringing more of them to life.

The air vibrated with a palpable hum of energy. The ground shook, and soon it was returning to life, too, the dust giving way to shoots of green grass, tiny dots of pale-yellow magic hovering over it like fireflies.

Nova finally stirred in my arms and opened her eyes, looking up at me from under her lashes. "I...tried to tell them you would be better than any magical pendant," she said, the words slurring a bit. "And I was right."

My jaw clenched. "This was a dangerously foolish way to prove a point."

A predictably chaotic little grin inched up a corner of her mouth. "I knew you'd find your way to my side," she said, attempting a shrug that made her wince.

"Must you always be so damned optimistic?"

"It's a curse, honestly," she mumbled—her last words before her strength seemed to fail her completely. She went limp against my chest. Panic briefly seized me. I placed a hand over her heart and forced my breathing to slow so I could watch hers until I was satisfied that it was steady enough.

Securing her in my arms, I rose to my feet and turned to find her brother, Thalia, and a handful of others racing down to meet us and the risen army.

The air had turned warmer. The scent of dust and ash was fading, giving way to the sharp, almost electric scent of new growth. Bodies moving, life unfolding...the scene was astounding, I vaguely realized. But I felt too numb to take in much of it, my eyes narrowed on the Regent of Rivenholt, and the Regent, alone.

Blood still streamed freely from his nose.

I didn't regret a drop of it.

I wished I'd done worse.

We stared at one another for a long, tense moment. A protective urge that bordered on feral wound its way through me, tightening my muscles, drawing Nova more completely against me. There were a thousand choice words I could have said to her brother, but all I managed to grind out was, "You better hope she makes a full fucking recovery."

I didn't wait for any response.

Without a backwards glance, I carried Nova up the hill to where my horse waited.

I climbed into the saddle and, with Zayn's help, dragged Nova up as well, carefully situating her in front of me. Once we were fully balanced, she finally opened her eyes again, gazing up at me without lifting her head from my chest.

She said only one more word—only my name. It sounded like a complete sentence from her lips. A complete plea. A complete surrender.

"You're safe," I said, tightening my grip on her once more, gazing one last time at the magic laid upon the land behind us.

Despite all she'd brought to life, death still hovered at the edges. There were still hordes of shades who hadn't been revived. The sky was still streaked with bruise-colored clouds that matched the ones on Nova's face. The patch of green grass we'd created seemed small and insignificant, an island in an ocean of darkness, reminding me of how vast this world was—and how much more it would take to save it.

How much more they would ask of her before the end.

She curled closer to me, her hands clenching into the front of my coat.

"You're safe," I repeated.

Even though it felt like a lie.

Chapter Thirty-Six

Nova

I OPENED MY EYES TO FIND MYSELF BACK IN MY ROOM AT THE palace. It was early morning, judging by the light filtering in through the window—which meant at least another day had passed.

Had it been longer?

How much time had I lost?

Phantom lay on top of my legs, the way he always used to when I was ill, letting out a soft cry every time I restlessly changed positions. My head throbbed. My hands tingled. My arms were covered in faint, shadow-like bruises, and my mouth was so dry it hurt to swallow…but, otherwise, I seemed intact.

It took a few attempts, but eventually I managed to shift out from under Phantom's weight and sit up, at which point I noticed my brother slouched in a chair in the corner of the room, his face resting against one of his hands. I thought he was asleep until he jerked his head up at the sound of Phantom repositioning himself on the bed.

We stared at one another without speaking for a long, uncomfortable moment; it felt as if we were strangers all over again.

I sat up further, leaning against the upholstered headboard, trying to recall my last moments before I'd fainted. Trying to find something to say about the mission to Graykeep, a scene that was coming back to me in bits and pieces —but the details of it all were foggy, at best.

I fixed my gaze on his. "...I don't remember falling asleep, or much of what came before. What happened?"

He swallowed hard, emotion shimmering in his eyes. "I made a mistake."

"...A mistake?"

He came closer, settling on the edge of the bed. After a brief hesitation, he told me all that had happened—the warriors I'd brought to life, the pendant shattering, the swarm that had converged around me, the fight Aleksander had put up to get to me.

The way he wished he'd told me to stop before the situation had turned dangerous.

"Desperation is not an excuse." He exhaled a long, shuddering breath. "But I'm afraid it's the only one I have. I'm sorry, Nova."

The silence stretched on as I searched for the right response to this—if one existed. "I'm sorry, too," I said, tilting my head back to stare at the coffered ceiling. "I thought I'd be able to do more. How many of those warriors did I revive in the end?"

"It doesn't matter."

"Of course it does."

"You did more than enough," he insisted. "You were brilliant."

I snorted. "You sound like Eamon. If one more person insists I'm *brilliant* while the world around us continues to crumble, I might scream."

He took my hand, gently lifting and turning it to better examine one of the bruises along my forearm. "It wasn't fair of me to ask you to hold up so much of that world on your own."

I started to argue, but found I didn't have the energy—or the right words—for it.

"You did enough," he repeated. "And again…I'm sorry."

I pulled my hand from his, wrapping my arms around myself, trying not to wince at the pain even this slight pressure caused. "It's fine. Well, it's not *fine*. But it's the situation we're in, isn't it? It's not as though you had a lot of other options."

He sighed.

I went back to counting ceiling tiles.

After a long, uncomfortable silence, he said, "It doesn't make up for all that happened, but I was thinking…you should take the rest of the day off from training and dealing with the pressures of this palace."

I lowered my gaze back to his, my interest piqued.

"We have an important gathering happening here the day after tomorrow; I haven't said anything about it before now because I didn't think it would actually happen—I assumed the invitations I sent would go unanswered. But at least some of the leaders from what's left of our world have answered the call; they'll be joining us to discuss the upcoming Equinox. And to meet you, of course."

My heart skipped several beats, but I kept my face impassive.

"You should go into town and buy whatever you'd like to wear to this meeting. It will be good for the people of Tarnath to see you, anyway—with escorts, of course."

"I don't need the palace guards to escort me anywhere."

"You can't go alone."

"Aleksander will go with me."

He stood, walking over to the dresser and fidgeting with the tray of food and drink in the center of it. He poured himself a glass of water from the silver pitcher but didn't drink any of it, merely clutched it tightly in his hand as he thoughtfully rubbed his chin.

I cleared my throat. "If he's willing to punch *you* on my behalf, imagine what he'd be willing to do to any average person who might threaten me."

"...A fair point," Bastian conceded with a wry smile. "And something tells me he would have done a lot worse to get to you. So I'm considering myself lucky." He carefully touched his swollen nose and took a long, slow sip of his drink, considering. "The two of you together, then. But there will be guards, as well—I'll command them to keep a respectable distance."

The thought of them at *any* distance was suffocating. But I'd seen very little of Tarnath since my arrival, and the idea of a relatively normal stroll through a city was undeniably tempting, so I agreed to these terms with little fuss.

We sat for a little longer, chatting mostly about the upcoming meeting with our world's leaders. Servants flittered in and out, bringing more trays of food and drink, trying to coax me into eating it. I struggled with this; I couldn't remember the last time I'd had so little interest in food.

Once I'd finally managed to eat enough to relieve my brother's concern, he stood and grabbed his coat from the chair in the corner before turning to leave.

"Enjoy the evening," he said, glancing back at me one last time as he adjusted the sleeves of his coat, "but promise me you'll keep your eyes open and your guard up. I am not the only desperate person in this city."

A FEW HOURS LATER, I had regained enough energy to prepare for my outing, and so, with the help of two maids, I bathed, pulled a pile of garments from the closet, and began to get dressed.

Some days ago, I'd casually mentioned to Aveline that my favorite color was orange. Unsurprisingly, a beautiful gown that heavily featured the shade had shown up in my wardrobe soon after; this seemed like the perfect opportunity to wear it.

While the maids worked to tame my hair into a half-updo, I stood before a large mirror, admiring the dress and fighting the urge to twirl in it. The main body was a warm shade of ivory, flaring out into a feathery sort of fabric at my hips. The skirt fell in various, lightweight layers, a mixture of ivory and a brilliant cascade of orange that shifted from a pale, golden amber shade near the waist to a darker, fiery shade toward the hem. It was somehow both delicate and intense, as though woven from the first rays of morning sunlight. The sleeves were long and sheer, almost weightless, like gossamer wings resting on my shoulders.

My hair was soon finished, the top half swept back and gathered at the crown, where it was loosely pinned with delicate golden combs, while the bottom half fell in large, loose waves—a perfect blend of elegance and ease.

The bruises caused by my magic were mostly faded. What hadn't faded had been artfully disguised with subtle swirls of golden paint, complimenting the shimmering powder on my eyelids. The artistic swirls were courtesy of Brynn, who had appeared in hopes of playing with Phantom, and had instead gotten distracted by the vast array of cosmetics strewn across my vanity. She was a surprisingly talented artist, given her age.

At last, the collaborative effort was finished, and I was allowed to give the dress a proper twirl. It seemed to take on a life of its own as I did so, its layers floating gracefully, its fabric shimmering and gleaming like sunlight caressing water.

"The very picture of elegance and fire," said Sylvia, Aveline's niece, clapping her hands together in delight. "You look lovely."

"Beyond lovely," said Aeris, the one responsible for my hair.

I thanked them all as I slipped on a comfortable pair of flats, ivory in color with subtly shimmering embroidery on them. They filed out, giggling amongst themselves. Phantom went with them, shifting into a large enough dog that Brynn was able to ride on his back.

"Be careful with her," I called.

(*I'm* always *careful*,) he retorted.

No less than five seconds later, the sound of her squeals —half terrified, half delighted—echoed from the hallway.

I sighed but let them be, checking my reflection one last time in the mirror before heading out the door myself. On my way out, I caught sight of the tonic Aveline had left on my nightstand. After a moment of deliberation, I swallowed it in a few gulps. Just in case.

The strange burning sensation the tonic caused in my chest distracted me as I left the room; I nearly ran into Thalia as a result. We shared a moment similar to the one my brother and I had shared when I'd first woken up—an uncomfortable, uncertain moment where I had to remind myself that we were not strangers, even though the space between us felt as if it had widened.

Then she surprised me by blurting out an apology.

"…I'm fine, really," I insisted, having no desire to repeat the awkward conversation I'd shared with my brother.

"Bastian told me he already apologized," she pressed, "but you should know that I was the one who was urging him to keep pushing you. So I owe you an apology, as well. Perhaps even more-so than him."

"There's no need for it. I agreed to the risks involved with the mission; it isn't as though either of you physically forced me into it."

She took a step closer, her expression pinched with concern. Then she surprised me again—this time by wrapping me in a quick hug. She let go of me almost immediately; I might have been offended by the brevity of it if it had been anybody but her.

I gave her a crooked little smile. "That was difficult for you, wasn't it?"

"I don't like touching people. Or being touched." She

shrugged, but the motion seemed heavy despite her indifferent tone.

I couldn't help wondering if she might have felt differently, had her father been around to embrace her when she was growing up. A smaller tragedy in the greater wars surrounding us, maybe, but it still hurt to think of it.

"Let's create a signal instead, then." She looked at me like I was babbling nonsense, but I continued: "Next time a situation calls for an embrace, we'll just do…this, instead." I placed my hand flat over my heart and patted twice.

Her brows lifted, half skeptical, half amused. "*If* we find ourselves in another situation where I feel the need to embrace you, then I suppose I can manage that."

"It's settled, then."

We both smiled, something like warmth budding between us. "Be careful in the city," she said.

"I will," I said, tapping my hand against my heart.

She rolled her eyes at my liberal use of our new signal, but smiled and returned the gesture before walking away.

I'd sent a messenger to Aleks soon after receiving my brother's blessing to do so, asking him to escort me into the city when evening rolled around. And as I made my way to our meeting point, a quiet, insecure part of me considered what I would do if he didn't show up. It seemed silly, given all the other, far more questionable horrors he'd accompanied me to over these past weeks—an evening in the city hardly seemed like an extravagant ask.

But I'd been ignored and overlooked so often in my lifetime, my old insecurities still clung to me despite my best efforts to wield logic against them.

He showed up, though.

Early, in fact—he was already in the palace entryway, waiting for me.

At the top of the stairs overlooking that entry, I remained unnoticed, so I paused to take him in. He sat on a marble bench, reclining with his head tilted back and his eyes closed. The pose made me think of the first time I'd seen him in this world, of all that had happened since that moment, and of how much had changed.

How had so much changed?

The last light of the day filtered in from the high windows, casting him in a soft, glowing gold. He was beautiful beyond the point of fairness, really—a statue carved to worship the human body.

He stood up. I inhaled too sharply in response, drawing his gaze. He went almost perfectly still as he spotted me, only his eyes moving, taking me in as I made my way down to him.

As I approached, I lifted the skirts of my dress and gave them a little flounce. "It's a stunning dress, isn't it?"

He eased back into his usual confident, relaxed stance, his gaze traveling the length of my body, admiring every dip and curve before settling on my face. "I hardly noticed the dress."

I couldn't stop the heat that flooded my cheeks.

"The night is young," he said in a low voice dripping with amusement, "and I already have you blushing."

I avoided meeting his gaze—though dropping my eyes to his body wasn't much better.

His attire was effortlessly regal, blending comfort with understated elegance. His fitted tunic of soft white linen, draping gracefully over his broad shoulders, was embroidered with subtle silver thread along the collar and cuffs.

He'd paired it with grey trousers, perfectly tailored to his lean yet muscular frame and tucked into polished boots. One hand was shoved into his pocket, a coat hanging casually in the crook of his arm.

His other hand curved around my side, steadying me and drawing me closer in the same motion. Warmth spread from beneath his touch, settling in all my most sensitive places, and already I was considering canceling our plans in favor of dragging him up to my bedroom instead.

I sensed people gathering nearby, staring in our direction.

I took a step back to gather myself.

Aleks laughed softly. "Are you going to be able to keep your queenly composure in my company this evening?"

I smoothed a non-existent wrinkle from my dress. "It shouldn't be a problem."

"No?"

"I know your tricks at this point—I can guard myself against them."

He grinned a lazy grin that accented his dimples. "All of them?"

"I can't be flustered by you."

"That sounds like a challenge, my dear Chaos."

"Shall we bet on it?"

"Only if I get to name my prize for whenever I inevitably win."

My core clenched, my mind circling back to the last time he'd claimed his *prize*.

Before I could answer him, we were joined by the guards my brother had insisted on.

"Our chaperones have arrived in full force," Aleks said under his breath, "we'll *really* have to be on our best behavior, won't we?" The devious gleam in his eyes suggested he had no intention of doing anything of the sort.

Already trying to fluster me, I realized.

I guarded myself against another twinge of desire and presented my arm to him. "Let's go, escort."

He let out another quiet laugh at my business-like tone, hooking his arm through mine.

Chapter Thirty-Seven

Nova

A SHORT ROAD CONNECTED THE GROUNDS OF THE PALACE with the royal city. A carriage was offered to us, but we decided to walk, and soon enough, the city of Tarnath unfolded like an enchanted map before us, full of a seemingly endless number of points I wanted to visit.

We swept from one point to another in a rush of eager curiosity—between stores full of glittering trinkets; to bustling market stalls full of colorful produce; to artisan workshops where beautifully-dyed fabrics hung from the rafters; in and out of crowded taverns with hearty laughter spilling from their doors...

Everything seemed alive, vibrant, pulsing with the rhythm of a thousand intricately intertwined lives all being lived out in tandem.

And this was likely another reason Bastian had insisted I come into this city: To remind me that there was life here, just as there was in the Above.

I could only imagine what it would be like to see this entire realm blooming with vitality once more—a hundred cities, each pulsing with their own unique heartbeat, each salvaged and snatched back from the darkness that might have destroyed them. I wanted the chance to visit them all.

To see them *all* come back to life.

The possibility made all the pain of these last few weeks seem worth it.

Word had apparently spread of my feats at Graykeep; I kept catching whispers about it, and about my rising army. I gained more and more followers as the evening went on, too. People wanted to speak to me, to ask questions, to parade me before their skeptical friends and prove I was real. In some cases, they merely wanted to touch my hand.

Both Aleksander and my guards grew a little more uneasy with every citizen that approached me—and I began to understand why Bastian had insisted on so many escorts—but I couldn't bring myself to turn anyone away.

It was so…different from my old life, to not only be accepted by these people, but also welcomed by them.

Admired by them, even.

But there was a bittersweet side, as well.

Because most didn't seem to know the whole story of what had happened at Graykeep. None of them mentioned the way Aleksander had fought his way to my side—the way his magic had combined with mine to create an even more impressive display. They rarely acknowledged him at all, and when they did, it was with the same sort of suspicion and uncertainty he faced from most of the people in the palace.

With every encounter, I found myself growing more confident in my ability to lead and save these people, but less certain about what that salvation meant for Aleks and me.

He had to have been thinking of similar things. Yet he smiled as he watched the citizens of Tarnath fawn over and flatter me—as long as they did it from a safe, respectful distance. And he never left my side.

Happy for me, regardless of what it meant for him.

The crowd around me thinned somewhat as it grew later. Realizing the day was slipping away, we hurried to the dress shop, arriving minutes before they closed. I hastily picked out patterns and fabric, had my measurements taken by a sleepy seamstress, and then we were sent on our way once more.

I was exhausted, by this point, but not ready to return to the palace. We strolled for an hour or so longer before finding ourselves completely enraptured by the scent of sugar and freshly baked bread. Following our noses led us to a quaint little bakery squished between two bustling shops.

A bell chimed as we pushed our way inside, where we were greeted by wall-to-wall display cases that held an assortment of delicate fruit pastries, beautifully frosted cakes, and other sugar-glazed delights. The air was warm, heavy with the rich aroma of butter and vanilla.

The baker was more than obliging once he recognized me, nearly tripping over himself to offer us anything we wanted. I couldn't choose between all of the delights he presented us with, and so we ended up with multiple boxes full of goods to take home with us—which a few of our guards agreed to carry, albeit with some disgruntlement.

The night deepened, bringing a slight chill with it. Aleks draped his coat over my shoulders and we walked on, pausing on a small bridge that curved over a tiny stream, watching the colorful fish darting about in the water.

I was eating my second cupcake of the evening, trying and failing to slowly savor the fluffy chocolate base and the salted caramel frosting swirled delicately on top of it.

"If the upcoming battles go poorly, I want to be buried in a coffin full of this frosting," I declared.

"Noted. And yet, you've wasted half of it by missing your mouth," Aleks said, grinning, as he trailed a finger near the swirl of salty sweetness gathered in the corner of my mouth.

"If you'd tasted it, you'd understand my sloppy haste to get the rest of it inside me."

He arched a brow. His fingers slid down, cupping my chin and angling my mouth toward his. He kissed the patch of messy frosting slowly, dragging his tongue as he pulled away, licking off the stray line of it that had smeared toward my cheek.

"You're right," he said. "It's delicious."

I closed my eyes for a moment, enjoying the lingering, buzzing warmth his mouth had left on my cold cheek, all while thinking of the other parts of me he'd savored with that tongue.

"Okay," I breathed. "Okay. I concede defeat. My composure is lost. I'm...*flustered*."

He laughed—a low, rich timbre that sent another hum of warmth through me. "Come on," he said, taking my hand and weaving his fingers through mine, "there's more I want to see."

We ignored our aching feet and continued on, lost among the quiet conversations and sparkling lanterns of the city after dark. I soon forgot about the guards trailing us;

the questions of what came next; the eyes of Tarnath's citizens that watched us so closely. It was only me and him and wherever the night wanted to take us—the possibilities seemed endless.

Hours later, though, I could fight my exhaustion no longer; my steps finally began to slow. I'd just agreed with Aleksander's suggestion that we head back toward the palace, when one last spot caught my attention: A music shop.

In the window, several instruments were displayed on tarnished stands and faded cloths, with a scattering of yellowed sheet music in between them. In the center of the display was a violin. Its body was a rich, golden brown, the varnish on it worn in places, suggesting it was well-loved and responsible for a lifetime of melodies.

Aleksander came up beside me, his expression curious. "Do you play?"

"...I used to. My mother—my adoptive mother, that is—was a talented violinist. I was never as good as her, but I enjoyed playing at her side. It...it felt like we were breaking down barriers between us when we practiced together, sometimes."

The clouds shifted, a sliver of moonlight filtering through their grey blanket, casting a momentary glow on the shop's window. The shopkeeper noticed me staring at the violin, and he was just as obliging as the baker had been, encouraging me to pick it up and take a closer look.

But I hesitated.

"Go on," Aleks encouraged.

My fingers itched for a chance to relive my playing days, but I couldn't bring myself to reach for it. I'd started playing because I so desperately wanted to have more in common with the woman I called Mother. I'd eventually come to love the music I created for other reasons, too, but it hadn't come easily to me—and I feared that would show if I attempted to play after all this time.

Aleks watched me for a moment longer. Instead of pressuring me to pick it up again, he walked into the shop and took a closer look at some of the other instruments. He settled before a piano in the corner, lifting the hinged lid that covered its keys, testing out a few notes.

And then he began to play.

He started slowly, fingers skimming the keys with quiet, purposeful deliberation that soon gave way to more confident, fluid movements as he relaxed into the piece. He played with surprising tenderness, each chord imbued with emotion that rarely broke through his stoic exterior.

I drew closer, mesmerized as I watched his long fingers dance across the keys with ease. For a moment, it felt as though time itself had suspended its relentless march. The night wasn't slipping away. War wasn't looming. There was nowhere else I needed to be.

And as the melody unfolded around me, my heart unfolded, as well, spilling all of the doubts and fears that had clenched it up so tightly.

I returned to the violin and tentatively picked it up. The shopkeeper offered me a finely-made bow, as well. An ache settled in my arms as I took it, almost as if my body was somehow reliving the many long hours of practice it had taken me to try and keep up with the Queen of Eldris.

The fear of looking foolish remained, even if it wasn't as loud as before.

Taking a deep breath, I drew the bow across the strings anyway.

The initial note was harsh, jagged—like a wail of protest. I cringed, wanting to stop, but the longing in my fingers refused to settle now that I'd started.

I tried again.

Like a rusted wheel grinding into motion, I pressed on, and soon the notes began to flow with more certainty.

Aleks paused to listen for a moment, his expression unlike anything I recalled ever seeing on his face. An almost soft, pensive...*desire*. He closed his eyes, seemingly allowing himself to sink more fully into the notes I was playing.

His hands rose to the keys once more. A few soft, tentative chords to feel out my song...and then we were playing together in earnest, the melody growing richer, rising and falling in an aching refrain that transported us far away and back again, leaving my stomach fluttering and my heart pounding.

Before long, a crowd began to gather around us. They packed into the small shop, pressing as close as my guards allowed, their smiles wide and their eyes bright with admiration as they applauded and requested a longer show. We obliged, each of us showing off with short solo performances until we settled on a tune we were both familiar with and played it together—an old folk ballad that spoke of love and loss, a melody as timeless as the stars.

When it was finished, I ended with a flourish, my final, lingering note echoing over the enraptured crowd.

Aleksander played on, softer now, while I leaned against the wooden counter next to the piano, taking in all of the happy, admiring faces around us. And I realized something: I was happy, too. The happiest I'd been in some time, despite all the worries and uncertainties pressing in.

Because I felt like I belonged here.

The realization overwhelmed me so much I could no longer focus on playing. I put the violin back on its cushion, thanked the shopkeeper, and gave a slight bow to the crowd before slipping outside for some fresh air, multiple guards on my heels.

Aleks lingered behind after I left, speaking with the shopkeeper—one of the few in the city who hadn't regarded him with suspicion or uncertainty; more proof of music's ability to break down barriers, just as it had between me and my mother.

While they talked, I went across the street to the florist shop. It was closed, but the front of the building was worth a visit, anyway; lush greenery, vibrant flowers and climbing vines formed a beautiful exterior display, spilling from the windows, weaving along the porch railings, wrapping around the door.

I knew when Aleks was approaching, because the flora reacted as his magical energy met mine—leaves shivering; petals shifting toward us; a few of the withered blooms perking up slightly. Subtle enough changes that most probably wouldn't have even noticed.

He reached for one of the more withered blooms—a lily of some sort—and gently cupped his hand over it. Once its petals were fully open and full of shimmering, colorful veins once more, he plucked it and handed it to me.

"A gift for a successful performance," he said.

I took the flower, smiling slightly as he pressed a lingering kiss to my cheek.

For the second time that night, I found myself slipping back into a memory of our past—into the garden at Rose Point, this time. I could still clearly picture the way his magic had brought a flower to life then, too.

I'd seen the possibility of a future with him that night... and then it had all imploded in a rush of bloodied blades and breaking earth.

Would this time be any different?

I'd gone silent without really meaning to. My smile had slipped away, and by the time I realized it, Aleks was already tilting his head in concern.

"Are you alright?"

"Just tired," I lied, forcing the smile back on. "We should get back to the palace."

His concerned expression remained, but he nodded, wrapping an arm around me and steering me back toward the main road. I huddled closer to him as we passed through the sleepy city, trying to focus only on the solid feel of his body against mine.

Nothing was breaking in this moment.

But as the city grew quieter, my thoughts grew louder, and one question rose above all others—

How do I choose between him and this world I want to save?

Chapter Thirty-Eight

Nova

It was after midnight before we finally returned to the palace. We moved like we'd spent the night at the tavern; stumbling about, our voices low and filled with laughter. Aleksander's arm was hooked loosely around my waist, helping me balance on increasingly tired legs. Or maybe I was helping *him* balance; it was hard to say.

I was thinking only of how I didn't want the night to end when Aleksander's arm suddenly tightened protectively and drew me to a stop.

The happiness I'd been trying to cling to burst the instant I saw them—three men standing by a window at the end of the hall. Two, I didn't recognize, but the third…

"Kaelen?"

He turned at the sound of my voice, giving a slight bow as our eyes met.

I fought the urge to reach for my shoulder, even though

the wound I'd sustained in his city had been healed for weeks now.

Cautiously, I approached and allowed him to introduce me to his two companions, Jorath and Marek—also keepers of sanctuary cities like Erebos, though their own cities were much smaller, if I recalled the lessons Thalia had given me correctly.

"We were just talking about you and your impressive magic," Kaelen said.

I nodded slowly, as graciously as I could. There was a reason my brother had invited him here, despite the messiness of my last encounter with him; he was powerful, and a potentially invaluable ally—even if he'd made questionable choices.

Most of the people around me had made questionable choices, my brother included. I hadn't forgiven them. But I could understand them. I'd only been in this world a short time, and already, I could feel the desperation permeating my soul, threatening to skew my own judgment.

Meanwhile, they had been watching the decay of this world for decades. Their entire lives must have felt like being trapped on the edge of a cliff, feeling the ground trembling beneath them as they waited for the inevitable fall—and they were simply grabbing on to whatever they could.

Kaelen's gaze traveled over Aleksander. "And I see you're still keeping close to her as well."

"Yes," Aleks replied, coolly. "It seems escaping your attempts to murder us really brought the two of us closer together. I suppose I should thank you for that."

A muscle twitched in Kaelen's jaw. "You twist the truth, Lightwielder."

I put a hand on Aleksander's chest, angling myself between him and Kaelen before either could speak another word. "It's late," I said, pointedly, "and *all* truths are in danger of being twisted at this hour, I'd say. Let's leave our conversation for our more official, planned meeting, shall we?"

The Noctarisan leaders didn't argue. All three offered polite bows before we turned and walked away.

"I don't trust him," Aleks muttered.

"I don't, either. But I'm tired of talking to other people tonight; I just want to go somewhere more private."

He gave my hand a small, understanding squeeze. We didn't look back. He walked me to my room, following me inside without uttering another word about Kaelen or anyone else.

As I slipped off his coat and moved to drape it over a chair, I noticed a gift waiting for me in the center of my bed: The violin from the music shop, freshly polished and adorned with an orange ribbon.

"That old shopkeeper moved impressively quickly," Aleksander commented.

I turned to him. "You did this?"

He shrugged, but a sly grin flirted with the corner of his lips. "I merely arranged for it to be delivered. The shopkeeper was happy to gift it to you; he fell in love with you, I think. Much like everyone else in the city."

Everyone else...including you?

The question rose in my mind before I could stop it, but I couldn't find the courage to ask it out loud.

Instead, I picked up the violin and its bow, smiling as I untied the ribbons around them. I'd smiled more tonight than I had in what felt like years; my cheeks were starting to ache from it.

"Thank you," I told him.

"It's really a selfish gift," he said. "I just want to hear you play it more, that's all."

I blushed slightly, taking the gift and carrying it out onto the balcony, sighing happily as the crisp night air caressed my cheeks.

One of my favorite places to practice back at Rose Point had been atop the roof of the observatory that stood on the edge of the expansive grounds. It was always a transformative experience, especially at night—to send melodies with love into the open air, far away from the main manor, with wild woods stretching before me and stars wheeling overhead…it was one of the few times in my old life that I'd truly felt *free*.

And though it wasn't as private, this balcony had become one of my favorite places in this palace. It was larger than it seemed at a glance, wrapping around the outer wall, and the spot around the corner felt secluded and set apart from everything else. I'd even slept out here a few times, curled up in one of the chairs or sprawled out on the larger lounge sofa, buried in blankets, letting the twinkling stars lull me to sleep.

This time, I stayed in the main part of the balcony, staring out at what I could see of the road that led to the front of the palace. There were riders approaching the gate. Five of them, in all.

More leaders, like Kaelen, who were answering my brother's summons?

They must have been, given how calmly they were welcomed in at such a late hour.

"More company," I muttered.

Aleks stepped to my side, bracing his hands against the railing and staring up at the nearly full moon. "Eleven days until the Equinox, isn't it?"

Instead of replying, I settled the violin on my collarbone and steadied the bow in my hand, trying to remember the first notes of the ethereal, haunting tune I wanted to play—an old favorite of mine. I just wanted to go back in time for a moment. To ignore the grim uncertainty we faced for a little while longer.

The music came easier than it had earlier; maybe because I had a smaller audience, and I was less afraid of making a mistake in front of Aleks. The notes flowed smoothly into the delicate, swirling melody, casting a spell over the space, and for a moment—just a heartbeat—everything seemed to vanish except for the sound; the hum of strings; the glide of the bow; the deep, rich timbre of my instrument.

Aleks turned and leaned his back against the railing, hands in his pockets, listening to me play with a slight smile on his lips. He didn't speak even after I'd finished. But he stepped toward me as I set the instrument aside, and he wrapped his arms around me from behind—an even more satisfying distraction than music.

His hands moved with the same artistry he'd possessed when playing piano, fingertips skimming over my body with a smooth, easy confidence. They roamed along the curves accented by the bodice of my dress, eventually settling on my hips, holding me in place while his lips swept down my neck and across my shoulder.

There was no music—the stars provided our only symphony, and they were silent and cold—but after a moment, he took my hand, spinning me as if we were in the middle of an elegant waltz. We ended up facing one another. He brought my hand to his mouth and brushed a kiss across my knuckles, then several more up the length of my arm before pulling me in and softly meeting my lips with his.

His eyes caught the moonlight when he pulled away, their golden color shimmering with a beauty that seemed almost inhuman. The sight transported me once more to the last night we'd spent in the Above together. To his radiant, handsome figure approaching me in the dark garden, smiling at me despite the grave-dirt on my hands. He'd kissed my hand then, too, and I'd been caught up in his gaze, and in the possibility of *us*—but for different reasons.

Now my reasons felt deeper, heavier, far more frightening than the prospect of a political marriage I'd faced all those years ago.

My heart raced. He must have felt it, because his head tilted as he absently stroked my knuckles with his thumb, and he asked, "What are you thinking, my Chaos?"

I hesitated. "About a conversation I had with Zayn the other day."

"...Oh?"

"He mentioned..." I trailed off. Swallowed hard. Tried again. "He pointed out that I favor Calista."

The answer clearly surprised him; he didn't seem to know how to reply.

"And I wonder if...as his descendant...if you favor Argoth," I said.

The meaning behind my words seemed to slowly dawn on him. "Nova..."

"In a way, it feels like we're living out the love story they never got to finish, doesn't it?"

He brushed aside a tendril of hair that had escaped from my partial-updo, letting his fingertips linger against my cheek.

"Just…" My voice grew thick. "Just tell me we aren't a tragedy like they ended up being."

His brow furrowed in thought, but he didn't answer right away.

Nearly a full minute passed.

It wasn't a fair question, I decided; who could really answer such a thing?

"Sorry," I whispered, starting to turn away. "It's late. I'm tired and speaking nonsense. Never mind, I should—"

He grabbed my arm, spinning me back toward him. My heart leapt into my throat.

No man had ever looked at me the way he was looking at me in that moment.

"There is nothing *tragic* about the fact that I met you here in this world," he said, taking my face in his hands. "Or about the way I feel when I kiss you, or when your body curves next to mine when we sleep. Nothing I could possibly regret about the way I find calm in your chaos and solace in your shadows, and if we end up ripped apart and ruined, it will still have been worth it all." He gripped me tighter and bowed his head against mine, as if in prayer. "And so no—no, I don't consider us a tragedy. At all."

I'd stopped breathing at some point; his hands, still clutching my face, were the only things that kept me from toppling over as a wave of dizziness struck.

I managed to take a breath. And then to swallow. To lick the dryness from my lips. His gaze followed each of these subtle motions, the hunger in them growing with every passing heartbeat.

I'm not sure who moved first.

I blinked, and suddenly our lips were together, our hands fumbling, trying to simultaneously peel off clothing while touching every inch of one another.

After several deep kisses, he drew back and managed to focus enough to grind out a breathless command: "Turn around."

I did, and he immediately started to undo the ties along the back of my dress. Despite the desperate world and war we'd found ourselves in, his hands didn't feel desperate against my body. They felt deliberate. Careful. *Reverent* as they stripped off my clothing, piece by piece and layer by layer.

The chill still lingered in the air, but it was less noticeable as his fervent energy tangled with mine, as I felt his magic rising in response to my quickened breaths and pounding heartbeats, creating a cocoon of warmth around us.

And I forgot about the cold altogether when I turned and saw him unbuttoning his shirt and tossing it aside, slipping off his belt, letting his trousers hang deliciously low on his hips.

If I could only memorize this image of him, I might never be cold again.

The moonlight hit his bare chest at all the right angles, skimming over hard ridges, across all the scars he'd endured, highlighting the muscular lines that drew my eyes down to the impressive bulge hidden just beneath his low hanging pants.

The heat spiking through me became unbearable; my

hands were on him before I realized what I was doing, my fingers clawing at what remained of his clothing, stripping it off. My lips collided with his; I felt him smiling at my eagerness just before his grip on me became ruthless, his hands digging into the fleshy backs of my thighs before he lifted me with ease, wrapping my legs around his waist.

Every point of contact between us was agonizing, heavenly, maddening—somehow both too much yet not enough.

He carried me around the corner, toward the lounge and the pile of blankets waiting there. He started to lay me down, but I stole a kiss as he did so—one that quickly turned deeper, his tongue dancing against mine, his moans vibrating down my throat.

The next thing I knew, my back was against the wall behind the sofa, his mouth continuing to ravage mine until I was gasping, begging for breath.

He drew back only inches to allow that breath, and he continued to tease my lips with gentle nibbling and sucking for a moment before he paused long enough to say, "You have no idea how close I came to doing this in front of every citizen of Tarnath, our guards included."

My toes curled at the thought.

"No idea how badly I wanted this." He loosened his grip somewhat, allowing my feet to fall back to the ground, so that his hand could slip more easily between my legs.

I gasped as his fingers plunged inside of me, the resulting pleasure that throbbed through me nearly making my knees buckle.

"As badly as you wanted it, too," he said, huskily, "judging by this sweetness pooling between your legs." He withdrew his fingers and brought them to his mouth, licking them clean with the same enthusiasm I'd devoured the cupcake frosting with earlier.

He dropped to one knee. Lifted one of my legs and balanced it over his shoulder, opening my thighs so he could press his face between them. My hands tangled in the waves of his hair, gripping tightly as he worked his tongue against me—slow, languorous licks and gentle breaths before darting it more fully, more forcefully inside.

I was melting into the wall, oblivious to its cold roughness. Arching my back, despite the sharp bite of its bricks, trying to pull him in more deeply. Bracing one hand against the palace while the other stayed in his hair, trying to maintain balance among the waves of heat and ecstasy rocking through me.

He started to draw back minutes later—just as I felt the beginning of a release and started to chase it—and I gasped out a series of curses in response.

The wicked gleam returned to his gaze as he straightened back to his full height, cupping my chin and tilting my gaze up to his. "Are we already getting impatient?"

I replied by taking his hand and leading him toward the lounge, easing him back onto the cushions.

Crawling on top, straddling his body, I leaned down and claimed his mouth with mine. My hair loosened further from its clips, falling in a messy curtain between us. He shoved one hand into the waves, gripping my head and pulling me harder against his mouth, deepening our kiss. His other hand smoothed its way down my back, over the curve of my ass, cupping me between the legs. His fingers stroked, pinched, and gently prodded until they were fully coated with my arousal. Then both of his hands were gripping me, guiding my hips lower, dragging my center across his hard length.

The first brush against him nearly had me collapsing into a quivering heap against his sweat-slicked chest. But I stayed upright, rocking my hips, chasing more. As I increased the pressure, he sucked in a sharp breath, and the sound brought me perilously close to release once more.

I drew back, wanting to make this last as long as possible.

I kissed a trail from his neck over his chest, taking the time to press my lips against every scar. Then lower, down across the hard ridges of his abdomen, before finally letting my tongue dance across the tip of his cock. After a few teasing lashes, I took him farther into my mouth, my eyes lifting toward his face to watch his reaction.

It was an incredible thing, that reaction.

His head tilted back. His eyes fluttered shut, his normally tense brow relaxing as his lips parted slightly.

I'd never seen him look so close to…*surrender.*

His fingers tangled in my hair once again, holding me in place as he rolled his hips, pushing himself deeper into my throat. After a few more thrusts like this, a sound somewhere between rapture and ruin tore through him. He grabbed my face in his hands once more, dragging me up across his body, bringing my mouth to his and into a sloppy, savage kiss.

Then his arms wrapped around my waist, pulling me against him, keeping my knees on either side of his thighs as he sat upright and planted his feet on the floor.

I settled into his lap, somehow fighting the urge to immediately start moving my hips once more.

As we balanced there, a tangled mess of pounding hearts and throbbing need, he paused, swiping the hair from my face, tucking it behind my ears. He looked mesmerized, almost. He began to kiss me more slowly—everything he could put his lips on. Every inch of heated skin he could taste. My face, my throat, the hardened peaks of my breasts.

"You lost our bet earlier," he murmured in between kisses against my neck.

"I did."

"Which means I'm due another prize."

"It does, doesn't it?"

"Mm." He dug his fingers into my backside, tightening his grip, pulling me more firmly against him. "And that means this ends with me inside of you."

"...Somehow, I don't feel like I'm *losing* in that scenario."

He smiled, lips back against my neck once more. "Now, I just have to decide how I want to take you."

My breath caught and my eyes fluttered shut, imagining the possibilities.

"I've thought about bending you over almost every piece of furniture in this palace..." He lazily traced the shapes of my breasts before letting his touch trail down my sides, then lower, sweeping it along my legs, which were still tucked beside him. "But I like you on your knees like this, too."

With no more warning than this, his hands slid under my thighs, jerking me up into a more upright kneeling position.

I draped my arms around his neck. While I balanced above him, he wrapped a hand around his erection, stroking it and teasing it across my entrance before slipping just the tip inside of me.

I leaned back slightly, trying to adjust to the thickness of him. His free hand reached up, fingers splaying across my throat, clawing down across my chest and stomach before settling on my hip, guiding me more fully onto him.

"Sit on it," he instructed, his fingers digging deeper into my skin.

I sank against him, slowly, moaning softly as he filled me inch by inch. His thickness felt even more impressive than it had looked. Both of his hands settled on my backside, helping me balance while caressing and stretching me, encouraging me to sink lower.

"So perfectly tight," he said, his grip on me strengthening, muscles flexing as he lifted me up and down on his cock in a slow, perfect rhythm. As I began to ride him more confidently—more smoothly—he lifted his hips to meet me with harder and harder thrusts, the sweet, slick sounds of our joining echoing through the night air.

He palmed the back of my head and pulled my face toward him, bringing his mouth to my ear, and growled, "Brace your hands against the back of the sofa."

I did, leaning forward and burying my face in the side of his neck with the same motion. It felt both primal and intimate, curving against him while his motions grew rougher, faster, bringing us together with increasingly reckless passion.

The heat between us roared hotter. The sofa creaked beneath our shifting weight. The air filled with swirls of shadow and light, intertwining so tightly it was impossible to say what belonged to whom. For a few blissful minutes, it didn't *matter* which magic was which—I was his, he was mine, and the world around us blurred, all its different sides and division undone by the sheer force of *us*.

As the first cries of my release rose in my throat, Aleks wrapped me in a powerful embrace, jerking me against him, burying himself more fully inside of me. His hands hooked over my shoulders, holding me to him as he followed me over the edge, and together we rode the waves of bliss to their peaceful, trembling end.

Once the last bits of my orgasm had shuddered through me, I crumpled against him, arms hanging around his neck, pulse still pounding. He leaned against the sofa's backing, dragging me with him while reaching for a blanket to wrap around us.

We existed in a state of perfect contentment for a little while, oblivious to anything outside of the two of us.

Eventually, I untangled myself from him. He offered me his shirt. I slipped it on while he pulled his trousers back on, and then I promptly tucked myself back against his chest. He let his chin rest upon my head, his arm circled loosely around my waist, while I closed my eyes and slipped into a dream filled with music and a world that was bursting, vibrant and alive with color.

"I'm really earning quite the collection of prizes, aren't I?" he said after a few minutes, the words whispering over my scalp, sending a pleasant tingle across it.

"And I've never been so gracious over a lost bet," I replied, yawning.

His fingers skated up my spine before settling against the side of my head, stroking my hair. "Anytime you want to lose again, just let me know."

I responded with a soft, sleepy laugh, closing my eyes once more as I nestled closer to his chest, burying myself in the comforting scent of him, and I tried to think of nothing else.

I WOKE to the sound of bells in the distance. Loud, pealing notes that ran through body like a cold wind. It was a traditional call to welcome visitors; my brother had mentioned it during our conversation yesterday. Warned me of it.

Aleks was already up, perched on the edge of the lounge, staring at the sky, which was the murkiest it had been since we came to this palace. When he noticed I was awake, he beckoned me over, wrapping me up in his arms and one of the heavier blankets we'd taken from my room.

We sat for a long time without speaking. It was tempting not to acknowledge the new day and the challenges awaiting us in it—as though ignoring these things would make them go away.

"The sky seems darker than usual, doesn't it?" I whispered, more to myself than him.

He didn't answer immediately, except to shift our position so he could slip his hand out from under the blanket. He twisted his wrist and subtly bent his fingers, drawing faint wisps of magic into his command.

A moment later, I watched a slant of light cut through the shadows on the wall beside us, casting a dazzling pattern that—at least, for a moment—distracted me from the dark and ominous sky.

I smiled softly at the memory of the last time he'd done this, and, just like when we were children, I found myself compelled to join him. My hand lifted as well, calling shadows into my palm, which I directed toward his floating fragments of light. They wove gently together, changing the patterns being projected on the grey bricks, creating a show of fluid, shifting shapes—shapes that seemed to be alive; a living tapestry of magic.

And as the different shades of our power danced, rising and falling together in an intricate harmony, I realized something.

I had fallen in love with him.

Everything seemed to still, just for a moment, including my heart.

If only I could have just *stayed* still.

But in my head, I knew better. The world had not stopped. *Nothing* had stopped. Not the Above. Not the Below. They were both careening toward a collision, toward battles I still didn't know how to fight. Tomorrow was coming, and tomorrow I would have to face a room full of people who expected me to lead them. To save them. Regardless of who I loved.

I lost my focus on my shadows; they scattered, taking most of Aleksander's light with them.

Another bell rang out, the sound low and hollow and cold, and my heart felt as if it might shatter.

Chapter Thirty-Nine

Nova

My dress had come together even more beautifully than I'd hoped it would—an incredible feat, given that it had only been a day and a half since Aleks and I stopped into the shop for measurements and materials. Somehow, the seamstress had managed to interpret my vision despite the rushed process, and now I stood on a stool before one of the mirrors in my bedroom, admiring the end result of her work.

The a-line dress appeared deep crimson at first glance, but black beading along the bodice and a sheer layer of dark tulle over the body made its true color impossible to pin down; it shimmered between shades depending on the lighting and angles, an ever-changing fusion of blood and shadows—a tribute to the dress I'd worn on the night of the Moonweaver Festival, only longer and sewn together with heavier, higher quality fabrics.

I'd felt strong that night. Decisive. And I had a feeling I

was going to need that kind of strength tonight, so I had purposefully tried to recreate the dress with hopes of recreating the feeling it had inspired.

Aeris had left my hair down in large, loose waves, save for a braided piece held away from my face by a delicate clasp that resembled a raven's wing. Heeled boots completed the ensemble, along with a small knife strapped to the inside of my thigh.

I hoped I would have no need for knives, but...old habits.

Once I was ready, I fell into another old habit, kneeling in front of Phantom and wrapping my arms tightly around him—an embrace for good luck, the way we'd always done before enduring our royal duties back at Rose Point.

"We can do this, right?"

(*Do we have a choice?*) he replied, cocking his head.

I sighed, straightening his collar—a regal, jeweled piece he'd insisted I have made for him alongside my dress so that he could look his best for our visitors. Giving him a quick scratch between the ears, I stood and faced the door.

Just another royal obligation, I tried telling myself. *Just like old times.*

My brother met me as I was making my way downstairs. He was alone, which was surprising, given the number of guests and palace dwellers alike who had been fighting for his attention all day yesterday and today.

"I managed to escape," he said, reading the surprise in my expression, "and I wanted to come check on you."

"There was no need; I'm fine."

"Well, it gave me an excuse to get away for awhile," he said, grinning.

"Glad I could help, then."

"You look lovely, by the way."

"You clean up quite nicely yourself."

"Yeah?" He gave the collar of his embroidered doublet an exaggerated tug. "It feels a bit like I'm being slowly strangled to death. But Aveline insisted it would give off the proper regal impression, so..." He shrugged.

"No one escapes her iron-fisted rule around here, do they?"

He returned the slight smile I gave him. "Not a single one of us. You know, I've even offered to just give her the crown a few times, but she refuses to take it. Says it would clash with her hair."

My smile widened.

He stopped fidgeting with his clothing and offered me his arm. "We have an hour or two before our guests will be joining us at the dinner table," he said. "Perhaps you'd like to see the progress our army is making before we get started on the evening's agenda? Hopefully, it will inspire some confidence for us both."

The idea filled me with trepidation and uncertainty. But, somehow, I managed to take his arm, walking alongside him without hesitation as he headed toward the wing that overlooked the training grounds, where most of the revived Graykeep soldiers were currently being housed.

Along the way, we stopped to collect Grimnor. It had been returned to its chamber for safekeeping while I recovered from the events at Graykeep, but both my brother and I agreed it should be at my side for the evening's meetings; Aveline had already provided a means of carrying it that coordinated with my dress, even—a wide, ornate-but-lightweight belt that hung gracefully at my waist, supporting the sword without compromising the garment's flow.

Before we left, I found myself hesitating, my eyes drawn to Luminor.

My brother stopped as well, his gaze shifting between me and the Sword of Light. I expected him to tell me to focus on my own blade and the power I could control, but he surprised me and said, "Just so you're aware, I plan to bring up the subject of the Light King to our visiting council. The possibility of him wielding this sword should not be entirely ignored, I've decided."

"...Really?"

"After what he did by your side at Graykeep—and outside of Erebos before that—it seems foolish not to consider that maybe he could be an asset after all. I should warn you, though, that the idea likely won't be received well by most of our guests. They've seen the Above as the enemy for too long; they won't be quick to trust him, regardless of the bond you two have developed."

My skin heated with frustration, but I nodded, knowing he was right.

"I've already spoken with Aleksander about this as well," he added.

I was momentarily speechless.

They'd *spoken* to one another.

And agreed on something, at that.

Maybe there was a glimmer of hope for our future after all.

"I suggested he sit out this first meeting, to avoid adding more tinder to what will be an already-combustible gathering," Bastian said, "and he agreed to this. But there will be an opportunity to explore his role in things in the days to come, I think."

The thought of facing this initial trial without him

made my chest feel uncomfortably tight, but I would manage, somehow.

I finished securing Grimnor at my waist, while also watching and taking mental notes on how my brother sealed the chamber shut behind us, and then we continued on.

We passed the kitchen, where the night's dinner was already being prepared; the scent of roasted meats, herbs, and freshly baked bread wafted through the air, making my stomach growl. Predictably, this was where Phantom left us, shifting into a smaller, less frightening form before trotting into the kitchen. He'd made an art out of convincing the palace servants that he was deserving of treats—I saw no less than three bits of food being tossed his way before he was out of my sight. I rolled my eyes but didn't call him back to my side; at least *one* of us was going to enjoy the feast tonight.

A steady roar of noise hit us as we approached the area around the training grounds, made up of the hacking and swishing of weapons; the clanging of armor; and the cacophony of chattering voices interspersed with shouted orders and grunts of exertion.

We made our way through the halls above and into the parlor that overlooked the grounds, peering down at the bustling hive of activity.

Things were being pulled from the armory and inventoried. Cleaned. Repaired. Groups of soldiers practiced swordplay and drills, shaking the rust from their muscles with swings and thrusts. Servants moved with purpose, preparing equipment, sharpening blades, and ensuring everything else was in order.

We stood for several minutes, watching. My wide eyes

darted back and forth, my mouth going dry as I tried to count and weigh everything I saw—as I attempted to determine how this waking army changed our odds.

"How many?" I asked my brother, quietly.

"Just shy of a hundred strong."

It had felt like more when I'd been surrounded by them at Graykeep. Such a small number to rest such a heavy task upon—a task we still hadn't worked out the details of.

Nine days.

Nine days to shape a formidable plan, to prepare our followers to carry it out. And I tried to keep my chin lifted and my spirits undaunted, but I couldn't help asking, "Will it be enough?"

My brother tilted his head toward me, his expression impossible to read.

My heart pounded and my body tensed, bracing for a grim reply.

No. No, of course it isn't enough. We'll be crushed the moment we step through the gate, but we have no choice but to attempt something.

But what he said was, "Do you feel the change in the air since we came back from Graykeep? Have you heard the occasional laughter among their preparations? The excited chatter between the servants tending them? It sounds like hope. Like a chance in the darkness, however tiny it might be."

I looked back to the crowd below us. Listening closer, now, to see if I could hear what he did.

"We are fighting for our future," said Bastian. "The ones who would stand in our way are clinging to the past. And they have everything to lose, while we have nothing—which gives us an advantage, I think, with whatever strategy we decide on from here."

I bit my lip, silently trying to will myself into believing he was right.

"There are several bright minds here to speak with us tonight; I've no doubt that together we'll figure out the best way to make use of the resources we *do have*." His gaze lifted toward the sun, gaging the time. Frowning, he said, "Speaking of them, I should probably go see if I'm needed anywhere. I'll meet you in the banquet hall in an hour, alright?"

I nodded, though I was tempted to admit that maybe *I* needed him even more than our visitors might have. And I didn't hate that he'd checked on me, after all. Whatever missteps we'd endured, he had become a familiar, comforting presence. But I couldn't ask him to stay, knowing all the obligations awaiting him.

He kissed my forehead and then left, and I continued to watch my army for a few minutes before heading back to the main wing by myself.

My spirits lifted slightly when, after a short stroll, I caught sight of another familiar face: Zayn, leaning against the wall directly ahead. As I approached, I noticed the painting across from where he stood—another portrait of Calista, this one done in impressionistic strokes that seemed to dance and shift with the light, giving her an almost dreamlike, ephemeral quality.

"I feel as though we've lived this scene before," I commented as I reached his side, cutting my eyes toward the artwork.

He chuckled. "It's a bit hard to *not* meet beneath a painting of the damnable woman, isn't it? This palace is rather obsessed with her."

"Very true." As before, the turquoise bracelet on my

wrist reacted as I stared up at the former Vaelora of Noctaris. The beaded bangle tightened to the point that it made me wince, and Zayn gave me a curious look.

I smiled through the discomfort, stepping away from the painting. Recalling my brother's theory that the bracelet reacted to large concentrations of pure Vaeloran magic, I scanned our surroundings, searching for some other sign of it. Perhaps the protective spells she'd laid over this palace were anchored in all the artworks of her, somehow?

Whatever the reason, I couldn't settle my powers enough to make any sense of it all. As the pain became nearly unbearable, I turned and continued my stroll down the hallway.

Zayn followed, his hands in his coat pockets and his expression thoughtful.

"Will you join us at dinner tonight?" I asked, still trying to distract myself from my restless magic and the bracelet that channeled it, which remained entirely too tight on my arm.

"Aleks didn't seem to think either of us should," he replied, keeping his gaze straight ahead. "He agreed to skip it after speaking with Bastian, as I understand it."

I could hear unspoken concerns in his tone, so I said, "There will be other meetings for him to attend."

"Perhaps."

"...I still believe balance is possible. That's the strategy I intend to suggest, first and foremost, at this first meeting. Once they've warmed up to the idea, we'll introduce Aleks and Luminor."

"And if the other leaders of Noctaris refuse to entertain *any* of these ideas?"

My tone hardened. "Then they don't get my cooperation, either."

He regarded me with a long, searching look, as though he was trying to determine how serious I was. Finally, he chuckled quietly and said, "You know, you turned out stronger than I expected, in the end."

I brushed the compliment aside. "Well, it's not really the end, yet," I said, focused on twisting the beads of my bracelet around. They felt oddly warm.

"No," he agreed, "I suppose it isn't."

We walked deeper into the main part of the palace. I caught the scent of the feast being prepared once more, reminding me that I was due in the banquet hall soon. We said our goodbyes, but I found myself hesitating, feeling as if things between us were unfinished.

"We'll talk later," I assured him. "And tell Aleks I'll find him after this is all done, too."

He didn't reply right away; his eyes had glazed over and a shadow of something unreadable flickered across his face, as though his mind had drifted far away.

"Zayn?"

"Sorry." He blinked, his eyes refocusing and his usual, easygoing smile returning in an instant. "It's just…your dress."

"My dress?"

"It reminds me of the one you wore on the night of the Moonweaver Festival."

So my efforts to recreate that piece had not been in vain.

"You were beautiful that night," he said, "and you're beautiful now."

I blushed, mumbling a thank you under my breath. I

started to turn away, unsure of what else to say—then a realization struck me, freezing me to the spot.

Slowly, I fixed my gaze back on his.

"Is something wrong?" he asked.

I swallowed hard, trying to dislodge the lump that had formed in my throat. "...How do you know what I looked like that night?"

He didn't reply, but that easy smile never left his face.

The rest of the room faded around us as I took a step back. "It was two years ago. You...you were trapped in the Below two years ago. You weren't...you..."

The ground felt as if it was dissolving beneath my feet. My stomach dropped like I was falling, plummeting through a nightmare, everything around me racing by while I desperately tried to grab hold of something to slow me down. I thought I might be able to jerk myself awake if only I could get my hands around something, *anything*—

But when everything finally went still, the Lord of the North Reaches was still standing before me. Still smiling at me.

Run, urged a voice in the back of my mind. *Run!*

But I refused to show my panic. "Please excuse me for a moment," I said. "I've forgotten something in my room."

"By all means." He gave a slight bow, and I escaped without another word, trying to move as calmly as I could despite the warnings screaming through me.

When I chanced a look over my shoulder, he was nowhere to be seen.

I picked up my skirts and walked faster.

As soon as I turned the corner, I broke into a sprint.

But to where?

I needed help, I needed answers, I needed to find Aleks and tell him—

Unless he already knew.

The possibility stopped me in my tracks so quickly I stumbled, catching myself against the wall. I heaved for breath. Thoughts and explanations tumbled through me, each more painful, more impossible than the last.

And I realized, all at once, where I had to go.

What I had to do.

I shoved away from the wall and ran, ignoring the few people I passed, pausing for nothing and no one until I reached the chamber where Luminor awaited. With trembling hands, I began to unlock the doors. The turquoise bracelet had gone still once I put space between myself and Zayn, but now it was alive again—not painfully squeezing, but gently lifting and pulling my hand this way and that, guiding my fingers over the ruts and glyphs until they began to glow.

Fear choked the breath from my lungs and made my legs feel like they were made of rubber, but I still pushed the heavy doors open and made my way inside. I had to be stronger than the fear. I should have been stronger before now. Should have divined answers from this cursed blade when I'd had the chance.

Whatever truths awaited within it, it was past time for me to see them.

Before I reached the center pedestal, it occurred to me that I had no idea how long it would take me to work the magic I needed to—I needed to secure this room first.

I turned, fresh terror gripping me as I realized Zayn was already there, quietly shutting the doors behind him.

Chapter Forty

Nova

I was reaching toward the floating Sword of Light, but I was rooted in place, my eyes fixed on the closed doors.

Zayn stepped closer, blocking my view of the exit, his hands still shoved casually into his pockets—as if this was just an extension of the stroll we'd been enjoying together.

"Go ahead," he said, nodding at the sword. "I think it's time you knew the truth."

I suspected I already knew it.

I forced myself to move closer to the center pedestal, anyway, reaching up and swiping for Luminor's grip with a shaking hand. The sword was surrounded by powerful energy that made my bones feel as if they might splinter as I pressed toward it, but I managed to push through, to gently grasp the handle and pull it lower.

I laid a few fingers against the base of the blade.

It was a testament to how much control I'd gained over

my abilities these past weeks, that I was able to focus on my task. To zero my thoughts in on the exact night, the exact moments I needed to see, ignoring the present moment even as Zayn drew nearer.

Show me, I thought, desperately. *Please, please show me what I need to see—*

Colors and shapes swirled behind my eyelids. Banners of blue and silver; a soaring white building overlooking a sweeping veranda with tiled floors; a night sky scattered with stars; vine-wrapped columns...

Rose Point.

I was back at Rose Point.

Bodies flickered into view. Most remained hazy in the background, their chatter an incomprehensible blur of noise. But I could feel the vibrations of their shuffling feet, could smell the spices of the food they were eating, along with the acrid sweetness of their wine...

I felt a pounding in my chest, and I wasn't sure if it was my own heart or the pulsing magic of the sword I was touching. Either way, it soon grew painful. Loud. Slowly, but surely rising, blaring out all other things.

Thump. Thump. THUMP—

Then it stopped, *everything* stopped, as the vision centered on a person holding Luminor. It was an odd angle, and the image of him was somewhat distorted—like I was watching the scene play out upon the reflective surface of the blade.

But I recognized the tattooed arms steadying the sword.

Zayn.

The familiar, complex tapestry of inked vines and thorns...but now I noticed a new symbol tucked alongside one of those thorns. It was glowing—a small circle that flared like a beacon in the fog. Radiating from its center were rays of light that grew progressively brighter toward the middle, and two crescent shapes curved away from the circle on either side, like blades protecting the light within it. The center of this symbol was the only thing that remained visible as smoke exploded through the memory, just as smoke had exploded on the veranda that fateful night.

I *felt* what happened next, as much as I saw it—as though the sword was *alive*, absorbing the emotions of its handler. And it felt like a thousand years of hatred rolled into a single movement, an almost unfathomable amount of fury all condensed to a single, powerful thrust. I could sense the moment the sword pierced flesh, too. The warm blood running down the blade, as if it was running down my own arm.

Except, it *wasn't* my blood.

It was my father's.

His face swam into the vision a heartbeat later. As distorted as everything else, yet the anguish in his expression was painfully clear.

I wanted to look away, to wake up, to escape this horror that I'd already relived a thousand times on my own, in my far-too-clear memories…

Then another person appeared in the vision, holding me in place—

Aleksander.

His hands closed around Luminor's hilt. Again, I could feel the emotions being channeled through the weapon. Memories of confusion, of shock, of pain. And now I realized he hadn't been the one to bloody that blade; he was only trying to assess the damage, to make sense of the chaos just as I'd been trying to.

My own face came next. I barely recognized the young woman shining in this dulled mirror of memory. I felt removed from the rage on her shadowed face, far away from her fear and floating somewhere high above.

Or maybe I simply didn't *want* to recognize myself.

Because what a fool I'd been.

I'd had enough. My eyes shot open. I stared at Zayn, heaving for breath, still in disbelief in spite of the evidence in front me. The tattoo on his arm was pulsing, its golden light brightest at the center of the circle, just like in the vision. I'd never noticed it before—but maybe I just hadn't paid close enough attention.

What else had I missed?

So many things I likely could have seen, if only I'd had the courage to open my eyes. But I'd been so afraid to see the truth about Aleksander—so afraid of being *wrong* about him—that I'd completely overlooked the horror standing right next to him.

"See anything interesting?" Zayn asked, with a knowing little smirk.

I swallowed, trying to clear a path for words. "You...you killed him."

"A murder that was long overdue. He never should have taken you in and gotten himself mixed up in this war. He was a king of the Above—why he agreed to help the Below, I'll never understand. He paid the price for it, though. And your mother will, too, before I'm finished."

"...You knew about both worlds all along."

"Oh, I know much more than that."

"*How?*"

He didn't reply, but the golden light of that symbol on his arm shifted, creating the illusion of movement, making me think of a serpent slinking its way out from underneath the vines it had been hiding amongst.

As I watched it glistening, a chilling, awful possibility burrowed its way into my heart and refused to budge.

"...What is that mark on your arm?" I whispered.

He glanced at it, as if just now noticing the way it pulsed and moved. "You had a similar one, before your keepers in the Above started working to shackle your powers, trying to convince me your magic was fading, that you weren't worth paying attention to—as though I would fall for their tricks."

My mind raced, desperate to remember all the things I'd learned since making my way into this palace.

What was it Thalia had said? The only beings who could travel freely between the two worlds were the Vaelora. Was this how he had seen me the night of the Moonweaver Festival? And all the other things I had no explanation for...the seemingly random reactions of my bracelet...the strange comatose states Aleks had suffered until I came along...and what else, what *else*—

"You look troubled, Princess."

My gaze darted up to his. "You're..." My words caught in my throat.

His smile grew, arrogant and cold, and the sight flooded my body with furious heat.

I lifted my chin and looked him directly in the eyes. I would say his name, and I would not be afraid.

At least in that moment, I refused to let myself be afraid.

"Lorien Blackvale." My voice came out hushed but

strong. "Your ability to take over different bodies isn't a myth."

"So clever. As I've come to expect from you over these past few weeks." He stepped closer. I started to reach for Grimnor's handle. But his focus shifted away from me—to the blade floating behind me, instead.

The edges of his body began to glow faintly, as if his magic was waking in the presence of Luminor. Or maybe he was simply no longer bothering to suppress it, to hide his true identity.

I didn't know how he'd hidden it from me these past weeks—how he'd hidden it from so many others for so long. But now my own magic was rising in answer to his; more undeniable evidence that he was harboring a power greater than anything I could have guessed at.

Little wisps of darkness lifted from me, and as I watched them twist and tumble, I heard myself whisper, "How is this possible?"

He dropped his gaze to mine. "I have prevailed through centuries, watching Noctaris fade away through a dozen different sets of eyes, waiting for the day when the last of its life-force, the last of its magic, finally expired. And it was so close to being *finished*.

"Calista should have been the last of the Shadow Vaelora. The ending I gave her should have made it impossible for her magic to be reborn." He rolled his shoulders, as though shifting the weight of all those centuries upon them. "Then, twenty-five years ago, *you* were born, somehow. I knew it the moment it happened, because I felt it through the bond the two Vaelora always share—your first breath was like a knife twisting in my chest. And your *magic*..." His gaze trailed over me, a slow probing that made my skin crawl. "It was something to behold, even while we were in separate worlds."

The sword was forgotten, all of Lorien's focus and intensity now on me.

I fought the urge to take a step back.

I will not show fear.

"They tried to hide you. To whisk you away to a place where your magic wouldn't grow as quickly or noticeably. But I found you soon enough."

Another icy realization crept down the back of my neck, and my composure nearly slipped. "...You're the one who tried to kill my brother and me when we were babies."

His smile turned into more of a snarl. "Emphasis on *tried*. But your magic combined with his and reacted in an unpredictable way." Another roll of his shoulders, and I had the crazy, unsettling thought that there was a more monstrous version of him contained within Zayn's skin, pushing and prodding, searching for a way out.

"It...*dismantled* me, for a bit," he continued. "But I still kept a foothold in the Above realm, thanks to my loyal servants who kept vigil."

"...The Light Keepers."

"*Three years.*" He circled me slowly, the movement casual yet predatory. "That's how long it took me to regain my grip on my powers. For three years, my spirit resided in Luminor's blade, healing and regenerating while kept under lock and key by the Keepers. Once I managed to fully regain my powers and consciousness, I found myself in need of a new body."

"So you stole Zayn's?"

"Well, he wasn't my *first* target."

The room shifted and spun, and my stomach twisted as it occurred to me who that first target had likely been.

My gaze shifted toward the door, calculating. Torn between a need to escape and a need to *know*. He seemed to be getting a sickening, arrogant sort of joy out of keeping me pinned here by telling me one horrifying thing after another, and—despite the warnings firing through me—I couldn't bring myself to run away from these answers I was finally hearing.

"By this point, my Light Keepers and I had a new plan," he said, "not to attempt to kill you, but to eventually steal you away to Elarith, pairing you with its future king, so that we might find a way to collar you and control your magic—rather than trying to destroy you and risk another setback like the one I'd already endured."

"The future king…you mean Aleksander."

He lifted a hand and guided a strand of light around one of my shadows, pulling it toward him. It hovered above his palm, casting a strange golden-tinged darkness over his eyes as he said, "Every other being I've possessed over these past centuries has succumbed immediately to my control. Only one has ever managed to fight back. To escape from my grasp."

The story Aleks had told me about his sickness and his scars—and all the nightmares that had followed—suddenly made perfect sense. "It wasn't an illness that nearly overcame him as a child…it was *you*."

Lorien crushed the tangle of shadow and light in his fist, and when he unfolded his fingers, a pure, brightly burning flame of gold had taken its place. "It would have been poetic, I thought—the descendant of Argoth in my control, luring the vessel of Calista's magic into my grasp, keeping her from intervening with the ultimate demise of Noctaris, adding to the tragedy of *them*."

"But he forced you out." My words came out hushed, again, this time from a mixture of astonishment and something aching and awful as I thought of how strong Aleks must have been to have fought back against such a powerful being—and how *frightened*, trying to make sense of these monstrous things when he was only a child.

The furious heat from before returned, burning so fiercely now that it blurred my vision.

"Yes," Lorien said, his smile finally falling a bit in the corners. "He fought back, forcing me to settle for his closest advisor and the next in line to the throne: His cousin."

"But you still allowed Aleks to live?"

"*Allowed?*" he scoffed. "Not exactly. He should have died upon my exit, but he didn't. And—you might have noticed—he has far more magic, and far more of a connection to *you*, than he should have."

More of the story Aleks had told me flashed through my mind, reminding me of how surprised I'd been to learn that his magic wasn't innate, as most thought it was; he'd developed it *after* the strange sickness he'd survived.

Of course.

"…Your magic is still tied to him, isn't it?" I breathed, terror squeezing my heart, even though I could only guess at the implications of it all.

How deeply—how dangerously—intertwined were they?

"Yes." His fist clenched, and the golden flame burned brighter above it, as if fueled by his anger. "So we did what we could to hone that magic and keep him under our thumb, so that he might prove a useful pawn to us, rather than a thorn in our sides. We figured we could use him as bait to lure you in, if nothing else."

I bristled at the idea of him being reduced to mere bait. My hand moved once more to Grimnor's grip, while my eyes stayed narrowed on the monster taking shape before me.

Lorien gave my hold on the sword a cursory glance, but continued without commenting on it. "But on the night of what should have been your betrothal," he said, "your father tried to back out of our agreement. I don't think he'd ever truly intended to go through with it; he was merely trying to draw us in so he could get closer to our secrets. He had suspicions about the Light Keepers, of course. I don't know how much he actually knew—but he was getting far too curious about me. My patience with him ran out. So, he was dealt with."

Dealt with.

I shifted my stance, preparing to withdraw Grimnor. "And you thought I would still agree to marry into Elarithian royalty after you killed him?"

"Of course not." He arched a brow. "But I am not above simply *taking* what I want when negotiations fall through. Whether as a future queen or a prisoner, we were going to leave Rose Point with you in our control. I tried to grab you before you made it to your father that night—you don't even realize the magic you unleashed in that moment, do you? How you protected yourself? You slipped through my grasp in the banquet hall, I followed you outside, and... well, we both know what happened next, don't we? Those damned shadows of yours sent me spiraling down into this hell."

My heart was in my throat, its relentless pounding

making it hard to breathe. The magic I'd loathed for so long, all the destruction and despair my shadows had caused…

It seemed they had only been sparing me from a far worse fate.

Lorien took another step closer to me, his gaze shifting once more to my hold on Grimnor, lingering this time. He seemed to be daring me to draw it out.

And those *damned shadows* of mine grew more restless beneath my skin, catching the fire building in my heart, whipping it into an even more frantic beat that pounded through my body like a war drum.

"I hope it hurt when you hit the ground," I snarled, locking my eyes onto his.

He chuckled darkly. "Don't worry—it did. My powers are weaker in Noctaris, and that, combined with the magic you struck me with, *and* my ties to Aleksander and Luminor…it's all made the last seven years *interesting*, to say the least. But I managed to slip back to the surface a few times —just enough to orchestrate things regarding the imposter on the Elarithian throne, and to watch you and the plans you were making."

"…You knew I was planning to come here?"

"I did. And I saw an opportunity to not only meet you here, but to regain some of my lost power. Because I knew Luminor had fallen, too, and I assumed it was being held somewhere within this cursed Below—but I was unable to find this palace on my own, due to the spell Calista protected it with."

Another realization crawled through me, and the horror must have been obvious on my face, because Lorien's smile brightened once more.

"That's right," he said. "If your foolish handlers hadn't feared you and your power so much, if they had just *left* you in this palace in the first place, I likely wouldn't have found you until it was too late. But they chose otherwise. So here we are. And I did want to thank you, dear Nova, for leading me into the heart of Noctaris's last stronghold, *and* reuniting me with my sword."

"…It was you who tried to break into this chamber," I gasped, gaze darting toward the Sword of Light, which had started to rock unsteadily in the air. "You slaughtered the guards…and silenced Rowen and Farren too, didn't you?"

"Clever again." The glow around his body flickered brighter, and his golden brown eyes seemed to take on a reddish hue—as did the center of his Vaeloran mark—as he said, "They knew too much. I've been periodically pulling out their memories with my magic over the years, so they didn't remember my returns to the Above, or other *sensitive* information, but the task of keeping them oblivious was becoming tiresome. I had to seek a more permanent solution."

I pictured the still bodies of Rowen and Farren. Their red-ribbon throats, their forever-silenced tongues, their pale skin and empty gazes…

I swallowed hard, forcing a calmness into my voice that I didn't in any way feel. "What are you planning to do now? And *why*?"

"Can't you guess?" His eyes—still disturbingly close to the color of blood—darted between Luminor and Grimnor before settling back on my face. "There isn't enough magic to sustain both worlds, and there never will be again. But there is a chance at creating something greater—imagine the Above in all its current glory, but with all that remains of Noctaris's power and magic added to it, as well."

"...And with you as its ruler?"

He was quiet for a long moment, his gaze calculating as he looked me over. "You could rule at my side, if you wanted to. The Vaelora are always stronger together, after all."

"You would sacrifice this entire realm, even after all the time you've spent in it? Even after seeing the life that still clings to it?"

His expression remained unchanged. "This world is little more than ash and shadows, anyway. And its survivors don't truly *want* you as their queen, by the way; they only care about what you can do for them. Their admiration will fade as soon as they believe their world is safe. It has *always* faded after the job is finished. For a millennia, our kind have been expected to sacrifice ourselves after fulfilling our duty, and so that is all we've been reduced to—mere tools to be discarded. But I am rewriting that narrative. Ending our servitude. And you could help me do it."

"And you *wouldn't* be using me?"

"No. Because I don't *need* you like this world does; I simply want you." He cocked his head, as though truly curious about my answer. Offering his hand to me, he asked, "Isn't there a difference between the two?"

I stared at his outstretched hand. At the ribbons of deeply golden light moving around it, drawing in my shadows like a flame ensnaring moths.

And I couldn't help considering his words.

Because there *was* a difference. I'd grown up painfully aware of that difference, surrounded by people who felt as though they needed to treat me a certain way, with a certain reverence, even though they didn't truly want me in their presence.

"We don't have to be enemies, Nova," Lorien said, his tone shifting into something oddly gentle and...*alluring*. Like a calm stretch of cerulean sea, begging me to jump in. To not worry about the jagged rocks that might be lurking below the surface.

I wondered what it would be like, to work side-by-side with someone who carried the same mark as me, who truly understood the weight of the magic that mark represented. A weight, a burden, that I feared would make it impossible for anyone else to ever truly *want* me—all of me.

I thought of reaching back.

Just for a moment, I thought of reaching back.

Then I withdrew my sword instead, easing the tip of it into his chest.

The glow around his body flashed brighter, sending a wave of electricity snaking up my sword, burning into my arm.

I refused to flinch.

Lorien kept his gaze leveled with mine, never once glancing at the sword or magic between us. "You really *do* favor her. No blood relation, but the dark magic weaving through your body has certainly left its mark."

I squeezed Grimnor's handle more tightly.

He tilted his face closer to mine, his lips barely parting with the words as he added, "And it's as I suspected: Wielding that sword makes you look even *more* like her."

He was too close, his eyes too hungry, and I had the unsettling feeling that he was no longer seeing *me* at all—he saw only the woman he believed had wronged him all those years ago.

The one he'd been plotting his revenge against for *centuries*.

"I am not her," I said in a quiet, seething voice.

"No," he agreed, leaning back slightly, "but I suspect ruining *you* will be almost as satisfying."

Chapter Forty-One

Nova

HE MOVED AS FAST AS THE LIGHT HE CONTROLLED—knocking my sword arm aside, catching me by the throat and slamming me backward.

I struck the pedestal's edge, my body bending over it with a gruesome amount of force. As stinging pain shot up my spine and radiated toward the tips of my fingers, my hold on Grimnor weakened enough that Lorien was able to drive it from my grasp with a well-placed kick.

He loomed over me, reaching toward the Sword of Light. I watched, terror blooming in my chest, as he beckoned—and as Luminor obeyed, dropping from the air into his grip.

I tried to scramble after my own sword, but Lorien beat me to it. His movements were graceful yet wild, impossibly fast but entirely controlled.

Inhuman.

"If I can't have *you*," he growled, "then I will make do

with your sword." He kneeled beside Grimnor, placing a hand over it.

The sword reacted to his closeness with a menacing hiss, the energies swirling within its blade darkening, forcing him to draw his hand back. The sight kindled a spark of hope inside of me; I felt, not for the first time, as if my sword was alive—which meant I at least had an ally in this chamber.

"But, as I suspected…" Lorien said, turning his hungry eyes upon me once more, "…I'll need to *borrow* a bit of your magic in order to make it easier to wield."

"You won't get a drop of magic from me," I snapped.

He laid Luminor beside its counterpart and then rose back to his full height, a sly smile sliding across his handsome features. It was jarring, how different those features looked without the warmth he'd been faking over the past weeks. How much sharper. How much crueler.

"I wasn't planning on asking *nicely* for it," he said.

I shifted into a more formidable crouch, grabbing for the knife hidden at my thigh and drawing it out.

He prowled closer, twisting his hand as he came, pulling light from his palm and guiding it out along his fingers—five separate lines of light that curved into sharp points at the end, extending like claws from his hand.

"I borrowed my ability to possess bodies from my dear Calista," he said, "and that power has endured all these centuries—so I believe I'm fully capable of taking what I need from the likes of *you*."

"Stole it," I said, standing and clenching my knife more tightly. "You didn't borrow it, you *stole* it."

He flexed his fingers, making the light at their ends shimmer and sharpen even further. "Same difference."

I sized up the distance between myself and my fallen sword, wondering if I could possess it and pull it into my hold quickly enough.

"This will be less painful for you if you don't resist me," Lorien said.

"I choose pain, then."

He huffed out an unamused laugh. "You would."

He lunged.

I sidestepped, narrowly avoiding his reaching hand. He doubled back in a blink and swung for me again. I stumbled as I avoided him this time, barely catching myself against the wall. Spinning around brought me face-to-face with him at the exact instant he slammed the claws of Light magic toward my chest.

I ducked. His hand—and his magic—struck the wall, leaving burn marks behind, sending sparks sizzling over the stone and dangerous heat washing over my skin.

My shadows lashed violently outward, briefly distracting him. I rose in a rush of cold fury, plunging my knife into his stomach, sinking it as deeply as I could and twisting until my forearms shook from the effort and my hands grew slick with blood.

He caught a fistful of my hair and yanked, throwing me to the floor.

He dove after me, but I managed to roll out from underneath him and stumble to my feet. As I put more space between us, he paused long enough to rip the knife out with little more than a pained hiss, flinging it across the room in the same motion.

Blood seeped from his wounded stomach, quickly covering the bottom of his shirt. He didn't so much as wince. His breathing remained evenly measured. His gaze was as fierce and focused as ever.

Did he even feel pain?

This monster had endured for lifetimes, and now...

I realized that I didn't know how much of him was even *human*.

As if he could hear the frantic questions in my head, he smiled. And then he demonstrated more of his supernatural ability, attacking so quickly that I had no hope of avoiding him. His magic-encircled fist struck my chest. I fell back, struggling to find my balance and trying to will my shadows into something that would protect me.

Before I managed either of those things, Lorien struck again, his fist unclenched, claws of light sinking in and slamming me against the pedestal in the center of the room once more.

I hit harder than before. The painful spasm that shot through my back was so intense that, for a moment, I feared I was entirely paralyzed. The shadows that had started to rise and gather around me scattered, and as their darkness parted, he was suddenly *there*—a terrifying figure wrapped in golden light that blinded me as he drew closer.

I didn't even manage a gasp before he sank the sharp strands of his magic into the side of my neck. They pierced like needles through my skin, burning as they delved deeper. I could feel them with disturbing precision, every twist and turn and subtle movement they made. It seemed as if they were hunting, almost, hooking themselves around each strand of my magic they could find, trying to rip it out of me—to separate it from my very soul.

Little by little, they started to succeed.

The pain was...*indescribable*.

It tore my mind from my body, pulling me away from all rational thought.

I don't know how much time passed before I became aware of myself again. Aware that I lay dazed and burned and bleeding like a sacrifice upon an altar, overtaken by a death-like stillness.

I *wanted* to be dead.

But no—I was still alive. I could feel my pulse, my shuddering breaths, my twitching fingers. And I could feel my magic—*gods*, the way that magic still twisted and curled, resisting every attempt Lorien made to pull it into his possession.

Its resistance did no good, in the end.

Like deeply-lodged thorns, those pieces of me still came out when he applied enough force, ripping painful tears through my flesh as they went.

An involuntary convulsion bent my body into an unnatural angle, and Lorien leaned closer, increasing the pressure on my throat.

"Don't move," he ordered.

I didn't move, because I *couldn't* move.

"Good girl," he said, his voice low and full of the same possessive hunger he'd watched me with earlier. The weight around my throat slid lower, needling and burning its way through my chest. Catching and pulling more of my magic toward him. His own power seemed to settle in the places where mine was ripped out, and my body grew heavier with each violent exchange, becoming more and more difficult to move.

A horrid image flashed in my mind—myself, sprawled over the stone, flayed open like a fresh kill with my heart and everything else laid out for him to feast upon.

I kept trying to move despite the heaviness. Until finally, *finally*, I felt something other than the pain, something beyond the blood and the cold stone underneath me…just the slightest itch upon my wrist.

The bracelet my father had given me, reminding me of its presence.

I closed my eyes, trying to remember his face.

Seven years.

Seven years with nothing but a memory of that man and the kingdom I once called home, all because of the beast who loomed over me now.

My hand was already shaking, my fingers still twitching from pain, from shock. I shook it all harder—on purpose—scraping my wrist against the stone pedestal, sliding the bracelet off, bit by bit. In that moment, I no longer feared what would happen if I removed it; it couldn't be worse than what I was already enduring.

It slipped over my hand, and almost instantly I felt a surge of cold power—a pulling, desperate power that urged me to lift my head, to turn my gaze in the direction of my fallen sword. I could *see* the energy sleeping within that sword, all of a sudden. The glow of it pulsed like a heartbeat that seemed to speed up to match my own.

I sensed Lorien moving above me.

Excruciating pressure followed, cutting toward my heart.

I summoned every ounce of strength I could to turn back to him, to meet his gaze without flinching as I growled, "Get your fucking hands *off me.*"

Knocking his touch away, I reached toward Grimnor and beckoned my fingers, bringing the sword hurtling toward us.

It nearly impaled him between the shoulder blades, but he twisted wildly aside at the last instant.

The sword flew over my head, clattering against the ground several feet away. Before I started crawling after it, I stretched a hand toward the knife he'd thrown away earlier. It was lighter than Grimnor. Easier to grab. It flew faster under my command, too, striking Lorien in the neck before he even realized it was coming.

As he stumbled away with a furious sound—still more from annoyance than actual pain, I feared—I again focused on Grimnor, crawling a few feet before reaching out and trying to pull it into my hand.

The sword hovered in the air, tipping toward me. But though my hold on it was firm, my control was shaky. I'd lost too much magic. Too much blood. I was too weak. Too slow. Too unbalanced. My attempt to reel it more precisely into my grip failed, dropping it at the feet of Lorien as he stepped back to me.

I tried to stand and ended up falling to my knees instead, the jolting motion making the blood flow more freely from the wounds along my neck and chest.

The room spun.

I would have vomited if I'd had the energy for it. Instead, I braced a hand against the floor and closed my eyes again, desperately trying to focus, to find another surge of power like the one I'd felt moments ago. It was swirling deep in my gut, like a deep, dangerous current hidden beneath calm waters. If only I could have reached it without drowning. Somehow, *I had to reach it*—

Lorien took a step toward me. A single step that echoed through the chamber. Through my very being. Then he stopped, and a strange noise escaped him—a sort of strangled laugh, full of disbelief and some other charged emotion I couldn't readily name.

I heard him...*retreating*.

I blinked my eyes open and gasped.

I was surrounded by shadowy figures. No less than a dozen spectral men and women had appeared in front of me, and they continued taking shape as I watched. Their forms shifted between solid and ethereal, like the lingering afterimage of a dream. But their eyes—those started sharp and stayed that way, gleaming with a bright, otherworldly clarity as they took in their surroundings.

After a moment of staring, mouth agape, I realized I recognized the one in the very center. She stood taller than the others, her silhouette sharp and distinct against the swirling mass of figures, her long, dark hair dancing unnaturally, as if caught in a phantom wind…

Judging by the way his face had drained of all color, Lorien recognized her, too.

Calista.

And all the others around her…were they *all* past Shadow Vaelora? Had I summoned them here, somehow? The weakness rapidly overtaking my body suggested as much—that they were made from, or at least tethered to, the shadows within me.

This was staggeringly powerful magic.

But I could already feel my hold on it slipping.

Lorien no longer seemed interested in trying to cut me apart. His attention had shifted to the shadows moving over his skin. Similar to the ones that appeared on mine, because they were caused by the same magic—the magic he'd *stolen*.

He didn't dare cross the line of my predecessors to resume his torture of me, but with my stolen shadows wrapping around him like armor, he managed to pick up Grimnor.

He looked to the door, calculating.

I struggled to my feet. Fear of letting him escape with that sword made me oblivious to the pain racking through my body. Indifferent to my exhaustion, my dizziness, to the dangerous amount of power I could feel building around him.

But as soon as I staggered forward, Calista's gaze jerked toward mine. Like the others around her, her eyes were the only part of her that remained focused and bright. As I stared into them, I stopped moving, as though under a spell, overcome by a sudden urge to save my strength. To focus on surviving and nothing else. And I would have sworn I heard a voice, soft and determined, though the shadow-specter's lips never moved—

This is not how it ends.

Calista turned away. She lifted her hands. The other figures followed her lead, and a veil of darkness rose up with the motion, driving Lorien farther back, pushing him more violently toward the doors.

Protecting me.

Reluctantly, I sank to my knees once more, reaching for my wounds. My hand came away covered in crimson. My breath caught in my throat, and I couldn't seem to resume my normal breathing, no matter how hard I tried. Every gasping attempt sent another wave of agony rushing through me.

The sentinels before me began to lose their shape, bleeding into the dark wall they'd created.

My chest felt as if it was cracking apart from the effort of trying to inhale.

So much blood.
So much darkness.
So little air.

The last clear image I saw before succumbing to the pain was of Lorien fleeing from the shadows, a fierce, wild expression in his eyes and both swords of legend gripped tightly in his hands.

Chapter Forty-Two

Nova

I woke up with my face buried in a rough forest of dark fur, dampened from a combination of sweat and tears. I inhaled sharply, and a low whimper vibrated against my cheek.

Phantom.

He curled more closely to me while I drifted in and out of awareness. Some time passed, and then I heard his voice, a whisper in the back of my mind—

(*Come back.*) Another whimper. (*Come back.*)

I moved my hands through his fur, weakly clenching my fingers into it, trying to ground myself and keep the world from spinning. He shifted his position again, pressing his forehead to mine. I scratched his chin, and the sound of his tail thumping uncertainly against the mattress woke me further. I felt life slowly creeping back into my body— enough that I managed to open my eyes and take in the familiar sight of my bed. My room. My dog.

I was still here.

I ached in every place it was possible to ache, yet somehow, I was still here.

But Grimnor was gone. To where, I didn't know—but it seemed far. I couldn't explain it, but I could actually *sense* its absence like a gaping hole in my chest, a missing piece that made me feel off-balance even as I was lying down. The vision of it being carried away played over and over in my mind.

Gone.

As was Luminor.

And Zayn…no, *Lorien.*

Gone.

And Aleksander—

I shot upright and tried to roll out of my bed, only to end up tangled in the sheets. I was weak. *Gods*, I felt so damn weak. The dizziness was overwhelming; I couldn't stay balanced. The white sheets tangled tighter and tighter around me, as if I were wrapped in the arms of angry, vengeful ghosts. I tumbled to the floor and struck my head against the bedpost.

"My lady!" Aveline cried, rushing to gather me up in her arms. Phantom gave a panicked yelp and leapt down to my side, shoving his cold nose between Aveline and me, trying to lick my cheek.

"*Aleks*," I gasped, as the room twisted around me. "Where is Aleks?"

"Let's get you back into bed," Aveline insisted.

I refused, clinging tightly to her, holding her down on the floor with me. "*Where is he?*"

She grabbed my arms, gently but firmly pushing me back, putting enough space between us to properly look me in the eyes. "He's still here."

"In the palace?"

"Yes."

"Alive?"

"Yes, of course, but—"

"I need to go to him."

Her grip on me tightened. "He's in the prison holds down below. No place for you to go in your condition. And besides—"

"How long?"

"...You've been in and out of consciousness for almost five days."

"*Five days?*" Another wave of dizziness overtook me, worse than any before it. I could no longer find the strength to fight against Aveline; she was surprisingly strong.

As I went numbly still, her hands moved to the sides of my face. She captured my gaze and held it, her blue eyes shining with emotion. "Five long, terrible days. When they brought you to me, I thought…I thought you were dead."

Dead.

I should have been focused on how *not dead* I was, maybe. Grateful that I'd survived to fight another day. But all I could think about—out of all the terrible things that were happening—was Aleksander.

How he and Lorien were tied to one another.

How he'd been lied to, manipulated, betrayed by the one he thought was his *family*…

I had to go talk to him. We needed to sort through all of these latest horrors together, and I needed to make sure he was okay, that he was eating, that he wasn't being tortured for a crime he didn't commit.

"He doesn't deserve to be locked in a dungeon," I said.

"My lady…"

"They've got it wrong. Zayn is the one they want; Aleks did nothing wrong."

"Nothing at all?"

I shook my head as vehemently as I could in my dizzy, weakened state.

Phantom leapt back onto the bed, settling down with his head resting on his paws, watching us and letting out the occasional anxious growl.

Aveline sighed as she rose to her feet, carefully pulling me up with her, guiding me to sit on the edge of the bed. She contemplated my words for a long moment before she asked, "Can you be certain?"

I didn't answer right away. Not because I didn't know the answer, but because it felt so…*big*. Like the sort of answer that cleaved a life into two parts. There was the before—before I realized how wrong I'd been.

And now came the after.

My gaze swept over the violin Aleks had gifted me, resting in its case on a shelf. Then I looked toward the balcony, transporting myself into the memory of playing that instrument while he watched in quiet awe, and then everything that had followed after—exchanges of heat, of breath, of words that had settled upon my heart like a vow…

I don't consider us a tragedy. At all.

I'd seen the truth in Luminor's blade. But a part of me, I think, had known it long before that. He was not my enemy.

Our worlds *wanted* us to be enemies.

But the worlds had gotten it wrong.

"Yes," I told Aveline. "I'm certain."

She again took a long time considering my words, busying herself with folding a basket full of freshly laundered towels.

"Well," she finally replied, "the Regent had no answers for what he stumbled upon in the swords' chamber. The Elarithian lord went missing, along with the swords, and you were half dead and in no state to explain anything. You're lucky your brother insisted on merely locking Aleksander up; the other leaders of Noctaris have been calling for much worse. They're furious, that lot. Looking for someone to blame. And it's only going to get worse, what with—"

"I have to speak with him."

"You have to rest," she countered.

"*Please*," I whispered, my voice strangled and desperate. "Please don't ask me to sit here and do nothing. Too much is at stake for that."

She pursed her lips. Folded a few more towels with tense, jerking movements that slowly gave way to easier, resigned ones. "…At least wait a little while longer. Eat something. Drink something. Make certain your strength is truly returning. You woke briefly two days ago, and we made the mistake of thinking you were truly recovered—you ended up fainting again, and worse off than before."

I didn't remember waking up at all…which, of course, made it difficult to argue against her point.

Part of me still wanted to make a run for the door, but my limbs felt too heavy and the room spun faster every time I started to stand.

So I sat. And I sat, and I sat, while Aveline restlessly continued her folding, and then she moved on to bringing me one tray of food and drink after another, until I finally managed to stomach some of it.

Slowly, the dizziness subsided. The heaviness persisted, but I managed to get to my feet, and I paced, and I paced and I paced while Phantom slept, snoring loudly, and Aveline continued finding chores to keep herself busy with while still staying close to me.

Eventually, I found myself in front of the standing mirror in the corner, taking in my disheveled and broken appearance.

My skin was gruesomely pale, the tired circles under my eyes as dark as bruises. The entire right side of my neck was covered in bright, angry scars. The worst of it was concentrated there, but those scars stretched beyond my neck, too; ugly, jagged marks of ruined pink skin creeping over part of my face and crawling down across my throat and my chest.

I wanted to rake the scars off. To create my own to cover these, as if I could erase the memory of Lorien's touch if I just carved deeply and violently enough. Because staring at them made me feel…*dirty*. Violated. Empty.

What magic had he taken from me?

And how could I reclaim it?

Could I reclaim it?

Gingerly, I traced the paths of ruin his magic had left behind. They didn't seem real. *Nothing* that had happened in that chamber seemed real.

My bracelets rattled against one another as my hand moved. I vaguely remembered the turquoise one slipping from my wrist in the sword chamber, and the surge of magic that had followed. The ghosts of Calista and the other Shadow Vaelora…had I imagined them all? Had I been hallucinating from the pain, delirious from the loss of blood and magic? Or had I really had such power inside of me all along?

What else could I do?

All of these bracelets, binding my power so precisely, so neatly, so fearfully…

"I did what I could with your wounds, but I worry they'll leave some sort of permanent mark, anyway," Aveline said, gently, making her way to my side. "Magic scarring is…complicated. And I have little experience dealing with what Light magic leaves behind."

It's okay, I wanted to say. Because for so long, that had been my mantra. My way of surviving—pushing the pain down. Hiding it. Shackling my real fury and feelings with bracelets and smiles and a bright, never-breaking optimism.

It's okay. It's okay. It's okay.

But I couldn't get those words to leave my mouth this time.

And I was shaking from a sudden urge to rip my bracelets off and throw them in the trash.

"I'm sorry," said Aveline. Then, in a tighter, colder voice: "We should have known those Lightwielders couldn't be trusted." Clearly flustered, she went back to her chores.

"…If I'd trusted Aleks, none of this would have happened." I was speaking to my reflection as much as to Aveline. To this bruised and battered version of me who was finally waking up to all the things that were *not okay*.

Aveline turned back to me, but I kept my eyes on the woman in the mirror.

"I love him," I told that woman, my voice breaking slightly. "I love him so much I was afraid of something—*anything*—that might tear us apart, and so I closed my eyes to what I didn't want to see. I've risked an entire world because I was too busy trying to pretend everything was fine, even when I knew it wasn't, because I was afraid that digging for the truth would hurt too much. And it…it does. It hurts. It…" I trailed off. My breaths were coming in short, erratic bursts, making it difficult to speak clearly.

I moved away from the mirror, unable to look at myself any longer.

I felt Aveline watching me as I stumbled back to sit on my bed. She finished arranging the throw pillows on the couch and then came to sit beside me. Phantom woke up and wiggled his way over to my other side, dropping his head into my lap.

"It isn't just my fear of what might become of me and Aleks," I said, numbly stroking Phantom's head as I stared at the ground. "I'm afraid of my power—whether it's divining memories or waking the dead, I've *always* been afraid. And I've spent most of my life hating it all, focusing only on how lonely and different it made me.

"*Trust yourself*, Orin told me before I came to this world. *And don't be afraid of your darkness.*" I held up my wrist, studying the amethyst jewels in the last bracelet he'd gifted me. "Since coming here, I've felt a stirring, a deeper connection to my magic than ever before. I could have truly embraced it and gotten so much stronger, if only I'd dared. I could have seen the truth so much sooner…but instead I kept shying away, kept choosing the path of least resistance, only doing the bare minimum, and now…" I trailed off, unable to put into words the crushing sense of regret settling over me.

Phantom lifted his head in concern. I buried my face against his while Aveline rubbed my back, offering a comfort I didn't feel like I deserved.

"There's nothing wrong with being afraid, my love," she said, softly.

"Maybe not," I whispered. "But fear won't fix anything."

She was quiet for several minutes, her hand still moving absently up and down my back, before she said, "Then it's a good thing there is more to you than fear, isn't it?"

I said nothing to this, but I let the words sink over me as tears ran silently down my face.

In time, I lifted my burning, bloodshot eyes to what I could see of the outside world through the partially drawn curtains. The faint orange glow of the setting sun barely cut through the shadows around us. Another day slipping away. Another day closer to Equinox—to what felt like inevitable ruin, now that Lorien was on the loose with *both* swords in his possession.

Where had he gone?

What was he planning to do next?

What could *I* possibly do to stop him?

I started to collapse back into my blankets and pillows, but Aveline caught me in her arms and held me against her instead. I gave into her embrace, as I usually did, letting her comforting scent carry me away into a softer, kinder world. I let her brush my bedraggled hair and braid it. I didn't fight her when she insisted I get up and bathe and change into clean clothes.

At least another hour passed. My tears finally stopped. The aching in my gut didn't subside, but I made myself move, more and more, in spite of it. I had to keep moving. I still didn't know what I was going to do. And I was still afraid—the fear would always be there, I suspected.

But maybe Aveline was right.

Maybe I was not made entirely of that fear.

I went to my wardrobe, taking out my boots and belt. Grabbed my favorite knife from the nearby dresser—the same knife that had been bathed in Lorien's blood just days ago. I still had it, at least. A reminder that I could still fight, no matter what he had stolen from me. I secured it at my side before turning around to find Aveline watching me, her expression unreadable.

"I have to go," I told her, quietly.

She didn't protest this time. She only beckoned me toward her, taking a silver pin from her own hair and using it to better secure the crown of braids she'd woven around my head.

"Be careful, my Queen," she said, kissing my cheek.

I headed straight for my brother's office, Phantom trotting at my heels.

Bastian spent more time in this office than in any other place within the palace—and this was exactly where I found him, as expected, sitting at the head of the long, marble-topped table that took up half the room.

But he was also surrounded by several of our own court, as well as the visiting Noctarisan leaders. The sheer size of the audience made me pause, briefly, and reconsider the words I'd been prepared to say. The demands I'd been a breath away from making.

Several of those leaders caught sight of me. The mood in the room immediately shifted from a quiet, smoldering tension to something far more volatile and ready to erupt, as if I were an ember tossing myself into a pile of dry kindling. A few stood, moving as if to approach me. Their expressions ranged from grim curiosity to outright anger. One of them—Lord Marek—started toward me, his eyes full of far more vitriol than the others.

Phantom growled threateningly at my side.

My brother was on his feet in an instant, catching Marek by his jacket and jerking him to a stop. Marek twisted violently from his grasp. An uneasy ripple raced through the rest of the room, bringing almost everyone at the table to their feet.

Bastian shoved Marek back toward the others and stepped purposely, protectively in front of me.

"Excuse us one moment," he said to the group, placing a hand on my back and guiding me away from them. We walked out of the room and down the hall—well out of hearing range—before he stopped and looked me over.

"Thank the gods you're awake." He placed his hands on my shoulders, studying me for a moment before wrapping me in a quick embrace. "I thought I'd lost you again." His gaze lingered on my new scars as he pulled away, and he swallowed hard. "What *happened* in that chamber?"

So many things I needed to tell him. But I knew how he operated, by this point; if I spilled all of the information he wanted, he would start making decisions and plans without hesitation—plans that almost certainly wouldn't involve releasing the Light King. Because leaving him to rot in the dungeons would be the *safer* thing.

"I'll tell you all of it," I said, "but I want Aleks present for this conversation."

He massaged the space between his eyes. "Nova…"

"I'm not changing my mind on this."

"We need to consider—"

"Those are my orders." My words were sharp-edged

and swift, cutting without restraint through the tense air between us. "Am I the future queen of this kingdom or not?"

He didn't reply right away; it was the first time I'd openly spoken of taking the crown he'd offered me weeks ago, and the words seemed to catch him off guard.

In the corner of my vision, I saw Thalia stepping out of the office, pushing her way through people, striding toward us. I could feel her gaze narrowing in my direction, but I didn't take my eyes off my brother's.

"If you do not release him, then I will find a way to do it myself," I said.

We glared at one another. My heart pounded. I realized I was holding my breath, and I forced myself to exhale slowly. Calmly.

He started to shake his head, but I cut him off with a pointed look. "Don't test me, Bastian."

He looked as if he was considering doing precisely that —until his gaze fell upon my scars again. His hand moved absently to his own scars, fingers lightly tracing the dark marks splitting up his arms. Different from mine—as his had been caused by his own Shadow magic, by a desperate attempt at defense—yet Lorien had been indirectly responsible for those, too.

"We don't have much time," I said, a pleading edge to my voice, now.

He kept silent.

Reaching us, Thalia cleared her throat, jerking her head toward the room she'd left behind; several figures were now gathering in the doorway. Creeping closer, trying to hear our conversation—and not bothering to be subtle about it.

Looking to Thalia, my brother said, "Take her somewhere safe. We'll talk later."

Before I could argue, he turned on his heel and marched back toward his office.

I darted after him, but Thalia grabbed my hand and dragged me in the opposite direction. Phantom barked in warning, but Thalia's hold remained relentless, yanking me around the corner and out of sight.

"*Let go of me*," I hissed.

"Be quiet," she shot back, gripping even tighter.

Desperation and anger brought shadows to the surface of my skin. They felt strange, muted and...*dazed*, almost, after my encounter with Lorien—which only made me angrier. I knew it was dangerous, but I let them rage recklessly for a moment, anyway, until the entire hallway was shrouded in cold energy that extinguished the lights in the wall sconces, wrapping us in darkness and filling the air with the scent of smoke.

Thalia was unfazed by my furious display. She shoved me against the wall, bringing her face close to mine as she snapped, "I am not your enemy, you fool."

Phantom snarled, the sound vicious enough to shock me back to my senses. I continued fuming but held up a hand, forbidding him from coming closer to us.

With effort, I called my shadows back.

Casting a wary glance at Phantom, Thalia pulled me away from the wall and led me onward without another word.

I fell into step beside her, deciding not to make another scene. For now. But I was plotting my next move as we walked, preparing for the moment when I could slip away.

But where could I go? How could I get Aleks out of whatever prison they'd thrown him into?

I was so lost in my own thoughts and plans that it took me several minutes to ask, "Where are you taking me?"

"Where do you *think*?"

I was quiet for a few more minutes, curiosity overtaking me. Down, down, and farther down we went, past flickering torches casting long shadows on damp stone walls. Deeper than I had ever been before. The air turned heavier, thick with the stench of mold and iron. The steps underneath us became less polished, more uneven, more treacherous.

We were heading toward the dungeons, I realized.

"...Are you planning to lock me up alongside of him?"

Thalia laughed, the sound hollow and without any real humor, as she relaxed her grip on my arm. "Wouldn't *that* be the easier thing," she muttered.

"Does this mean you're going against my brother's orders?" I pulled the rest of the way from her grip, still eying her suspiciously. "I assumed you would always take his side."

"I *am* taking your brother's side—and the two of you are also on the same side, make no mistake. He tries too hard to keep the peace, sometimes, and it can make him seem...short-sighted. And stubborn."

(*That's putting it mildly,*) Phantom interjected, a growl rumbling in his chest.

Thalia gave him another wary glance before continuing: "Surely you realize, though, that he can't agree to release Aleksander when every other leader of Noctaris is calling for his head? And it wouldn't be wise for *you* to release him, either. But I can let you see him, at least."

My heart felt as if it might pound out of my chest as we

quickly but carefully continued our descent down the weathered stone steps.

"You'll need to be fast," Thalia said. "Tell him what you need to tell him, and then figure out what your next move is. Our time is short. With Grimnor no longer at the center of our palace, I'm not sure the protections Calista laid upon our sanctuary are going to hold. There are already signs of it deteriorating."

My breaths quickened at the thought. "That sword feels…far away. My connection to it is strained."

"I feared that would be the case." She looked troubled as she paused in the center of diverging hallways, taking a lantern from the wall and gathering her bearings for a moment before continuing straight onward. "Our search for the swords and the thief has led us only to dead ends; I fear he isn't in this realm anymore."

A horrible realization struck me. "He took both swords…the Nerithys Gate will yield to someone wielding them together, won't it?"

"That was our thought, as well. So we visited that gate a few days ago."

"And?"

"There were signs he'd been there. But it's closed itself off, now, and…" She trailed off, her eyes full of uncertainties, questions she couldn't seem to give a voice to.

But I didn't need her to elaborate—I understood.

If he was inside the Nerithys Realm, could we even follow him?

Did we stand any chance at stopping his plans, whatever they were?

"Wait here a moment," said Thalia, coming to a halt at the head of a small, narrow corridor. Peering down the dark passage, I saw two guards stationed at a set of double metal doors at the end, their armor glinting in the low-burning lanterns on either side of them.

Thalia walked straight to these guards, her uncertainty giving way to her usual confident stride. Her conversation with them was tense, but I couldn't bring myself to focus on it. I was too busy picturing horrible images of the Nerithys Gate crumbling to dust, taking all of our hope with it. Of the realm beyond that gate filling with a cold, bright light that grew farther and farther away until a final death, a final darkness, fell upon Noctaris and its people.

Thalia's sudden reappearance startled me. The guards she'd been arguing with filed past us a moment later, taking up a new position in the distance.

"The keys," she said, offering them to me, along with the lantern she'd been carrying. "And those guards shouldn't bother you. But keep your wits about you—with all the extra guests and turmoil filling this palace over these past days, there's no telling what trouble you might run into."

Phantom fixed his softly glowing eyes in the direction of the whispering guards. (*I'll keep watch,*) he assured me.

"You focus on this," Thalia said, nodding toward the metal doors, "and I'll work on your brother, in the meantime."

I took the keys and lantern from her, gripping them tightly, forcing my hands not to shake. "Thank you."

She studied me for a moment. Slowly, her hand lifted and tapped twice over her heart.

Then she was gone, leaving me to face the darkness of Aleksander's prison alone.

Chapter Forty-Three

Aleksander

THE ABYSS HAD ALWAYS BEEN MY LEAST FAVORITE punishment.

That was what the Light Keepers had called it—that small, circular room deep in the belly of Duskhaven. One we didn't even subject most of our prisoners to, because it was considered far too cruel. We didn't want the outside world thinking we were barbarians, after all. No; the Kingdom of Elarith was a place of light. Of learning. Of perfect order.

They'd thrown me into the Abyss more often than I liked to think about, for the slightest transgressions, and they had always acted as though they were doing me a favor by choosing this particular punishment—giving me another chance to prove my worth, they would usually claim. To see how long I could keep producing Light magic while in such a dismal, dark setting.

It had been…effective. In a sense. Because when my

light went out in that place, the darkness and the cold became absolute, and so the fear of being swallowed up by those things was usually enough to keep me summoning magic far past what I *thought* was my limit.

Far past the point of being safe, or rational.

Sometimes, I managed to stay conscious until they came back to let me out.

Other times, I failed, and the only thing that saved me from madness was giving into unconsciousness, slipping away into a protected corner of my mind where the warmth and the light never faded.

But there was nothing quite like the horror of collapsing to try and escape the dark, only to wake up and find yourself still in it.

This was not the Abyss.

I kept reminding myself of that.

And yet.

And *yet*.

Several times since I'd been thrown into this prison, I had woken up to find myself still in the dark. My powers waned a little more each time I shifted in and out of consciousness, keeping the encroaching void at bay for less and less time. The silence here was stark, but the memory of the Light Keepers' voices rang through my skull, loud and unceasing. Cold, cruel, mocking voices.

The darkness only wins if you fail to conquer it.
Don't fail us, Aleksander.

I'd lost track of the minutes, the hours, the days.

I'd lost track of the number of times I'd failed and slipped out of awareness, only to resurface in an even weaker state than before.

I was getting close to slipping again, now. No more light

came to my hands, no matter how hard I tried to summon it. The room was fading around me, its shadows deepening, consuming everything in their path.

Maybe I can just stay unconscious, this time, I thought—no, I *hoped*.

Then a door opened somewhere in the distance, the groan of metal dragging over stone pulling me back into awareness. I blinked, and I saw a figure approaching me.

Nova.

For a moment, I thought I'd already fainted again; that she had taken up residence in that quiet, safe corner of my mind that I escaped to. It was a comforting thought, being able to meet her there.

Except, I wasn't…*there*.

I was awake. The stone beneath me was solid. Cold. And Nova's face was clear, her features sharp—not like the hazy, drifting details of my unconscious mind.

She carried a small lantern, dispelling the darkness as she came. Without any hesitation, she dropped to my side and started examining me, pushing the hair from my face, cupping my jaw, trying to get my eyes to meet hers. I didn't realize how cold I truly was until I felt her warm hands upon my skin.

Setting the lantern down, she frantically searched the space around us. She seemed to be trying to figure out what to do next. Her lips quivered. Her eyes were bright in the grimness, the anxiety in them clear.

I'm fine, I said—at least in my head. I don't think the words actually made it past my dry, cracked lips.

She fixed her gaze on a metal cup near my boot, grabbing it and bringing it carefully to my mouth.

I managed a single sip before turning my head away. It

was water—some repressed, rational part of me knew that—but it burned like poison as it slid down my throat.

She reached for the plate of bread, next. A stale loaf sliced into rough, but relatively even pieces. I didn't remember breaking it into those pieces, but I suspected I'd been the one to do it. My bleary eyes scanned the plate. My fingers twitched as I fought the compulsion to continue scraping at that crusty bread, to create more even lines. I should have been neater to begin with. More precise. More controlled.

"You haven't been eating, have you?"

I'm fine.

"Here," she said, pushing a piece gently into my hands.

I caught it tightly between my fingers—panicked at the thought of letting it hit the ground, for some reason—but I didn't lift it to my mouth.

"Please," she whispered.

I'm fine.

"I know it probably feels like you need to control this, like you might not have another chance to eat anything else, but they aren't going to starve you like the Keepers did. I won't let them."

She pressed her hand to my jaw once more.

The warmth of her palm was…overwhelming.

I attempted to focus on it. But her face was rapidly becoming a distant, blurred canvas of shadow and light. Her words grew more and more muddled—as if I was underwater, sinking away from her. I tried to swim back. But my body was too tired, too heavy. The water pulled, wrapping me up, dragging me deeper and deeper, down into the depths, where I was met with voices. Familiar voices rebuking me with familiar lines.

You've failed.

Then my own voice joined them, repeating the line, as if it was a lesson I had to recite over and over until I got it right—

I've failed.
I've failed.
I've failed.

Hours passed.

I kept expecting Nova to leave me alone.

They had always left me alone when I failed them.

We'll come back when you've learned to be stronger than the dark.

The light will come back when you find a way to bring it back, and not before. Endure. Outlast. Prove yourself to us...

I still had not summoned even the faintest spark of anything resembling light.

But for some reason, Nova was still there, sitting in the darkness with me.

My head rested in her lap. Her hands combed through my hair, gentle and soothing. Her scent was clean; soft powder and the delicate sweetness of wild rose. A stark contrast to the stench of this damp, dirty prison and my own filthy self.

And I had a thought, like I so often had these past weeks, of a flower blooming in Hell, its roots somehow taking hold in a dead land. Taking hold in *me*.

What a foolish, reckless flower, I thought, *to plant herself here in the dark.*

But another thought struck me almost as quickly—a memory. That fateful night, seven years ago, when I'd found her on the grounds of Rose Point, clutching a glowing flower between her dirt-stained fingers. Her words whispered through my mind, as soft and certain as the scent enveloping me now.

Some things bloom brighter in the dark...

She was shivering. A particularly violent tremble went through her, and I found myself moving automatically, reaching to take her hand in mine. Light flowed from my fingertips, leaving warmth in its wake as it traveled along her arms. The effort left me breathless, even more tired and sick feeling than before, but I didn't care; I would have given my last breath to keep her warm.

Her shaking eased. I started to curl toward her, to drift away again, until I felt a tear drop onto my cheek.

"Chaos," I mumbled. "Why are you crying?"

She took a long time answering. Or maybe it was only seconds. Time had lost all meaning in this place.

Quietly, she said, "Everything is all wrong."

"Everything?"

"Your cousin is gone."

"I heard."

"And he's not who he seemed to be."

"Yes; I gathered as much."

"It's worse than anything you could imagine."

The fear in her voice woke up some primal instinct in me, giving me the strength to drag myself upright. I leaned against the wall beside her. Fighting the urge to close my eyes, I tilted my face toward hers, swallowed away the lump in my throat, and said, "Tell me everything."

Her hands were trembling again, but not from the cold

this time, I suspected. She tried to hide their twitching by keeping them busy, clumsily gathering up the cup of water and the plate of bread in front of us.

"Drink," she insisted, lifting them before me, "and eat. And then I'll talk."

There was no negotiating with that tone. And my need to listen to her fears proved greater than my need to ration and control the meager nourishment I'd been given, so the bargain was struck—I placed the cup aside but lifted a scrap of bread to my mouth. It felt like swallowing glass, forcing it down my throat. But I pushed through it, as she inhaled deeply before launching into a breathless recap of the things that had befallen this palace over the past several days.

So many impossible, dangerous things.

As she spoke, I was overcome by a storm of emotions. Shock. Anger. Doubt. But also a strange sense of relief, as questions that had been gnawing at me finally began to make sense. There was something to be said for having a clearer target to hit, I supposed.

"Five days since he fled," Nova said, bowing her head and covering her face with a hand. "Through the Nerithys Gate, we assume. But we aren't certain."

Five days.

She'd been suffering for five days, while I'd been down here, useless and rotting in this godsforsaken prison.

"I'm sorry," she said. "I should have trusted you. I could have seen the truth about Zayn, long before now, if only I hadn't been afraid of my magic, and I just…I…"

"They made you afraid." The words slipped out in between my attempts to choke down sips of water.

She lifted her head away from her hand, slowly looking back at me.

My gaze fixed on her bracelets. "They put those shackles around your wrists, and they treated you as if you were something to fear. So of course you learned to be afraid."

She didn't argue.

A humorless laugh almost escaped me at this; we were clearly past the point of broken, if she no longer had the fire to disagree with me.

She shifted, leaning more fully into the wall and stretching her feet out before her, bracing her boots into the dust-coated ground. "I wish I could say I wasn't afraid now, but…" Her eyes stared straight ahead at nothing. She started to reach for her face again, but seemed to lose her nerve halfway through, dropping her hand and wrapping her arms around herself instead. "But it would be a lie."

I gathered my strength and summoned a small orb of glowing gold, so that I could better see her, and see for myself what Zayn—no, *Lorien*—had done to her.

Rage burned through me as the first flickers of light landed upon her newly scarred skin. I swallowed it down, forcing myself to keep inspecting the damage. Carefully, I reached toward the branching marks along her jaw.

She flinched.

I drew my hand back into a fist, magic and fury twisting in a violent dance in my gut. So much godsdamned magic and fury that, had I unleashed it in that moment, it likely would have ripped apart the entire palace and everyone in it. And I wouldn't have fucking cared. I would have destroyed it all in my next breath—

If not for her.

Somehow, I found her gaze and I held it.

Somehow, I calmly said, "He did this to you."

She nodded, anxiously tucking a few loose strands of hair behind her ear, only to immediately untuck them, allowing them to fall over her face and partially hide the scars. "I don't really know how much magic he was able to steal, what I gave up, I…"

I caught her unscarred cheek as she tried to turn away. "You *gave up* nothing," I said, firmly. It seemed like the most important thing in the world right then, making certain she heard me clearly. That she was meeting my eyes as I said, "This wasn't your fault."

She stared at me. No—through me. Her eyes were glassy, her thoughts traveling down some path I couldn't follow, no matter how desperately I wanted to. Her lips parted several times before she finally managed to blink, to truly look at me again as she said, "I just want to fix all of this."

"We will," I replied, the words coming so fiercely, so *violently* that they surprised even me.

For so long, I had kept up my role of the stoic, unbreakable ruler. Lesson after lesson, punishment after punishment, mission after mission. Anger served no purpose, I'd been taught. Fury was for fools. Kings endured in silence and did what was expected of them without question.

But now, I'd found something worth being furious for.

And whatever Lorien had taken from her, I was going to take it back—and then some.

Chapter Forty-Four

Nova

"Look at this," said my brother, waving me over to him.

We were pacing along the outermost wall that surrounded the palace—one connected to the main gatehouse. It was late, though I couldn't gauge the exact time of night, as the sky had been the same color all day: Dark, dreary grey. This dreariness had apparently washed over the palace shortly after Lorien disappeared, and it hadn't cleared ever since. Between that and the strangely thick fog rolling across the landscape, I didn't expect to be able to see much.

I braced a hand against the battlement, nonetheless, peering in the direction Bastian was pointing in.

Fear squeezed the breath from my lungs as I caught sight of ghostly white figures in the distance—shades. They had gathered in countless groups along the expansive fields encircling the palace, their ethereal forms twitching with unnatural movements, dancing like pale ribbons caught in a restless wind.

"They're getting closer every hour," Bastian said. "The wards that Calista put into place are beginning to fail, and now they can sense the life we've been protecting within our oasis. They likely sense you and your power, as well. I doubt they understand what's happening here, but it draws them in, all the same."

An unsettling question occurred to me. "How did they end up outside of these walls in the first place? How did Calista—and the leaders who served alongside her—decide who would be protected within this sanctuary, and who would be left out?"

"I'm not sure. I've spent hours scouring all of the literature and notes we could find about the shades, but there's nothing conclusive about her decision-making process."

The question continued to eat away at me, until a horrible sound—a low, unearthly hiss—rose from the crowd of shades, jolting me back into the present.

"There are so many out there," I said, hugging myself against the chill that rippled through me. "Enough to cause problems if they get inside, even if they aren't sentient and organized…"

My brother nodded in solemn, silent agreement.

It explained why both the gatehouse and the rampart we stood upon were more heavily secured and guarded than I'd ever seen them.

Such defenses had been unnecessary ever since Calista's magic had made this refuge impenetrable and impossible to overtake, or even *find*. As a result, the structures themselves were in varying states of disrepair. All day long, there had been a flurry of activity around them—attempts to reinforce crumbled sections, to cover openings, to shore up weak points. Not just against the shades, but against whatever other calamities awaited in the days to come, whether by Lorien's hand or otherwise.

The preparations continued, even now. The thumping and clanging of tools echoed in the eerie, foggy night, along with the sound of footsteps and the shouting of orders and plans.

It made me want to imagine this palace in its prime, back when Rivenholt was a proper kingdom surrounded by other proper kingdoms. It must have been a grand sight, at one point—all these towering walls, majestic arches, and imposing fortifications. I wondered briefly at the history of Noctaris and all its secrets, the untold stories woven into ancient stones like the ones we walked upon. There was still so much to learn about what had been lost, and what we might still be able to salvage in the future.

Yet my gaze never strayed far from the present situation. "Our walls are being reinforced here, but what about Tarnath?" That royal city would be overrun in no time, should the shades manage to flood into its streets.

"The citizens have been warned not to leave their homes. Eamon and a few of the other feyth like him are heading up efforts to reinforce things. There are old, lesser remedies to fend off shades, too—special herbs and salves that can be burned, charms that can be fashioned from blessed obsidian and bone. They don't last indefinitely, but they should buy a little time."

My gaze drifted back to the shades, whose movements seemed increasingly desperate.

"What will become of them, even if we manage some sort of victory?" I wondered. "They're different from the wraiths who are partly sustained by the flames in places like Erebos, or the more protected shades we revived at Graykeep, right? They've been wandering in the Deadlands for so long, bereft of all magic...will they be able to return to human existence, if so much has been lost, even *with* the aid of the Aetherstone's magic?"

Bastian didn't answer right away, but I could tell by the way his jaw tightened and his fingers twitched restlessly against his crossed arms that he was giving the question serious consideration—and the tired lines around his eyes suggested it wasn't the first time he'd wondered about it.

"It's...daunting to think about, isn't it?" I said, my voice hushed.

"It is." His eyes closed for a moment, as if he was searching his mind for some last lingering shred of optimism. "Brynn came back, though," he eventually said.

"Yes, but she didn't wander out in the Deadlands for very long, compared to many who have been out there since the initial fall of Noctaris. And she had Aetherkin parents, besides."

Bastian sighed, but he didn't disagree. He watched me for a moment before giving my shoulder a comforting squeeze. "We'll find a solution for all the fallen beings of our kingdoms, whatever their state, when we reach that point. One step at a time, hm?"

"I suppose."

His troubled gaze swept over our surroundings. "The sky is honestly the more disturbing thing to me at the moment. And also...*that*." He directed my attention to a distant stretch of ground, where I saw a crack starting to form. Still small, barely noticeable, but it seemed to grow even as we watched.

The very world threatening to break apart, right under our feet.

I gripped the stone battlement more tightly. "The darkness, the breaking, the failing wards…is it all simply because Grimnor has been stolen from us? Was so much of Calista's protective spell truly reliant on that blade? Or do you think Lorien has done something else within Nerithys…something to speed up the decay of this realm?"

Bastian shook his head. "I wish I knew. I think both things are likely playing a role, but to what extent…I can't say."

Neither of us could.

We were only guessing at what we truly faced, and it was maddening—like trying to suit up for battle in an armory that was pitch dark.

But I'd told him everything *I* knew, at least. Everything Lorien had tauntingly shared while in the swords' chamber.

And, in exchange, Bastian had released Aleks from the dungeon. Although he'd refused to let the Light King move freely through the palace, as he once had, we'd reached a compromise: Aleks was now considerably more comfortable, tucked away in a small room in a forgotten corner of the palace. That room was still heavily guarded, but at least he was safe. He'd been moved covertly, too, so most of our would-be allies still believed he was in the dungeons.

Of course, I would have preferred him by my side.

And he *would* be back at my side, before long—I wouldn't be marching into any battles without him.

But I could only fight so many things at once, and knowing he wasn't suffering made it easier to focus on the bigger picture alongside my brother, for the time being.

"I don't think we can wait for Equinox," I told Bastian.

"The Aetherstone may be easier to manipulate during that time period, but I think the pressing thing is to get into Nerithys and do what we can, while we can. The longer we wait, the more time Lorien has to lay traps and further destabilize things."

Bastian nodded slowly, the movement heavy and resolute. "Agreed."

The decision hung in the air like a stone.

"We'll only be two days early, if that," I muttered. "Close enough, right?"

"Let's hope so."

I hugged my arms against myself, searching the sky for the moon that had been lost within the foggy darkness. "Will the other Noctarisan leaders follow us into battle?"

"Most will, I think. They have no real choice, after all. This is…" He trailed off, inhaling a sharp breath, as if that stone in the air had landed on his chest.

The end, I finished in my head.

But neither of us said it out loud.

It went without saying, really. What else could we do, now, aside from march to our inevitable ending, whatever it was? Lorien had made his intentions clear. Either we stopped him, somehow, or the world we stood in was finished.

A terrible feeling squeezed my heart as I thought of Tarnath, of all its people smiling and waving at me. Of the army I'd raised, and how hard they'd been training and trying to organize on my behalf. Of the palace and its people—Aveline, Brynn, Eamon…all these things that had started to feel the tiniest bit like my true home. My true life.

All of it in danger of just being…*gone*.

"I'm sorry I led him here," I said, quietly. "I'm sorry I

brought this end upon you all even sooner than you'd feared."

Bastian shook his head. "Thalia led you here—and on my orders. We missed the danger right under our noses, too, and Thalia is the most discerning person I know. No one could have seen the truth about Lorien; there's a reason he has survived for all these centuries. A reason he managed to murder Calista all those generations ago. He's a cunning snake."

I kept my eyes on the distant crack in the ground, unconvinced.

"We knew there was something strange going on with the Light King and his brethren, besides," he insisted. "We should have investigated the whole situation more thoroughly to begin with."

I tilted my face toward him. "I did wonder about that. When I first met Thalia, she seemed surprised that Aleks and the others were awake and with me, but not particularly surprised that they were all in this world."

"We found them all shortly after their fall—well, we found Aleksander and a few of his soldiers, anyway. The one you called Zayn was nowhere to be seen at that point. Aleksander was close to death, as were the others with him; we assumed they all would perish in the decaying air of this world, given a little bit of time. Especially once we took Luminor."

"So, you took the sword and left them for dead?" It seemed a cruel choice, even if Aleks and the others were clearly in league with the Light Keepers—clearly enemies.

Bastian shrugged, though the movement was heavy, making him seem less indifferent than he was trying to appear. "Traveling outside of this palace and its immediate surroundings is dangerous enough on its own; we didn't need to drag the extra weight of them with us."

The back of my neck prickled at him calling Aleks *extra weight*, but I held my tongue.

"Their deaths should have been quick. They shouldn't have been able to survive for years like they did...and when some of them *did* survive, we opted to secure the area and occasionally send people to study the magic at work, instead. Our curiosity got the better of us, I guess."

"How different things might have turned out, if you'd killed them," I mused.

"Yes; I think about that often."

I leaned over the wall, staring again at the fissure in the distance. Imagining all the different paths this world could have followed, as if they were branching cracks in the ground—some far more destabilizing than others.

"I still have a lot of questions about what Lorien was doing over the past seven years," my brother said. "How he came and went, how much of his power is tied into Luminor and Aleksander. But, in hindsight, the fact that you ended up being drawn into the grove where they all were should have made us all wary."

"...Because the Vaeloran are always connected and drawn to one another." Recalling Lorien's words—how he had felt me the moment I was born, I shivered.

I didn't *want* to be connected to him.

And now that he'd drained my magic and left these scars on my body...just how deep did our bond go?

Could he feel me at this very moment?

Could I have felt *him*, if I'd tried to?

As if he could sense my distress, Bastian added, "I suppose it gives us some hope, that your connection to

Aleks seems at least as strong as any connection you share with Lorien. Maybe the amount of magic he retained from Lorien's attempt to overtake his body will give us the edge we need to tip things in our favor."

"Hopefully." I tried to sound optimistic, even as a voice in the back of my mind whispered—*but at what cost?*

I couldn't imagine any scenario where Aleks and me being so connected to Lorien didn't end poorly.

Tragically.

My brother's voice remained solemn, his eyes troubled, as he said, "Anyway, my point is the end was coming soon, either way. So there's no sense in wasting your time apologizing about it."

I forced myself to talk a step back from the wall, to stop obsessing over the breaking ground. We were quiet for a few moments before Bastian spoke again.

"Although, as long as we're apologizing…"

I glanced over and saw him studying the scars along my face and neck.

"That wasn't supposed to happen," he said. "I should have stayed closer to you the other night. I should have kept you safe."

I waved the apology away, same as he'd done with mine. "You've kept this palace and everything around it safe for nearly twenty-five years," I pointed out. "For what it's worth, I think it's time you gave yourself a break."

He chuckled softly. "You think we have time for breaks?"

I grimaced. "No, I guess not." I tilted my face toward his. In a quieter, more serious tone, I added, "But I'm here, now, at least—so it isn't all on you anymore. You don't have to do things alone."

He exhaled a long, slow breath, his gaze fixed on the cloudy sky, before acquiescing with a slight nod.

I elbowed him in the side and added, "But you *do* have to stop bossing me around—and stop trying to protect me so damn much."

He rubbed at the spot where my elbow had jabbed him, his mouth curving in one corner. "I'll try."

"Promise?"

"Promise."

We stood for a while longer, watching the lighting shift under the strange sky, discussing potential plans and battle strategies. It was growing darker. Quieter. The air itself seemed to be pulling in around us, like the world was inhaling one last time before a deep, dark plunge.

I yawned, and—just like that—the concerned demeanor overtook my brother once more as he nodded me toward the palace. "Go get some rest."

I arched a brow.

"Or don't," he amended, grinning as he held up his hands in surrender. "Sorry. Old habits."

I laughed, declaring him a hopeless cause before bidding him goodnight and making my way down through the gatehouse and heading into the palace.

THERE WAS ONLY one place I would be able to rest, I knew—and it wasn't my own room. I risked drawing attention to Aleks if I went to his makeshift prison, but I didn't care; I needed to be near him.

The guards outside that prison tensed as I approached, their breathing quickening, their eyes narrowing.

I drew my shoulders back and fixed them with the most queenly stare I could manage. "I'll be staying in here tonight. You won't disturb us unless I summon you."

They exchanged a quick look. The tension in their limbs held for only an instant longer before they bowed and stepped aside.

My heart pounded. A simple command...but it had worked. They kept their gazes lowered respectfully as I passed, silently and obediently falling back to their posts as I closed and locked the door behind me.

I'd never been one for commanding people, even when I'd reigned as the Princess of Eldris. It would take some getting used to, this role I was expected to step into—assuming both this world and I survived the next few days.

My mind had started to spiral, thinking of all the reasons we might *not* survive, when I caught sight of Aleks emerging from the attached washroom. A soft, relieved sigh escaped me. My racing thoughts slowed, all my questions about the future fading into the background, leaving me to focus on just...*him*.

He looked as if he'd just finished bathing; his hair hung around his face, water droplets shining on the ends; his shirt was unbuttoned and hanging open, parts of it clinging to his still-damp chest. It was amazing how different he already looked, after just half a day removed from the dungeons. But then, I supposed he was used to bouncing back quickly from hellish situations, given the world he'd grown up in.

His eyes immediately brightened at the sight of me. We didn't speak at first—we had no shortage of things to talk about, yet words didn't seem important as he stepped to meet me, taking my hand and drawing me closer. His other hand cupped my cheek and guided my mouth to his, and for a few, blissful moments I was aware of nothing beyond his scent; his taste; the warm, buzzing thrill of his tongue dancing with mine.

Then he pulled away and asked, "You spoke with your brother?"

I nodded, quickly filling him in on the things Bastian and I had discussed outside.

As I finished speaking, Aleks went to the window, studying what he could see of the disturbing gloom I'd mentioned—though it wasn't much, as this room opened only to an interior courtyard, which was shaded from the sky by a ceiling of tinted glass. He stared at it all for several minutes, lost in thought, while I moved restlessly over the scantly-furnished space, picking up a few books from otherwise bare shelves, flipping through them only to set them back down without reading anything.

"There's something Lorien said that I can't stop thinking about," I said.

Aleks glanced over his shoulder at me, listening.

"You are the only one who has ever managed to force him out of your body. And your magic is still deeply connected with his, somehow. So I wonder…"

I let the thought hang in the air.

"If we can use these things to our advantage?" he guessed.

"…What if you could force him out of Zayn, too? Maybe seal him back into Luminor, where he ended up after you ousted him from your own body."

He turned away from the window, making his way to

the chair by the unlit fireplace and slowly lowering himself into it, his expression troubled.

"And perhaps I could help, too," I pressed. "I can use my abilities to possess objects, so if I could gain control of his energy, his life-force, and make it an easier target somehow…"

"He's not an object," Aleks pointed out, frowning. "And his energy is far more powerful than anything you've ever tried to control. It's also…*messier*. We don't know what his actual powers are at this point. The Light Vaeloran have always had somewhat predictable abilities, as I understand it, but what abilities has he stolen from you and Calista? And if he's in Nerithys, like we believe, and he's been in contact with the Aetherstone…"

Every point he made was like another stone piled onto my shoulders, until the weight became painful. Frustrating. But I knew he was right. I was just grasping at threads—at something, *anything* resembling a plan.

"It's not a bad idea. It's just…" He raked a hand through his hair, sinking farther down into the chair cushions.

"A dangerous one."

"Yes." He tilted his head back and closed his eyes, his brow scrunched in thought.

I went back to my restless wandering. But my gaze kept finding its way back to him. Kept getting caught on the thoughtful part of his lips. The rise and fall of his chest as he took deep, calming breaths. The way his body folded over the chair, his form a beautiful study in contradictions —relaxed yet poised, graceful yet powerful.

He must have felt me staring, because he eventually

cracked one eye open, a ghost of a smile appearing on his lips.

He beckoned me toward him.

I moved as if connected to his hand by an invisible chain, crossing the room and settling into his lap. I curled into all the arcs and edges I'd just been admiring, exhaling a soft, contented breath at the way my body molded so perfectly to his.

His arms slipped around my waist, drawing me more fully into his embrace.

For a few minutes, I merely relaxed there, letting his strength envelop me. But soon I found myself intimately aware of every breath he took. Every heartbeat. Every move of his fingers as they grew bolder, more deliberate in the way they touched me.

"I thought of this while I was in the dark," he mumbled against my shoulder. "Of your body, pressed against mine. My hands on your skin." He slipped one of those hands beneath my shirt, the cool, rough pads of his fingers making me sigh as they caressed my stomach. "It helped keep me sane in that prison, thinking I had to hold on if I wanted to have you in my arms like this again."

My heart clenched at the thought of him locked away in the darkness.

But he seemed to have escaped that hopeless place—at least for the moment; all of his focus was on me. The intensity of his gaze was nearly overwhelming, stealing my breath, bringing every nerve in my body to life.

"What a tragedy it would have been," he said, fisting the fabric of my shirt and gently pulling it downward, partially exposing my chest, "to never witness this perfection again." He pressed his face into the valley between my breasts, dragging a trail of kisses through it, then upward over my throat. My head tipped back, granting him better access, my elbows balancing on the wide arm of the chair.

"And we are not a tragedy," I whispered, recalling his words from the balcony a few nights ago.

"Exactly," he replied, shifting a hand under my back, holding me steady so he could kiss me more passionately, more fully.

His mouth eventually settled against the hollow of my throat, tongue flicking against that sensitive spot. I moaned softly, and a shiver went through his entire body in response.

"*Gods*, that sound," he breathed, the words hot against my skin.

"Something else you thought of to save you from the dark?"

"Yes," he said, with a rough little laugh. "Though, it's dragging me back toward madness at the moment."

I lifted my head, fluttering my lashes at him. "Both your salvation and damnation, rolled into one?"

He smiled, trailing his fingers over the warm spot his mouth had left on my throat. "We've been a contradiction from the start, haven't we?"

Light followed his touch, coaxing my own magic to the surface. I didn't resist its rise, relaxing against him and letting my shadows out to play, watching as the light and dark wove around one another.

Slowly, we began to mirror their intimate waltz: bodies pressing closer; limbs tangling tighter; hands clasping together and fingers intertwining until there was no beginning or end—only the single, magical force of *us*.

He brushed the back of his hand across my cheek, then

into my hair, gently weaving his fingers in among the waves. As they tangled deeper, he tilted his face closer, letting his lips hover just above mine. The brush of them brought a shock of warm power with it, as if he were somehow directing all of his magic to this single point where we collided.

Again and again, we collided, each kiss growing firmer, hungrier. His teeth nipped at my bottom lip, adding to the bite of electricity already tingling through me. Another soft moan escaped me, a breathless whisper of need spilling directly into his mouth. His fist tightened in my hair, and his entire being coiled with the same motion—an attempt at restraint. At focus.

"Tell me to stop if you want me to stop," he said, drawing back far enough to meet my gaze. "We can keep discussing our battle plans, if you'd rather."

It did seem foolish, with the world falling down around us, to be thinking of anything other than those plans.

Or, maybe it wasn't.

Maybe it was *exactly* what we needed to do. To rebel. To refuse to let Lorien dominate our every thought and feeling. He had taken so much from me already. He was threatening to take so much more.

But he wouldn't take this.

He wouldn't take *us*.

"Don't stop," I said. "I don't want to think about all the possible ruin awaiting us. I don't want to think about anything else at all."

Aleks shifted me from his lap to the chair and stood, watching me for a moment with a mischievous little smile on his lips. In the glow of our still drifting, dancing magic, he looked...otherworldly. Like something from a dream I never wanted to wake up from.

He shrugged out of his shirt and tossed it aside. Then he reached for my hand, pulling me to my feet as well, drawing me in so close our noses touched. His fingers traced my mouth, parting it. His tongue swept over his lips, and I trembled, desperate for it to caress my lips next.

"Please..." I whispered. "*Please* don't stop."

"Oh, Chaos." He spun me around, pulling me flush against his bare chest. His fingers snaked along my throat and then higher, gripping my jaw, tilting my face so his mouth brushed my ear as he said, "The pleading is unnecessary. Because it will be a privilege to fuck you into a state of oblivion."

Chapter Forty-Five

Nova

MY ENTIRE BODY CAUGHT FIRE AT HIS WORDS.

I was burning and breathless beneath his touch as he lifted my shirt over my head and threw it to the floor, as he undid the supportive bindings underneath and his lips moved across my shoulders, along the back of my neck, across the shell of my ear.

Once my breasts were bared, he cupped them, his possessive grip drawing me even more tightly against his chest. I felt his arousal, hard and throbbing, against my lower back. Without thinking, I lifted up and down on my toes, shamelessly trying to ride his length.

His hands roamed over my naked stomach, eventually settling on my hips, helping me rise and fall against him. It felt sinfully good, even with too many clothes still separating us.

Far too many damn clothes.

My hand fumbled for the corner of the chair we'd been

sitting in. I clutched it, desperately holding on, barely resisting the urge to beg him to take me completely right then and there.

As if my desires were written across my flushed skin, he clenched a hand into my hair again, drawing my face back toward his with a grip just shy of painful, and said, "You want me to bend you over this chair, don't you?"

My knees buckled at the low, hungry growl in his voice.

I didn't manage a coherent response.

"Soon enough," he promised, sweeping me into his arms, carrying me to the nearby bed and tossing me onto it. His hands fell again to my hips, peeling off the rest of my clothing and jerking me toward the edge of the mattress in the same motion.

His mouth crashed to mine, the force of him making the bed and the floor underneath creak and groan. I hooked my arms around his neck, pulling myself upright and more fully into the kiss. As his tongue went deeper, my hands strayed lower, fumbling with the drawstring of his pants.

He laughed with his mouth still against mine, the sound vibrating down my throat. "So eager," he murmured. "I appreciate the enthusiasm—but you aren't supposed to be *thinking* of anything at all." He caught me by my arms, his strength overtaking mine easily and pressing me back down toward the bed. "Isn't that what you said you wanted?"

My words caught in my throat as his golden gaze burned into mine, but I managed a nod.

"So that means I'm in charge." His fingers raked along my arms, caressing and guiding them up above my head, pinning my wrists against the mattress with one hand. The other hand smoothed its way down the length of my body, settling with a light, teasing amount of pressure between my thighs. "And you don't move without my command."

I was too transfixed by the feel of his fingers moving, playing at my entrance, to reply.

"Agreed?"

The thought of *agreeing* was both thrilling and maddening. His touch was growing more precise, deliberate taps and circles and pinches against that most sensitive bundle of nerves I possessed, and I would have done *anything* in that moment if it ended with him inside of me—yet I wasn't sure I could manage what he asked. To not think, to relax as if the world outside didn't exist, to trust him to carry me completely away from it...

Aleks let out a quiet, dark laugh, clearly sensing my questions, my building vexation. "Why doesn't the challenge burning in your beautiful eyes surprise me?"

"I'll never be done challenging you," I informed him, breathlessly.

"Gods, I hope not." His smile turned wicked. Any answer I might have uttered was cut short by that expression, and by the realization that he was dropping to his knees, aligning his mouth so it could follow the pleasurable paths his fingers had been mapping out. "But maybe, just this once...trust me, and I'll make it worth your while."

Trust me.

I couldn't remember the last time I'd trusted anyone this way—if I ever had. When you spent most of your life feared and hated, you became wary by default. For so long, there hadn't been anyone *worth* trusting with such conviction, with such potentially devastating certainty.

Not until him.

I exhaled a shaky breath. "You make a convincing argument with your head between my thighs like that."

His smirk somehow turned even more devious. He dipped his head lower, pressing a kiss to my center—a slow, lingering kiss, the tip of his tongue dipping inside of me and drawing a faint, needy sound from my mouth. His gaze stayed on my face the entire time. "I could stay here all night, trying to convince you," he said, planting a far more innocent—but no less searing—kiss on the inside of my thigh.

I studied his face a moment more. The familiar strong lines juxtaposed against the faint dimples. The particular softness that came over his eyes when he looked at me, and *only* when he looked at me. Every little thing I'd fallen in love with. Every unspoken promise I'd somehow started to trust.

Slowly, I let my head sink into the mattress. My eyes closed. My arms relaxed at my sides, and he immediately claimed them, pressing them against the bed, holding me down as his mouth came back for more. His tongue worked tirelessly between my thighs, darting and licking until I was soaked and squirming beneath him.

He pinned my hands more firmly into the bed. My legs moved where my arms couldn't, spreading further and encouraging him to taste me more fully, more deeply.

"There it is," he mumbled, approvingly. "Open wider for me."

My hips lifted as I obeyed, pressing myself harder against his mouth. He seemed to lose control for a moment, his hands moving away from my arms and digging into the fleshy backs of my thighs instead, lifting me even more completely to him. The savageness of it brought a cry of near-release to my lips.

He jerked away, his composure quickly returning.

I let out a protesting whimper, but he merely leaned up, kissed my pouting lips and said, "It's much too soon for that."

He rose to his feet, pulling me with him. The room spun slightly around me, making me feel like I was floating.

"The chair," he reminded me, his harsh, lustful tone causing chills to erupt across my body.

I should have been self-conscious, maybe, crossing the room wearing nothing except the bracelets that jangled at my wrists. But I had never felt more confident than I did in that moment, striding to that chair while Aleksander's eyes drank me in. I felt his gaze like a caress. Sensed every slow, deliberate step he took after me. The air between us literally shimmered and sparked as he closed in—our magic still reacting to one another's, despite all the work we'd done over these past weeks to better control it.

"Put your hands on the armrests," he ordered.

I did, shivering with anticipation as he circled closer and admired me from every angle, occasionally brushing a hand over my displayed body; slipping it between my legs; tracing my curves; fondling my breasts and pinching their hardened tips.

He paused as he came close to my face, fisting a handful of my hair and using it to lift my lips to meet his.

"You are so godsdamn beautiful," he rasped, in between kisses. "Just in case you weren't aware."

I regarded him from underneath my lashes, breathing hard, as he pulled away only to immediately bring his lips back to my skin, dragging them along my neck and up to my ear before growling out another command: "Now bend lower."

I did, and I was rewarded with another touch—a slow, confident trailing along my spine, over the curves of my backside, into the dampness waiting between my legs. His fingers circled and teased through that dampness until my knees were in danger of giving out, my arms shaking despite the support of the chair.

Then he stepped away.

I felt his searing gaze still watching me. I heard the sound of him continuing to undress, of the rest of his clothes hitting the floor beside his discarded shirt. Then he was back to me, his hand trailing one last featherlight touch between my thighs before coming to rest on my right hip—steadying me for what came next.

I inhaled sharply as he guided his cock between my legs. Like his touch, the movement was smooth, just barely a brush of velvet and heat and hardness. He slid it back and forth, adding the slick of his own arousal to mine, while his hands guided my legs farther apart.

His touch skated down my body, shifting the hair from my back over my shoulder, leaving a bare expanse of skin for his fingertips to slowly stroke as he asked, "Are you relaxing for me?"

My pulse was pounding, but I managed a breathy *yes*.

He let his length rest between my legs, pressing just close enough that I could feel every throb and twitch, every tiny movement that sent more coils of needy heat twisting through me. "Still mine to do whatever I wish with?"

"*Yes.*"

"Good." He drew a few more mesmerizing patterns along my back and shoulders. Gentle. Smooth. Precise. As if painting his name, his vows onto my skin, before finally letting his touch slide lower, grabbing my sides, digging his fingers in.

With a powerful thrust, he drove himself into me, jerking me back against him in the same moment. I cried out at the sudden, almost unbearable fullness of him. His hand was over my mouth an instant later. He kept it there as he continued to thrust into me, muffling my cries of pleasure and occasional gasps of pain.

I moaned against his palm when his pace slowed. He bent me back over while he leaned forward, drawing close enough that his lips brushed the curve of my shoulder as he teasingly whispered, "Quiet. We don't want the guards outside thinking you need any help in here."

The guards.

I'd forgotten they even existed.

And I didn't give them another thought as Aleks twisted my arms behind me, pulling my body more upright before pushing into me once more.

He fell into a powerful, easy rhythm as he moved inside of me, each push and pull of his hips more devastatingly good than the last. I started off trying to match his movements, but the waves of euphoria rippling through me made it difficult to keep up. My knees still felt weak. My raspy attempts at breathing were leaving me lightheaded. I started to sink against him, and he hooked an arm around my throat, further arching my back and better supporting my body with his strength.

His free hand snaked around my waist, dipping between my legs, his fingers finding their way to the swollen bud that was desperate for his touch. He stroked until I was rocking against him, chasing the continued rise and fall of his hips with whatever desperate, chaotic efforts I could manage, all my inhibitions lost as I felt my release building.

I pushed against him with particular force, and a feral sound ripped from his throat—something caught between a growl and a groan. He jerked me tighter to him, nuzzling his face into the waves of my hair, his mouth moving over my neck with slow, slightly dazed kisses.

His strong hold merely supported me for a few minutes, letting me ride him however I wished—a breach in our agreement that didn't last long before he was back in control, flipping me around, pinning me underneath him in the chair.

One of my legs draped over the armrest. He took hold of the other, moving it aside as he guided himself back into me. My eyes closed and my head tipped back as he sank in, and I grabbed for the armrests, clenching tightly as he found his rhythm inside of me once more.

"Open your eyes."

They fluttered open.

He braced one hand against the chair, then caught my chin with the other, forcing my gaze up to his. "I'm the only thing you're looking at right now. The only thing you're thinking about."

It wasn't a question, but I found myself nodding anyways, completely mesmerized by the sight of him on top of me. By the way he moved with increasing fervor but never looked away. By the soft part of his lips; the breaths rumbling through his broad, sweat-slicked chest; the way his eyes seemed to shift through every shade of gold imaginable as they watched mine, studied them, memorized them.

"Keep them open," he said, his hand moving from my chin to the small of my back, lifting it as he pushed even more deeply inside. "I want you to meet my eyes when you come for me."

His lips found mine—and this was what tipped me over the edge. Not the frantic, powerful pounding of his hips. Not the feel of his hands moving over me, finding every sensitive spot that made me gasp and convulse a little more wildly. Not the rasp of his breaths or the pure desire dripping from his words.

It was the soft and certain way he kissed me and then pulled slowly back to watch what came next—as if there had never been a doubt between us and there never would be. I was his, he was mine, and there was no questioning it.

Mine.

As that thought crashed over me, so did the waves of my release. Those waves caught him, too, drawing him alongside me, deep into a pool of final, untethered bliss.

He came with a roar that vibrated deep in my bones, sending a second surge of my own release spiraling through me.

I floated in that blissful space with him, toes curled and muscles pleasantly taut, for several long moments before the room came back into focus around me. Even then it seemed brighter, more vibrant than before.

Aleks gathered me in his arms, and for a few minutes, we returned to the quiet repose of earlier—curled in the chair together, heartbeats racing, skin sensitive and shivering at every point where we touched.

Eventually, we unfolded from one another and stumbled into the tiny washroom to clean up. He brought me one of his shirts to use as a nightgown, and then he crawled into the bed while I lingered by the sink.

My gaze had gotten caught on my reflection in the

mirror above it—on both the scars on my face and neck, and on the shadows Aleks had drawn out, the latter of which were still lazily drifting around my skin.

I watched as one of those shadows caressed the widest scar on my throat and then swept toward my arm, circling it and eventually winding around the turquoise bracelet at my wrist. The movement felt deliberate. Sentient.

I realized I was holding my breath, and I forced myself to exhale slowly.

"What's wrong?" Aleks asked, his voice slightly slurred, heavy with sleep.

Nothing, I started to say.

"…Were you telling the truth earlier," I asked, instead, "when you said you thought of me while you were imprisoned?"

He took a moment to answer, clearly losing his battle against sleep. His eyes were closed, his face halfway buried in the pillows, but his eventual reply was quiet yet certain: "I thought of you and your shadows," he said, "and somehow the darkness around me didn't seem so terrible."

My response caught in my throat. I wasn't even sure what I'd been planning to say; I couldn't name the emotion choking me, much less put into words all that I felt in that moment.

By the time I found my voice again, his breathing had slowed and his muscles had relaxed more completely. His eyelids occasionally fluttered, but he was obviously fully lost to whatever dreams had been waiting for him.

I moved quietly into the room, settling onto the very edge of the bed, not wanting to wake him. I didn't mean to stare, either.

But I couldn't help myself.

Out of everything we'd done and said and survived together, something about those words he'd just spoken shattered me—and then reformed me—more than anything else.

He didn't simply accept my shadows.

He found...*comfort* in them.

One of those shadows was still tightly woven around my turquoise bracelet. I stared at it, thinking of the moment that bracelet had slipped from my wrist in the swords' chamber. Of the things such a small act had unleashed, and of the power bound within me—power I was going to need for the battle that lay just ahead.

Taking a deep breath, I pulled the bracelet from my wrist and placed it on the bedside table. The urge to put it back on struck immediately, but I resisted, turning away and huddling closer to Aleks instead.

His arms wrapped tightly around me, pulling me against his warm chest. Despite his heat, I shivered. My magic was shifting wildly inside of me, a storm of frigid wind and overwhelming energy.

But Aleksander's hold stayed secure, drawing me away from the cold and the dark, just as he had that night at Lake Nyras, and countless times since. Every time I thought I might give in to the desire to reach for the binding on the bedside table, he would pull me in again and kiss my forehead. Still asleep, I thought, and yet, more than once, I would have sworn I heard him say the same words he'd said to me that night in the water—

I've got you.

I finally let myself believe it.

And I finally slept.

Chapter Forty-Six

Nova

A FAMILIAR VOICE WAS WHISPERING IN MY EAR.

Are you coming or not?

The room was dark. It smelled of ashes, though I didn't remember lighting a fire. I felt pressure against my side—a hand. Its grip was strong, almost crushing.

Come along, Nova. Wake up. It's time to go.

Lorien's voice, I realized. The words settled over me like cold stones, trying to weigh me down. Trying to drag me to him.

"I'm not going anywhere with you," I heard myself mumble.

The hand against my side gripped even more tightly, fingers digging in, each added ounce of pressure making the panic in my chest coil a little tighter, until I could barely breathe because of the pressure on my lungs.

Are you afraid to face me?

I rolled from his grip and stumbled to the nearby chair, snatching up the knife that was piled with the rest of my clothing.

I wasn't afraid.

I *wouldn't* be afraid.

"...Nova?"

I spun to face the dark figure rising from the bed, my knife raised.

You should be afraid, said the voice.

"I'm not afraid," I hissed back.

With a furious cry, I swung.

The dark figure ducked my attack, darting from the bed and sliding gracefully behind me. I spun after him, swinging even harder this time—but he caught my wrist, halting the blade inches from his neck.

"Nova, what the hell are you doing?"

I set my stance and kept shoving, my stare locked on the life-giving veins of his neck.

"It's me! Aleks!"

My hand shook violently as I tried to push the knife forward.

His fingers tightened around my wrist, nails pinching in. The bite of pain caught my attention. I blinked, and the fog of confusion and panic began to lift—just enough for the face before me to take on its true shape, transforming from the shadowy visage of a nightmare figure into something clearer. Something safer.

"*Your* Aleks," he whispered. His eyes were wide, pleading, and...golden. A pure, warm gold. Like a sun-drenched wheat field. Not like the reddish-brown blood of Lorien's eyes.

"...Mine," I breathed, slowly lowering my arm.

"Yours," he repeated, leaning his forehead against mine and gripping the sides of my face. "If there was any doubt left in your mind about that...banish it."

A tremor overcame me as I realized what I'd almost done. I dropped the knife and buried my face in Aleksander's chest, my stomach churning with a sickness that made my mouth water and my body break out in a cold sweat.

It felt like a long time passed before I managed to calm my racing heart enough to say, "I heard his voice. He was... talking to me."

Aleks drew back, looking confused for an instant before understanding dawned in his eyes, followed by fury. "What did he say?"

I shook my head; I barely remembered the actual words. Only the feel of them creeping over my skin, trying to burrow themselves into my mind. My heart. "I thought he was here. I thought he was you. Or me. Or..."

I pushed away from him, stumbled to the washroom and immediately vomited into the sink.

Again and again I went back to that sink, until there was nothing left in me to throw up. Even then, I wanted to keep going, until I somehow managed to expel whatever bond I shared with Lorien.

Aleksander followed me after a moment. He didn't speak. He merely held my hair back, and then helped me into the shower after I collapsed into a sweaty, panicked heap on the cold tile floor. Once I was clean, he dried my scarred skin and squeezed the water from my hair, wrapped me in a blanket, picked me up, and carried me back to the bed.

I was exhausted, but I couldn't even think of going back to sleep.

The sun was rising. Still barely penetrating the gloom that had overtaken the sky, but enough cool light filtered in to highlight the beads of the bracelet I'd placed on the nightstand.

Aleksander's gaze shifted between it and me, questioning.

"I took it off last night," I explained. "Which is probably why Lorien's voice was able to reach me. Our connection is part of my magic. Not shackling myself with that bracelet makes my power stronger, but it leaves me vulnerable to things like this, I guess."

He picked the bracelet up, turning it around in his hands, tracing the markings on the beads with a thoughtful touch. I shivered as if he were touching *me*—which brought to mind a slew of daunting questions. Was there no undoing my connection to it or my other bracelets? Had I worn them too long? Was I really so inseparable from them?

"I'm sorry I attacked you."

Aleks glanced up at me, giving me that slight, sly smile of his—the one that accented his dimples. "It wouldn't have been the first time you'd stabbed me."

I exhaled a deep breath. "Yes, but I thought we were past that stage in our relationship."

"Me too." He shrugged. "I *do* love that you're full of surprises, though."

I huffed out a quiet laugh. His face brightened briefly at the sound, but his smile faded as his attention shifted back to the bracelet. "Nova, if wearing this keeps you safe from him..."

"I think we're well past the point of *safe*, regardless," I said, quietly.

He looked ready to disagree, but I took the bracelet and slipped it back on, causing him to fall silent—at least for the time being.

And, at least for the time being, I would pretend this piece of jewelry could actually shield me from everything I faced. I needed to be able to think clearly, anyway; to not risk Lorien invading my mind as I worked out the final details of our battle plans.

But the time was fast approaching when I would no longer be able to shy away from him, or from any of the other horrors looming on the horizon. When I would have to face it all—and wield whatever power I could, whatever the risks.

Aleks and I both knew that moment was coming, even if we didn't speak of it.

And if it came down to keeping this world or myself safe, we both knew which one I would have to choose.

A SHORT TIME LATER, Aleks and I strode confidently into the palace training grounds, side-by-side, escorted by several guards.

My brother waited at the entrance of these grounds, surrounded by our various allies and fellow leaders. He regarded us calmly as we approached—ignoring the immediate confusion and commotion that rippled through the rest of his company as they caught sight of Aleks.

Bastian was expecting us, because he and I had made a decision last night: We were going to attempt to pass through the Nerithys Gate this evening. We would enter that in-between realm and make our way to the Aetherstone, controlling whatever we could to hopefully salvage and restore what was left of our world. And whatever danger awaited, whatever traps Lorien had set, we would face it all head on.

All that was left to do was convince the others of our plan—a plan that would require them to trust both me *and* Aleksander, whether they liked it or not.

I squared my shoulders, bidding my brother and the others hello with a curt nod. Aleks did the same, and then we both proceeded to ignore them, instead turning our attention to the small army of soldiers running drills across the sweeping training grounds.

They looked more and more alive every time I saw them, the light in their eyes returning; their movements becoming more fluid; their voices less like whispers of wind and more like the confident chatter of seasoned warriors.

But their numbers seemed lower than they should have been.

"Are we missing some?" Aleks wondered quietly.

My brows pinched together in concern as I tried to do a quick headcount. Some were clearly not here; were they simply resting, or was something more sinister to blame?

Was this another symptom of Grimnor disappearing—of the protections over this palace failing?

My power, along with Aleksander's, had initially brought these soldiers back, but it was the steady magic flowing through the halls here that had allowed them to continue awakening and regaining their humanity. Perhaps some of the weaker beings were already losing their grip on that humanity again.

I hadn't checked the fissures around the palace walls this morning, but something told me they were likely getting larger, too.

"More evidence that we're running out of time..." I muttered.

Aleks frowned, but kept his voice light. "Let's focus on what we have left, then."

I nodded in agreement, forcing myself to take deep breaths.

Overseeing the drills was Captain Darien Voss, who was also one of the shades we'd brought back at Graykeep. A man who towered well over six feet tall, with white-streaked, dark auburn hair and a permanent gaze of ice, he spoke little but commanded respect merely with his intimidating demeanor. It was all the more intimidating to think of how he'd existed in this world for so much longer than me—hundreds of years longer—even if he *had* spent most of that time as a shade.

I must have seemed like an outsider to him—to *all* of the soldiers and leaders I needed to somehow convince to follow me into battle.

Despite my doubts, I lifted my chin and cleared my throat. "Captain Voss."

He gave me a slight bow. "Lady Nova."

I was hyper-aware of all the heads turning toward us—my brother and all the ones with him, along with dozens of soldiers who slowly ceased their activities to watch and listen. But I kept my gaze level with Voss's green eyes, trying not to let it wander along the scars that slashed paths across both his cheekbones.

"You remember who brought you back to life," I stated —not a question; I was leaving nothing up for debate, and I spoke loudly enough for all of our onlookers to hear me.

Voss glanced between Aleks and me, then gave another slight bow of his head.

"And now we require your service. Your sworn oath. I need the best of your regiment ready to go at a moment's notice."

His expression hardened even more than usual—but then he glanced over his shoulder and called out a simple command: "Form rank!"

I held my breath as the soldiers moved with precise, practiced discipline, the sound of their boots against the ground a symphony of controlled clicks and stomps. Captain Voss watched them with cold, calculating intensity. Once they had formed a long, unbroken line, he faced me once more.

A sense of authority tingled through me as our eyes met —the same feeling that had overtaken me last night, when the guards outside Aleksander's room had moved aside at my command.

"By life or by death," Voss said, crossing an arm over his chest, "by light or by dark, our swords and services are at your command."

He kept his arm crossed over his heart, speaking to Aleks and me as though we were one entity—a united king and queen hailed in this realm and every other—and I decided right then and there that he was one I could trust.

Maybe it truly *was* the magic that tied those of Graykeep to Calista—a power still flowing, still tying his loyalty to the Shadow Vaelora all these centuries later. I couldn't explain it, but I was grateful for it among the sea of uncertainty I was swimming in.

I did my best to keep my expression stern as I gave him an approving nod.

"Our young queen seems to have a plan," came Lord Marek's cynical voice, shattering the solemn silence. "I wonder if she cares to enlighten the rest of us?"

I turned to glare at him. And with my soldiers still standing at attention behind me, I wasted no time launching into a fiery declaration of what I intended to do.

"The Nerithys Gate awaits us," I said. "I am leaving for it this evening, with my army in tow. If you wish to prove yourself as a leader of this realm, then you'll join us as well."

He didn't reply.

Silence swept over the other gathered leaders, as well, and the soldiers behind me seemed to be holding their breath, making the moment feel tense and tightly wound—like it might snap at the first wrong word or movement.

"…The gate requires a great deal of magic to open," said a woman with intelligent eyes and a steady, calm voice—Lady Zara, sovereign of the sanctuary city known as Durnhelm, if I recalled correctly. "A great deal of *balanced* magic."

"We're aware," said Aleks.

"You truly think you can open it?" Zara asked me.

"Your future queen is more than capable of the required magic," Bastian said, his tone a quiet warning.

"But we're not worried about *her*, are we?" asked Lord Marek, his gaze shifting to Aleks.

Aleks cut his eyes toward him. His smile was confident

—that familiar smirk bordering on arrogant. Magic simmered just beneath his skin, little cracks of it burning bright in the dreary daylight, and the combination of those things made my heart stutter. He looked undeniably powerful, even after all he'd endured in this realm that he didn't truly belong to, and a spark of hope flared through me as I stared at him.

We might have both been outsiders in our own way, but in that moment, at least, I felt invincible at his side.

"I stand a better chance of opening it than any of *you*, don't I?" he asked Marek.

Lord Marek scowled, but he couldn't seem to think of a retort to this.

"And if the gate fails to yield to us?" asked Lady Zara. "What then?"

"Then it fails to yield," I replied, tersely. "And we sit and wait for our demise."

"As opposed to doing *nothing* and sitting and waiting for our demise," Thalia added, pointedly. "Even if all of these plans fail, are you *really* content with the alternative of doing nothing? Of continuing to live as you are now, with your cities full of wraiths just barely clinging on to what makes them human? The end approaches either way. We have a chance to shift that ending in our favor, and we must take it, whatever the odds."

A solemn hush fell over the crowd, until my brother said, "The time has come for action, clearly. No one can argue that."

There was a general murmur of agreement, however reluctant it might have been.

"The gate doesn't open without these two working

together," he continued, nodding toward Aleks and me. "It requires a delicate balance of magic, as Lady Zara pointed out. As for the Light King? He has sworn his allegiance to Nova. That's good enough for me. And so all that remains is to decide on a plan."

Chapter Forty-Seven

Aleksander

Hours later—after a series of tense discussions and difficult decisions—the Nerithys Gate loomed before us, a towering archway of weathered stone with a dark wooden door encased in its embrace. The intricate symbols etched into the door caught what remained of the dreary daylight, shimmering like eyes slowly blinking open, awakening at our approach.

The air was thick, saturated with a scent that had become all too familiar—ash and dry earth. It clung to everything Lorien and his magic had touched, I was noticing. It had lingered in the chamber where we'd found Nova days ago. It had been present this morning, too, when he tried to invade her mind. I hadn't told her, and I wouldn't, but I couldn't ignore how the smell seemed to have twisted even her natural clean, floral scent. Now there was a smoky undercurrent, a subtle but undeniable mark left on her—

another scar to accompany the ones Lorien had left on her skin.

Days had passed since he had physically moved within this realm, but his presence remained, an ever-present shadow that only thickened the sense of unease surrounding us.

There were no signs of life here, save for our own, but soon, a low, hissing wind stirred the heavy stillness. Faintly, almost imperceptibly, I thought I heard a voice drifting within it—a whisper that swelled and ebbed, sometimes rising to a note that made the hairs on the back of my neck prickle.

I couldn't tell if it was beckoning us forward or warning us to turn back.

"Do you hear that?" Nova asked, softly, her hand steady against Phantom, who stood alert, his ears flattened, fur bristling with dark energy that spiraled from his coat like smoke.

"I was hoping I was imagining it," I said, gaze fixed on the gate ahead.

"It sounds...*angry*."

The other leaders of our group soon joined us, their anxious chatter drowning out whatever wind-swept whispers we might have otherwise heard.

Our small army folded around us as well. I resisted the urge to count them again; the number grew no more impressive, no matter how many times I added them up in hopes that they might have miraculously turned into more. The crumbling, increasingly useless spells over the palace had left fewer and fewer souls standing as the day had pressed on; by the time we left out, only three dozen soldiers had been deemed fit enough to make the journey with us.

All together, we totaled less than fifty.

Less than fifty souls standing against the greatest threat the realms had ever known.

I breathed in deeply through my nose, trying to settle the squeezing sense of panic that kept trying to rise up and take hold of my heart. Again and again, I settled it. Glancing at the scars on Nova's skin proved helpful, too; the sight of them reignited my furious, burning resolve every time.

We would make our way to Nerithys—to Lorien—even if it meant I had to pry this damn gate apart with my bare hands.

"The gate opens easiest at Equinox, of course," Thalia said to the crowd pressing closer to us. "But enough magic can open it at *any* given time, and it gets progressively easier to do this with every day closer to Equinox. So…"

"So we'll manage," said Nova, moving closer to the gate.

I stepped forward alongside her, masking my usual skepticism; it wouldn't do us any good, now.

She took a deep breath before cutting her eyes toward me. "Together?"

"Together."

We moved before any more doubt could creep in.

If nothing else, getting away from the Rivenholt Palace—and the lingering protections Calista had left—had been a positive move for my own magic; it no longer felt like it was being suffocated. It rose easily from my outstretched palms.

Nova mirrored my movements, and soon we'd both

managed to call forth equal amounts of our respective powers. They rose as shimmering tendrils of light and dark, slowly drifting toward one another, rising without hesitation despite the heavy air.

What had once been a chaotic meeting of clashing energies now moved with purpose and grace, effortlessly weaving in and out, twisting tighter and tighter together until there was no space in between. The threads of twisting power combined more fully above the arch, shaping into a spiraling column that was illuminated and shaded in turn. It spun for a moment before dividing once more into two strands—ribbons that each carried a predominant magic, but also a hint of the opposite magic, now.

With precise guidance from our hands, the ribbons dove and skimmed along the stone arch. There were pedestals on either side of this arch—places meant for the Swords of Light and Shadow to rest and channel their power. Our magic sank into them, filling in the grooves and awakening the ancient mechanisms hidden within.

All the symbols on the door flared brighter. The stone arch lit up with equal boldness. As we shielded our eyes, a loud, sharp sound rattled through the area—like ice cracking and snow shifting on a mountaintop, echoing through a deep valley.

When it all settled, most of the arch remained, save for a few chipped shards.

But the door lay in a thousand splintered pieces upon the dusty ground.

A path of some kind was clearly opened; a swirling mass of grey and white energy now waited where the wooden door had once stood.

Beckoning us.

But to enter it meant stepping over the shattered remnants of the once imposing gate—a pile of sharp, broken things that seemed ominous, at best.

If we stepped into that chaotic-looking portal, could we come back the same way?

We all hesitated.

Nova crouched down, carefully sifting through the broken splinters of wood and bits of stone. "What have we done?" she breathed. "What does this mean?"

Bastian knelt beside her, his expression grim. He started to speak several times before seemingly deciding on an explanation. "The realms, and the paths between them, aren't as they once were…and you two aren't exactly like the Vaelora of centuries past. I wouldn't expect everything to go as smoothly as it once did for the usual incarnations of those beings. Especially without the Swords of Shadow and Light in your hands."

"Either way, the path is open, right?" said Thalia, taking a cautious but determined step forward. "No turning back, now."

Nova straightened, her eyes shining a strange shade of blue as she stared down the glowing portal. "Onward, then."

Despite the unanswered questions hanging over us, no one disagreed.

Phantom bounded ahead of us all—only to stop just shy of the gate, pacing and whining.

"He's gotten used to being solid and normal in this realm," Bastian said. "The energies in Nerithys might not react kindly with his…interesting, shifting existence."

Alarm overtook Nova's face. "Could it permanently harm him?"

Bastian didn't answer, but the concerned furrow of his brow betrayed his thoughts.

The dog started to force himself closer to the portal anyway, but Nova caught him by the ruff around his neck and pulled him away. She hesitated before kneeling before him, her voice shaking slightly as she said, "Stay. I'll be back before you know it."

Phantom growled his disagreement but ultimately obeyed, slinking away. Nova clenched her hand into a fist and braced it against the ground, bowing her head as she collected herself. She took only seconds to do so; too many eyes were on her, waiting for her to lead them.

I offered a hand and helped her to her feet.

Side-by-side, we stepped through the gateway.

A feeling of falling immediately struck—like I'd missed a step on a steep staircase. I didn't tumble far, but the landing was still jarring, and it was pitch dark at the bottom. So unnaturally dark that, for a moment, it seemed like I was the only being in existence. Like nothing else could *possibly* have existed in the nothingness around me, in this dark that swallowed up all scent and sound and sensation…

Twisted though it might have been, I was suddenly grateful for my time spent in the punishing Abyss back at my old palace; my experiences kept me from panicking, at least. I merely closed my eyes and searched for that calm place I kept buried deep inside of myself.

As I drifted within that still, inner place, I heard a faint breath in the darkness. Then a heartbeat. Then a pulse of magic that I recognized, even as all my other senses were dulled or outright failing me. My own magic answered automatically, lighting its jagged paths through my skin, cutting through this new abyss to answer that distant pulsing.

I took a few steps forward, following the pull of my magic, and I soon spotted Nova's hand reaching out in the dark. Her eyes were slightly wide with fear as they met mine.

She glanced at the low ceiling my light had revealed. It was covered in hanging, crystalline structures, their sharp edges both beautiful and menacing; we appeared to be at the mouth of a cavernous tunnel of sorts. A relatively clear path stretched before us—the only way out. A palpable relief washed through us at the sight of our obvious next steps.

That relief lasted only seconds.

The light rising from my body was acting strangely, rapidly gathering near the ceiling, as if being pulled in by those odd crystals. They captured the light and magnified it with incredible, unnatural force, and our surroundings went from being shrouded in total darkness to being flooded with so much light that it was equally disorienting.

Blistering heat rapidly followed the eye-watering brightness.

Then came the sound of one of the crystals popping, followed by glistening shards raining down, pinging against the rocky ground.

Cursing under my breath, I attempted to pull some of my magic back. It did little good; even the slightest flicker of light was caught and reflected back with blinding ferocity and heat.

Meanwhile, one after the other, our allies were following

us through the portal, cramming into the space and immediately finding themselves lost among the unbearable light and heat. Their sounds were strangely muffled—making me more and more certain unnatural spells and protections were at work here—but the panic rolling off them quickly became palpable.

Just as that panic started to sink its claws into me, I caught sight of a shadow rapidly encircling one of the crystals above. It pressed into the middle of the translucent structure like ink blossoming in water, dimming the light beaming from its center.

Understanding dawned over me. I closed my eyes and focused, no longer trying to pull my magic back, but instead holding it in place while Nova added her shadows to it.

The searing heat slowly cooled. Stillness overcame our crowd of allies. Curiosity overtook panic, and I opened my eyes to find Nova standing directly in front of me, cast in a soft, delicate light.

She was carefully studying the hanging crystal closest to us, her upturned gaze reflecting the swirling mass of our magic now balanced in its center. With precise movements of her hands, she continued to guide her shadows into other crystals near and far, until they were all filled with both our magics, and the entire tunnel was cast in the same muted, pleasant light and warmth that directly surrounded us.

"Traversing this path *also* requires balance, apparently," she whispered, her tone a mixture of lingering panic and building awe as she lowered her gaze and looked around.

It was impossible *not* to be awed by the sight now surrounding us.

The balanced glow of our magic slowly, fully revealed

the short tunnel ahead—the strange, colorful flowers along its floor, the walls lined with smooth, iridescent stones. There were faint, glowing symbols etched into some of those stones, pulsing with an energy that felt ancient and alive—much like what we'd witnessed on the gate itself.

The world beyond the passage beckoned. The mere glimpse we were able to see from where we stood revealed a wide expanse of fields, trees, and a smattering of rooftops, all bathed in an otherworldly white light.

Nova jogged ahead to get a better look. I followed closely behind, emerging more cautiously from the tunnel to find myself on top of a hill overlooking the ruins of what appeared to have been a sprawling city at one point. Vast plazas lay cracked and overgrown, connected by the shattered lines of an elaborate road system. The remains of houses were dotted along those broken roads, most of their walls sagging and crumbling into the earth, choked by vines and creeping ivy.

At the bottom of the hill lay a twisted, rusted, and half-buried gate that led into a barren courtyard. The courtyard was long and narrow, with the ruins of multiple walls dividing it. A central path led through it, up to a massive structure of battered stone and cracked marble...

The remnants of a palace.

Its shattered towers jutted up like broken bones, only partially visible above the outer defensive walls—but the main building appeared to be more or less intact, its bricks weathered but standing firm, the majority of its arched, ornate windows unbroken.

Beyond it all, far past the palace and the city behind it, lay a wide expanse of glimmering grey. A sea, perhaps. Its shimmering seemed oddly out of place in this otherwise still and silent world, and I briefly wondered what the rest of this place might look like under the light of a normal sky and sun.

"The Palace—and Kingdom—of Midna," said Bastian, coming up behind us. "Or, what's left of it, anyway. It was once the most powerful, most central kingdom in existence, back when Noctaris and Soltaris were part of one singular world. Some legends say the last King and Queen of Midna played a role in the formation of the Aetherstone—that they were duty-bound to the gods themselves to see that artifact created and protected." He scanned the ruins, his eyes lighting up as they fell over what remained of the main palace. "This is actually in better shape than I expected; I imagine its rooms are full of all sorts of interesting things we could study…"

"Not really what we're here for, unfortunately," Thalia reminded him. "Though maybe we'll survive long enough—and balance things well enough—that we'll have a chance to explore and unearth more knowledge."

"We survived getting here," Nova said. "That's a start, isn't it?"

Her brother nodded. "We're lucky we had you two back there." Glancing over his shoulder toward the tunnel, he added, "The path to this realm and its Stone were meant for both of the Vaeloran to walk together, so that likely won't be the last time we'll need both of your respective magics."

"It also further explains why Lorien needed to steal Grimnor, and Nova's magic, to better balance his own powers," Thalia said, already making her way down the hill.

Nodding in agreement, Bastian followed her.

Nova hesitated, her eyes glazed over in thought, the corners of her mouth drooping. I could read her well enough by now to guess at what she was feeling—guilt and regret over letting Lorien escape with that sword and everything else.

"Whatever he took," I said, placing a hand on the small of her back and urging her onward, "it isn't as powerful as you are. And he won't be able to wield it as you can. He used it to get into this place—and for nothing more, for all we know."

She gave a barely perceptible nod; it was the only response she had time for before the rest of our company caught up to us, forcing her to shift her expression into something more formidable. Something our doubters couldn't question.

We crept carefully down the steep hill, making our way through the dilapidated entrance and into the skeletal remains of the courtyard. As we passed under what remained of the entry arch, the sky suddenly shifted, its milky white glow giving way to churning clouds of dark purple and blue.

Several members of our party gasped at the dramatic change in lighting, drawing to a stop.

The earth began to shiver beneath us. It was so subtle, at first, that I wondered if I was imagining it. But then it grew more violent, forcing me to brace a hand against what remained of the nearest wall. Little chips of stone rained down, joining loudly rattling piles on the dusty ground. One of the few trees still standing snapped with a series of startling *cracks* before falling forward, nearly striking two of our soldiers as it did.

The quaking lasted at least a minute.

Another minute passed before our party regrouped, gathering around and looking expectantly at Bastian for an explanation.

"...The lack of balance—and proper Vaelora—has clearly taken a toll on this realm as well," he said.

We continued on. No one spoke. Most seemed to be trying to quiet their steps, their rattling armor, their very *breathing*. There was a lingering sense of something monstrous sleeping just beneath our feet, and no one wanted to wake it up.

But as we passed beyond the final defensive wall—into the innermost yard of the palace—silence seemed impossible. Gasps and confused whispers rang out at the sight that greeted us: *Soldiers*.

Countless soldiers frozen in various poses of action and stillness, all caught in a moment of time they were never allowed to finish. And the way they were all dressed...

"These are old uniforms of the Elarithian Army," I said. My stomach twisted as I pointed to the sleeve of one of their jackets, which featured a crescent shape cradling a single, radiant star at its center, the star's light spilling outward in sharp, clean lines. Swallowing away the sudden dryness in my throat, I added, "And this symbol is sometimes used by the Light Keepers."

"...Is this Lorien's army that we were so worried about encountering?" wondered Lord Kaelen, stepping forward. "An army of frozen ghosts?"

"These look like the cursed figures back at Rose Point," Nova said, quietly. "Like...like my mother."

Bastian moved closer to one of them, tentatively circling the stoic figure. The buttons on the soldier's jacket glistened with a hint of movement—no more than a breath, the faintest hint of life beneath its condemned shell.

"That aligns with the theory we've discussed," said Bastian. "This kind of curse seems to befall those who are caught in the crossfire of warring energies from the separate realms. As for what's happening here…" He looked to the sky as it began to ebb back to the soft shade of glowing white from earlier.

"It's nothing *but* warring energies in this realm," I thought aloud.

He nodded in solemn agreement. "I suspect if we stayed here long enough, we'd end up as similar victims of those energies." He lowered his voice toward the end, but the damage was already done; urgent chatter broke out among our own soldiers, and some of them looked back toward the hill we'd descended, likely wondering if it was too late to retreat.

Cowardly, maybe, but I couldn't exactly blame them. We had no way of knowing how much time we had before the ill effects of this realm—whatever they would be—started to take hold.

"So it seems the realm itself has done its part to slow Lorien and his minions down…could we really be so lucky?" wondered Captain Voss, carefully weaving his way in between the frozen figures.

I frowned but held my tongue. It saved us a battle, maybe, but nothing about this seemed *lucky*. And it felt as if these living ghosts were all still watching us—more monsters just waiting to spring to life at our first misstep.

"Let's hurry up and find the Stone before our luck runs out," Thalia suggested.

Another slight tremor shook the earth, and I found

myself quickly agreeing with her. "We should divide into groups and start searching. It's somewhere within the palace grounds, correct?"

"According to almost every account I've read on the subject," Bastian confirmed.

Nova was hesitant to divide our forces, but another dramatic shifting of energy in the sky ultimately convinced her. "...Make sure each group has a necromancer among them," she ordered, "so they can send shadows—a signal of some kind—for any discovery or trouble they run into."

The details were settled, the groups decided on, and Nova and I were joined by Captain Voss and a few soldiers as we made our way to the left side of the palace. We were forced to sweep wider and wider in an effort to avoid more and more rubble, as well as great craters that looked as though they could have—*should* have—swallowed the entire palace whole.

The destruction only grew worse as we continued to explore. It was a wonder any of it was standing at all, and a challenge just to get close to it, much less to thoroughly explore it.

Captain Voss pressed on with a methodical, tireless determination. His soldiers followed his example. Nova appeared equally dauntless on the outside, but I could sense her frustration growing, her magic becoming more and more restless with every dead end we reached.

I started to suggest we head back to the central courtyard, and perhaps reconvene with some of the others, when a strange light caught my eye—a flare of gold that illuminated a corner we'd yet to explore.

Searching for the source of that light proved fruitless. And there was nothing that immediately stood out in this forgotten corner, even as I moved closer...only a staircase, half-buried in the debris of the collapsed palace, its steps partially obscured by a tree that had grown twisted and bent around it.

Yet, something about it called to me.

As I ascended the stairs, I realized the palace had once soared much higher than its ruins suggested. At the top of the steps, I entered what had clearly been a vast room on a second story; fragments of marble flooring inlaid with delicate gold patterns lay scattered about, and broken columns stood at even intervals.

The walls had all crumbled away, allowing my gaze to spot an interesting sight in the distance: Some fifty feet away, a massive, circular chamber jutted out, seemingly untouched by the cursed energies that had destroyed so many other parts of the structure.

It stood high in the air, held aloft by four towering marble pillars branded with markings that gleamed brightly. A narrow bridge of carved stone, worn with age but still sturdy-looking, connected it to the main palace—to one of the few sections of that main palace that also seemed to still be sturdy.

I heard Nova following me up the stairs. She gasped as she reached the top, catching sight of the suspended room. She rushed closer, tripping over pieces of debris in her haste, her gaze never leaving the strange, circular structure.

Captain Voss and our soldiers caught up as well. While Nova continued to explore the room and the pillars holding it up, we searched the surrounding areas for any potential threats.

Once I was satisfied no one was hiding in the rubble to ambush us, I joined Nova in the shadow of the room. I paced between the columns, brushing my fingers over the strange symbols etched in gold, trying—unsuccessfully—to decipher their meaning.

"This could be it," Nova said, her eyes locked on the bottom of the chamber. "Look at that." She pointed to an engraved circle with lines radiating from its center and a crescent shape curving away from it on either side. "It's similar to the mark of the Vaelora that I saw on Lorien's arm. And that one next to it…"

I studied it along with her. It featured a crescent shape, as well, but one turned horizontally, its open ends curling inward as if trying to close the gap. Suspended within that gap was a black teardrop. "The mark of the Shadow Vaelora, maybe?"

Nova was quiet for a long moment before seeming to make up her mind. Looking to the bridge, she said, "I want to go inside."

A warning skipped through me at the words, but I made myself nod; we'd come too far to turn back now.

It took a bit of exploring, climbing over crumbling walls and leaping across precarious patches of flooring, but we eventually found a way into the palace, and then up to the room that allowed us to access the bridge.

Our footsteps echoed and stirred up dust, regardless of how carefully we stepped. The space on this side of the bridge was vast, its ceiling dizzyingly high. It looked like it had been a grand entrance atrium at one point—to a throne room, perhaps; through a crack in a pair of doors hanging crooked on their hinges, I saw a room with an ornate chair in its center, its back high and trimmed in threads that shimmered faintly in the dim light.

I turned away from it, focusing on the bridge. But as I

braced my hand against a leaning column, fighting off a cough triggered by dust, an odd image flickered into my mind: Those crooked doors behind me swinging open to reveal the throne in all its splendor—no, *thrones*.

There were two.

Two empty thrones draped in flowers, centered in a room filled with people silently bowing their heads.

My curiosity almost won, urging me to turn around and look closer, to see what visions I might be able to draw out of the other pieces of this broken palace.

Nova's voice stopped me at the last instant: "Are you coming?"

Captain Voss joined us at that moment as well, and he nodded toward the bridge, which Nova had already stepped onto. "We should stay together."

I agreed, though the urge to glance back followed me onto the bridge, along with the growing sense that we were missing something. It was only the three of us—with the rest of our search group scattered close by in the ruins below, keeping a lookout—but suddenly I felt as if the entire realm were pressing in around us, intently watching our next moves.

Before I could speak any of these fears aloud, I lifted my eyes to the room ahead.

And I immediately forgot about everything else.

Because the way into that circular, suspended room was clear, with both Grimnor and Luminor balanced on either side of its open door.

Chapter Forty-Eight

Nova

"This feels like a trap," said Aleks.

"It does," I agreed. And yet, I couldn't stop myself from stepping forward, even knowing Lorien had been here, that he'd left these swords for us to find—who else could have done it?

Grimnor hummed as I approached, sending a pleasant tingling through me. My chest flooded with warmth, as if I'd spotted an old friend from across the room; all I wanted to do was run and grab ahold of her, to never let her go again.

But I forced myself to move slowly.

Aleks did the same, cautiously reaching a hand toward Luminor, but not quite touching the blade or the ornate holder it rested within. "It feels like both swords are channeling their power into this structure," he said, his gaze sweeping over the walls of the suspended room.

"I wonder what will happen when we pull them out of the holders?"

"No telling. But we should probably brace ourselves for the worst; nothing about this realm feels stable."

I considered the two swords and the open door between them. As much as I longed to feel the weight of Grimnor in my hands once more, I didn't want to risk disturbing whatever magic was currently keeping our path unobstructed and everything around us relatively sturdy.

"...Let's leave them be for the moment," I suggested. Looking to Captain Voss, I added, "Stay out here and keep watch, please."

He agreed with a bow, gripping the pommel of his sword as he paced to a better vantage point.

I hesitated only long enough to send up an alert to my brother and the other search groups—the shadowy circle that we'd agreed upon; a signal that we'd found something worth everyone's attention.

Pulse pounding in my ears, I gathered my courage and stepped into the room, Aleks following closely behind.

The energy that greeted us was nearly...*indescribable*. A hum that reverberated throughout my chest, a pressure that was almost unbearable, yet somehow invigorating. Like the very weight of existence, the fabric of life itself, was being woven together in this room. I shook from the mere effort of breathing it all in.

What had seemed like a large room from the outside now felt limitless—a small palace unto itself, with vaulted ceilings soaring dizzyingly high above us and walls draped in dark, velvety tapestries that made me think of an endless expanse of night sky. Competing scents of smoke and rose mingled in the air; a burning hint of decay tumbling with the richness of life—another reminder of the fragile balancing act that had led us to this point.

Across the middle of the vast space, a circular dais rose up, its face inlaid with scattered, precious stones and its edges etched with various runes, some of which glowed in the light streaming in from small cracks and gaps near the ceiling.

And at the center of this platform, the Aetherstone waited.

A relatively small pedestal held it above the dais. Surrounded by such vast opulence, it seemed oddly small. Unremarkable. But as I stepped toward it, the pressure in the room increased until I could hardly breathe, and I found myself fighting the urge to sink to my knees—to bow before it.

Aleks and I both took only a quick closer look before putting space between ourselves and that legendary object, studying the multitude of other interesting things around it instead.

"The openings seem very precisely carved," Aleks said, after a moment, his eyes on the ceiling. "…To create specific patterns of light on these rune markings, maybe."

I looked again at the light filtering in, and I realized he had a point; what had at first seemed like weathered cracks caused by time and neglect were actually purposeful, clean-edged openings of all different shapes and sizes.

Following the closest beam of light, I knelt before the rune it was illuminating and considered it more closely. Running my fingers over it, I could feel the pulse of some ancient magic on the cusp of awakening, I thought. Something I felt a deep connection to, even if I couldn't fully explain it.

I stood and walked along the edge of the dais, studying the symbols, trying to imagine different patterns of light and shadows falling over them.

"I wonder where the light falls during Equinox..." I thought aloud. "According to most legends, the Stone is easiest to control on the dawn of that day. Maybe because of something these runes reveal in that specific lighting?"

"Maybe," Aleks agreed. "But we're still too early to see, aren't we?"

He was right, yet my mind continued to stubbornly plot, turning over one unlikely plan after another until I settled on a possibility. "Perhaps we can simulate it?"

He gave me a curious look, but then caught on quickly, lifting his gaze to the openings above once more. "...Your shadows could block the light coming in."

"And you could create only the light we need, casting it on specific runes." His curiosity gave way to doubt, but I continued before he could interrupt: "We're very close to the dawn of the day we need," I pointed out. "Wouldn't a glimpse of a future image that's so close be easier for you to see?"

"...It's worth a try, I guess," he relented, making his way toward the platform's edge, kneeling and running a hand over the same markings I had.

He closed his eyes and went almost perfectly still for a long moment—until the slightest twitch of his facial features suggested that he'd seen...*something*. Then he moved on to the next section without a word.

Several times, he did this, making his way around the entire circle before he finally turned back to me with more confidence shining in the golden depths of his eyes.

I didn't speak, not wanting to break his concentration as

he scanned the entire dais and all its symbols one last time, seemingly locking in whatever patterns he'd seen in his vision.

He tilted his face toward me and gave a single nod; an unspoken cue.

I reached toward the ceiling, fingers twisting and pulling thick tendrils of shadow into existence. With as much precision as I could manage, I sent my magic upward, fixing it over every hint of light I saw.

As I covered the last opening, we were plunged into a deep, all-consuming darkness. My heart skipped a few beats as I found myself reliving the horrible moments when we'd first touched down in this realm. But just as he'd done then, it wasn't long before Aleksander calmly summoned his light.

He guided each spark of it methodically along the circle, putting it in its proper place, until he'd set a dozen of the etched runes aglow.

At first, nothing happened. But then a few adjustments, one rune dimmed, another illuminated…

The dais rumbled, and it seemed to twist—first one way, then the other—only to fall back into place so smoothly that I questioned whether or not it had actually moved at all.

But *something* was happening beneath the shiny surface of it, of that I was sure; I could feel the energy of it shifting, raising chill bumps along my arms.

I held my breath, watching as the gems within the platform's polished face lit up one by one. Each illumination revealed a new image in the marble; they rose up like ink bleeding through a page—symbols that resembled all manner of things, from towers to forests to crests of ocean waves. Alongside each cluster of symbols were markings that vaguely resembled letters, a script that seemed to be some ancient, stylized version of the common one I'd grown up reading in the Above.

It took a moment of studying before I managed to read them—to recognize the name of a familiar kingdom.

Eldris.

And several more names became obvious, the closer I looked at them: *Elarith. Rivenholt. Midna...*

"It's a map," I realized, stepping back to the edge so I could get a more complete view. "A map of both the Above and the Below, with this realm we're in—marked by the Aetherstone—in the very middle. Each of those jewels represents a kingdom." A sense of awe blossomed in my chest as I stared at our world in its entirety...followed by a rising sense of despair.

It was strange to see all the realms united in one circle like this.

Aleks stepped onto the platform, walking between the kingdoms, considering each in turn.

"What about these empty spaces near the Stone?" he wondered, pausing next to a groove carved into the dais, far away from any kingdom. It looked almost like a wayward slash left by a careless hand—I hadn't even noticed it before now. But there was an identical one on the Noctaris portion of the map, which made me think there was nothing random about it.

Curious, I went to Aleksander's side. Bracing myself for whatever I might see, I crouched down, pressed my fingers firmly against the groove, and closed my eyes in search of its past.

It took several deep breaths before an image flickered into my mind: One of the Sword of Light impaling this spot, and then the Aetherstone glowing to life behind it. The sword took on the same glow, briefly, before sending cracks of white energy outward. Some branched toward the kingdoms, but most of it went northward, settling in an orb on display just beyond the platform.

The vision lasted only an instant before another vision seemed to be trying to push its way in. Then another, and another, and—

I felt a hand on my shoulder, squeezing tight.

"Nova?" came Aleksander's concerned voice.

Slightly dizzy and breathing hard, I shook my head, blinking away the last bits of the chaotic vision.

"...Luminor has sank into that space more than once," I told Aleks. "The memory was...strangely broken up. Like an overlapping of several different, but similar, impressions. But I saw the sword working as a conduit, guiding energy from the Stone across this platform...most of it went to that." I pointed to the orb above the Soltaris portion of the map. It stood in a shadowy recess within the wall and, like the Aetherstone and its pedestal, it was small and unassuming, easy to overlook.

Aleks walked to the orb my vision had highlighted, circling it, tentatively running a hand over it—an action that made its center pulse with a dull light. "So is this the main way energy is fed into the Above? It's linked to Soltaris in some way, I guess..." He looked across the dais and asked the same question I was thinking: "Where's the one for Noctaris?"

Instead of answering, I made my way across the room, to the point exactly opposite of where he was standing. It was one of the only sections of the marble walls not covered by a tapestry, I noticed.

The source linked to the Above was already clear and on display; that wasn't surprising. It had been for centuries, presumably, while the one for the Below had been shoved aside, hidden and buried.

But this room, and all the magic it represented, was about balance. Which meant there had to be a counter piece to Soltaris's power source here, somewhere.

Aleks joined me, summoning a bit more light to help me inspect the wall more easily. Within the glow of his magic, I quickly spotted two diamond-shaped symbols etched deeply into the stone, their edges smoothed by time.

I pressed a hand to both of them. My bracelets shivered—all of them, at first. But the turquoise one continued to move long after the others had stilled. I stared at the word spelled across that bracelet, thinking of the meaning my brother had shared with me weeks ago.

Kindred spirits…souls that are bound to one another…

I carried the force of an untold number of those ancient bonds, of countless lifetimes and the magic they had wielded across thousands of years.

And together, we were going to find a way to save our realm.

The surge of Shadow magic that followed this thought was violent and swift, sweeping over the wall with a force that left the nearby tapestries hanging haphazardly and sent me stumbling backward.

Aleks caught me against his chest. I stood perfectly still, bracing myself against his strength, as we watched the wall begin to glow with symbols that had been invisible before.

They were faint, their glow more like foggy moonlight than the brilliant blaze of the runes we'd illuminated earlier. But soon that moonlight was shifting, pulling away from the symbols and etching out a tall, rectangular shape against the marble.

I still didn't move, even as parts of the wall slid open, revealing the Noctaris orb.

I scarcely breathed as the moment settled, along with a silence that felt ancient and deep, and I slowly realized what I needed to do next—a relatively simple next step, in the end.

Almost too simple, whispered a quiet, wary voice in the back of my mind.

I shook the warning off.

"The swords…" I said, finally breaking free of my stupor and looking to the door.

Aleks nodded, but neither of us moved right away, as if struck simultaneously by the weight of what we were about to do—or *attempt* to do.

I still had far too many questions.

Far too many doubts.

But we'd had two main goals when we'd stepped into this realm: To stop Lorien, and to keep Noctaris from fading beyond repair before it was too late. We were perhaps moments away from accomplishing at least one of those things. I had to do what I could with this orb—to pour magic into it, somehow—and start rebalancing things. I refused to think beyond this.

With renewed determination, I marched to the doorway and reached for Grimnor.

Sounds of distant shouting stopped me in my tracks.

My gaze jerked to the bridge, seeking Captain Voss. He emerged from the doorway of the palace, his eyes trained on the yard below. His gaze was stoic, but his lips were tightly pursed—as if he'd just held in a gasp.

I followed his line of sight, and I didn't bother holding in my gasp when I saw what he did: A host of enemy soldiers pouring into the yard.

My brother and some of the others had obviously seen my signal—they'd joined my own search party, swelling the number to at least twenty—but they were still outnumbered.

I took a few steps toward Captain Voss, panic gripping my throat. "We have to help them!"

He moved to follow this order while I turned and grabbed my sword. Aleks already had Luminor in his grasp. He was standing on the very edge of the bridge, watching the violence unfold. But he hesitated to follow the captain—

And so did I.

Because the Aetherstone still beckoned.

I bit back a curse, knowing I couldn't fight every battle at once, yet unable to make myself abandon my soldiers so readily—not when the number of enemies below seemed to have doubled in the span of seconds. "There are so *many...*"

"You didn't think I'd finish off this last part of my plan all on my own, did you?" came a cold, amused voice.

I twisted around, heart leaping into my throat.

And there he stood on the other side of the bridge, leaning against a broken slab of the palace wall: Lorien Blackvale.

A visceral reaction curled through me at the mere sight of his smiling face. A dozen different responses to his words flashed in my mind, each more violent than the last—he sauntered forward before I could decide on any of them.

"Now, while they stay busy below, let's step back inside

and finish what you started, shall we?" he said, nodding to the Aetherstone's room.

Aleks moved between us, lifting the Sword of Light, pointing it threateningly at Lorien's chest.

Lorien's gaze drifted lazily toward him. "Don't worry. You can come, too—you and I are far from finished, anyway."

"We're not going anywhere with you," I snapped.

"It wasn't an *invitation*," he replied, lifting his hands.

My first instinct was to grip my sword more tightly, expecting him to try and rip it from my grasp.

Aleks held just as tightly to Luminor.

But rather than trying to steal the swords back, Lorien merely struck out with a wave of shadowy magic—*my* magic—possessing the blades and sending them hurtling backwards into the room, dragging us with them.

Aleks and I both hit the ground with a jarring thud, our bodies crashing into the cold, unforgiving stone floor.

The door began to close as soon as the swords crossed the threshold, two great, wooden slabs groaning and shifting into place with a deafening screech.

Lorien stepped through just before they closed us off completely from the outside world.

I rose alongside Aleks, the blood pounding in my ears. Both our swords shimmered with energy as the Aetherstone itself flared to life behind us, flooding the room in a storm of light and shadow.

Chapter Forty-Nine

Nova

"Once again, you've been a tremendous help," Lorien said.

I backed farther into the room, my muscles tensing as his gaze fell upon the orb I'd uncovered.

"Because I couldn't have reached that without you."

I stepped in front of it.

"And in order to finish stealing away the last of your pathetic world's energy and directing it into the world *I* intend to rule over," he said, "I needed to be able to access that last remaining reservoir."

"You aren't accessing any of it," I snarled. "You're finished. I'm here to bring the balance back, and there is no room for *you* in the world *I'm* going to be ruling over."

He cocked his head, his lips pulling into a smirk. "A noble goal. But one that will be difficult to achieve without your sword, won't it?"

A vicious jolt of pain accompanied his words—like he'd

taken hold of my wrist and tried to snap it in half—and Grimnor was ripped from my grasp before I had time to register what was happening. As it soared precisely into his hold, I realized with horror that he'd managed to possess *both* my arm and my sword at the same time.

I'd had no chance to hold on to my weapon.

I was lucky he hadn't controlled me into doing something far worse.

I stood up straighter, pushing past my fear, shoving aside all my horrible questions about just how deep his well of power went.

"I've gotten very good at this trick," he said, while twisting and balancing the sword, "thanks to the possessive magic I stole from your predecessor, which was, of course, reinforced with what I stole from *you*. So again, allow me to extend my sincerest gratitude. Now, if we—"

He was cut off, forced to spin and meet the powerful swing of Aleks and Luminor.

The swords collided with a sound like cannon fire, sending waves of wild energy radiating through the room.

Lorien's counter was equally wild, slicing toward Aleks with so much force I nearly cried out, anticipating an inevitable strike and a spray of blood.

Aleks brought Luminor into a guard position at the last moment, but the blow was enough to knock him back several feet. More magic erupted at the contact, and this room that had once felt massive suddenly seemed to be collapsing in on itself, sinking from the weight of too much power in too small of a space.

I darted out of the path of the most turbulent twists of energy, dodging reckless swings and trying to get into a clear space to catch my breath, to think through my own next move.

The Aetherstone continued to hum with more and more energy, coming fully to life now that both Lorien and I—along with the swords—were present. In the rapidly building mayhem around us, it seemed like a beacon, a lighthouse I kept spotting no matter how high and wild the waves of other magic roared.

Aleks moved like a man possessed, meeting Lorien step for step in an increasingly furious dance of flashing blades and crackling arcs of power. I didn't know how long he could keep that up, but I was confident he could buy me some time, at least.

I made up my mind and ran for the center of the dais. I needed to take what I could from the Aetherstone while it was awake and practically calling for me; there was no telling how unstable it might become as our battle with Lorien raged on—or what he might do to prevent us from manipulating its energy.

I didn't have Grimnor, but I could still guide some of that energy into my world, surely—enough to keep it going, if only until we could come up with a more permanent solution.

Pausing only a moment to steady my hand, I reached for the Stone.

Shadows bled from my palm without any real effort from me, falling onto the Stone, which crackled in response. The shadows merged with the current of steady, pale blue energy enshrouding the Stone, turning it to a deep shade of purple. Then my magic was flowing back into me as easily as it had fallen out, except it was clearly...*changed*.

It snaked around my arm, light and cool as a breeze but buzzing with a power that hadn't been there before. With as much poise as I could muster among the battles raging around me, I guided that torrent of energy to the orb at the platform's edge, watching as it settled and ignited a soft glow in its center.

Again and again, I did this, watching the glow become more and more visible. A flickering candle transforming into a glowing ember—steady with promise, even if its light was still faint.

It wasn't as efficient as I imagined the sword would have been, but it still seemed to be *working*, however slowly, so I pressed on.

Until the earsplitting sound of metal scraping stone caught my attention.

Out of the corner of my eye, I saw Lorien backing Aleks against the wall. Aleks managed to duck a second swing—leading to another cringe-induing slice of steel across the stone wall—but Lorien followed with magic, this time, launching an assault of shadowy daggers with a wide sweep of Grimnor's blade.

Aleks fell to one knee, hastily bracing Luminor in front of him. As he was swept up in the storm of sharp shadows colliding with his shield of light, our enemy turned and moved back toward me.

Spotting the currents of magic I was attempting to channel, Lorien paused.

And he laughed.

"That won't be enough to save your dying world, you foolish woman."

"Then why do you look so concerned about me doing it?" I shot back.

His darkly amused tone held as he took a few more

steps toward me and said, "Habit, I suppose. It's such a pity for one of our kind to waste their energy on something so trivial; I'm only looking out for you."

"I have plenty more energy to spare," I lied, letting more shadows bleed from my skin to prove my point.

"And yet, I can't help my concern for you."

His gaze fell far too intimately on my face with the words, and I resisted the urge to recoil. He was only trying to get under my skin, I knew.

I wouldn't let him.

He kept trying. His next words were a whisper in my thoughts, an attempt to exploit the Vaeloran link we shared, as he'd done this morning. I blocked him out well enough that I couldn't understand what he was saying, but the mumble of his words was like a physical prodding against my mind, sharp enough to be painful along with unsettling.

"Stop it," I commanded, my shadows darkening with the words.

He gave me a crooked smile—the one I had associated with Zayn for so long.

How many had he charmed with that stolen smile?

My hatred for him only grew at the sight of it, and he must have sensed this, because his tone became mocking as he said, "The offer to rule alongside me still stands, by the way."

"I would kill myself a thousand times over before I ruled at your side."

He chuckled. "Once will suffice."

I braced a hand against the Aetherstone as he stepped closer. And without really thinking, I squeezed.

The Stone reacted to my violent grip by sending an equally violent surge of magic shooting into my body.

Reflexes channeled it into a javelin of shadows, which I flung from my other hand, striking Lorien in the chest and knocking him backward.

Grimnor nearly slipped from his grasp as he caught himself awkwardly against the ground. I saw my chance, but I was dizzy from the amount of power that had just rushed through me—my attempt to repossess my sword came too slowly.

He gripped it tighter and launched toward me.

Aleks cut him off once more, exploding through the lingering shadows I'd created, Luminor's blade burning brightly as it slammed into its darker twin.

"Eyes on me, motherfucker," he growled at Lorien, his expression bordering on feral—a look that was only heightened by the blood trickling down his face.

Lorien staggered beneath the force of the collision. He tried to rebalance Grimnor, to ready his own attack, but Aleks was relentless, forcing him to move so quickly he scarcely managed to block, much less attack.

"Didn't you hear her earlier?" Another powerful *swish* and *thwack* of Luminor and its light, knocking Lorien further off balance. "We're both *finished* with you."

Lorien met the next swing more fully, letting out an annoyed roar as he began to fight back in earnest. He dove under the next swipe, and then cut upward with Grimnor, sending a current of both light and shadow flying upward.

Aleks danced back and away, narrowly avoiding another shower of shadowy daggers.

They resumed their battle on the other side of the room. Aleks seemed to be purposely leading him away from me and the Stone—but I found myself torn between continuing my work with that stone and chasing them down.

The Noctaris orb was still glowing steadily, yet faintly. A start, but only a start—it needed more.

I needed to do so much *more*.

But the blood on Aleksander's face kept flashing in my mind. He'd looked prepared to fight to the death.

But I wasn't prepared to *let* him.

I started toward him at the exact moment he and Lorien collided in their most violent show of magic yet.

I shielded my face from the explosion of light and dark that followed, covering my eyes as the room was engulfed in a dark cloud shot through with twisting bolts of white-hot power. The floor shook. The walls rumbled, shedding tapestries and layers of dust and bits of the ceiling, and between that rain of debris and the mass of magic, I couldn't see more than an arm's length in front of me.

The settling haze was so disorienting that, for a moment, I didn't realize how perfectly silent everything was becoming.

I could hear my own heartbeat. I could hear the hum of the Aetherstone, and a crack splitting through the beams across the ceiling, and the shower of dust causing a weak cough that sounded oddly far away.

I backed away from the Aetherstone, reaching for the knife sheathed at my hip while simultaneously letting shadows rise from my skin and wrap me in a protective cage. I tried to make that cage into something formidable—only to realize, then, that I'd given too much of my power to the orb, too quickly, and now I couldn't force my magic into something solid no matter how hard I tried.

Lorien erupted from the haze, slamming a light-wrapped hand into my shadows.

He broke through my defenses quickly, catching me by the throat and throwing me against the wall. I stayed on my feet, dazed as I was, but my vision split—three different Loriens followed up his initial attack.

I dodged the wrong one.

His hand slapped across my jaw, knocking my head sideways into the wall. Black dots swam in my vision. I slumped to the floor. I saw nothing else for a long moment—but I *felt* Grimnor moving toward me.

At the last instant, I managed to reach out, to possess my sword for a heartbeat, making it veer aside and miss my chest—barely.

Lorien was thrown off balance for a few steps. I was too stunned to make much use of it. I was able to scramble to my feet and put a bit of distance between us, nothing more, before he was upon me again, scourges of his light reaching out and snapping at my legs like the teeth of hellish hounds.

My head throbbed and my limbs ached, but I twisted around and somehow brought forth precise strikes of my own, whipping my shadows around his magic and jerking until the light waned and scattered.

Looking back to the path ahead, I realized I was out of space to move. The walls rose up before me. The haze lingered behind. I couldn't see Aleks. I couldn't see the Stone or the platform it stood upon—I could barely see Lorien, even though the sound of his breathing told me he was still close.

He'd slowed, moving with more deliberate steps—a panther stalking its prey. As our gazes met through the fog, he tossed my sword aside and focused on gathering magic into his hands. He drew from the mass of it already hovering all around us, whipping all the lingering energies into a renewed frenzy before taking a more exact hold on the jagged lines of heat flickering through it all.

He summoned more, and those lines became like the solid cage I'd been trying to make with my own shadows—bolt after bolt wrapping me up in a burning embrace that sank into my skin, paralyzing my muscles, numbing me to the point that I didn't realize, at first, that I was being lifted several feet off the ground.

Then I was flying, careening across the room.

I hit the door hard enough—wrapped in enough of Lorien's violent magic—that the ancient wood cracked as I collided with it. An entire section of it splintered away, falling with me to the hard stone floor.

Chapter Fifty

Nova

DAYLIGHT AND DUST FILTERED DOWN OVER MY BATTERED body.

The opening my collision had created was large enough that I could have crawled through it—could have gone for help, maybe.

But I couldn't make myself move.

I couldn't even find the energy to speak.

The sounds of clashing steel and thundering voices drifted up from somewhere, and I vaguely remembered the battle waging below. My brother. Thalia. All the soldiers who were desperately fighting down there. The last hope of our dying world.

I'd failed them.

With a painful twist in my gut, I realized that Lorien had been right to taunt me earlier.

It wouldn't be enough.

I wasn't enough.

My attempts to change the fate of my world felt pathetic in the face of his power, in the wake of all the destruction surrounding me.

I tasted blood on my lips. I smelled it in the air, along with the tang of magic. So much chaotic, ruinous magic. Mine, or his—it didn't seem to matter. We were intertwined, and so our fates seemed to be equally tangled, a knot that only grew tighter when I tried to pull it loose.

And if anyone could have stopped him, it should have been me.

When I laid my head against the cold stone and closed my eyes, trying to make the throbbing in it go away, he was there. A splinter beneath my skin that I couldn't ignore. I sensed him moving back across the room. Getting closer to the Noctaris orb, I suspected. No—I *knew*, somehow. As if that orb was his current, all-consuming thought, and I had no choice but to be aware of it through our connection.

He was going to destroy it if I didn't make myself *move*. If I didn't somehow take back the sword he'd ripped from my hands and the very breath he'd ripped from my lungs.

Tears squeezed from my eyes as I shifted onto my side and tried to lift my head, searching for something, anything that I could use. Every tiny twitch of my muscles was agony, but I kept searching. And searching, and searching for…

Nothing.

There was nothing here to save me.

Nothing except my knife, which had fallen from my hand when I'd struck the door. It lay on a piece of the broken door, shining in the faint bit of light trickling in from outside.

I took a deep breath. Gritting my teeth, I crawled to the knife, taking it in my trembling fingers. Then I held up my wrist, sliding the blade between my skin and the beaded turquoise bracelet.

It no longer felt like enough to merely take that bracelet off.

With a swift jerk, I severed the cord holding it together. I gave my wrist a shake, sending the beads scattering. Every one that bounced across the floor seemed to coincide with another thundering beat of my heart, and then...

With *shadows*.

Another shadow exploding for every beat and breath, until I was surrounded by them—that protective shield I'd been trying and failing to summon earlier. I kneeled within it for a moment, gathering my strength.

A cool breeze brushed the hair from my bloodied, sweat-streaked face.

Lifting my head, I caught a glimpse of Calista standing above me. She was there only for a moment, just long enough to offer her hand and pull me to my feet. Then she was gone.

I stood alone in front of the broken door, my shadows blocking out the day.

No—not alone.

Aleksander was on his feet as well, standing on the opposite side of the room. Light surrounded him, steady and pulsing, revealing his figure even through the chaos. His light was different than Lorien's. Warmer, more golden.

The light of a sun rising, reminding me that we were not finished.

He still held Luminor. Somehow, he was still holding on. His eyes were still seeking mine, and as they found me, I thought of his voice, a whisper between the nightmares, within the cold, dark waves—*I've got you.*

I ripped the rest of the bracelets from my wrist, letting them fall to the ground behind me. With every one that dropped away, I felt another surge of my power rising. Each one slightly different than the last. More dangerous than the one before it. And every one hovering just barely within my control.

But I only had one target left.

And I was in control enough to strike it.

Whatever it took, I was going to going to strike it.

I took those shadows shielding me and used them to hit the doors behind me first, tearing a wider opening. As the section of stone and wood crumbled away, the hovering haze of violent energies in the room was sucked toward the open air, leaving a clearer battlefield before me.

And I spotted Lorien precisely where I'd expected him to be: Preparing to strike the Noctaris orb. He paused as the light and magical remnants around him shifted, looking toward the opening I'd made.

His eyes narrowed as he lowered them to me.

I focused on my sword—which was back in his hand—with a single word pounding through my thoughts: *Mine.*

I searched for the familiar pulse of Grimnor's essence, finding it easily. Wrapping my focus and power around it, I clenched my fist and pulled.

The blade soared toward me, leaving a shimmering trail of dark energy as it came. That same energy continued to build around it once I caught it and balanced it in my hand. It wound up my arm and over my shoulders before cascading down, draping around me like a layer of armor forged from a dazzling night sky.

Lorien turned more fully to me. His eyes seemed to take on a reddish glow as the mark of the Vaelora flared to life on his arm. I felt another prodding against my mind, a whisper that quickly took on a physical weight—but I'd been prepared for him to try that.

I wasn't listening.

I focused on preparing my next strike to drown him out, holding my ground as he stalked closer. Just as I'd done with my sword, I sought the center of his being, that pulsing beat that I could possess and control.

And I felt...*two*.

A gasp slipped through my lips as I realized that Zayn was clearly still in there—but I didn't let it distract me for long. That second essence was much fainter, buried beneath the tumbling, violent being that had overtaken it so many years ago.

I exhaled a slow breath, and I imagined my magic constricting with the inhale that followed, closing around the powerfully beating heart of Lorien's life-force.

He stumbled. Froze. His eyes dropped to his stomach, his hand grappling over it and then up to his chest—as if looking for the blade I'd stabbed him with.

"There is no blade," I informed him. "There is only *me*."

He started to reply, but I gave a vicious twist of my power, pulling my hold tighter, choking him into silence.

His magic rose in furious response, coming precariously close to overpowering mine.

Sensing an impending eruption I might not be able to contain, I looked past him and quickly found Aleksander's eyes once more. "Ready your sword!" I cried.

Any doubt and fear about this plan we'd only hastily discussed disappeared in that moment. His expression mirrored mine—grim determination and acceptance.

We moved now or never.

As I squeezed my own sword more tightly, letting its power wash over and steady me, Lorien stumbled a few steps closer—close enough that only I could hear his whisper.

"If you take me, I'm taking Zayn with me." His smile was back—savage and slightly unhinged. "And don't forget the connection I share with Aleksander. Maybe I'll drag him down along with us."

"No," I growled, taking a step even closer to him, refusing to cower. *"You won't."*

I didn't listen to his reply—I was done listening, determined to never hear his voice again.

I wrapped my power more tightly around him.

And I held.

I held, even as his magic tried to break me. As my entire body shook and waves of nausea rocked through me. As pain and exhaustion blinded me. As his voice battered against the walls of my mind—not just words, but awful, inhuman screams, hissed threats, wild roars.

I couldn't focus on much beyond steadying my own magic, but through my glazed over eyes I saw light lifting from Aleks. From the sword he held. I focused on that light with every ounce of resolve I had left, knowing my shadows would call to it, that I could lead him to the monster, to the bitterly black heart I held in my control.

Lifetimes seemed to rise and fall before I finally felt it: A warm current of magic fighting its way in, relieving some of the pressure against my insides. It circled the cage I'd made around Lorien's life-force, like a serpent preparing to strike.

Hold it steady, said a voice, deep in the back of my mind. My own, or Aleksander's, or some ancient entity trying to guide me—I didn't know. But it was calm and certain, and I couldn't help but listen to it.

Hold, it whispered, over and over. *Hold!*

And so I held, and held and held, until Lorien gave a final, guttural cry as he was thrown from Zayn's body.

That body collapsed. For a moment, Lorien's essence appeared like a phantom before me, a volatile shape of the man he had once been. It was gone in a blink, gathering into a smaller, more solid shape that immediately shot off toward the shattered doorway.

I caught it in ropes of quickly-summoned shadows, dragging it back.

It fought, twisting and writhing with enough force to drop me to my knees. But even as I hit the ground, my magic held firm, shadows coiling more firmly around all that remained of Lorien Blackvale, reducing him to a mere wisp of red-tinged energy.

And then my shadows found their way back to the light—back to Aleksander and the sword he held at the ready.

Carefully, I guided our prisoner into Luminor's blade.

The steel turned solid black, trembling violently, and for a moment, I feared we'd made a mistake, thinking it could hold him.

Aleks kept his hands tightly wrapped around the hilt just the same, fierce concentration furrowing his brow, drops of sweat mingling with the blood drying on his face. The blade slowly shifted from black, to the reddish-colored energy of Lorien, to the warm hue of Aleksander's magic.

Another minute passed before it finally began to pulse with its normal shades of pale gold and soft blue.

It stopped shaking.

I managed a breath.

Finished.

It was finished.

Aleks let Luminor clatter to the ground, and only then did he let his body give in to the obvious pain and exhaustion coursing through him. He tumbled forward, barely catching himself before his face hit the stone floor. But before he'd even caught his breath, he was already moving again, crawling to his cousin's side and checking him for life.

I swallowed hard. "Is he...is he..."

"...He's breathing, at least," Aleks confirmed.

I fought my way over to him, settling at his side. We leaned against one another for support, after both trying and failing to stand. I found his hand, intertwining our fingers.

Zayn's chest rose and fell steadily—he looked as if he might have merely been sleeping.

I still couldn't believe we were all alive.

We had only a moment more to take in our victory before the sound of footsteps racing across the bridge reached us. I braced myself for the worst, my hand slipping from Aleksander's and reaching toward my sword.

When my brother's face appeared in the doorway, I had to choke down a sob.

He rushed to my side, Thalia and several soldiers following soon after. While they assessed wounds and staunched bleeding, we recounted the battle that still didn't feel as though it had happened.

Luminor remained on the ground several feet away. Its energy was still calm, yet no one touched it—and it was a long time before anyone dared to approach Zayn, either, as if some wicked essence of Lorien might still be lingering within him, too.

"We'll take him back with us and do what we can to heal him," Bastian said, directing two of our soldiers to carefully pick up his unconscious body. "I'm sure he'll have some…interesting information to share once he wakes up."

If he does wake up, I couldn't help but think.

"Can we get back to Noctaris the same way we came?" Aleks asked, fighting his way to his feet.

"We don't need to," Thalia said.

"What do you mean?"

"Come see for yourself." Bastian helped me stand, then beckoned us to follow him back to the bridge.

Looking down from the center of it, I took in the aftermath of what appeared to have been a bloody battle. One we'd been victorious in, but at the cost of at least ten soldiers—that I could *see*. There were at least as many of our enemy scattered about, but somehow that didn't make me feel any better.

Of the living, only our soldiers remained in the yard, now. And most of them were gathered around an area of strangely wavering air in the center of the yard. Occasionally, clear images formed within this shimmering air—glimpses of Noctaris, I realized after a moment.

"Energy started to gather there during the middle of our battle, right about the time one of the symbols along the bottom of the room lit up," Thalia said. "Whatever you did, whatever you channeled, it seems it was at least enough to create a temporary link between this realm and ours. We're hoping that passing through it will take us home."

Home.

The word settled warmly over me, and for a moment,

all we'd done actually started to feel like a victory. Because whatever happened next, I had created a path home.

And Aleks and I were going to be able to walk it together.

"Though that makeshift portal has gotten fainter just over the past few minutes," Thalia said. "So we should hurry."

I looked to the Aetherstone's chambers. The pull of *home* was fierce, but the pull of duty proved stronger. "I need to see the Stone and the orbs again, first—a moment to study it all in peace before we head back."

Bastian hesitated, his gaze darting briefly to our fickle route out of this realm, but he nodded. "We need to more fully secure Luminor, too. Though I'm not sure how— maybe something within that chamber can help."

Despite my aching body, I jogged for that chamber, determined to gather as much knowledge as I could, as quickly as I could. The war for our world wasn't over, but I was confident I could make my way to the next step, now. I just had to keep going.

That confidence faded abruptly as I made my way deeper into the room, and I realized…something was wrong.

Luminor wasn't where we'd left it.

Instead, it was floating high above the Aetherstone's pedestal. Its blade was black once more—but now there were fissures of red light spreading from its center. The sound of metal expanding and beginning to crack echoed in the stillness.

I managed only a single, breathless cry before it *shattered*.

The blackened shards flew in all directions, but with controlled, deadly aim—as if they were arrows loosed from a skilled archer. At least one of them landed upon the dais, striking the groove where Luminor had once stood as a proud conduit of magic and life. Another struck the Noctaris orb. Both triggered a violent crackling of energy, and I was still staring at it all in frozen horror when I realized there were more shards hovering in the air, taking aim.

In the next breath, they were hurtling toward me.

Aleks moved faster than I could.

He knocked me to the ground, shielding my body with his.

They missed us.

Gods, they *should have* missed us.

Except, it was clear, now, that the remains of Luminor were being controlled by the very demon we'd tried to trap within it.

And one after the other, those shards turned in mid-air and struck again, impaling Aleksander's body, each strike sending a current of magic rippling through it until we were both swallowed up in a raging sea of cold light.

Chapter Fifty-One

Aleks

I DIDN'T REGRET ANY OF IT.

Not for a second.

We were not a tragedy.

And as darkness slid over my vision, a thought struck—that even if we *were*, I would have lived that tragedy over and over and over, in a thousand different lifetimes, if it meant I had a chance to meet her again.

Chapter Fifty-Two

Nova

Little by little, Aleks lost the battle to stay upright. His body slowly collapsed against mine, and I did my best to support it with my numb arms, to at least keep his head off the ground.

Light continued to flare around us, creating a dome that cut us off from the rest of the room. Through the veil of its energy, I saw the vague figures of our soldiers rushing frantically about. I heard my brother's voice, equally frantic, commanding them to secure the space, to find a way to get to me, to seek out any more of Luminor's pieces.

But something told me there were no more of those sharp fragments to be found. The ones that had pierced Aleksander's body were the last—the final, desperate strike.

Six of those shards. And something was happening around the puncture wounds they'd created...something strange: A soft glow of reddish-gold light pooling, a trembling radiating out across his body and pulling that light with it, sweeping an unnatural pallor across his skin.

With a shaking hand, I pulled one of the fragments free. There was hardly any blood to be seen—only a dark rim around the edges of the wound.

A flare of light engulfed it.

And then the skin...*healed*.

Silent tears dripped down my face, dropping onto his.

"Chaos. Why are you crying?"

My nickname.

But he had spoken it in a different voice.

Lorien's voice.

"No," I whispered. "*No*."

His body shook with silent laughter. A great sigh followed—like he was settling into a pleasantly familiar place after a long journey—and the rest of the shards slipped from his body. They were no longer black as they hit the ground; there was no sign of any magic in them at all.

"*Finally*," he breathed.

I dug my fingers into him.

"Let go."

I didn't.

I...*couldn't*.

He moved with inhuman strength, snatching my shirt and throwing me down as he pushed himself up. He glared at me, then rolled the stiffness from his shoulders and looked toward the center of the room.

The dome of magic around us expanded outwards, until it encompassed the platform and the Aetherstone. A stone that was alive once more, feeding into the shard of Luminor that had landed in the groove close to it. A powerful current of magic streamed between the shard and the Stone, making the platform beneath it all tremble.

Lorien forgot about me, moving toward the crackling bridge of energy without a backwards glance. As he approached it, he seemed to pull some of that energy toward himself. To absorb it. And for an instant, he appeared to shift, to grow into a beastly, beautiful shape that made the room and all its magic pale in comparison. A god given form and flesh.

It wasn't just the influence of the Stone creating this effect, I realized—it was all of his power being concentrated into this form, no longer divided between himself and Aleksander and the Sword of Light.

The world shook as he reached into the current of magic before him.

I fought my way to my feet. I had little strength left, and no sword or any other weapon within the dome he'd trapped us in—and I doubted I could have wielded any of those things against him, even if I'd had them.

But I found myself staggering toward him all the same.

He started to swirl his hand through the current, forming some of the energy into a solid shape.

My steps grew quicker. More desperate. More clumsy. I threw myself at him, trying to wrap my weight around his arm and drag him away from whatever he was planning.

He overpowered me easily, slinging me to the ground, my shoulder striking hard enough that I felt something in it shatter. The shard from Luminor flew into his hand. He stepped after me, looming over my crumpled body for a moment before he dropped, pinning me on my back and easing the piece of the broken sword into the hollow of my throat.

"You've been so useful to me," he murmured, "but now you've become nothing but a *nuisance.*"

I closed my eyes. Tightly. I didn't care about the pain in my shoulder or the sharpness at my throat.

It was his face I couldn't bear to focus on.

Not while he was speaking in that awful, *wrong* voice.

He was quiet for a long, horrible moment, dragging the broken sliver of the sword across my skin.

I tried to calm my breathing. To focus, to reach for the essence of Aleks I knew was still buried within him. But it was impossible; I felt him—I could have felt him no matter the chaos between us, I thought—but the heart of him was warring so violently with Lorien's that it was impossible to truly grab hold of it.

And what would I have done, even if I could have caught him in my grasp?

I squeezed my eyes tighter, sending fresh tears streaming over my cheeks.

"Still crying?" He *tsked*.

I opened my eyes and forced myself to look at him, to not give him the satisfaction of knowing just how broken—how *finished*—I felt in that moment.

He leered down at me, tapping his makeshift knife against my skin, his lips curving cold and cruel on his stolen face. "Do you want to know my favorite part of all this?" Another tap. "It's that he can see everything I'm doing to you."

My heart seized so tightly, so violently, I feared it might shatter into even more pieces than Luminor had.

"I wish you could hear him begging me to spare your life." He cocked his head to the side. "He really loved you, you know."

"He still does," I whispered. "We are not past tense."

"Give me a moment to fix that," he replied, his eyes flickering between shades of gold and red as he lifted the shard, walking it casually, expertly along his fingers and into a more secure grasp.

He plunged it toward my neck.

It struck the ground directly beside me.

How?

How had he missed?

His gaze was suddenly full of a rage unlike anything I'd ever seen. It was so painfully *not Aleks* that I couldn't breathe as I looked into it. Combined with the pain radiating through my shoulder, it was too much. I closed my eyes again. I was drifting, fighting just to stay conscious. All I wanted to do was leave this moment.

A whisper brought me back: "Run, Nova."

My eyes flashed open.

He'd sounded like Aleksander again.

He was still in there.

He was still fighting.

How could I possibly leave him to fight alone?

"*Damn it, Chaos, RUN!*"

I started to shake my head, to reach for him—

He jerked me upright and shoved me into motion himself, throwing me toward the wall of magic that separated us from the others. That magic shifted, closing in on us but then parting for an instant—just long enough to allow me to safely stumble through to the other side.

I immediately spun back around, but I was already too late.

The wall had closed, and I could just barely make out Aleksander's shape through it. He was on one knee, a hand over his face. His body was shaking with obvious effort. Still fighting, trying to take hold of himself once more.

I had to get back to him.

I summoned every shadow I could. Again and again, I slammed them against the wall of light, trying to pierce it. But they only scattered and fell uselessly away. I was too exhausted. The power before me was too great—and only growing more dangerous, more out of control as the energy around the Aetherstone continued to feed into it.

That stone flared so brightly that Aleks disappeared within the blaze. The ground rumbled, and suddenly it felt like the entire realm was in danger of cracking apart.

Someone was shouting, trying to get my attention—*the portal! The portal is closing!*

Strong arms closed around me a moment later—my brother.

"LET ME GO! I have to help him!"

Bastian held tighter, dragging me backward.

"NO! *NO!*" My screams were lost within another violent quake, within the clatters and crashes of falling stone that followed it. Every attempt I made to fight my way free made the agonizing pain in my shoulder worse, and soon I was blacking in and out, losing entire moments to that pain.

Somehow, I found myself on the bridge, tumbling over the edge of it and into the waiting arms of someone down below—Captain Voss, I realized, after surfacing from another moment of blackness.

My next slice of clarity came far too late; we were already at the portal. Its energy washed over me, soothingly cold and familiar. The energy of Noctaris. Of home.

But I couldn't go.

No, I *wouldn't go*—

I managed to twist back toward the Aetherstone's chamber, just in time to see light-filled cracks forming all over its walls. It was breaking. Collapsing.

I screamed again as someone pushed me forward, and then I was falling, lost in a haze of pain, hoping the impact with the ground would kill me quickly.

Chapter Fifty-Three

Nova

I WAS STILL SCREAMING WHEN I HIT THE GROUND IN Noctaris.

The pain was the only thing that eventually managed to silence me. It took so much of my strength as it rocked through my body, that soon I no longer had the energy to scream, or even to whimper.

But I did not die, however badly I wanted to.

My brother arrived soon after me, Grimnor clutched in his hand, blood and bruises covering him. He set the blade aside and dropped to his knees beside me, gathering my battered body carefully to his.

"I'm sorry," he whispered. "I'm so sorry."

I didn't reply. I just let him hold me, numbly watching as the rest of our army returned.

One after the other, they staggered in. Two of them carried Zayn's still unconscious body. They were followed by Thalia, who came immediately to my side, her steps uncharacteristically unsteady and her eyes bleary with emotion. She laid a handful of things she'd collected at my feet—my knife; my remaining, unbroken bracelets; a single shard of Luminor's shattered remains. She pressed a hand to my cheek, a warm, wordless gesture before she turned her back to my brother and me and proceeded to stare off into the distance, her arms wrapped tightly around herself.

I watched the fading portal for a few minutes, until I couldn't stand to look at it—at anything—anymore, and then I buried my face against Bastian's chest and I wept, no longer caring about appearing strong.

I want to die.

Please, just let me die.

The minutes passed. I kept breathing. It was the hardest thing I'd ever done within an entire lifetime of hard, cruel things, but I kept going.

Breathe in.

Breathe out.

"Nova…look," came my brother's voice.

The heaviness in my limbs felt almost insurmountable, but I managed to lift my head.

And I saw *life*.

The portal had faded away entirely, but a new energy was settling over the land all around us. It drifted down from a periwinkle sky like a fine mist, making everything it fell upon shimmer. Some of those shimmering things slowly began to glisten with their own inner light, with their own waking energy.

In the distance, a massive tree bloomed on a hilltop, its flowers unfolding into a bright display of white and gold.

There was still a cast of twilight over it all. The edges of things seemed dark, even as undeniable life pulsed within them. Not a dead world any longer, maybe, but one still fragile and fighting under the threat of decay.

But it seemed all the more impressive for its willingness to live in spite of the shadows, I thought.

Some things bloom brighter in the dark.

Some things were not given a choice.

I stared at that distant tree for a long moment. Imagining its roots—the way they had clung so stubbornly to life. They must have run deep.

So did mine.

My kingdom would bloom in spite of the darkness.

And so would I.

I would find a way to thrive in spite of it—no, *with* it. And the darkness I was going to unleash on Lorien the next time we met would be unlike anything he had ever seen.

I would not be afraid any longer.

Aleksander and I would not be a tragedy, because *I* was the one writing the story now, and this was not how it ended.

I would get him back.

Steeling myself, I crawled out of my brother's protective embrace. I picked up the things Thalia had left at my feet, wrapping what remained of my bracelets around my knife with slow, but steady movements. Then I stood and marched my way to the top of the hill.

Wincing from the pain in my shoulder, I knelt and stabbed the blade into a hard patch of ground at the base of the tree. And this was where I left it—a memorial to what I'd once been. What I no longer was. What I was becoming.

Shadows erupted around my body when I stepped away

from it all, and I let them trail freely alongside me as I walked toward my palace without looking back.

The story continues in . . .

What Echoes in the Dark

Discover your next thrilling romantic fantasy obsession with S. M. Gaither's Shadows and Crowns series . . .

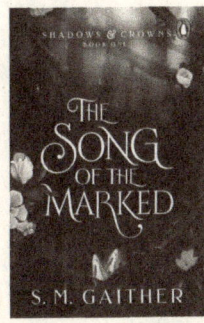

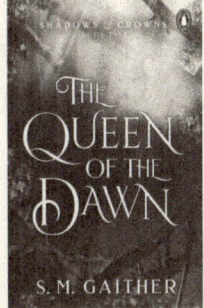

AVAILABLE NOW